The Secret Bureau:
The Marquis de Lupiano
(Vol. 4)

ALSO TRANSLATED BY NINA COOPER

Fortuné du Boigobey. *Two Crimes*
Emile Gaboriau. *Monsieur Lecoq; The Casebook of Monsieur Lecoq*
Jean Petithuguenin. *The Adventures of Ethel King, The Female Nick Carter*
Charles Rabou. *The Secret Bureau* (Vol. 1); *The Brothers of Death* (*The Secret Bureau,* Vol. 2); *The Bloodied Girl* (*The Secret Bureau,* Vol. 3)
Antonin Reschal. *The Adventures of Miss Boston, The First Female Detective*
Pierre Yrondy. *The Adventures of Therese Arnaud of the French Secret Service; The Adventures of Marius Pégomas, Marseille Detective*

Charles Félix Henri Rabou

The Secret Bureau:
The Marquis de Lupiano
(Vol. 4)

translated, annotated and introduced by
Nina Cooper

A Black Coat Press Book

Acknowledgements: Thanks to Charles Griggs for his reviews of all drafts and his helpful critique of each. Thanks to the Henneveux Family for their loyal support, as well as to Daniel Auliac for his always invaluable help. Thanks to Professor Henri Rossi for his kind assistance in providing scans of the original edition from the Bibliothèque de l'Arsenal.

English adaptation and introduction Copyright © 2018 by Nina Cooper.

Visit our website at www.blackcoatpress.com

ISBN 978-1-61227-761-5. First Printing. July 2018. Published by Black Coat Press, an imprint of Hollywood Comics.com, LLC, P.O. Box 17270, Encino, CA 91416. All rights reserved. Except for review purposes, no part of this book may be reproduced or transmitted in any form or by any means, electronic or mechanical, including photocopying, recording, or by any information storage and retrieval system, without permission in writing from the publisher. The stories and characters depicted in this novel are entirely fictional. Printed in the United States of America.

TABLE OF CONTENTS

Introduction

The first volume of the saga of the Secret Bureau (in French: *Le Cabinet Noir*) was first published in Belgium by A. Lebègue in 1859 in a truncated version; the complete edition was then released in France in five small volumes by L. de Potter in 1856. Its sequels, *The Brothers of Death* (*Les Frères de la Mort*) and *The Bloodied Girl* (*La Fille Sanglante*), followed in 1857, and the story eventually concluded in *Le Marquis de Lupiano*, released in 1858.

Volume 1 of *The Secret Bureau* starts with the son of E.T.A. Hoffmann, the author of the celebrated *Tales*, Frantz Hoffman, a medical student in Paris, who agrees to help a man seemingly risen from the dead, François-Maximilian Kormer, a.k.a. the Marquis de Lupiano, to publish his memoirs which include the history of the infamous *Secret Bureau*. The Marquis takes part in all the episodes of the story, but changes names frequently, using the various aliases of Marquis de Samaniego, Marquis de Saint-Faust, Salvador Arbib, etc., but always retaining and elaborating on his evil designs, plots, and influence.

At the beginning, *The Secret Bureau* mostly tells the story of the Hulet family, for centuries the custodians of the French Government's spy system. This secret system, called in English the "Secret Bureau," opens and examines all domestic and foreign correspondence, including those written in code. The secret position is inherited, going from father to eldest son when the latter reaches his majority. If the son is not fit, stupid, or irresponsible, he will be imprisoned, killed, or, if he refuses to assume his inherited position, he will be watched throughout his entire life, never allowed to succeed in whatever he may attempt.

When nearing his majority, Henri Hulet, whose principal characteristic is ambition, has contracted a relationship with the daughter of a rich friend of Hulet the elder. It is advantageous and a love match. Hulet the elder refuses to give his permission, but without any reason, except that their fatal inherited burden would, by that match, draw a new family into the Hulet fate.

To try to avoid his mysterious fate, the details of which he has not yet been told, Hulet junior enters the priesthood, rises in the hierarchy, is punished because of his pride, ambition, and inordinate severity, and sent back to his monastery, hidden as if he didn't exist. But when the Revolution of 1789 begins, he is defrocked, enters political life, and marries his former intended fiancée, now a nun who has forsaken her vows. He rises in political life to become part of the National Convention Assembly that decided the fate of King Louis XVI. He casts the deciding vote at the Convention for the death of the King. During the Reign of Terror, both he and his father are imprisoned. After the death of his father, who is taken to the guillotine in his place, Henri Hulet is released and leaves public life, retiring to the country.

During his time in the country, he is a model father and useful medical practitioner. Hospitality given during a storm to a passing couple leads to the kidnapping of one of his sons and, finally, to his being summoned to the office of Joseph Fouché, who had recommended the death of Louis XVI, without a vote. Fouché is now the head of Napoleon's secret police. He is aware of the function of Hulet's father, and wants to enlist the younger Hulet in the same service for the government he now represents. He has a file in the handwriting of Hulet's father detailing the secret history of the Hulet family, beginning more than a hundred years before. He places Hulet in a private room and gives him a key to the file and leaves him to read his family history.

The saga then returns to the Hulet story some ten years later, when Henri Hulet is now the head of the Secret Bureau. A chance encounter in Napoleon's office antechamber with another petitioner, whose description matches that of the Marquis de Lupiano, again casts him into the disasters awaiting him.

Volume 2, *The Brothers of Death*, continues the Hulet family history and reintroduces the Marquis de Lupiano into the story. When it opens, Rabou tells a short tale of a young man who, for a small mistake, is mustered out of Napoleon's army. He tries to commit suicide, but is deterred by a stranger and is inducted into a secret society. Then he fights bravely out of uniform with the military. He is again inducted into the military, rescues a rich young woman, whom he has seen and admires, from a burning building, is offered her hand in marriage, but refuses, even though he loves her. When commanded by the Emperor, he marries her, but on his wedding night he receives a note which causes him to commit suicide. The stranger he met was, of course, the infamous Marquis de Lupiano, who has now organized a group called the "Brothers of Death," whose members commit suicide by lottery.

In the third volume of the saga, *The Bloodied Girl*, Rabou finally answers to some of the reader's questions, as he had promised to do in the first volume. He also solves some of the mysteries we encountered in the two previous volumes. At the end of *The Brothers of Death*, Rabou had revealed the identity of the author of the *Memoirs of the Secret Bureau*, now identified as a man called Carbonneau. He had also identified the editor who is now interested in publishing the remainder of Carbonneau's secret history. The editor wants to find the missing volumes which followed the previous two. He and a psychologist friend have been told that the remainder of the documents might be in Germany, where young Frantz Hoffmann returned after completing his medical studies in Paris. At the end of *The Brothers of Death*, the two men were contemplating going there to search for them.

Most importantly, Rabou draws together some of the earlier plot threads involving not only Henri Hulet but also the Maltese man, Gregorio Matiphous, both of whom, at the end of *The Brothers of Death*, were working for the Secret Bureau.

He also reintroduces, and reintegrates into the plot, Matiphous' enemies from the two previous volumes, including the Marquis de Samaniego, a.k.a. the Marquis de Lupiano, as well as Henri Hulet's ubiquitous nemesis, the man who once stole his infant son under the identity of Rempailleux. Finally, Rabou also brings back Herminie Daliron, Georgiana's confident from Volume I.

As an employee of the Secret Bureau stationed in Italy, Matiphous has discovered that two of his former acquaintances are now colleagues and have forgotten the valuable help he gave them in England in the past. With his skill as a surgeon, Matiphous kept the criminal Broughton alive after he had supposedly died from hanging. He was also instrumental in releasing a man named Fauntleroy from Newgate Prison, where they had met. Broughton the boxer, and Fauntleroy, alias the Prince of Asturias, are now corresponding by letter about a counterfeit scheme they are operating. Broughton, in his letters, sheds light on what happened at the lighthouse of Bell Rock in Scotland after Matiphous left.

In this, the fourth and last volume of *The Secret Bureau,* Rabou continues tying together events and characters as he promised in Volume1. Addressing the reader, he then wrote:

"In the vast and arduous development of what might be called an imbroglio, whose curiosity and mystery must be one of the principal elements of interest, would the author be showing himself too demanding of those who want to follow the deduction to ask patience, which will always be given, for everything? Could he also be asked to pay attention to how the plot of the many incidents is developed, and finally asked to keep in mind some of the facts already recounted which will be echoed or repeated in a distant part of the story?"

The reader must remember that Rabou frequently changes the name, or lets the character himself do so, of a central character throughout the four volumes. One of the main characters is called the Marquis de Lupiano in Volume 1. His name is later changed to the Marquis de Samaniego. A note left later in a mortuary cave of three individuals fleeing from

Matiphous, said, "Follow up to the Hamburg ossuary," the work of the Marquis de Samaniego, here left by a character who called himself Salvador Arbib, the Duke of Venice; but he is merely another incarnation of the Marquis de Samaniego, Marquis de Saint-Faust, and, now, again Marquis de Lupiano.[1]

Another central character begins, in Volume 1, as the leader of a band of thieves in the Orgères Forest, where Henri Hulet, at that time the next head of the Secret Bureau, has settled under the pseudonym of Vandel. The band was called les *chauffeurs*, alluding to the fact that they used extreme methods of torturing their victims to force them to reveal the hiding place of their valuables. Their chief, Dulac, also called Rempailleux, returns to the story in the last two volumes using the name Comte de Saint-Rambert.

The Prince de Bevillacqua, a man from Genoa, also called Montalvi, is the former head of the French National Lottery, and a man who sold his wife's daughter to a flesh dealer, who then sold her to an Oriental harem, from which she migrates from one man to another. She is Georgiana, the so-called "Bloodied Girl," who reappears here as a friend of the Marquis de Lupiano. The two had met in Vincennes Prison, where he had sent by Napoleon and from which he was released after his fall.

The reader will remember that in the preceding volume, Henri Hulet, then head of the government spy bureau, the Secret Bureau, had been sent, with his wife and daughter, to a group of exiles in Texas with all those who, at the National Convention, had voted for Louis XVI's death.

Another central character, Gregorio Matiphous, the man from Malta, after escaping from the Bell Rock Lighthouse changed his name to Deschamps and had been almost convicted of a crime he did not commit, but was convicted of leaving the lighthouse unattended. He was sent to prison in Australia.

The Secret Bureau, vacant because of the deportation of Henri Hulet, is now headed by the criminal, Dulac/

---

[1] See footnote 5, page 13, *The Secret Bureau*, Volume 1.

Rempailleux, now called Saint-Rambert. Kitty Ketch, the daughter of the London hangman, who, with Matiphous, had resuscitated the supposedly dead boxer, Broughton, was rescued from falling into the sea off Bell Rock. Then, married to an old Scottish nobleman, she had an assignation she believed would be in a darkened theatre box with a Russian master equestrian who had asked Matiphous' black servant Britannicus, to arrange it. Unknown to her, Britannicus has taken the place of the Russian equestrian. From that encounter, she had produced a mulatto, whom she had, after several years, given to Britannicus, who was overjoyed to have her. He returned with the child to his native African country of Madagascar. Kitty then married Rempailleux, who, although an escaped criminal, soon became the new head of the Secret Bureau.

Both Rempailleux and Matiphous are searching for the treasure hidden at the Bell Rock Lighthouse by the Jew Ephraim, who was the keeper of the documents of various international secret societies sworn to overthrow all governments.

With Volume 4, which begins in 1816, Rabou shifts his story to the situation following the exile of Napoleon, carrying it forward with a new character introduced at the end of Volume 3, Commandant Lefebvre. However, to move his story along, he must remind the reader that he had already introduced one of the characters, the Marquise de Camembert, in an earlier part of the story.

Like many former soldiers of Bonaparte, Lefebvre is on half-pay and unemployed in 1816 and in dire circumstances economically. He accidentally meets a woman to whom he is immediately attracted, even though she is more than thirty-years-old and bears the marks of smallpox. She is Herminie Daliron, who returns from Volume I, where she had revenged herself on a rich man who had seduced her, making her his mistress, then abandoning her when she contracted smallpox. She became the mentor and companion of Georgiana, then mistress of the same rich man. In preparing his downfall, she also prepares that of Alexis, son of Henri Hulet.

Approached by Lefebvre, Herminie refuses his advances, partially because she is in love with a young man she has never met, a young secretary who works for a politician/banker and lives on the same street where her apartment is located. Preoccupied with the thought of the necessity, if he is successful in his conquest, to provide for two households when he can barely afford one, Lefebvre meets a former fellow soldier who is now employed by Rempailleux at the Secret Bureau. With some reservations, Lefebvre agrees to join the Secret Bureau, which will guarantee him a large and sufficient income. However, Herminie, to avoid Lefebvre's advances, has moved to another neighborhood, leaving no address.

When he is not working for the Secret Bureau, unsealing and reading private as well as government correspondence, Lefebvre uses every means to continue stalking her. He finally finds her address and sets up a location for an ambush across the street from her new apartment. One day, he sees the back of a man, who appears to be young, carrying flowers and entering Herminie's apartment. He waits for a while, but finally determines to confront the two. When he does burst into the apartment, he finds that the intruder is the young secretary— his own son, Alfred. Rabou ends Volume III with this startling surprise.

Now, read on...

Nina Cooper

PART I: THE CALICOT [2]

I. The Calicot

The next day following his encounter at the Place de l'Estrapade, Lefebvre was at his son's apartment at a very early hour. It would have been difficult for him to pose as a moralist because there should always be a certain harmony between the conduct and the words of the preacher, which would have been lacking in his sermon. But broaching the subject in a less risky way, he said:

"Alfred, my child, I didn't come to reproach you. You're amusing yourself; that's normal at your age, but I wonder how, with all your advantages, you can look at a woman who is more than thirty-years-old and who is disfigured by small-pox."

"But, father, the young secretary answered, "it seems to me that, more than anyone else, you should be aware of the reasons for my attraction."

"Oh! Me, that's different. An old wreck like me can't be too demanding. But when I was at my best, although I was far

---

[2] In Rabou's original plan, this section was entitled *Le Champ d'Asile*, in reference to the French settlement in America; see note 137 p. 267 of Volume 3. Calicot, or Calico, is a plain-woven textile made from unbleached and often not fully processed cotton. The fabric is far less fine than muslin, but less coarse and thick than canvas or denim, but it is still very cheap owing to its unfinished and undyed appearance. The fabric was originally from the city of Calicut in southwestern India, hence its name. In 19th century in Paris, a "calicot" was a seller of novelties for female customers. Neither are particularly well-chosen titles for this section.

from being your equal in intelligence, education, and physique, I would never have given a glance at such a conquest. But I know what happened. She made advances to you and you took advantage of an opportunity."

"Oh, no!" Alfred replied, laughing. "You shouldn't say bad things about her charms. There are very desirable sides to that woman, and you saw them as well as I did."

"But you can't think of holding on to her! That would be depravity, against nature! I gave you, yesterday, a beautiful opportunity to break it off. Now that your fantasy is satisfied, you would be an idiot not to take flight."

"You want me to leave the table and try to persuade myself that I have no more appetite?"

"Yes! When will that be? Handsome, young, attractive as you are, women must be running after you. I can very well ask you to leave me a poor faded flower that I was going to pluck, if you had not thrown yourself in the way."

"First of all, father," the young secretary answered, "it hasn't been proved to me that, even if I left you a free field, I could be assured of the success of your enterprise. The woman that you are coveting is one of those who use their charms as resources..."

"What! And you are not ashamed, with your twenty years, to let yourself be enticed like a naive old *roué* who thinks he can buy affection?"

"We became acquainted very quickly," Alfred answered, "and it was entirely disinterested on her part. But I have since learned that her methods of existence couldn't be more precarious and that I could become an obstacle to more serious arrangements. I had then decided, after having made her accept some tokens of my very modest generosity, to let that relationship die out."

"Marvelous!" Lefebvre said pleasantly. "That's behaving like a gentleman."

"But you, father, with your very limited resources, how do you expect to be able to provide the necessities for that costly liaison?"

"Don't let that worry you. I'll know how to take care of it."

"I'm sorry, but it's my duty to be concerned, because yesterday, coming back from our apple of discord, I found a letter from my mother asking me to come and see her, since you have apparently been absent from the conjugal household for almost two weeks. You have left her in a terribly difficult situation."

"What is she complaining about? I sent her money, telling her that she shouldn't be upset about my absence, that my business would perhaps keep me away for a while."

"But, father, two weeks is a long time. And I, who knows the nature of your business, can't refrain from pointing out..."

"You're mistaken! You don't know anything. For some time now, I have had some very serious and time-consuming functions which have forced me to put aside all other distractions."

"I'm very happy to learn that, but if these *functions*, which seem hard for you to explain, make it necessary for you to live apart from my mother, then it seems to me that you should inform her of the situation, instead of leaving her in the present distressing situation."

"All right; I will go and talk to her."

"Right now, today, because otherwise, despite some other pressing work, I would feel obliged to go reassure her myself."

"Don't do that. I will go immediately to Belleville. Now, promise me not to see Herminie again!"

"After what has happened, that almost goes without saying. But if I dared, as a respectful son...

"Ah! You're going to talk to me about morality. My son, everything in this world is relative. Because of the fact that I am a great deal younger than your mother, who tells me I am an old fool when I want to speak the language of love to her, I cannot live without an attachment. Well, then, isn't it better that I seek out a quiet girl, already settled down, who has a worthy side, that of a young brother she is bringing up, has educated, and in whose interest it is sure she will always behave properly?"

"But, father, are your functions so well paid that you can calmly think of taking on the responsibilities you are going to assume?"

"Yes, I can honorably pay for the upkeep of two households. I will tell you about that later; but now, get out of my way."

"What about my sister, Amanda, who has been for some time of an age to be married?"

"I am telling you that everything will be taken care of, but you have to let me go about it and stop harassing me."

"It's not necessary, then, that I give you what I would have given to my mother from my small savings?"

"Keep your money. You aren't yet rich enough, because that miser, Martin Lambert, has probably not raised your salary."

"True, and I won't even ask him to, for a reason that I will later tell you."

"All right, it's agreed then. I will hurry over to Belleville, kiss your mother and your sister, and you will cut short a folly that, as you can plainly see, would end by making you look ridiculous."

"Good luck, father," Alfred said, "but I don't know that it will be very easy for you to get the benefit of my neutrality."

"It's a conceited man," replied Lefebvre, smiling, "who believes that no one can replace him."

And delighted with the turn the negotiations had taken, which he had believed would be more difficult, the Commandant took a cab to Belleville.

He expected that he would be greeted by a tempest. Therefore, he was agreeably surprised to see his wife throw herself into his arms. Seeing that two big tears were rolling down the poor neglected woman's cheeks, he said affectionately:

"Well, here I am. I wasn't lost, but I had so many things to do! Fortunately, I didn't do them badly and, from now on, we will be sheltered from need."

"Here everything hasn't taken place the same way," Madame Lefebvre answered. "Amanda has been very sick, and she still is."

"What's wrong with her?" Lefebvre asked.

"A female problem."

"A female problem! That's very unusual. She has always been very healthy and all her, er, *functions* have worked very well."

"What do you expect? Women are like machines that can easily go off track."

"Then she is better?" asked the Commandant, about to enter her bedroom.

"No," said Madame Lefebvre, "don't go in there so suddenly. She is still weak! Let me tell her of your arrival."

"Then that female problem was serious?" Lefebvre asked with anxiety. "What does Doctor Bompard say?"

"It wasn't Doctor Bompard who took care of her. It was Madame Irénée."

"What! Madame Irénée—the midwife?"

"Yes, Doctor Bompard was not available at the time of the accident and, as midwives also know much about those things…"

"Go tell her I am here so I can see her," said Lefebvre with a movement of impatience.

Madame Lefebvre came out of her daughter's bedroom shortly thereafter, telling her husband that he was expected.

"What has happened to you, my poor Amanda?" asked Lefebvre, struck by the pallor and the haggard face of the sick girl. "I left you so beautiful and so healthy."

"Oh, it's nothing," said the girl. "I'm a great deal better."

"Well, aren't you going to embrace her?" Madame Lefebvre asked her husband, seeing him lost in contemplation of the ravages caused by the girl's sickness.

Lefebvre embraced his daughter. She kept him held tightly a long time in an embrace which had something convulsive about it; at the same time, she was sobbing.

"Well, Madame Irénée is all right," Lefebvre said, "but the sickness must have been very bad to have irritated her nerves so much. The consequences of these things are always dangerous. I want to have Doctor Bompard's opinion."

"Did you come here to scare us?" Madame Lefebvre asked sharply. "We were able, thank God, to do without you. Madame Irénée found her much better this morning, and she said that she would again be on her feet in three days. Forget about your Doctor Bompard, who will only make problems. Instead, tell us about that good situation that you have finally obtained."

Lefebvre, expecting that curiosity, had had time to make up his story.

"I can, my dear ones, tell you about it in confidence, but you must not spread it about. One of my former colleagues, who has entered the private sector, not being willing to serve under this government, is now the head of a large factory manufacturing military equipment. He needed someone to supervise it, so he hired me, instructing me not to speak about it because, since he is selling equipment to the Ministry of War, he must not seem to be assembling around him former soldiers of Napoleon. The police, who have already bothered him, would say that, under the pretext of doing business, he is plotting conspiracies. I am even working for him under a false name."

"Ah!" said Madame Lefebvre, "and you were so busy with that for two weeks that you haven't been able to spend an instant here?"

"Night and day at work, my dear love. And I had to bring myself up to date. As for bringing you to Paris, for the moment, that's impossible. My friend wants me to live at the factory. And he says that with women, no secret can be safe. It is therefore agreed that, for the moment, you will stay here to continue your little business; only I will make it possible for you to carry it on a little more nicely. After that, according to what he told me, it would be only for a while; then, I will have you come and join me, and we will think seriously of getting Amanda married, since her accident could very well be because it hasn't been taken care of until now."

"And how much does that new situation pay you?" Madame Lefebvre asked.

"Six thousand francs at the start; later, the salary could be doubled."

"Ah! That's not bad! And you will have enough to play your little games."

"Ah! As if I had time to think of chasing women! Day and night, I repeat, I am on my feet. Right now, we are organizing the Royal Guard, for which we must furnish all the accoutrements."

"That's something nice, the Royal Guards!" said Madame Lefebvre.

"After all, we can't act as if *the other one*[3] didn't do some stupid things, and, since there's money to be made, it might as well be by us."

"Are you eating well?" asked the housewife.

"Not really. I just ran in, because Alfred, whom I saw this morning, and he told me that you were worried. Now I must rush off... I don't need to give you any advice about Amanda?"

"No. Go on, then!" Madame Lefebvre answered in a voice half friendly, half scolding. "We know how to take care of ourselves without you. The next time you come back, her sickness will be over."

Lefebvre then embraced his wife and his daughter, and started on his way back to Paris. As he approached the barrier, his attention was drawn to an elegant carriage which was stationed at the bottom of the steep incline across which Belleville was spread.

---

[3] Nickname given to Napoleon by his former soldiers when speaking amongst themselves.

A young man with a most aristocratic appearance wearing a moustache and a *Légion d'Honneur* medal, jumped lightly to the ground, while a servant, dressed in a perfect jockey uniform, held the reins of the horse.

After giving some instructions to the servant, the unknown man began to climb the Paris road where Lefebvre lived just as Lefebvre was coming down it. For a moment, they walked past each other. They looked at each other and, after some twenty steps, both having turned around at the same time, they seemed to have the same thought, that of vague curiosity. A little further on, Lefebvre still glanced behind him. He then saw the unknown man enter a café that was on his path.

"That's unusual," he said to himself. "What could such a fashionable gentleman have to do in this slum? It's not the woman who owns that establishment that could draw him... she's a terrible peasant... He looked at me in a funny way; he turned around to see me again... It's obvious he went in there to keep me from knowing where he is really going..."

Once on the road to suspicion, Lefebvre's thoughts didn't stop. A man of that age and appearance, who seemed to be hiding, could only be attracted to Belleville by a lover. What if it were his daughter that he was looking for? His way of looking at him had been unusual...

The "accident" that had happened to Amanda... a female problem... That wasn't the ordinary sickness of a young girl— and they had sent for a midwife instead of their usual doctor, who didn't tend childbirth deliveries.

Moved by all those ideas that passed rapidly through his thoughts, giving in less to reflection than to a vague instinct, the Commandant turned rapidly into an intersecting little street and, after a few detours, came back to the street he had just left, a little above the place where his wife's boutique was located.

That maneuver worked marvelously for him. Lefebvre stayed there for ten minutes in a little alley, where he hid himself as well as he could, looking ahead. Finally, he caught sight of the unknown man continuing to go up the street where they had met; the stranger turned around from time to time as if to make sure that he was not being followed. He stepped to the middle of the street, facing the road he had left behind. Then, having made sure that nothing disturbing was on the horizon, he entered resolutely into Madame Lefebvre's lingerie shop.

In presence of a full clarification which seemed about to become a fact, the Commandant was afraid and didn't want to full explore the depths of his discovery. But after a moment, he went in.

"That's some ladies' man," he told himself, "who, to have an opportunity to see Amanda, has come to place an order for some linen."

He was expecting to see the decorated gentleman placing an order with Madame Lefebvre at the counter. Not finding either his wife or the customer inside, he no longer doubted that this was something serious. However, he was enough in control of himself to think that, in his daughter's state of health, a scene could cause her to have a serious relapse. He therefore limited himself to tapping on the glass of the door that separated the shop from the back, as if he were a client. In addition, that door was open and the empty room through which, apparently, the stranger had been taken by Madame Lefebvre, led into Amanda's bedroom on the upper floor; any other visit would have taken place either in the shop itself, or in a little room on the other side of it.

At the noise, the owner of the lingerie shop came downstairs, shouting from the top of the stairwell the sacramental: "I'm coming!"

When she saw the Commandant, Madame Lefebvre changed color and, although the trembling of her voice betrayed her emotion, she had the presence of mind to say:

"Ah, it's you! Did you forget something?"

"Yes, my handkerchief, that I left in Amanda's bedroom."

"All right, I'll go get another one for you," Madame replied said. "Your daughter is asleep and I don't want to go into her room to wake her."

"What happened to the gentleman that I saw enter here?" asked Lefebvre.

"A gentleman?" asked Madame Lefebvre, as if she didn't know what he was talking about.

"Yes, a gentleman, very well dressed."

"Ah!" said Madame Lefebvre, "you're calling him a gentleman? That's our cotton merchant's salesman, who has come to collect a bill."

"A salesman who wears a moustache?"

"Don't all salesmen wear one? Just because of that, they've been putting them in comedies at the *Varietés*, under the name of *Calicots*."[4]

"Then, where is that salesman?"

"Where?" Madame Lefebvre repeated.

For women, when they lie, defend their ground foot by foot.

"Yes, where? What did you do with him? I suppose you didn't take him into Amanda's bedroom, since she's sleeping."

Grasping at an invention that had just come into her mind, without knowing how, after that, she would get out of it, Madame Lefebvre said:

"On the contrary, it's just that. He is in Amanda's bedroom."

"Then she's not sleeping!"

"He asked to see her, and I didn't refuse, because I had an idea that he might make be a good husband for her."

"What! Without consulting me, you imagine that you can arrange her marriage?"

---

[4] Author's Note: "In *Le Combat des Montagnes* by M. Scribe, which was, in fact, at the first part of the Restoration." Also see Note 2.

"I would have told you about it later; it's something that I am considering, but which isn't far enough along."

"I want to see him, this gentleman."

"Er... No, I don't want you to see him. You would talk to him about the thing right away, and you would perhaps spoil everything."

"I can at least see his face without saying anything to him about your plans. I want to be sure of him, if he returns to me as a son-in-law."

"What's the use of that?" Madame Lefebvre asked.

"Come now, will you have him come down, or I'm going up," Lefebvre said in the tone of an ogre.

"What stubbornness," said the lingerie owner, starting on her way to her daughter's bedroom.

"Don't say in front of Amanda that it's me who's there," Lefebvre was careful to add. "In her condition, the least emotion could be dangerous."

"Don't worry," Madame Lefebvre said, shrugging. "As if I needed your advice! You would do better to leave rather than come here and act like a tyrant!"

A few moments later, Madame Lefebvre reappeared, followed by the so-called salesman.

"My husband, that you hadn't yet met," said Madame Lefebvre, introducing the Commandant. "He wanted to thank you for all the kindness that your business has shown to us."

"*Mon Dieu*, Madame, it's my boss who you should thank."

"Oh, no! Without you, he wouldn't have given us such an extension of credit."

"Monsieur has served in the military?" asked Lefebvre.

"Yes, Monsieur, I have had that honor," answered the Calicot.

"I wouldn't have doubted it, seeing your mustache and your ribbons... But... But..." Lefebvre added, suspending his sentence, "I would have sworn, when I saw you enter, that you had been decorated..."

"No, Monsieur," said the man, sighing with a constrained attitude. "It was perhaps the end of my scarf that I had in my side pocket and that had come out, that you mistook for a decoration?"

"Ah! That's what it was," Lefebvre said casually. "I was certain that I had seen something red. Well, Monsieur, since you have been kind enough to take an interest in my wife's business, I now have some money at my disposal and I wouldn't be unhappy to talk to you about certain ideas for expansion that are running around in my head. If you are going down to Paris, we could chat as we walked."

"Gladly, Monsieur."

"But I haven't finished talking with Monsieur!" said Madame Lefebvre, intervening.

"Well! What is it about? A bill? That's quickly settled. If you don't have the money, I have some on me."

"No, you will pay just what is written there, whereas we are behind with Monsieur."

"No, Madame Lefebvre," said the Calicot. "That bill is not pressing; I don't even have it on me. I just came in to have news of Mademoiselle Amanda."

"Well then, Monsieur, let's go, if you will," said the Commandant, "because I have some rather pressing business back in Paris."

"I will follow you, Monsieur," said the stranger.

After having bowed to Madame Lefebvre, he stood ready to leave.

"Aren't you going to give me a kiss?" the lingerie merchant asked with anxiety.

Lefebvre embraced his wife rather coldly, and joining his traveling companion, whom he had left in the street, he said, when he found himself far enough away not to be heard by his wife, who had remained at the threshold, watching them:

"Monsieur, you can put back on your *Legion d'Honneur*."

"How's that, Monsieur?" the Calicot asked with some emotion.

"Yes, you can understand that, in my house, because of my daughter's condition, I didn't want to make a scene, and that I appeared to believe everything you said. But I have good eyesight, and I saw a decoration in your lapel, and what's more, I noticed a charming cabriolet waiting for you at the bottom of the hill. Now, as it isn't very likely that cloth merchants pay their salesmen to go collect bills in carriages as elegant as that, it's not necessary to play a comedy with me."

"It was with the same feeling of caution for Mademoiselle Amanda that made me, please believe me, Monsieur, play with the unfortunate imagination of Madame Lefebvre."

"What else? When you are caught off guard, you get out of it however you can. But now, we can talk facts. As head of the family, you won't find it unusual that I ask you what you were doing in my house, hiding from me?"

"Mon Dieu! I had come to get news of Mademoiselle your daughter, in whom I have a strong interest."

"I can willingly believe that, but what is the nature of that interest? If, as my wife led me to believe, while disguising your social position, you have some notions concerning Amanda's future, it seems to me the moment has come for you to explain them to me."

"Madame Lefebvre is going a little too quickly. She doesn't know just to what point I can do as I like."

"Yet, I don't believe that you intend to make my daughter your mistress."

"Every day, Monsieur, people give way to badly thought out feelings before they first consider all the ramifications."

"Then, Monsieur, I will begin by telling you that a father has the duty to put order in badly thought out feelings. But when he is told about it, it's often too late!"

Saying that, Lefebvre stared into the face of the man to whom he was speaking.

"Without a doubt," replied the Calicot, made uncomfortable by that look. "It's something unfortunate... very regrettable..."

"I must not hide from you the fact that your attitude and that of Madame Lefebvre," continued the Commandant, "as well as the so-called *accident* that happened to my daughter, and the type of woman they got to take care of her, instead of our ordinary doctor, have given me the most unusual thoughts. I must ask you, in the name of honor, what has taken place between you and Amanda. You understand that certain things, once they have come to light, cannot remain hidden for very long."

"Well, one prefers that such things be guessed at rather than talked about."

"I understand, Monsieur, but then, I must ask you what your intentions are."

"You have caught me off guard Monsieur. I need to ask myself that."

"Your answer, Monsieur, could already be taken for a serious insult; and if I were not a father, and having with that title the duty of caution and reflection, I would ask you for immediate satisfaction."

"I'm in the habit of giving satisfaction to all those who demand it!" replied the stranger, finding himself on grounds more to his liking.

"I don't doubt it; and I know a number of persons who prefer that way of getting out of all the bad situations into which their honor had strayed."

"Monsieur!" the Calicot said haughtily.

"But I, who am a father, I repeat," Lefebvre said, "I, who have proved myself on the field of battle, and elsewhere, and who, with my gray hairs, must not give way to a first reaction, I prefer to wait until you have consulted with yourself, since you have stated that intention. If I were to act rashly, I could make it impossible for you to listen to the voice of your conscience, by seeming to have you submit to such pressures. It is therefore humbly that I ask you to reflect. At this moment, I expect only an accommodating attitude from you, that of being willing to tell me to whom I will be able to introduce myself to have your response after you have meditated on it."

"Here is my card!" said the man, who, for the moment, was delighted to end a conversation where he was playing such a terrible role

Lefebvre read: *Comte Albert de Lucheux, Brigadier in the Guards of Monsieur,*[5] *rue Saint-Dominique, 195.*

"Good-bye, then, Monsieur le Comte," said Lefebvre, bowing to the Count, who had reached the place where his servant was waiting for him.

"Good-bye, Commandant!" said the young officer, climbing into his carriage, which left, burning up the pavement.

II. Strike while the Iron is Hot

Two days later, Lefebvre received an explanation from his wife that brought him completely up to date on all the circumstances of their misfortune. Deciding that the seducer had had, to speak according to the code, all the time necessary to deliberate, the morning of the third day after their initial conversation, Lefebvre presented himself at the Saint-Dominique address which he had been given.

He was first met with a Swiss Guard, of a size equal to his importance.

"Monsieur le Comte," that man answered, "never receives anyone before lunch."

"At what time does he have lunch?" Lefebvre asked.

The Swiss Guard looked him up and down as if he had asked the most incongruous question, and he then let fall superbly this sentence:

"At what time do you think that anyone eats lunch? At noon."

---

[5] Title given to the brothers of the kings of France. In this case, it refers to the future king Charles X (1757-1836) who, for most of his life, was known as the Comte d'Artois, but was the younger brother to reigning kings Louis XVI and Louis XVIII.

"However, you yourself seem to do that earlier," countered the Commandant, seeing that the man, while he was talking, was busy spreading butter on a piece of toast.

The Swiss guard raised his head proudly:

"You call this lunch?" he asked.

"Well, then, what are you doing?"

"I'm having my coffee. Besides," he added, "I don't believe that you have any business with Monsieur le Comte. That big Champs-Elysées merchant brought him yesterday two dark chestnut horses, which seemed to suit him perfectly, and they are only waiting for a five hundred francs payment."

Lefebvre was dressed that day in the big blue overcoat that he ordinarily wore, and that, in fact, gave him somewhat the appearance of a horse dealer. His *Legion d'Honneur* decoration, would have prevented that misunderstanding, but just that morning, Madame Lefebvre had taken off the one he had worn for a long time in his lapel, saying that it was horribly dirty, and she had forgotten to replace it, so he had presented himself without this sign which demanded respect.

"What's that you're telling me?" he asked the Swiss. "Do you think I sell horses? Give me a piece of paper so that I can write my name. Give it to your master. I guarantee you that he will see me."

"I will gladly give you a piece of paper," answered the bad-tempered door-keeper, impressed by Lefebvre's tone of command. "But Monsieur le Comte is never awake at this hour, and his valet would never take it upon himself to wake him up."

"Give it to him anyway," Lefebvre continued. "Give him my little love letter when it's daylight for him. I bet that he will order that I be received politely when I return."

Seeing written on the paper that was given back to him the name *Commandant Lefebvre*, the Swiss Guard recognized the blunder he had committed, and, doing his best to repair it, said:

"Commandant, you can be sure that as soon as he is awake, the Count will have your note."

And he deigned to leave his box and accompany Lefebvre right up to the door of the townhouse that he took the trouble of opening and closing after him.

Having at least two hours to kill before he could hope to be received, the Commandant went to walk with his worries on the Boulevard des Invalides, which was near. There, in one of the public gardens, he recognized an old sergeant that he had had in the past under his command, and who had left one of his legs on the field of battle at Essling. Recognizing each other, they spoke of Austerlitz, Iena, Eylau, Friedland and of the *other one,* all of which made the time pass quickly and, for a moment, took away from Lefebvre's mind the memory of the terrible fight that he was going to have to defend his daughter's interests.

Finding a small café, the two companions-in-arms went inside, and a couple of *glorias*,[6]—a name rather fitting for those old remains of the Imperial legions—reminded them of the good times. At the cost of a leg or an arm, they had Russians and Prussians to tear apart at their discretion. After several hours thus spent agreeably, Lefebvre went back to the Comte de Lucheux' townhouse.

"There is the Count, coming out from visiting with his aunt," said the Swiss Guard. "He's walking with the friend with whom he just had lunch. He will be with you in a moment."

In fact, the Count, giving his arm to a woman who appeared splendidly beautiful to Lefebvre, was coming down the steps of his townhouse; and he accompanied her with an air of gallantry and familiarity to her carriage, which had been waiting for her in the courtyard.[7]

After having remained on the steps until the carriage was gone some distance, having given a friendly wave to its charming contents, the Count went across the courtyard and

---

[6] Alcohol coffee drink with a crème topping served in a glass.
[7] Madame de Camembert ; she will return later.

reached, on the side of the outbuildings, a little stairway leading to a mezzanine situated above the stables.

Meanwhile, the Swiss Guard had closed the door to the townhouse after the carriage. Ringing a bell, the Guard made a valet in a black suit and a white tie appear, to whom he presented Lefebvre, saying:

"Monsieur is the person the Count is expecting."

"If Monsieur will please follow me," said the valet.

A moment later, Lefebvre found himself in a tête-à-tête with the seducer in a drawing room more attractively furnished than he would have supposed, from the rather unattractive surroundings of that bachelor apartment.

"Monsieur le Comte," said the Commandant, after, with marked politeness, he had been asked to sit down, "I saw my wife yesterday, and she took so much trouble to hide the truth from me that I had to believe that she, like many mothers whose weakness for their daughters makes them commit imprudent acts, had something to reproach herself for what has happened to us. But she explained to me that she knew nothing until the last moment."

"That is perfectly true," said the Count loyally.

"She had to let Amanda go out alone," the Commandant continued, "because of the needs of the business that they operate together. She did not know that you had met that unfortunate child in the streets of Paris, that you had followed her, surrounded her with all your seductions, and that finally you had led her into a little apartment that you probably rented for just those sorts of exploits. And the imprudent girl succumbed."

"Commandant," said Monsieur de Lucheux, "you will allow me to point out a correction—an error in your exposé of the facts. I don't deny having forced myself right into the heart of your daughter, whose beauty had made the greatest impression on me. But as for having lured her into a kind of bachelor's pad, as I think it is called, nothing is less exact. Your daughter and I were in love. We were tired of meeting out in the open. I rented an apartment for the sole purpose carrying on our relationship. There, between two people in love, opportunity created a slippery slope."

"But you're not claiming that my daughter made advances to you? You were obsessed with her; you sought her out."

"Mon Dieu! I did what any man would do when he's in love; what perhaps you would have done in my place. I'm not claiming that Mademoiselle, your daughter, threw herself at my feet, nor even that she could be reproached for not having defended herself. But, after all, she is twenty-years-old, and I didn't entrap her in any way."

"You would agree, however, Monsieur, that when that attraction, which seems so simple and so natural to you, resulted in certain consequences, the man who finds himself its author must be ready—if he is a man of honor—to bring reparations?"

"There is still one thing that it's necessary to establish," replied Monsieur de Lucheux, without answering the question directly. "That is, between Mademoiselle Amanda and me, there was never any question of marriage. She didn't make a condition for me that I should promise her that."

"But, Monsieur, in certain circumstances, I repeat, that method of reparation speaks for itself, because there is no other possible."

"I agree," the Count replied, "when, for two lovers, to the tie that formed their attachment between them, another comes to add to it, as a living testimony of their weakness... It is then possible for the mean of which you are speaking to..."

"Do you mean to say," Lefebvre quickly interrupted, "that because Amanda's life was put in danger by the accident that brought to light her shame before term, you are now free of all obligations to her?"

"I am far from saying that. However, that accident, that leaves the entire secret of our liaison between us, at least permits us to think and not do anything hastily."

"You can't bargain about a duty of honor, Monsieur, and if, as you claim, you love my daughter..."

"It is exactly because I have a great deal of affection for her that I hesitate and think about it. You see, Monsieur, how I am lodged, like a true son of the family. My aunt, of whom I am the sole heir, creates my present position by her generosity, and this same generosity is all my future. She then has the right to ask me to account for all the decisions that I take in all the important circumstances of my life. There, where she would see an evident necessity, she would perhaps pardon me for what she might call a misalliance, but with the proof of an inflexible duty being presented to her, there is no possible illusion—that would mean an irremediable rupture with her."

"Eh! Monsieur, what are all these considerations beside the honor of my daughter!"

"I find, Monsieur, that they deserve much attention, even more so because nothing about all this is known publicly. Your daughter, Madame Lefebvre and you are the only ones who know."

"And your compromising visits, do you think that they haven't been noticed?"

"I'm almost sure of the contrary. Mademoiselle Amanda had wanted to see me for a moment. In the perilous situation in which she found herself, I couldn't refuse her that consolation. But you yourself saw with what precautions I surrounded my actions."

"But what about the midwife that it was necessary to involve in this secret—do you count her for nothing?"

"With money, one can be assured of her discretion; besides, that is in the duty and the habits of her profession. That will be no sacrifice for me, and please believe me, by remaining on good terms with my family, I am in a much better position to be useful to Mademoiselle in the future, than by lowering myself with her to a limited existence short of money."

"So, Monsieur, you refuse to give your name to the woman you have seduced?"

"At the present, that seems impossible."

"Yes, you want to gain time, and one fine morning, Madame your aunt will write to us to offer a dowry and the hand of your valet."

"Monsieur!" said the Count, "you have a very harsh way of speaking!"

"Yes, Monsieur, I get to the bottom of things. Your insinuation of services that you might later render to your victim is merely a new insult added to the one that I had decided to ask you to account for. Please know that we are not the kind of people whose honor you can buy with money. We want nothing from you. All the means of reconciliation have been exhausted; now, it only remains for me to reclaim from you the favor that you cannot refuse me, and which you said you have never refused anyone. In a few hours, I will have the honor to send you my witnesses."

"First of all, let me point out to you," the Count answered calmly, "that this violent procedure goes directly counter to the secrecy that is so useful to manage this sad occurrence. Four witnesses are going to put into our confidence."

"No, Monsieur, we merely jostled each other in the street and then we had words. We are hot-headed, and we fight."

"So be it then, we will fight. It would be a miracle if you killed me, but if fate decides the contrary and I kill you, there will be a family deprived of its head just at the precise moment when misfortune is weighing heavily on it."

"That should have been considered before bringing said misfortune," said Lefebvre. "Besides, I do have a son who will avenge me."

"You don't know me," replied the Count. "You don't know that two or three successful duels have given me the reputation for being a rather formidable adversary."

"Come now!" Lefebvre shouted. "Do you hope to scare an old soldier like me?"

"To scare you, no. I'm not thinking about that the least in the world. I only want to prove to you that I, myself, am not afraid in refusing the encounter that you wish. That is my only intention."

"What! You are refusing! When the other day, you conceitedly told me that a proposition of this kind was always to your taste?"

"Yes, I am refusing," the Comte de Lucheux answered calmly, "and I would be happy if you would please not ask me the reasons for such refusal."

"*Parbleu*! Those reasons are easy to guess. Either you are a miserable coward..."

"Monsieur!" Lefebvre's adversary said quickly.

"...Or you are acting generous by not seeming to want to add murder to the desolation that you have already brought to my household."

"Believe me, Monsieur, when I say that a duel between us is impossible. Don't insist that I explain myself any better."

"Not only must I insist, but if you stubbornly do not speak, I must tell you that I will see that as the subterfuge of a coward—and will make it publicly known."

"You are wrong, my dear Monsieur, to push me."

"And you, my dear Monsieur, to want to play games with a man of my caliber."

"You will not have it? Then, here's what happened. Just this morning, foreseeing the regrettable extremities to which you might want to go, I judged it proper to be sure of the participation of a friend. I had the same idea as you. While asking him the assistance that probably would be necessary for him to lend me, I mentioned one of those stupid quarrels, which everyone is likely to pick up in the street..."

"To that point, everything is fine," Lefebvre said.

"You won't be astonished that my witness wanted to know the name and the social position of my adversary."

"That goes without saying. It's necessary to know with whom you find yourself on the dueling field."

"I then identified you as Commandant Lefebvre, former head of a battalion."

"Yes. So?"

"Well, I have the greatest possible regret to be forced to tell you this to your face, but my friend, who is Head of Foreign Affairs in the Cabinet of Monsieur, being in a position to know a great deal of secret things, upon hearing your name, told me...and these are his own words: 'Commandant Lefebvre! You don't fight with a man of that type, nor with anyone in his family.'"

"Your witness is insolent!" Lefebvre shouted.

"Insolent, maybe, but quite ready to support what he said, because he added: 'I cannot let you know the character of his indignity, but I swear to you, if that man doesn't understand you, tell him to come find me and, man to man, I will make him acknowledge that he is not a suitable adversary."

"Yes, certainly, I will go. Where does this gentleman live?"

"You are certain to encounter him at the Ministry of Foreign Affairs if you go there after you leave."

"I will go there immediately," said Lefebvre, rising. "But do not believe, Monsieur, that you will escape me by this evasion. If you refuse to give me satisfaction, I will resort to some public and sensational insult to force you to abandon the position behind which you are trying to hide."

"In any case, Monsieur," the Count responded, "I would find it prudent if you were to give some rest to your resentment. Mademoiselle Amanda's health seems to me to demand great attention, and before she is completely back on her feet..."

"You are truly full of attention," Lefebvre ironically interrupted. "I could almost believe that you have a heart."

"Let's leave it there," said Monsieur de Lucheux. "In the terms where we are now, we shouldn't harm each other."

"Yes, if you, a man who looks for shameful means of escape, refuse to fight me."

"Monsieur, I am in my own house. I ask you to remember that, and I am not alone."

"Then call your valets," said Lefebvre, who more and more spoiled the dignity of his position. "Their heart is in a better place than yours."

Monsieur de Lucheux did nothing but go into another room. Left alone, Lefebvre departed shortly thereafter, slamming doors behind him, but that excitement wasn't long in dying out after some reflection. It wasn't possible to misunderstand what he had been told. The Secret Bureau had several of its members detached to the Ministry of Foreign Affairs. That Ministry could therefore know the names of the personnel attached to the Bureau. And obviously, in that way, his own. When the Count's friend had said that one could not accept as an adversary either Monsieur Lefebvre or any member of his family, he had alluded to the stain that the infamy of that function had placed upon his name.

The unfortunate Commandant then understood the depth of the abyss into which his love for Herminie Daliron had led him. He no longer even had the right to get himself killed in order to protect the honor of his own family, and his son was enveloped in the reprobation that he had attached to his life!

He thought of going and finding that Head of Foreign Affairs and asking him if the magnitude of the injury done to him didn't absolve him in this matter, bit if that action wasn't crowned with success, it would have served only to disclose his daughter's dishonor. To reject his shameful functions, he would have done that with unbelievable joy, even if he was again placed in that poverty that had been so cruel for him, but the lair in which he had let himself be drawn wasn't the kind of prison from which one could leave, or even ever wash away the defilement that it brought.

Finally, as he had threatened, he could, in a public place, strike Monsieur de Lucheux in the face, but what would that accomplish if, instead of getting justice for himself, his adversary took the matter to court? He would receive an infamous condemnation, might be dispossessed of his functions without compensation, and for all that, his honor would still be forever lost. He might even see himself exposed to the vengeance of his sinister colleagues, fearing for themselves the exposure of their secret.

The unfortunate Commandant was then enclosed on all sides by a circle of fire, without even the resource of asking advice and assistance from a friend, without being able to reveal the baseness of his fall! He was alone, frightfully alone, against the greatest misfortune that could strike a man!

It's understandable then, that in the middle of the contemplation of such a sad situation, Lefebvre should have been visited by the idea of suicide, and, without a bizarre intervention of his lucky star, which destined him to an end further away, he would have, perhaps, succumbed to it.

In the excitement of his thoughts, after having walked for a long time without knowing where he was directing his steps, that evening he arrived in Bercy, by the banks of the Seine, and, worn out with fatigue, sat down not far from the restaurant of the Grand Maronniers. He only had to take a few steps to find the death which was flowing at his feet.

By one of those coincidences of which existence is full, just above the place where he had stopped, while he was caressing his deadly idea, happy companions were sitting around at a full table, by a window opened for a moment to refresh the atmosphere of the room where the reunion was taking place.

Across the silence and the solitude that the evening had brought, around him the noisy gaiety of the diners sent its laughter. At first, these cries of pleasure seemed to him rather annoying and unimportant, and a menace to speed up his resolution. He had just stood up, to escape them by going further away, when the fresh voice of a woman started the song *The Old Sergeant* of Béranger.[8]

The first couplet was this one:

Near the spinning wheel of his beloved daughter,

---

[8] Pierre-Jean de Béranger (1780-1857), French poet and songwriter. He was described as "the most popular French songwriter of all time" and "the first superstar of French popular music," but is mostly forgotten today.

The old sergeant distracted from his troubles,
And with a hand that a bullet murdered,
Rocked two laughing little twin grandsons.
Thus, tranquil at the threshold of the country roof,
His only refuge after so many battles,
He sometimes said, 'Being born is not all,
May God, my children, give you a beautiful death.

That refrain was an allusion too direct to the obscure and ignoble end that Lefebvre was then meditating not to move him deeply. He returned to refresh his ear, the memories of the great wars where he had taken his part of glory mingling with that refrain which seemed to speak to him, little by little, shook his resolution. At the end of the sixth couplet, when noisy applause recompensed the singer, he said to himself:

Yes, it would be wrong to die. Let's go back to my wife and my daughter. The morgue is too villainous a step!

He then started back on the way to Belleville, having the superstitious thought that, in his life, protected against himself in such a providential way, despite the storm that was currently passing over his head, there were still some beautiful days ahead.

III. But, after the storm...

On arriving home, Lefebvre found his wife at the door of her shop, saying goodbye to Madame Irénée, the mid-wife who had taken care of Amanda. It could have been nine-thirty at night, which, in Belleville, unless there was some extraordinary circumstance, was an hour a little unusual to visit the sick. Lefebvre then thought about some terrible complication, and anxiously questioned the matron.

"Not at all," Madame Irénée answered, "Mademoiselle Amanda is doing the best in the world, and tomorrow, she will be able to get up. But it was Madame Lefebvre who was on pins and needles when you didn't return. We chatted while waiting for you; and the evening went by quickly."

"You are coming back so late," said Madame Lefebvre to her husband. "I was afraid that you had gotten into a fight with that gentleman, the Count."

"No," answered the Commandant, "everything went as it should have, but we're dealing with a fellow..."

"Well, then, come in for a little while, Madame Irénée," said Madame Lefebvre, "and tell my husband what you told me, because you don't play games with a Lefebvre.

"The truth is," said the Commandant, "that I only came back this evening to reassure you, because tomorrow, I must report at the factory at a very early hour, so I must leave in an hour."

"The fact is," said the mid-wife, "that I didn't say I'd be staying. I thought I would stay only for a moment, but what if, during that time, someone had come to ask for me!"

"Bah! One hour more or less won't matter," said Madame Lefebvre. "Come in, my dear Madame Irénée, I'll make you some warm wine. And there's a man," she added, pointing to her husband, "you can't refuse."

Madame Irénée was of that respectable age where a gourmand appetite can become a determining factor. She therefore came back inside the shop. While Madame Lefebvre, in the back, began to prepare the seductive beverage, the matron, having sat down beside the Commandant, began telling him her confidential information:

"So, you were not satisfied with that handsome gentleman?"

"No!" Lefebvre answered. "I didn't find him to be a man disposed to do his duty. He hid behind some family obstacles, but in fact, it was easy for me to see that he was thinking of nothing but avoiding his responsibilities."

"That doesn't surprise me," said Madame Irénée. "I saw him beside the bed of your sick daughter, and, in my situation, I have often observed men do a similar jig. I noticed right away that he didn't want to marry her, and that he was very uncomfortable at the thought of a scandal. That's what made me pay more attention to a notion that came to me, and which I was just telling your wife before you arrived."

"What's that about?" Lefebvre asked with curiosity.

"I must tell you that, in my neighborhood, lives a young man, in the cream of youth. He's well-behaved, orderly, a good worker, has no women coming to see him, never spends a night out. Only on Sunday does he come in, at eleven o'clock at the latest. And you should see his little lodgings, how well kept, pleasant they are..."

"Well!" said Lefebvre. "And the young man?"

"For a long time, that boy has seemed to have a grief which shows on his expression. That doesn't keep him from being polite, and each time that he meets me on the stairway, he asks me how I am. But several times, when young girls I had as lodgers made overtures to him, it seemed to annoy him, and he never responded to their advances. I said to myself: 'I believe that Joseph—for that is his name—has some unrequited love in his mind.' And you're going to see that I had put my finger on it...."

"Yes, yes," said Lefebvre, "and then?"

"The morning that Madame Lefebvre came to get me for Mademoiselle Amanda, our young man was going out at the same time, and it seems to me that he saw me enter your house, because that evening, he came to ask me if the sickness of Mademoiselle your daughter was serious. 'Well!' I said to him, 'are you interested in Mademoiselle Lefebvre? So, you know her?' My young man blushed like a poppy, and told me he knew her from having seen her in your shop as he passed by, and that everyone is always interested in a pretty young girl.

" 'That's not it,' I said. 'You can't teach an old monkey to make faces; so admit honestly to me that you're in love with Mademoiselle Amanda, and that's why you're melancholy.' "

At that moment, Madame Lefebvre, bringing the wine she had prepared, came to join in the conversation.

"It doesn't astonish me at all," she said, "that this Joseph would be in love with our Amanda, seeing that several times, in the evening, I've noticed him looking through the shop window, but not arrogantly, and he left as soon as he noticed he'd been seen."

"Continue," said Lefebvre, in order to further the narration.

"The poor young man," Madame Irénée continued, "having been somewhat taken aback by my question, replied: 'All right, I'll tell you my secret, if you will tell me yours. What exactly is Mademoiselle Lefebvre's illness?' I looked him up and down, with an air to put him in his place, because I guessed what he was thinking about. 'It suits you very well, young man,' I exclaimed, 'to want to make a person talk about an art of which discretion is the first virtue! Don't women have a thousand complaints which are part of my art, and that should not be confided to men, and above all, not to brats like you?' "

"What did he answer to that?" Lefebvre asked with curiosity.

"This: 'My poor Madame Irénée,' h said, 'it's useless for you to act secretive. I know as much about it as you do, and I can tell you that you can no longer ignore the fact that Mademoiselle Lefebvre has a lover.' "

"But he's a nuisance, your charming young man!" shouted Lefebvre. "If he's not a policeman, he has everything it takes to be one."

"Him? With the police? Ah, I doubt it! He's known on the contrary for his opinions, which are rather those of being in conspiracies against the Bourbons."

"Go on," said Lefebvre.

"At the word *lover*, I exclaimed, telling him he had a viper's tongue, he was a slanderer, and that I would never have thought that of him. The young man then started talking and admitted that, for more than a year, he had been in love with Mademoiselle Amanda; he had thought of nothing but her, lived only for her, but that giving himself sometimes the pleasure of following her—not to spy on her, but only to enjoy her presence, even from afar—he had seen her, several times, get up into a superb carriage with a very elegant young man. From that he deduced that she was having an intrigue and that the unfortunate girl was lost."

"Quiet!" said Lefebvre, suddenly listening. "It seems to me that someone moved; it may be Amanda, who needs something."

"What? No," Madame Lefebvre said. "She is sleeping. I went up to see her moments ago. That was Minette who hears some mice."

"I beg your pardon for having interrupted you, Madame Irénée," the Commandant said. "Please continue."

"At that point," Madame Irénée went on, "having seen me called in all haste for your daughter, he couldn't doubt that she had committed a fault, and he was certain in advance that the seducer wouldn't marry her. Because of that, after much thought, an idea came to him by which, if I agreed, I could help him a great deal..."

"He wanted to ask you to ask me for Amanda's hand in marriage?" Lefebvre asked with barely contained eagerness.

"Just as you say, Monsieur Lefebvre. And that shouldn't appear extraordinary to you. I have seen men older than he and in more brilliant positions arrange marriages for themselves with a beautiful young girl who's had only a moment of forgetfulness. It's as if she were a widow. Besides, one shouldn't complicate matters when a man takes to it in a certain way."

"Certainly," Lefebvre said, "I myself have seen a great number of similar examples of passion. But what about that young man? What is his situation?"

"Ah! As you can imagine, he is not a peer of France. He is employed as a foreman in the chemical manufacturing firm of Monsieur Clérault, but it seems that he is the pearl among his workers. Orderly, as I told you, and already having some savings. But, what's more, he's gifted with knowledge and superior capacities; his nose is always in books. Because of this, Monsieur Clérault has great regard for him, and, according to general opinion, if from one day to the next, the owner retired, he would leave him his chemical factory, where they are already discussing the matter of giving him an interest in it."

"Assuredly," said Lefebvre, "if all the good things you have told me about that young man are justified, it's very clear that, after her mistake, that would be a very good marriage that Amanda should be happy to find."

"Exactly," said Madame Irénée, "this is what he told me: 'What am I? a poor orphan, brought up by charity, with no family, no support in the world, a simple worker, although I hope not to stay in that position forever. Could I hope to claim the hand of Mademoiselle Amanda, the daughter of a superior officer who knew Napoleon?' "

"Poor young man!" Lefebvre said with emotion.

" 'It took then," the young man continued, 'a miserable scoundrel that I would have a great deal of pleasure killing if he wanted to do me the honor of fighting with me, to render me the service of bringing down to my level that beautiful statue from its pedestal; otherwise I would never have stopped loving her, because that love is my life, and I would have always been unhappy.' "

"That's a little like the way it was with us," said Madame Lefebvre, speaking to her husband. "You were obsessed about me, and in the job from which you took me, there were a thousand chances that if you had not hurried, someone else…"

"No, no," said Lefebvre with importance. "When I married you, I was sure that you were well-behaved, and the more your position was exposed, the more merit you had in staying that way."

"Ah! My boy, you were smitten with me! Even if I had been a slut, you would have gone through with the marriage."

"That's' possible, but it's not a question of us now; it's a matter of considering Madame Irénée's proposition, which assuredly merits our attention. Now, we must inform ourselves more completely about that young man, and then Mademoiselle Amanda, even with her heart still full of that blackguard, who made her into his past-time, must completely understand the sacrifice that an honest man is prepared to make for her."

"But there's no need for that," said Madame Irénée. "My young man doesn't ask that Mademoiselle Amanda know of his devotion, and discretion. He doesn't want to embarrass her. As for the girl, after what happened to her, you know very well that she will no longer have the same pretentions that she might have had formerly."

"Besides," said Madame Lefebvre, "that boy doesn't displease her. When he came sometimes to wander about the shop, she didn't get angry and we sometimes laughed together. It was only since she fell under the thrall of greater things, that is to say into shame, that she sometimes said that, with his secret love behind the shop window, that suitor was ridiculous and boring."

"I don't understand that sort of things as you do, ladies," Lefebvre said, "but I don't wish for this decent young man, who is making such a heroic sacrifice, to appear a fool to his wife. Amanda must know that he has been told everything, and that, even knowing her weakness, he still wants her for his wife, and however little heart she has, she will consecrate every instant of her life to make happy a man who has so generously devoted himself to her."

"Yes, but he," asked Madame Lefebvre, "will he also make her happy? Once the first passion has passed, is he going to throw her mistake at her head?"

"If that's a concern, based on what Madame Irénée has told us," Lefebvre answered, "the same reproaches would escape him sooner or later, during some housekeeping quarrel, even if it was agreed that he would pretend to know nothing. If he is really a gallant man, he will never make even the most discreet allusion to her shame. The whole question now is to meet with him, to chat with him, to study him. How about tomorrow, my dear Madame Irénée? I will be here at about three o'clock. Tell him to come and talk to me."

"Well! As far as I'm concerned," said Madame Lefebvre, "I am still in favor of the young man pretending not to know about her situation. Amanda is proud; she will be uncomfortable with her husband if she thinks he knows. That will create coldness in the household, and then, think about it, Lefebvre, up until now, the poor girl has been confident that everything has remained hidden from you, but if, in proposing this marriage, you begin by telling her you have discovered the truth, that will deliver a blow to her morale and she might die of shame."

"We will wait until she is completely well," Lefebvre answered, "but certainly, I don't intend for her to live with the eternal dissimulation of what I have found out. That 'proud girl' needs a lesson, and besides, to cure her of the love that has dishonored her, she must know what has passed between me and her seducer. When he had the audacity to tell me that the fruit of his libertinage not having lived, there was no necessity for him to marry the mother!"

"Really? He said that?" Madame Irénée asked. "That's really a horrible thing to say!"

"And then, that so-called gentleman seemed to want to talk to me about arranging everything with money."

"You didn't strangle him?" exclaimed Madame Lefebvre.

"No, but I can very well tell you now, since it will not take place, that I challenged him to a duel, and the coward refused!"

"Is that possible!" exclaimed Madame Irénée.

"Everything is possible, Madame Irénée, with these cowardly weaklings. Amanda must learn the truth about her gallant lover, and then, if she is not the last of women, she will have as much contempt for him as she had love before."

"Oh! I agree," Madame Lefebvre said. "The madness she felt for that heartless man won't hold against his vile actions. She had already noticed that he seemed somewhat ill at ease during his visits, and she had mentioned it to me."

"Well!" exclaimed Lefebvre, becoming excited, "let her stamp out his memory; let her welcome, as she should, that worthy boy that Heaven has sent to save her. Then she won't have to fear my severity. I will still be the same father for her. I will embrace her, my poor strayed sheep, as warmly as I have always done in the past. And all the harm she has done us will be forgotten."

In pronouncing these last words, Lefebvre had tears in his eyes. His wife shared his emotion as she threw herself into his arms.

"Oh! *Mon Dieu!*" she suddenly exclaimed.

Lefebvre's eyes, and those of the mid-wife, followed the direction of her gaze. In the entrance to the back of the shop, where the door was slightly open, they saw a white kneeling form. It was the guilty girl. She had heard her father's voice, and tormented to know if he knew about her mistake, she had furtively come down from her bedroom to listen to the conversation, almost the entirety of which she had overheard.

"Unhappy child!" exclaimed Madame Lefebvre, running to her. "In your state, to leave your bed half-naked!"

And she tried to lift her up from her begging position.

"No," Amanda answered, "not until my father has forgiven me."

"You have understood very well that I have forgiven you, if you promise me to be a good girl again," exclaimed Lefebvre, running to her and taking her into his arms.

"Yes, father!" Amanda responded. "All that you will decide, I will agree with in advance."

"Thank you, my child!" Lefebvre answered. "You were well inspired to come and listen to us. Cruel explanations have thus been spared."

"Provided that she has not been harmed herself because of her imprudence," Madame Lefebvre observed.

"I think not," answered Madame Irénée. "Her poor heart feels now relieved, and she will spend a good, peaceful night. Contentment is better than any medicine."

"Until tomorrow then, my good Amanda," Lefebvre said, once again embracing his daughter. He embraced his wife also willingly, and then said to the mid-wife:

"Will you come, Madame Irénée? I shall see you home as I go to work."

"No," replied the matron. "I'm going to help the soon to be married woman to return to bed, just to see if she needs anything. I can very well walk home alone. I am often late in the streets, and everyone knows me."

"Good evening, then," said Lefebvre, "because my lodging in Paris is about an hour from here."

And he started on his way to be at the meeting of *the Secret Bureau* the next day. It will be remembered that they met in the mornings.

IV. The Solution

The next day, at three p.m., Joseph, the young foreman, was received by the Lefebvres. His appearance as well as his conversation justified all the good things that had been said about him by the mid-wife, and, if needed, he would have made the conquest of his future father-in-law just by the respectful enthusiasm he seemed to be filled with in the presence of a companion-in-arms of the Emperor. However, before committing himself definitively, the Commandant reserved the right to get some information from the employer for whom the young man worked.

Testifying thereby that the precaution had nothing about it which upset him, the suitor said:

"If you want to see Monsieur Clérault, you will find him now at home. He's often absent, and you would do well to catch him on the fly."

Lefebvre took advantage of that information, and some minutes later, he was at the home of the manufacturer. The information he received was excellent. Not only did Monsieur Clérault have only praise about his foreman, but he considered him a superior employee and had the project of making him a full partner in the firm. However, that project, he said, would have to be delayed until, by his savings, or by the goodwill of some protector, the young worker would have procured a little capital.

That last sentence gave Lefebvre something to think about. Was the industrialist conniving with his protégé, and might one not believe that this indirect request for a dowry implied a conditional promise of association? An appointment having been previously made to come back in the evening in order to know the result of the inquiry to which he had consented to be the subject, the suitor was cleverly made aware of the question of matrimonial support which still bothered Lefebvre. Approached in that not entirely frank way, it took away something of the heroism from the lover's devotion.

But that test did not diminish the high level of his sentiments. He was astonished that anyone could have a doubt concerning his love for Amanda, and when Lefebvre spoke, not of a capital, but of an annual annuity that he could put at the disposal of the young couple, his gracious intentions were respectfully declined by the young man.

Having noticed in the course of his life that the way in which a man dealt with the question of money was a measure of his moral value, the Commandant no longer hesitated. He welcomed the request of the young worker for his daughter's hand, and with no further hesitation, Monsieur Joseph—for unfortunately the only name that his position as an orphan would let him offer his wife—was taken to see Amanda.

The encounter went marvelously well. The young man, without allowing the least explanation of the past, spoke of the honor being done to him, as if, on his side, he hadn't made the least sacrifice, and his gratitude was phrased in terms of delicacy and humility of the condition of his social class that formed a most pleasant contrast and was entirely unexpected.

Things turned out so well that it was agreed that the marriage would take place without delay. Only fulfilling the formalities relating to its celebration would cause some delay. However, a cloud remained over the situation. Monsieur de

Lucheux hadn't wanted Amanda for his wife, but, wasn't it to be feared that, still wanting her for his mistress, he might want to claim the rights that, by her weakness, Amanda had given him over her? Such a man leaves a woman, who would be desperate if abandoned, without pity or remorse. But the handsome gentleman from the Faubourg Saint-Germain might very well, seeing Mademoiselle Lefebvre act so resolutely, suddenly feel reignited the fires that the glacial notion of a marriage had killed. And then what detestable steps might come about from the persistence of his passion, overexcited by an overpowering ego?

For example, having left Amanda ill, he might have the specious pretext to send someone, or even to come in person, to inquire about her condition, or he might write. In brief, that would be a past that hadn't been liquidated entirely, and the young foreman, a foreseeing and thoughtful boy, would be preoccupied with a way to obtain a definite resolution.

The first idea that presented itself was that Lefebvre would return to see Monsieur de Lucheux and let him know that he was forbidden henceforth to concern himself with Amanda, and at the same time, tell him of the marriage. But Lefebvre, knowing that his bellicose claims had been rejected, having been struck down by his adversary, was only in a mediocre hurry to find himself again in the Count's presence. He therefore easily accepted the *veto* of his intervention on the part of all those around him.

Another way to keep Monsieur de Lucheux at a distance was for Amanda to write to him, emphasizing their break-up by announcing her impending marriage. That procedure, however, had the inconvenience of putting in the hands of her former lover a definite and written proof of the relationship that had existed between them. And despite the bitter pleasure that Mademoiselle Lefebvre would have experienced to break up with her own words the last ties that remained, she had to understand that she couldn't suitably give herself that satisfaction. Far from that, there remained a rather large number of letters that she had written to him, and to get back that epistolary deposit seemed a great deal more urgent than to add a new and compromising letter to it. Amanda, for her part, had several letters from the Count and a gold cross set with little diamonds, a symbol of love that she had always hidden from her mother by wearing it as a relic under her corsage.

Her future husband took charge of all these remains from the past and he had them on him when he presented himself one morning at the Count's townhouse.

He was wearing his Sunday best, just proper without being elegant. The Swiss guard who had so badly received his future father-in-law did not see in him a very important person. His claim to see Monsieur le Conte was greeted with very little favor. And, in addition, to be let in, he had to give a reason which had to be believable. Monsieur de Lucheux was getting dressed to go to the Tuileries to fulfill his obligation as Brigadier of the Guards and his carriage was waiting, already hitched up to take him to his company's quarters.

The young foreman was still negotiating the terms of his admission with the Swiss Guard, who was beginning to lose patience, when Monsieur de Lucheux appeared, his helmet on his head, in all the brilliance of his grand, green Brandebourg uniform. Joseph didn't hesitate to take advantage of that opportunity, and, to the great scandal of the Swiss Guard who couldn't get over such audacity, ran to approach the Count just as he was going to climb into his carriage. During that time, the driver was holding the head of the horse. The foreman could, therefore, speak to Monsieur de Lucheux, without being heard by anyone else.

"Monsieur, I must talk to you about Mademoiselle Amanda."

"Ah! Very well," said the Count, with a blossoming smile that testified to the tender interest that the name still provoked in him. "How is she, that poor child?"

"Rather well, Monsieur, but you are not now in a position to receive her message. When will I have the honor of coming back without being turned away by your people?"

"That's true," said the Count. "I'm pressed for time. Nevertheless, in a few words, what's it all about?"

"I wouldn't know how to explain myself on the spot."

"Well, climb into my carriage with me. On the way, you can tell me what you've been charged with."

Figaro was right:[9] how usefulness brings people together! The young man declined, but the Count insisted:

"Yes, yes, do! Get in! We will have a good ten minutes to talk."

The foreman decided to take advantage of the unusual honor done him, and, a moment later, from the height of the carriage, he let a mocking look fall on the Swiss Guard, who, after having opened the door of the townhouse, stood respectfully, hat off, on the threshold of his booth.

When they had gone a short way, Monsieur de Lucheux, while giving his attention to the fast and spirited horse that he was driving, asked:

"Well, what do you have to tell me?"

"I am charged by Mademoiselle Amanda," Joseph answered, "to announce to you that she is about to be married."

"Ah!" said the Count, reacting with surprise to a news that was apparently little to his taste, because he began to treat his horse's mouth harshly. "And who is she marrying?"

"Me, Monsieur le Comte," answered the future husband in a perfectly calm manner.

"You! And you yourself are taking the trouble to come and announce it to me?"

"Yes, in order for you to know that I am making this marriage with a perfect knowledge of the situation."

"Ah! Mademoiselle Amanda thought she should let you know everything?"

"No, Monsieur le Comte, it is I who knew everything in advance. From the moment that I saw Mademoiselle Lefebvre

----

[9] Allusion to the clever servant Figaro from Pierre Beaumarchais' plays *The Barber of Seville* (1773) and *The Marriage of Figaro* (1778).

become involved in a liaison that I knew could only end badly for her, I decided to offer her my devotion when it would become necessary, and she deigned to receive it."

"That was very good on your part," said the Count in a somewhat constrained tone. "Would it be indiscreet to ask you what kind of fortune you are offering your fiancée?"

"The humblest possible. I am a worker; a foreman in a factory that produces chemicals."

"Then you will allow me not to be less generous than you. I haven't been able to do for Mademoiselle Amanda all that she wanted, but on the other hand, I am in the position to offer her..."

"Yes, since I'm going to be her husband, I am in a position to forbid her to accept anything. But my visit has a completely different object than that of bringing forth your pleasant memories. I have come to ask you to return Mademoiselle Lefebvre's letters and to bring you those that you wrote her."

"Those letters," Monsieur de Lucheux drily answered, "you understand that I don't have them on me."

"I don't doubt that, but you can set a day for me to come make that exchange, or, what might be simpler, you leave the sealed packet with your Swiss Guard and while coming to pick it up, I will deposit mine with him."

"But what if I nevertheless wished to hold on to those letters?" the Count asked, the dry and peremptory voice of his successor finally making him lose some of his calm.

"I do you the honor of believing that they are important to you, but to return them is a sacrifice that demands loyalty and justice, and you are too much a gentleman for me to be forced to insist."

"My dear Monsieur," said the Count, becoming more and more impatient, "I don't like people who gives me lessons and, from the height of your devotion for Amanda, you are using a tone that doesn't suit me."

"I don't believe, Monsieur, that there has been anything impolite in my words, while you don't show very good manners in calling Mademoiselle Lefebvre Amanda. As for my tone, it's that of a man who is neither your friend nor your admirer and who doesn't think he is obliged to kneel to reclaim the payment of a debt."

"Oh! I know," said the Count, "that there are workers today who are clever speakers and that impertinence is for them the first of instincts."

"Well, Monsieur le Comte, to set myself apart from my fellow workers, may I again ask you, with the deepest humility and without rhetoric, if you judge it proper to give me back my wife's letters?"

"I don't know about that," Monsieur de Lucheux answered, transferring his bad mood to his horse, to which he applied a vigorous whip lash.

Under that unmerited attack, the noble animal reared, making a prodigious bound. Then, starting off like an arrow, he dashed off furiously at full speed, that could only end in some catastrophe.

Feeling himself in the position of Hippolytus on his way to Mycenae,[10] while making great efforts to hold back his steed, Monsieur de Lucheux had become extremely pale. The passers-by on every side moved out of the way, and the rear of the carriage was in danger of being broken apart at the first obstacle. The driver cried out in vain with agony: *Stop! Stop!* No one made any effort to put his life against that runaway beast out control. The danger was becoming greater second by second.

"Is your horse of great importance to you?" the foreman coldly asked.

"At this moment, only moderately," Monsieur de Lucheux answered.

Then the worker took a small pistol out of his trousers' pocket, and aiming at the head of the furious animal, he pulled the trigger.

---

[10] Hippolytus was the grandson of Phaestus and had inherited his the kingdom of Sicyon, but Agamemnon of Mycenae led an army against him. In terror, Hippolytus surrendered.

The shot didn't hit its target, but the sound of the detonation and that of the bullet whistling between its ears astonished the horse to the point that it stopped short. Ten persons then ran to take charge of him, and all the peril vanished.

"It's fortunate," Monsieur de Lucheux said to his liberator, "that you are in the habit of carrying a weapon on you!"

"I carry one sometimes, and today that was a good precaution, because it seems to me rather dangerous to get into one of your coaches."

The worker got slowly out of the carriage, then added:

"Monsieur le Comte will be good enough to think about whether he wants to return those letters to me."

"Oh! After the service you've just rendered me, that goes without saying. You will find them tomorrow afternoon with the Swiss Guard."

"And I shall, at that time, give your letters back to you," said the foreman, who, by means of that generous trust, ended by having gotten the best of the encounter.

With his hands, Monsieur de Lucheux took a sealed packet that was like the testament of a love, the end of which he hadn't believed could be so close. In the interval, his driver had made sure that nothing in the harness had been damaged, and the carriage left rapidly.

While going in another direction, Amanda's suitor was thinking to himself that the retrospective fantasies of the Count wouldn't last long, and he could certainly be considered as warned.

V. The Mote and the Beam

While Lefebvre had remained preoccupied with the misfortune that had happened in his own house, his passion for Herminie, as if lost and buried by his immense paternal cares, had ceased to exercise its powerful domination over him. But as soon as calm on the side of Amanda had returned to his spirit, he found himself once more strongly obsessed by that *idée fixe,* and he went back to the Hôtel de Londres to see what chances there were for him after the elimination of the dangerous rivalry which he had come up against.

He found bad news at the Place de l'Estrapade. The day after his turbulent visit, the dove had again taken flight. And because they really didn't know, or didn't want to tell him anything, it was impossible for him to obtain any information about Mademoiselle Daliron's new domicile. Lefebvre then thought, with some likelihood, that his son could be better informed, and besides, he now had a serious reason for seeing him. He had to tell him about his sister's impending marriage and ask him to come and meet his future brother-in-law, before the day, rather close, of the ceremony.

One thing had been agreed at Belleville during a family counsel; that was that Alfred would not be told about the sad circumstances which had led to the marriage. Confiding the truth would have been useless and, in the future, it might present several inconveniences. So, when the elegant secretary of the banker learned that his sister was going to marry a mere factory worker, he was a little astonished, and asked his father if, by proceeding with less haste, a more suitable husband couldn't have been found for Amanda?

Lefebvre answered that the party the most concerned seemed to be satisfied; that a girl without a dowry was always difficult to marry; that between the foreman of an important factory and a little lingerie girl there wasn't a great deal of social disproportion. He hastened to add that the suitor was an intelligent young man, who, with his manners, belied the humbleness of his present station, and, in a short time, might even become the partner of his current employer. Alfred wasn't a vain boy; he didn't insist on his objections, to which Lefebvre found he had responded in a satisfactory way. At that point, the Commandant could broach another subject that was also close to his heart. He asked his son how the agreement set up between them after their last encounter had been carried out.

"The most religiously in the world," Alfred answered. "The very day of your visit, I wrote Herminie that, after what had happened, she must understand that our relationship had to end, and, at the same time, I sent her a hundred *écu* bracelet."

"And then?" Lefebvre asked, curious.

"She returned my bracelet," Alfred answered, "with a letter which saddened me."

"Women, when you leave them, always know how to take on tearful airs. You shouldn't be duped by their great despair."

"That of Herminie," the young man replied, "was expressed in terms too simple and too seemly not to be sincere."

"Did she tell you where she was going? Because you probably know that she has moved."

"She did tell me, in fact, that she had left the lodgings where your visit had compromised her, but she didn't tell me where she was going."

"Excellent stratagem to get you interested in her again," Lefebvre said. "Let me see her letter; my old experience will make me able to disentangle her feelings."

"Your old experience," Alfred retorted, "seems to me to be little related to an exceptional situation, for which, for my part, I am completely wracked by guilt."

"Well," said the Commandant, "let me see the epistle; we will discuss it afterwards."

Herminie's letter, given to Lefebvre, read as follows:

My Love,

If you had sent me a lock of your hair or the least 25 sou object from a boutique, I would have kept that as a precious souvenir, but you sent me a magnificent bracelet as one does to a prostitute when tired of her. I must therefore return that sumptuous but offensive article. Nevertheless, for this, as for all the rest, I have no hard feelings, since my love was working for another's account...

"What does she mean," Lefebvre interrupted.

"In a minute, in a minute, father, I will explain that to you."

...Since my love was working for another's account, I should not have hoped that it should leave me in possession of your dear person for a long time. In any case, a little sooner or a little later, I should have expected a separation. But the miserable intervention of your father cruelly hastened that denouement. Frankly, you still owed me some days of happiness and I doubt that the desired results could be obtained in so little time.

But she's talking in riddles, that girl," Lefebvre said, again suspending his reading.

"It was to me she wrote, father, not to you. I understand very well what she means, and you will know it in an instant. Do continue."

In stubbornly persisting to follow me, your father, who was hardly reasonable for his age...

"You see that!" said Lefebvre. "That didn't keep her from letting me enter her apartment when she took me for a general."

"Read on, father," Alfred said, impatiently.

...And he had the most disastrous influence on my life. Not only did he deprive me of you before it was time, but his brutal intervention forced me leave that house where he had already reduced me to seek asylum. Through the wickedness of the landlady, it rebounded to the family where I was giving private lessons. That scandal deprived me of the poor income that I used for the accomplishment of a sacred duty. That misfortune becomes so much worse, when, as short as our liaison was, it made me foresee what other women might perhaps call a burden and that I, despite everything, will call good fortune. That, my love, is what will be a better souvenir than a brace-

*let! And why is it necessary that I be so poor when that bless-
ing is mingled with worry.*

"But there hasn't been enough time for her to be sure of
what she is insinuating," Lefebvre exclaimed. "That's a car-
rot!"

"Enough, please, father," Alfred said, like a man who
could hardly control himself.

*If I am not mistaken by the first signs, my hope being re-
alized, what will I do? I hardly know. I'm going to begin by
selling my small amount of furniture. That should last for a
year at least, providing for my brother's schooling. Then I will
put myself in an institution up until the point that my state will
make the stay impossible. If it is then necessary to go to the
Maternity Hospice, that extremity doesn't frighten me. After
that, Providence will provide.*

*Don't look for me, my love, because I will take more care
to hide myself from you than you will know how to find me.
There is only one occurrence in which I would consent to give
you news of me. That would be if the Good Lord would wish to
take me out of this world before my task is finished. Then I
would commend "someone" to you, because it would be a
duty to ask for your generosity for "him" or for "her." Destined as you are for a brilliant existence, I will always know
where to find you, if it becomes necessary. Now, goodbye,
dear love of my heart. Try to keep some poor little memory of
me. As for you, you have been my only, my first love and I am
very sure that after you I will never love again.*

Herminie

After he finished reading, seeing that his son had tears in
his eyes, Lefebvre said:

"But, my boy, those are just words. You can be sure that
at the first opportune moment, she will be found."

"No, father, in the short time that I lived with her, I know
her well enough to know that she's a proud soul that will endure everything relating to me."

"Well, then, I will find her and will know very well how to tame her, I can promise you that."

"Permit me to tell you that now, you, less than anyone, are in a position to have her listen to you. Without you, everything would have come about in a conventional way and I would not have the terrible worry that I will continue to have."

"Did you swallow the story she told you?"

"Is that misfortune impossible? She is an upright girl that I never caught in the least lie. She hadn't even put the shadow of a doubt when she admitted that she loved me. And the first thing that she told you when you presented yourself as a *useful* suitor, was that her heart was taken."

"Me, I tell you that she's some clever girl, and I'm glad I intervened, because God knows where she would have led you!"

"She would have led me to the altar; that's what she had in mind!"

"What! You would have married that woman?" Lefebvre exclaimed, without remembering that, some days before, he believed it was his right to force his daughter upon her seducer, in a similar situation.

"You don't understand, father. It's never been a question of a marriage between me and Herminie. The event that could have made it a duty for me hadn't even been suspected by us."

"Oh! Come now! Are you joking" Lefebvre exclaimed. "Duty to a woman who, before you, had two or three lovers!"

"*Mon Dieu*! If I questioned my conscience, I'm not sure what it would have answered."

"A woman," Lefebvre sententiously responded, continuing not to perceive that his words were backfiring on him, "once she has had an affair, can no longer claim to carry the name of an honest man, and unless she can find some pathetic idiot to..."

"It's useless," Alfred said, "to discuss a question that has been so harshly settled by the victim."

"The victim! The victim!" Lefebvre repeated, shrugging. "But if not herself, then what was that marriage she wanted you to consider: another whore like her?"

"Would it seem to you that Mademoiselle Martin Lambert was a more desirable choice for me?"

"Mademoiselle Martin Lambert! What madness are you telling me?"

"When you wanted to remove me from your path, you talked to me a great deal about all the personal advantages that I was wasting. It seems other eyes, more disinterested, had seen me in the same manner, because very obviously the daughter of the house had singled me out."

"There is nothing impossible in that, after all, but what did Mademoiselle Herminie have to do with it?"

"She could make Mademoiselle Lambert, who, as a rich heiress, believes she is permitted every sort of caprice, not shunt me around constantly, going from the most engaging welcomes to the coldest and most unfriendly manners. As women understand very well among themselves: 'Make her type jealous,' Herminie told me, 'and soon you will see a more friendly disposition emerge.' And it was she herself who offered to be the riding crop to lash the other woman—herself with the most perfect abandon and the most complete selflessness."

"Didn't you see that it was a way for her to be near you?"

"*Mon Dieu*, father," Alfred continued, "because you have known, in your life in the army, many fleeting women, you believe you know them all, and you are disposed to think a great deal of ill of them. But in the heart of individual women there are impenetrable abysses. Please understand, that Herminie was a character apart. She proposed her bargain to me very conscientiously."

"I would have liked to see how you could have extricated yourself at the end!"

"The same way that you extricated yourself from me. It's just that the extrication would have been less violent and would have exposed me to fewer regrets."

"Well! What's done is done, and I won't think anymore about it. It remains to be seen what your beautiful fantasy schemes will finally lead to."

"Everything that Herminie had foreseen," Alfred responded. "Since I have stopped spending all my evenings in my employer's drawing room, and no longer made any attempts at pleasing Mademoiselle Lambert. Most of all, she has found out, through her maid—she having the advantage for me of being very gossipy and indiscreet—that one of the servants has frequently gone to carry my letters to a woman in a distant neighborhood. Now, the poor girl is out of her mind. Constantly obsessed with me, sometimes she seeks to sting me with sharp words; other times to surround me with kindness. She finally came to ask me for an explanation that I haggled about. Ten times already she has offered me some very nice entreaties, without my having been, so far, willing to accept them."

"The Devil!" said Lefebvre. "I agree; those are what I would call significant changes. But not everything is up to the girl's will."

"For a long time," Alfred said, "Monsieur Lambert has known my aspirations and is not hostile to them. Everything considered, he can't do without me; I'm his brain. To make sure of it in perpetuity by having me enter his family wouldn't displease him too much. As for the mother, that's different; she's totally hostile, but she has not had enough arguments to force me to leave the household."

"Well, my friend, you must move that along! To become Martin Lambert's son-in-law! Why, that would be magnificent!"

"Without a doubt, but now I feel rather cold about that denouement."

"Come now! I'm telling you that I will find your bad-luck Herminie. Wasn't I the first one interested in her? Well, when you are rich, if she doesn't want me to console her at all costs, you can have her back. There is only one thing that bothers me now..."

"What's that?" Alfred answered.

"The marriage of your silly sister. This is rather bad timing..."

"First of all, it's not necessary right now to make her part of this. And later I can perhaps help my future brother-in-law become an industrialist."

"Well, son, let's keep that thought on the back burner," Lefebvre said, rising. "For my part, I'm going to start a campaign to find the fugitive. And we expect to see you as soon as possible in Belleville."

"I will go there this evening," Alfred said, "but not a word about all this to my mother and my sister."

"Who do you take me for?" Lefebvre answered importantly. "Don't I know that discretion is soul of business and that nothing good happens because of idle chat."

VI. The Marriage Proposal

Several days after his daughter's marriage, where everything had happened in the most satisfactory way, Commandant Lefebvre took up again the search for Herminie Daliron.

His first action was naturally to pay a visit to the concierge at the Rue de Provence, but there, he found only confirmation of the facts contained in the letter to his son, to which he had appeared to accord so little belief. After having given up her apartment, Mademoiselle Daliron had gone ahead with the sale of her furniture and nothing further had been heard of her.

Another risky visit to Monsieur Simonnet served only to confirm the old professor's anger against his former *protégée* that the Mistress of the Hôtel de Londres had completely ruined in his opinion. He said he knew absolutely nothing about her, and he added disdainfully that he didn't care to learn anything more about her.

Lefebvre next had the idea to go to the Lycée Henry IV. There, he found that the tuition and boarding of the young Daliron boy had been paid in advance for the entire year. The child, called to the parlor, could give him only one piece of information: that his sister had come to say good-bye to him, telling him of an absence to which she herself could not assign a duration.

Thus, up to that point, the program of the poor abandoned woman had been religiously followed.

The enthusiasm for the kind of chase that Lefebvre had undertaken, didn't, however, make him lose sight of the great interest of ambition and future that he had to handle carefully for his son. In continuing his system of coldness and indifference towards Mademoiselle Lambert that had already succeeded so well for him, Alfred, to tell the truth, was no longer playing a role. By the sweet and courageous resignation of Herminie, by that possible paternity that she had made him foresee, perhaps also remembering those ardent emotions with which their short liaison had been filled, he had felt himself thrown completely to the side of the absent woman, and no longer gave any but the most lukewarm and distracted welcome to the loving entreaties of the banker's daughter.

But the more Alfred' lack of interest showed itself, and after having acted out a comedy, the more she showed her real self, the more the heiress put passion into triumphing! Going straight to the heart of the matter, and not worrying about compromising her dignity, she finally made to her former *ugly duckling* the most explicit admission of her sentiments and, without any reticence, brought up the subject of their marriage. That act, so frank and flattering for the ego of the young secretary, brought about a new turnabout in his feelings. He now told himself that Herminie was very entirely lost to him and, besides, continuing that liaison would have led to an impasse, whereas Mademoiselle Lambert's love opened infinite horizons in his future. At that point, sometimes with his would-be fiancée, sometimes with her father, a question often returned as the order of the day: how to vanquish Madame

Lambert's resistance, which could be expected at the thought of their union.

Judged very difficult to handle, here is how, one fine morning, that question was tackled by Commandant Lefebvre.

Martin Lambert and he did not know each other. It had been without any intervention from him that Alfred had entered the financier's household. The former officer on half-pay and the rich *député* lived on very different levels of the social edifice to have had any natural opportunities to meet. It would have been necessary, therefore, that Lefebvre make a premeditated visit to Monsieur Lambert. But despite seeing the dowry of Martin Lambert's daughter glittering before his eyes, the Commandant, because of his ideas of the supremacy of the military, having only mediocre esteem for people of money, taking it as a fact that the position of his son had been filled—and well filled—without his efforts, believing that any show of deference toward the banker would have no useful result, let their two existences continue to move in their respective spheres, without trying to create any relationship between them.

On morning, however, *ex abrupto,* without consulting his son, Lefebvre had himself announced at Monsieur Lambert's house. Lambert was just then in a foul mood; he had just learned of the disappearance of one of his colleagues who, fleeing abroad, had taken with him for a sum of nearly 1.5 million francs which belonged to Lambert. So, then, when his servant came to tell him that a Commandant Lefebvre was asking to see him, the man of finance, being so preoccupied, didn't even notice that the name Lefebvre was also that of his secretary.

"I don't know that gentleman," he answered. "Tell him to make known the purpose of his visit in writing."

It's known that among highly placed people and those who wish to appear to have great occupations, that's the standard formula to dismiss tiresome people.

Lefebvre insisted, saying that he had a most urgent communication, which could not be written down. In addition, he added:

"I am the father of the young Monsieur Lefebvre that Monsieur Lambert has as a secretary."

After this, the Commandant was introduced, but preferring to explain his foul mood rather than suspending its course, the banker said to him:

"I beg your pardon, Monsieur, for having hesitated to receive you, but I am dealing with a very frustrating situation. I have just learned of a very important bankruptcy and have serious measures to take. Please tell me in a few words what brings you to me."

"I've come to thank you for your kindness toward my son."

"If that's all it is, I will consider your gratitude as sufficiently expressed. You son is a charming employee with whom I am very happy and I will give you ample praise of him on a better occasion."

Even though he had been dismissed, Lefebvre didn't leave.

"But, Monsieur," he continued, "I would also like to speak to you about his future."

"Oh! That would be a long chapter; your son is barely twenty-three-years old!"

Seizing the transition on the fly and, as one says, putting his foot in it, The Commandant continued:

"Mademoiselle, your daughter, if I'm not mistaken, is eighteen. In the case that it might be a question of following up on certain hopes of which Alfred has already spoken to me, there would be a proper rapport of age between the two young people."

The banker looked at Lefebvre with stupefaction.

"I have told you, my dear Monsieur," he repeated, "that I don't have a moment to lose, and truly, to talk about such hypotheses which are as gratuitous as they are ridiculous, is a strange way to spend your time."

Martin Lambert then walked toward the door, which was a clear way to show his annoying visitor the way out.

"Let's cut short, I ask you, a subject, rather extraordinary in itself, and the time that you choose to deal with it with tiresome insistence truly takes on a character of irrationality."

"But, my dear Monsieur," Lefebvre said without being moved, "my son has 1.5 million francs in dowry. You won't give as much to your daughter and you can't deny that Alfred is a boy with great intelligence. I myself am a superior officer in retirement. I don't therefore see what there is so irrational in my approach."

"You are giving 1.5 million francs in marriage to your son?" the banker, incredulous, asked.

"Yes, Monsieur, that is exactly the sum that you are about to lose and, what's more, that explains your somewhat distracted reception, but I don't hold it against you."

"But how do you know that I stand to lose that very sum? The amount of the theft is not yet known, except by me and my bookkeeper. Do you know this because of his gossip?"

"I don't know your bookkeeper, but chance allowed me to know that a ruthless financier just fled the country taking with him the sum of 1.5 million francs. Now, that sum, I will be powerful enough to replace it in your hands, but it's a matter of *quid pro quo.* Our children love each other; let's get them married. That's what I came to tell you, and you can see that the moment was not entirely ill-chosen."

"Then," Monsieur Lambert said, "you know where my money is?"

"Yes, I do, and with that information and the telegraph, the police will soon be able to recover it."

"But how were you able to find out...?"

"The *how* is not what should interest you, right now; the important thing is that I know, and as soon as you clarify your intentions on the question of this marriage, I will prove to you that my information is correct."

"So," said the banker, weighing his words, "my daughter's hand for my secretary, that's the condition that you make for your information?"

"Yes, because, one more time, you are not ignorant of the fact that these two young people please each other and even without my contribution, there would be nothing improper about that union."

"But we can't, however, celebrate it here, in my study, before you have consented to explain yourself."

"Ah! You know that the word of Monsieur Martin Lambert will be enough for me."

"I must admit, however," the banker continued, without answering directly, "that I would be curious to know a little more about the source of your information. Since you are making it a business deal, that would be a way for me to check it out."

"Well! To lift the corner of the veil a little for you," Lefebvre answered, lowering his voice, "I will tell you that there's a woman mixed up in all this. But I can't tell you anything further without compromising her."

"Ah! I understand!" said Martin Lambert.

"So much the better if you can guess," the Commandant replied, "but I must point out to you that time is pressing, and you appear to be amusing yourself, if I may speak bluntly, with trifling matters."

"All right, it's a deal!" said the banker. "We will be uniting our young people. Now, tell me where my thief is?"

"At Vaugirard."

"Vaugirard? But you were talking about telegraphing!"

"Only to take advantage of the common opinion that bankrupts flee to Brussels. Yours is a great deal smarter. He has not left Paris. Take this!" Lefebvre added. "Here on this sheet of paper is the name of the street, the number of the apartment, the password, with which you can reach him. Have yourself accompanied by two or three strong lackeys, and just any case, take some weapons."

"Oh!" Martin Lambert said, "I know whom to take with me."

"Only," said Lefebvre, "don't let my name be mentioned in connection with this, I beg of you, and let even my son Alfred ignore that..."

"That's understood," said Martin Lambert, ringing for his valet to bring him his hat.

Lefebvre accompanied him to the bottom of the stairs and saw him get into a carriage which was already harnessed and waiting under a shed. Then he left the millionaire's house without asking to see his son.

The reader has probably already guessed that a letter, passing through Lefebvre's hands, while he was working at the Secret Bureau, had procured for him the information that he had just used with such determination.

Under the honest and somewhat puritanical administration of Hulet, that prevarication would have been a fact of the highest gravity, but under the administration of Dulac, a.k.a. Rempailleux, it was no more than an opportunity to be cleverly seized. The way in which, in fact, this casuist with his rather flexible moral background would have reacted to such an act, had he known it, would have been to label it praiseworthy, because its intent was to take the money out of the hands of a dishonest man and restore it to its rightful owner.

A Laverenette[11] and other recruits of the same nature couldn't reasonably be asked to have the discretion and inflexible and rigorous honesty that turned unsealing and reading letters into a kind of tomb where all the confidences and all the mysteries are to be buried. With those men without morality, the principles of absolute and impenetrable secrecy that had been the rule of the Secret Bureau, had be replaced by an abdication of conscience, and certain accommodations, depending on circumstances, when they could be permitted to

---

[11] Laverenette is Lefebvre's former army colleague who was given a dishonorable discharge for theft and recruited him into the Secret Bureau. See Vol. 3, p. 271.

forget their vow of silence. That type of doctrine of freewheeling compromise was part and parcel of the style of the new Secret Bureau, and Lefebvre hadn't proceeded under any other impulse. Sovereignly dominated by his passions, which altered in him the extreme delicacy of moral sense, he had persuaded himself with very good faith that, in working to impose his bargain on his son's employer, he had done the simplest and most natural thing in the world. And when the revelation, that his actions intended for the profit of his paternal ambition, had also led to the restitution of a stolen sum, far from thinking himself guilty, he had instead regarded himself as a zealous and clever magistrate who, by procuring the arrest of a fraudulent banker, had just rendered a valuable service to public order.

To say the least, his expectation was to have Martin Lambert indebted to him, and thinking that he had not sold his information to him at a very high price, when he saw the banker in a subsequent meeting talk to him about some obstacles that the immediate realization of their bargain might encounter, he took a very high and threatening tone with him. With a man infatuated with his millions and his high social position, that was precisely the way to cloud everything. The reason given by the banker for obtaining some delay had, however, a very respectable side.

"As far as I'm concerned," Lambert said, "the marriage suits me and the proof of that is that, having been informed by Madame Lambert of an understanding that seemed to have been established between the young people, I, nonetheless, kept Alfred in my household. But my wife is strongly opposed to the idea of taking your son for a son-in-law. I well know that, in the case of a difference of opinions, that of the father must have the last word. However, I cannot, right off, and for a marriage that would astonish the public, go to the violent extreme of ignoring maternal consent. Only time can overcome that resistance, and everything considered, there is no peril in delay, because my daughter is only eighteen-years-old, and your son twenty-three."

The day following his invasion of the banker's home, Lefebvre had come joyfully to announce to his son, without, of course, telling him his method of success, that he had taken the bull by the horns and had gone to ask the hand of Mademoiselle Lambert for him, and that his request had been accepted.

Alfred, then, like his father, took the thing as done, but he nevertheless admitted the necessity as well as the propriety of the delay, and that opinion was also shared by Mademoiselle Lambert. Lefebvre then saw himself obliged to be patient and to return to Herminie, whom he searched for with all his mental activity. But he was no luckier in that direction. It was in vain that he said to himself that the poor girl was acting out a comedy of retreat, and that he could put his hand on her whenever he wanted to. She continued to be unfindable, so that, little by little, for Alfred as well as for himself, she no longer remained anything but a tender and sad memory.

VII. *Madame de Camembert*

We have seen the woman who bore that name [12] in some preceding chapters, on the steps of the townhouse of Lucheux, where she had just had lunch with the old Duchess, the dowager of that name. She was then holding the arm of Monsieur Albert de Lucheux, the nephew of the duchess and the great deal too happy lover of Amanda, to whom Commandant Lefebvre had just come to demand an accounting of his happiness. But in a part found in Chapter II of the Prologue, [13] a great deal further away from this story, Madame de Camembert had already been shown to you, selling the Marquis de Lupiano an historic townhouse where she lived on the Notre-Dame-des-Champs and which had belonged to the Controller

---

[12] Barely. See Note 7 page 31.
[13] See Volume 1, pp. 49 seq.

General, the Abbé Terray.[14] The sale of that building took place about the year 1819 and, at the same period, a living dead woman, the Marquise de Camembert, after having buried an old gouty and septuagenarian husband, disappeared from society, where she had played a brilliant and active role, to go bury her twenty-five years and resplendent beauty at the Convent of the Dames du Sacré Coeur in Turin. At the moment that the continuation of our drama brings her back on the scene, we are still only in 1816. Therefore, we have, as they say in law courts, to give an accounting of how she spent her time during the three years which will go by up until her entry into religion.

When Lefebvre saw her conducted to her carriage by Monsieur de Lucheux, he had been struck by the rare charm that shone in all her personality. But that day, the Commandant was too worried about the interview that he was going to have with his daughter's seducer to give any woman the attention that he ordinarily had at the disposal of the entire sex. The Marquise, in addition, had only passed in front of him; he had then kept, at the most, a vague memory of her.

Some weeks later, a Sunday, Lefebvre was walking toward the Louis XV Bridge. It was the hour the expensive carriages came from the Bois de Boulogne and went down the Champs-Élysées, coming out in every direction into the Place de la Concorde, a great danger to the pedestrians caught in a jumble of horsemen and vehicles of all kinds, in the middle of which they had a great deal of trouble disentangling themselves. Suddenly, the Commandant heard himself hailed by a coachman in a powdered wig, with golden cords hanging from his epaulets. The carriage had just missed running over him. Lefebvre then did what everyone in such a case does: he became outraged against the man that who had warned him to step aside, called him a vile scoundrel, and began to brandish

---

[14] Joseph Marie Terray (1715-1778), Controller-General of Finances during the reign of Louis XV and agent of fiscal reform.

his cane. His passionate pantomime drew the attention of a woman in the carriage. She was apparently of a happy disposition and the agitated and threatening attitude of the old soldier had something comic about it, because she took the great liberty of laughing in his face.

Exasperated by that impertinence, the Commandant ran after the vehicle, that a traffic jam had forced to stop shortly thereafter. He had seen the form of a man beside the laughing woman and was about to call him to account. When he was close enough to be aware of the adversary he came to accost, he perceived an old man buried under a blond wig with large curls and in the last stages of decrepitude. As for the lady, despite her offensive behavior, she seemed to him to be of rare beauty and distinction. But to the subject that Lefebvre already had to complain about, there was joined another grief. As if she feared an attack from him, or if she was offended by the impudence of his look, she quickly made a show of raising the window of the door.

"That's unusual," Lefebvre said to himself, seeing, almost at the same instant the vehicle departing at high speed, removing any idea of following it. "It seems to me that I have seen that insolent woman somewhere!"

Then his anger calmed down, and there remained for him only the interest of knowing where and when he had seen that proud beauty. Everyone has experienced that prolonged torture that certain faces one believes he is not seeing for the first time bring to the memory.

Two weeks later, Lefebvre continuing to live as a bachelor in Paris, attended, as a middle class man, sitting in a Feydeau[15] orchestra seat, as it was then called, a production of

---

[15] Georges Feydeau (1862-1921), a dramatist who wrote witty and complex farces, considered a forerunner of the Theater of the Absurd- Here a theater named the Feydeau. A Théâtre Feydeau was founded in 1789 under the patronage of the future Louis XVIII). In 1801 it merged with, and took the name of its rival, the Opéra Comique.

that opera of *La Gioconda*[16] that had made its first appearance at the noise of the canons of Champaubert [17] and Montmirail,[18] without the Parisians, excited with the gay refrains of Nicolo, appearing to perceive anything of the muffled cracking sounds of the Imperial Throne. During the intermission, standing up, his shoulder turned toward the stage, he glanced toward a ground-floor box, and, in the half-light created, not without premeditation in those sorts of places, he recognized, this time without a lapse of memory, the beautiful impertinent woman whose face, that had, once already, intrigued him so much. Behind her, and in a still more indecisive light, stood a man whom he could only recognize as being young, without making out his features. But the lady, probably having something to show to that handsome shadow, the man left his corner of obscurity for a moment and brought half of his body into the light. Then Lefebvre recognized Monsieur de Lucheux. That discovery was an illumination for him.

"Ah!" he said to himself, "I now understand. That's the Marquise de Camembert, the woman that fellow was conducting to her carriage the day I went to see him. I was certain that she was not entirely unknown to me. In fact, I saw that he was using great signs of intimacy toward her. A tête-à-tête in a

---

[16] Opera in four acts by Amilcare Ponchielli set to an Italian libretto by Arrigo Boito (as Tobia Gorrio), based on *Angelo, Tyrant of Padua,* a play in prose by Victor Hugo, dating from 1835. First performed in 1876, *La Gioconda* was a major success for Ponchielli, as well as the most successful new Italian opera between Verdi's *Aida* (1871) and *Otello* (1887).

[17] The Battle of Champaubert (10 February 1814) was the opening engagement of the Six Days Campaign of the Napoleonic Wars.

[18]. The Battle of Montmirail (11 February 1814) was fought between a French force led by Napoleon and two Allied corps. In hard fighting that lasted until evening, French troops defeated the Russians and compelled them to retreat to the north..

ground-floor box! That speaks for itself. So, that miserable man already had her as a mistress when I went to see him to talk about Amanda!"

Finding thus united two objects of his aversion, so long as the intermission lasted, and it was long, Lefebvre couldn't look anywhere else but at the ground-floor box. Monsieur de Lucheux was sitting in such a way that that he couldn't easily see that obstinate and indiscreet curiosity. Besides, if he had seen it, Lefebvre would have hardly cared. And, as the ground floor was at that moment three-quarters empty, the beautiful Marquise could notice perfectly well the persistence that Commandant Lefebvre gave to honor her with his attention. That time, either because she was not in a laughing mood, or because she remembered his face from their earlier encounter, or possibly because she was one of those flirts who like to amuse themselves by gathering glances from however humble a place they might come, the fact was that Lefebvre thought that his persistent glances didn't seem to displease her. So, his eyes, that at the beginning wanted to take on an expression of irritation or insult, were not long in becoming languorous and tender without any ill will accompanying that transformation.

Analyzing his good fortune, that the earlier encounter had not made likely, Lefebvre replayed in his mind the events that had taken place on the Place de la Concorde. Dressed in his eternal blue frock coat, without his decoration, muddy, and carrying his big cane, he had been surprised into showing excessive anger, ending up, in fact, looking rather ridiculous; while, that evening, more careful of his dress, having his *Legion d'Honneur* decoration in his button hole, firmly seated in his box, wearing evening dress and a waist coat gallantly open showing the imposing beauty of his chest, he appeared to his advantage and couldn't be taken for the same man. While enjoying his good fortune, Lefebvre had the presence of mind to calculate that, after the curtain had opened, from the place where he was seated, he could no longer continue to exercise his power of fascination over her. As a consequence, since that evening every place was full and not a single unoccupied corner could be found, he struck up a negotiation to change his seat, and chose the one he came to occupy so well that, seated at the base of the desired box, by holding out his hand, he could touch the arm on which the beautiful Marquise was leaning.

In that already favorable situation, he had some fortunate luck. Either by chance or kindly clumsiness, Madame de Camembert dropped a bouquet she was holding, and in returning it to her, Lefebvre was repaid with the most caressing smile that any woman had ever given him. During the intermission that followed, without waiting for the end of the play, the Marquise left her box and the bold Commandant didn't hesitate to follow her. As a conqueror that nothing can disturb in his triumph, Monsieur de Lucheux, having on his arm his splendid mistress, was accustomed to ignoring the flighty men that might be drawn by the brilliance of her charms, and Lefebvre could at leisure brush against the new lady of his thoughts right up to her carriage, at that moment relegating Herminie Daliron a thousand leagues away from his memory.

Standing under the theatre's peristyle while the valet opened the carriage door, the man in love received a long, languorous look that the Marquise, turning around, gave him as a good-bye.

"She is mine!" Lefebvre said to himself, all the while having trouble persuading himself that such good luck was reserved for him. It's useless to add that, regaining his domicile, he didn't walk, but strutted; happiness had given him wing, and he couldn't close his eyes almost all the night.

Rather early the next morning, he was at the Faubourg Saint-Germain, and the first household supplier whose shop he entered on the Rue du Bac to ask for information about Madame the Marquise de Camembert could point out to him her townhouse, Rue de l'Université, two steps from the Rue des Saints-Pères. Lefebvre immediately ran to reconnoiter the place, in order to find a way to achieve his aims. For certain, Heaven must have been on his side, because, while he was at his observation post, the door of the townhouse opened, letting out a woman, and that woman was his dear Marquise, leaving alone and on foot in an elegant morning outfit.

As she passed by, her eyes modestly lowered, and not seeming to see anything around her, the heart of the panting Commandant lacked the courage to take the audacious step of speaking to her, and he settled for following her. She led him to the Church of Saint-Thomas Aquinas, where, as she did every day, she heard Mass. Lefebvre entered after her and, as from time immemorial he had not done, he took a place in front of a prie-Dieu at a distance to be seen by the beautiful worshipper. But that was a pure waste of time. She did not lift her eyes from her book and prayed with a fervor that made it difficult to comprehend her tête-à-tête the evening before in a box at the Opéra Comique with Monsieur Lucheux.

The Mass over, she was approached in the nave by two or three women of a most aristocratic appearance with whom she exchanged a few words. A little further, as she was leaving, she had to endure the eagerness of an old Chevalier de Saint-Louis who, to Lefebvre's great despair, offered her his arm to descend the church steps. But as he left, shortly thereafter, at a turn into a street, the man in love persuaded himself that, desiring to be approached, she did not want the old gallant to accompany her to her residence. Yet, although at almost every ten steps, the beautiful Marquise was greeted by some people of her own social class, the Faubourg Saint-Germain being a kind of little village where everyone knew each other. It didn't occur to Lefebvre that people might go to Mass every day. Telling himself that if he didn't take advantage of the opportunity given to him, it would perhaps be a long time before it presented itself again, he therefore resolutely took a chance. Approaching the elegant young woman with an appearance of respectful hesitation, which didn't, however, leave out a little air of the conqueror about him, he said to her:

"The opera of *La Gioconda* didn't seem to please the Marquise very much, because she left the theater before the last act."

Madame de Camembert, without answering, looked at the man who had said that to her with such perfect surprise, that Lefebvre thought he should add:

"Don't I have the honor, Madame, to be recognized by you?"

"Oh, but of course, but of course," the Marquise answered, "and I am delighted to see you, so I can tell you that I am very unhappy."

"Already?" the amorous man replied shrewdly.

"What do you mean, *already*? Do you have to use a saddle twice to see that one is badly seated on it?"

In his turn, Lefebvre was stupefied.

"A saddle?" he said. "I don't understand."

"What do you mean? Aren't you Monsieur Ferlut, my saddle maker?"

"I would have thought that this ribbon..."

"Well! That's exactly what caused my error. Monsieur Ferlut served in the caissons, the charrettes, the charrois, I don't know what you call it... and he is also decorated."

"My military career was a little more brilliant. I had the honor to command a battalion."

"What! So, you're not one of my suppliers? That would have already been rather bold, but if you're not, how dare you approach me!"

That was said in the most disdainful tone. Madame de Camembert decided to cut the situation short by crossing the street, to reach the Rue du Bac, immortalized by Madame de Staël.[19]

---

[19] Anne Louise Germaine de Staël-Holstein (1766-1817), commonly known as Madame de Staël, was a French woman of letters whose lifetime overlapped with the events of the French Revolution and the Napoleonic era. Known as a witty and brilliant conversationalist, often dressed in flashy and revealing outfits, she participated actively in the political and intellectual life of her times. Her works about love, life, and oppositional politics made their mark on early European Ro-

Lefebvre was stung by that action; he made a movement to follow her. Seeing that action, she stopped a servant in livery who had just crossed the street and greeted her respectfully, and said to him:

"Pierre, how is the Duchesse?"

"She is a great deal better, Madame la Marquise."

"Tell her I will go see her this evening."

Then, as Lefebvre had also halted some steps away, she added, raising her voice:

"Please tell that gentleman, who seems to be waiting for me, that I don't receive visits in the street."

The servant turned around to see the man the Marquise pointed to him and looked at Lefebvre, laughing. Then, as the Marquise walked away, hastening her steps, he continued on his way because he understood that his commission had been sufficiently done and thought that, perhaps, there might be some danger in pushing the Commandant's threatening and ruffled look any further.

After the cruel insult by way of the valet the Marquise had wanted to direct to him, as if setting a dog on a beggar, there was no longer any illusion possible for Lefebvre. He could very well have explained his mistake as the fantasy of a *coquette*, who had wanted to pass a half-hour with her languorous airs, without later finding it good that there was a follow up to that charitable feminine recreation. But in his terrible disappointment, Lefebvre didn't stop at such a simple analysis. In the behavior of the Marquise, he chose to see the result of a plot. Monsieur Lucheux had probably recognized him, and it was he who had pushed his mistress to play that cruel act, the affront of which he had just suffered. Once that idea was in progress, since he couldn't have the consolation of using his sword to fight that man, with whom he already had such a large account to settle, his frenzy of hatred and his furious ideas of revenge were understandable.

---

manticism. She lived at No. 97 Rue du Bac, formerly the Hôtel de Ségur from 1786 to 1798.

What is certain is that Lefebvre's amorous follies didn't have happy denouements, and his constant attacks on conjugal fidelity were, it has to be admitted, rather thoroughly punished.

VIII. An Unpleasant Visit

Nothing was less true than what Lefebvre thought. Monsieur de Lucheux was in every way a stranger to his misadventure. As for Madame de Camembert, the most outrageously disdainful woman it was possible to imagine, the ground floor of a theater was, to her, a kind of swamp swarming with a population of salesmen, grocer boys and lower middle-class people, that she would never have called gentlemen. In the middle of that performance, she had seen Lefebvre giving her his attention. It had the effect of a toad looking at her. Instead of being fascinated by him, a faculty that is commonly lent to that kind of amphibian, she amused herself by looking at him and letting him follow her right to her carriage.

That's what the unfortunate Commandant called a conquest! And the next day, the Marquise no longer remembered anything about her experiment in natural history, and it was in good faith that she had taken this pretended conqueror of the evening for Monsieur Ferlut, her saddle maker. She hadn't, in the same fashion, remembered that bold man who had dared to speak to her on the Place de la Concorde. Like all Parisian women, she was accustomed to that kind of insolence. Her attractive beauty even made them rather frequent when she walked out alone, and, provided that these collisions remained within certain limits, she was more disposed to laugh about them than to be frightened by them.

Lefebvre then, remaining for her as if he didn't exist, two days after the poor Commandant's escapade, she left with her old husband for Crôsne, near Villeneuve-Saint-Georges. She had a chateau there that the hot breath of the first days of June had made her decide to go and take up residence there.

One beautiful morning, she was alone in one of the most romantic sections of her park, busy reading a volume of Alexandre Soumet[20] one of the first poets of the Royalist Pléïade[21] that created the literature movement of the Restoration, when a maid, only a few days in her service, announced that Monsieur Ferlut, her saddle maker, was in the chateau asking to speak to her.

"All right," she said, annoyed, "let him talk to Tomès (her English coachman). Why do I need to see Monsieur Ferlut?"

"I don't want to bother Madame la Marquise," the chambermaid again said, "but he insisted, saying that it was absolutely indispensable that he see Madame and Monsieur le Marquis, who was passing by while I was refusing to announce him, and ordered me himself to come and tell the Marquise."

"Then show him here," the Marquise said, and she became absorbed again in the reading from which she had been so disagreeably distracted.

"What is it, Monsieur Ferlut?" she asked without lifting her eyes from her book, interviewing the man the chambermaid had brought to her.

The fake Ferlut, the reader must be told, was no other than Lefebvre. He waited until the chambermaid had left to answer in a mysterious manner.

"An important piece of information that I wanted to communicate to Madame la Marquise."

"What do you mean, an important piece of information? You are talking like a lawyer."

---

[20] Alexandre Soumet (1788-1845) wrote poems in honor of Napoleon. He joined the Académie Française in 1824, and is best known for his tragedy *Norma, or the Infanticide* (1831), adapted into an opera by Bellini.

[21] Originally a group of seven 16th century poets; the 19th century Royalist Pléiade was another group of poets who wanted to reform the French language.

Then, continuing to look at that face which she vaguely remembered:

"Ah! My dear Monsieur Ferlut," she added, "explain to me why you never seem to have the same face when you show yourself to me."

"That's because there are two of us, Madame," Lefebvre retorted.

"What do you mean, two of you? Do you have a brother?"

"No, Madame, there is the real Monsieur Ferlut and the one in your imagination."

"Explain yourself better. I don't understand you."

"That's because Madame la Marquise doesn't have a memory for faces. I am the saddle maker that she greeted so graciously the other morning on the Rue du Bac, and whom she told Pierre, the servant of a Duchesse, to get rid of for her."

"Ah yes! Now, I do recognize you! What could have given you the nerve to come here?"

"The desire to render a service to Madame la Marquise."

"To oblige me?" said Madame la Marquise in a disdainful voice.

"Madame la Marquise sometimes writes very compromising letters!"

"And what do you know about my letters?"

"I read them when I have the opportunity. It is certainly impossible to be wittier. But to speak to Monsieur de Lucheux in the familiar *tu*[22] and to speak very casually about certain intimate details, why, that is, Madame, a great deal of imprudence!"

---

[22] French has two words for the English word "you." The familiar *tu* is used for family members, lovers, close friends, servants and animals. The formal *vous* is used for everyone else.

"What are you saying about Monsieur de Lucheux?" Madame de Camembert exclaimed, becoming as red as a cherry, with the degree of emotion that can be imagined.

"I am saying, Madame la Marquise, that in writing to him in that way..."

And at the same time, he took from his pocket a letter that he began to unfold.

Madame de Camembert jumped toward him to snatch the letter from his hands.

"Ah, ah! No! No!" said Lefebvre, putting it securely away. "I really want to return it to you, and that's why I came, but first of all, a little explanation is necessary."

"Go on, Monsieur; I'm listening," the Marquise said, sitting down again.

She felt herself somewhat trapped in the hands of Lefebvre, but being a woman of energy and unusual resolution, she let no other expression show on her face except that of calm contempt.

"Madame la Marquise sometimes amuses herself," Lefebvre said.

"Not at this moment, I believe."

"And in a way that people don't like. She encounters them at the Feydeau theater, flirt with them, then the next day, when they want to see a little closer what it's all about, she throws them to the first valet who passes in the street."

"And where did you see, Monsieur, that I was flirting with you? I remember that it was you who, for a long time, followed me with your eyes. When one feels one is being stared at, one gives way to a sort of magnetism, despite oneself."

"Madame, I have been around a considerable part of the world, and I have observed that, throughout Europe, when a woman looks at a man in a certain way, that, without the intervention of the Abbé Faria[23] has a generally recognized meaning."

"But it's exactly that which you thought you saw, that I deny most vehemently."

"That is to say that perhaps I don't have the honor to please you and that you found it comic to make me believe I did. But whatever your intention was, the misfortune nevertheless happened, if that must be called a misfortune, and I have stupidly fallen madly in love with you."

"I have, Monsieur, all the regret in the world," the Marquise said, "and believe that it happened without my will. In any case," she added with a nuance of caressing, "when one loves someone, one does not think of causing them pain. I therefore suppose that you are going to give me back that letter, fallen I don't know how into your hands."

"To give it back to you is all that I desire, because you will undoubtedly accept the condition that I intend to put to that restitution."

"A condition!" exclaimed the Marquise, proudly raising her head.

"Yes, Madame. As a military man, I have been present at the taking of more than one stronghold, and I have always seen that those besieging imposed conditions to the besieged."

"So," said Madame de Camembert, trying to laugh, "you consider me a citadel?"

"Yes, Madame, a true Danzig, a real Gibraltar."

"You are very kind, and I think you won't offer me too harsh conditions? All right, what is your condition?"

"One always does very nearly what he desires for a lover."

---

[23] Abbé José Custódio de Faria (1756-1819), a Luso-Goan Catholic monk who was one of the pioneers of the scientific study of hypnotism, following on from the work of Franz Mesmer. In the early 19th century, he introduced oriental hypnosis to Paris.

"Yes, but not for a lover who is not, er, the chosen one, and who knows that one's heart is occupied somewhere else."

"It's exactly that *elsewhere,* Madame, that could prevent you from getting as good a capitulation as you might desire, because Monsieur de Lucheux—it's appropriate that you should know this—is my mortal enemy. I believe that it was he who excited you to make that little teasing overture which troubled my reason."

"Monsieur de Lucheux didn't even see you on the evening you're talking about, and he has never opened his mouth to me about any person who resembles you."

"That's possible. He has his reasons for that, but I have still other motives to detest him, and because of that, I got it into my head to take his place for a while."

"Are you're saying…?" Madame de Camembert asked, with a disgusted expression.

"I'm saying, to take his place for a while," Lefebvre repeated firmly. "That thing often takes place between friends; a stronger reason is for it happening between those who wish harm to each other."

"I suppose you understand, Monsieur, to whom you are talking, since I have the honor to receive you in my house?"

"Perfectly, Madame la Marquise. I know that I am speaking to the wife of the Marquis de Camembert, a venerable old man, who, as much at the end as he is, wouldn't calmly learn that he's been given a successor while he's still alive."

"Monsieur," said the Marquise, "you are a scoundrel!"

"Expressed better, Madame, a monster. Yours won't be the first pretty mouth from which I have received that word."

"But if, with that threat, you believe you will lead me to the point you have supposed, you are far short of your target. A separation, even criminal prosecution, which could be the outcome of your vile revelation, would be less horrible to me than your... ridiculous condition."

"So be it, but, as the letter couldn't be read in open court, because certainly the King's Prosecutor would demand a closed-door hearing, I will take care in advance to have some copies made up to distribute in the noble Faubourg Saint-Germain."

"Leave my presence, Monsieur," Madame de Camembert shouted. "A criminal wouldn't practice extortion with treachery so base."

"I am leaving you, Madame," Lefebvre said without showing any emotion, "because the case, in fact, merits being studied in solitude, and then examined with Monsieur de Lucheux. Because, you see, for what I am demanding, it is mostly he you should blame."

"All right, I will tell Monsieur de Lucheux myself."

"As for the charming inspirations of your good little heart, after having toyed with people's peace of mind, you are now surprised that the annoyed tomcat shows his claws?"

"I have told you to leave!" commanded Madame de Camembert, interrupting him. "Must I call someone?"

Lefebvre bowed with ironic humility and departed, not without looking back several times to see if, after thinking about it, the Marquise wasn't going to call him back.

Two hours hadn't passed when Madame de Camembert, whom the old Marquis left absolutely in charge of all their business, used as a pretext a letter from a notary, decided to return to Paris.

Immediately called, Monsieur de Lucheux didn't have to pretend to be astonished when the Marquise spoke to him about a letter that had gone astray. Since her departure for the country, he hadn't received any kind of news from her and affirmed that in a way so as to be believed.

"Ah!" said the Marquise, "I can explain what happened. Before leaving Paris, I fired a maid whom I suspected of theft. She was the one I gave that letter to put in the mail. She must have misappropriated it and gave it instead to that awful man, who must be her lover."

"What awful man?" the Count asked.

"A man whom I don't know who said that he's fallen in love with me, and he had the audacity to tell me that himself once in the street. He claims, in addition, to feel a great deal of enmity towards you."

From question to question, and with a circumstantial description, Monsieur de Lucheux finally assured himself that the man in question was none other than Commandant Lefebvre. He understood, better than Madame de Camembert had, the vengeance the former officer was planning in all its harrowing refinements. When they began to discuss the method of getting rid of that dangerous jouster, the Count said:

"With anyone else, I would have proceeded in the way that any brave man has at his disposition to get justice for himself, but his hatred for me comes precisely from the fact that I refused to cross swords with him."

"You, Albert?" said Madame de Camembert, somewhat astonished.

Monsieur de Lucheux had been very careful not to tell her the real subject of his quarrel with Lefebvre; instead, he told her how, on the point of agreeing to a duel with Lefebvre, he had been diverted from that notion by his friend who was the Head of the Cabinet at the Ministry of Foreign Affairs.

"Obviously," the Marquise exclaimed, "that odious man is an employee of the police. Could the Minister be asked to intervene?"

"First of all," the Count retorted, "in knocking at that door, you have to be sure it's properly done."

"Go and see your friend. He didn't want to tell you what was that stain he advised you to be concerned about, but if you make him understand that the reputation of a woman highly placed in society is at stake..."

"My friend Edouard," Monsieur de Lucheux interrupted, "is at this moment en route to Naples, where he has just been nominated Secretary to the Ambassador. As far calling on the intervention of the Minister of Police without knowing if this fellow is under his purview, you will judge for yourself if that is possible for me, who is creature of the Pavilion Marsan[24] to

---

[24] Part of the Louvre that temporarily housed the police.

whom Monsieur Decazes[25] is blatantly hostile. Instead of stifling it, he would do his best to stir up the scandal."

"Something, however, must be done about this, because that unfortunate letter must not be made public, and it probably doesn't suit you to make this thuggish soldier part of a *ménage à trois*."

"Assuredly, that ferocious beast must be muzzled, but how do we go about it?"

"Sometimes, people like that are made to disappear…"

"That's true," said Monsieur de Lucheux. "In the old days, we could have asked for a *lettre de cachet*.[26]

"I know very well that the time of *lettres de cachets* has passed, but there are other ways to dispose of such a man."

"Yes, my dear love, in Corsica or Sicily, but we are in Paris, and that miserable man may well be part of the Police. Besides, foreseeing what might be done to him, who knows if that man hasn't arranged to leave his venom after him? Only one thing is possible: leave your old husband behind, and come to Italy with me to wait for the hour of your delivery."

"A similar scandal!" Madame de Camembert answered, "when for a long time we have made so many sacrifices to comply with the opinion of society."

"That scandal, would you prefer it was for nothing?"

---

[25] Élie-Louis, 1st Duke of Decazes and Glücksburg (1780-1860), French statesman and leader of the liberal Doctrinaires party during the Bourbon Restoration.

[26] Letters signed by the king, countersigned by one of his ministers, and closed with the royal seal, containing orders directly from the king to enforce arbitrary actions and judgments that could not be appealed, often ordering that a person be imprisoned without trial and without an opportunity of defense (after inquiry and due diligence by the Lieutenant de Police) in a state prison or an ordinary jail, or in a convent or the General Hospital of Paris, or transported to the colonies, or expelled to another part of the realm, or from the realm altogether.

"I don't like leaving the game so quickly," said the Marquise. "That man has terrible leverage in his hands. But I will speak to his reason. With that, Elmire got the best of Monsieur Tartuffe!"[27]

With that, the conference was over and the two lovers separated.

IX. There are Traps in that Enclosure

Eleven o'clock sounded at the clock tower of the Chateau de Crôsne, to use an Ann Radcliffe[28] metaphor, where Madame de Camembert had arranged for a great number of society members to come together. The old Marquis was playing a lively game of checkers with the local priest, while, beside them, two serious onlookers followed their game. Music occupied the rest of the guests.

After a long list of romantic pieces and various songs, Madame de Camembert had urged both the virtuosos and the listeners toward those well-known songs that are usually massacred in a group and in which everyone believes himself authorized to take a part, causing a great disaster to the ear. In the middle of the famous *Frère Jacques, dormez-vous?*, that inevitably crowns that sort of musical orgy, the Marquise said to one of her friends:

"I can't stay up any longer. I have a terrible migraine! I'm going to go to bed. Please be kind enough to make my apologies."

On leaving the drawing room, without being noticed, thanks to the noisy tumult that she herself had organized, she went up to her bedroom, and almost immediately sent her maid away. After having put together necessary items in a flat

---

[27] Molière's play (1664).

[28] Ann Radcliffe (1764-1823), English author and pioneer of the Gothic novel. Her technique of explaining the supernatural elements of her novels has been credited with enabling Gothic fiction to achieve respectability in the 1790s.

suitcase, she reached the park by means of a hidden stairway, where she began to cross the darkest alley, walking toward a goal. That goal was a small door cut into the estate wall, opening onto an isolated path.

As soon as she had placed the key she had brought in the lock, the door opened to show a person wrapped in a cloak.

"*Mon Dieu!*" she said, laughing, "a cloak in this kind of weather!"

(It was June, and the weather was superb.)

"It's a way to avoid being recognized," answered the man.

"Yes, and a way of drawing attention to yourself from people who, without that beautiful precaution, would have let you pass by them unnoticed. A Spanish rendezvous!"

"Be quiet, you wicked thing!" the *Caballero* responded, seizing the Marquise' waist and stealing a kiss, at which she didn't flinch.

Seeing the suitcase she was carrying, the man in the cloak asked:

"What's that?"

"I will show you in a moment," the Marquise answered. "Come!"

Followed by the nocturnal visitor, she walked to the edge of a little house where she slowly climbed the steps. She pushed open the door and went across a little bedroom that lead to a fully room, the blinds of which had been carefully closed, in order to not let any light be seen from the outside. A profusion of flowers, a thick carpet, an ottoman upholstered with satin Chinese fabric with fantastic designs, which also formed the covering of a round mosaic table and a vast armchair where one could sleep stretched out as in a bed, made up one of those little tiny, cozy rooms where one comes to dream, relax, and sometimes hide.

Now, by the light of four-branched candleholders filled with rose-colored perfumed candles, we could now recognize the cloaked man as Commandant Lefebvre. He took a careful inventory of the room into which he had been introduced, with rather marked curiosity.:

"Almaviva [29] wouldn't be afraid," the Marquise noted with humor.

"Afraid?" Lefebvre responded, taking off his cloak. "I saw the great retreat from Moscow without emotion, my dear lady."

"However, the place and the hour would be favorable for a surprise. So, to reassure you, I have brought weapons."

And going to open the small suitcase, that, upon entering, she had placed on the mosaic table, she said:

"Look, My Lord, they're made by Lepage[30] and there's everything here that's needed to load them."

"You would be very charmed, you wicked thing, if I made myself that ridiculous!"

And he tried again to embrace the beautiful chatelaine, but this time, she escaped his embrace and said:

"Come now, behave, and let's talk."

Saying that, she sat down on the ottoman, where Lefebvre wanted to take a place beside her by putting his arm around her waist.

"Not at all, not at all!" said the Marquise, who had gotten up and had rolled the massive armchair some distance from the ottoman. "You are going, if you please, to sit down in this big armchair like a Pope, and I'll sit here."

Lefebvre let himself be guided, counting very well on that arrangement not being of long duration.

"Now," the Marquise added when they had taken their places, "it's your turn to talk."

"It's then to tell you, my charming one," Lefebvre answered, settling himself into his big armchair, "that I find you as adorable on the side of wit as on the side of physique."

"I haven't said anything yet," the Marquise remarked.

---

[29] Another character from Beaumarchais's *Barber of Seville*, that of a Spanish grandee in love with Rosine.
[30] Dynasty of French firearms manufacturers founded in 1717.

"No, but you have done something! I think that writing to me as if I were Monsieur Ferlut, your saddle maker, to ask arrange this encounter was nothing but ingenious."

"You're the one, my dear Commandant, who gave me the idea by coming here under that alias to tell my maid to tell me that if I sent you away again, and decided to forget about you, you would talk to my husband."

"The truth is," Lefebvre said contentedly, "that wasn't too badly played, because I wanted you to abandon your high and mighty disdainful attitude, and, without pushing things to the extreme, you couldn't have been warned more discreetly or more cleverly."

"So you didn't actually intend to give my letter to the Marquis?"

"Of course not. That would have been too villainous a role for me to play."

"I'm astonished then that you didn't choose a more generous action which would have impressed me a great deal more."

"Doing what?" Lefebvre asked.

"Giving me back my letter the same evening of our first meeting when I asked for it. Once I gave my word to come here, as I am in fact here, there would have been something disarmingly courteous in you trusting my integrity entirely."

"Certainly, that would have been a beautiful trait, but women are so capricious; with them, you have to be careful about giving them temptations. So, to tell you the truth, I didn't think about acting in such a gallant fashion."

"What about now?" asked the Marquise, caressingly. "There would still be time."

"To give you what I'm holding?" Lefebvre asked, seeming to think. "On my word, no! It's said that proofs before the fact are always the most beautiful."

"You're being witty, my dear Commandant. I must ask you to observe that, if you defy me, I am no longer paid for having absolute confidence in you. We're going to find ourselves at an impasse."

"How could you think that, once overwhelmed by my kindness? After the truly exemplary patience that I have demonstrated, would you think that I would hesitate to fulfill my part of our bargain?"

"You suppose very well, but would you, paying no attention to your feelings, doubt that once the letter has been put in my hands, I would deny my debt?"

"Oh! That's very different," Lefebvre said.

"Yes, different in the sense that all the advantages are presently on your side, since I don't have the means to deceive you. Giving up what, until now, has made your strength, you would still be the master of the situation. We are alone here, at night, in a place where my cries wouldn't be heard. You are a man; I, a frail creature that you could break like glass, and what's more, I have brought you some weapons. If that isn't the total demonstration of good faith!"

"Then," Lefebvre answered, "you are asking me for that letter?"

"Yes, and I don't understand why you are hesitating to give it to me, if only to take away the scent of violence from our encounter, which, you must understand, revolts my feminine delicacy."

"That's amusing," Lefebvre said, "since you are arguing beautifully, and I don't want you to be proved right."

"Let's break it off there, Monsieur," said the Marquise with dignity. "I suspect that I am asking you for the impossible."

"The impossible, no; but for something I wouldn't do voluntarily."

"I repeat the word 'impossible.' Besides, you probably don't have my letter on you."

"Ah! That's a little strong!"

"Obviously, you were afraid of a trap, and that the letter would be taken from you by force, so the simplest thing for you to do was to leave it at home."

"I have already told you, my dear love, that an old soldier of Napoleon is never afraid. I have promised to give you back your letter; therefore, I have it here on me, and if you doubt it," he added, rummaging in his pockets, "…here it is."

"Let's see it," said the Marquise. "Oh! At a distance, of course, I don't want to get it by trickery."

"See, you incredulous person," Lefebvre said, unfolding the paper by the light of a candle.

"In fact, that is certainly my letter.. Will you have the heart to put it back in your pocket?"

"Yes, that's my instinct, but see, my beautiful one, it's very easy for you to have it pass into your hands…"

At the same time, he stood up.

"Ah! Stay where you are," exclaimed the Marquise. "Your passionate behavior frightens me. I don't like cavalry charges, and the long way around is the one that must be taken, I warn you."

"Then you're going to act as a timid maiden," Lefebvre said, going to sit down again.

"What is the color of your eyes?" the Marquise asked.

"Gray-green, I believe," Lefebvre answered. "I'm not too sure, but come look for yourself."

"You think I'm joking, but I attach extreme importance to that detail. Everything about people's character is there. And the nuance in your eyes will tell me if the promise you made me not to pursue me any longer and to leave me in peace after this evening has passed, will be kept."

"Well, my darling, come and take a look," Lefebvre answered, putting his head back and showing himself in a kind of seated military "present arms" position.

Madame de Camembert approached him cautiously, being careful to use one of the arms of the chair as a guard against any of Lefebvre's impertinences. Then, as she was leaning over his face, she slowly passed her hand behind the back of the piece of furniture and pushed a spring.

Caught like a wolf in a trap, the gallant Commandant felt himself instantly trapped by a complex system of steel wires and springs; each attempt he made to escape their pressure only tightened it more strongly over all his members, so that, after several seconds, all movement was made impossible for him.

"You bitch!" shouted the unfortunate Commandant.

"Be calm, my sweet friend, be calm," the Marquise said, "because nothing is more beastly and brutal than a mechanism, and if you continue to struggle, this one will strangle you, so much more quickly since it's from Birmingham, an English fabrication."

"I will pay you back, you shrew," Lefebvre shouted, stopping, however, his fish-like leaps that he had begun with, since he perceived that the steel wires were strangling him more and more.

"You are going to begin by giving me back my letter," the Marquise said, rummaging through the prisoner's pockets.

Not being able to do anything better, in his fury, Lefebvre spat in her face.

Once the paper was in her hands, Madame de Camembert took it to the flame of a candle. When it was consumed, she said aloud:

"It cost me thirty thousand francs to procure that trap; but that wasn't too expensive."

However, Lefebvre continued to vomit the crudest insults against her.

"My dear Commandant," she said, "we're going to see if you will be as staunch here as you were during the great retreat from Moscow."

Taking a cartridge that she tore open with her beautiful teeth,[31] she loaded the primer of one of the pistols and came over to place it on Lefebvre's forehead, watching his face with curiosity.

---

[31] The Marquise is using a percussion cap pistol which replaced the flint lock pistol. The percussion pistol used black powder struck by a hammer. The Marquise tore open with her teeth the packet containing the black powder.

The old soldier showed no emotion; but he had stopped swearing. The solemnity of the moment seemed to have recalled him to more dignity.

"Well, decidedly," said the Marquise, lowering her weapon, "Napoleon's soldiers are brave and that atones for their small amount of gallantry. Here is how," she added, "we are going to resolve this situation. In an hour, if you continue to remain calm, the resorts will relax by themselves and you will again be free to move around. One of these windows opens onto the countryside, and it isn't very high above the ground. By holding onto it with your hands, you will have to jump down only two or three feet to get to the ground. Me, I'm going back to my bedroom, where I will, I think, sleep rather calmly. And, above all, dear Almaviva, don't forget your cloak the color of the wall. I could be compromised tomorrow if the servants, coming to put everything back in order, found it here."

Having said that, she opened a window, snuffed out the candles and, carrying the pistols, she took care to double-lock the door through which she disappeared.

X. Aunt Aurora

Madame de Camembert, as can be seen, was a woman of rare strength. With all the exterior signs of the ordinary, including religious devotion, she was, in fact, without morals, and had a taste for the extraordinary and for adventures. Attracted by an immense fortune, she had resolutely associated her life, the highest and most unexpected destinies, with that of a decrepit old man. She had welcomed the overtures of Monsieur de Lucheux, an elegant ladies' man, but she actually didn't feel for him one of those deep attachments which, in any event, would have been very unlikely in a woman of her caliber. She lived too much by her intelligence to love anyone strongly, even with her senses.

In the battle that she had just left victorious, she had found that Monsieur de Lucheux had shown himself to be rather ineffective. She had organized her triumph all by herself. She had listened to an old *roué* of the former court that she had often made recount the vices and the scandals of the period before '80, who had said that, in the past, in the *little houses,* there were pieces of furniture constructed in a way so as to get the best of the most savage men. She then had sent to England an old servant, in whom she confided all the secrets of her life, that she trusted more than her maid. Pretending to be a dentist who needed a piece similar to the one we have seen in action, that servant, paying without bargaining, had in several days obtained the clever mechanism from Birmingham, a master piece of his art, and we have just seen with what cleverness and with what dexterity she had put it to use, trying it out on her insolent persecutor.

The next day, when she appeared before Monsieur de Lucheux, she told him:

"Now, the hardest thing has been done, but we must get rid of that Lefebvre. He's certainly going to bark, since he couldn't bite, and for two reasons, you must leave immediately for Naples."

"For Naples?" Monsieur de Lucheux repeated. "To leave each other when the peril has been taken care of?"

"That's indispensable," Madame de Camembert repeated. "And if you don't decide to take this voyage, I don't yet know how I will persuade the Marquis to go there, but certainly I will do that."

"Can you at least tell me why that's necessary?"

"First of all, for your sake—that of not being here when that man will mingle your name with mine in the gossip where his wrath is sure to lead him. Then to question your friend, the Embassy Secretary. Seeing you take the trouble to come such a great distance to get that information, he will understand that you *absolutely* have to know what that mysterious stain is that makes Lefebvre an impossible adversary for a gallant man. Once we know his corrupt side, we will be strong, and the tiger will find himself solidly muzzled."

"What a nice arrangement you've imagined there," said Monsieur de Lucheux, who, although allowing himself periods of escape with *grisettes*[32] on the side, prized his arrangement with the Marquise. "To be separated for a month at least, and not having even the means to write to each other!"

"What! Not to write to each other? What would be the obstacle?"

"Didn't all our trouble come from a letter that had gone astray?"

"Undoubtedly, but as you won't give the letters you address to me to a fired valet, I don't see the least danger in pursuing our correspondence. Besides, you can send me your epistles under the cover of the Minister of Foreign Affairs, who would be only too happy to forward them to me."

Monsieur de Lucheux still had many more objections, but the Marquise was peremptory and, three days later, he arrived in Marseilles, ready to sail for Naples.

Nothing more had been heard from Lefebvre. Following the instructions he had been given, he had left the pavilion, the stage where his pride had been deflated, through the window. If he had sought to spread gossip, it was useless, because the members of his class operated in a sphere far too low to raise him to the level of the Marquise.

"That poor Commandant," the Marquise had said to herself several times, laughing about the figure he made. "However," she said, "he didn't blink an eye under my pistol. It's understandable that, with such fellows, Bonaparte had Europe at his feet."

Once in Naples, Monsieur de Lucheux wrote to tell her of a pleasant voyage, lamenting a great deal about the sorrows of her absence, reporting that, with respect to the information he had come to seek, he had not yet mentioned that important matter to his friend, the diplomat. The diplomat himself, hav-

---

[32] Working girls who were also prostitutes in addition to their regular job.

ing just arrived, was busy getting settled and he had not been able to see and talk to him, except about very casual matters.

After she received that letter, Madame de Camembert went three weeks without seeing a second missive arrive, and that tardiness was not long in being eloquently explained to her. One day, in her presence, without suspecting the blow that as being dealt to her, since she had kept her love affair with the Count very secret, people began to talk about a dancer who was, at that moment, causing great excitement at the San Carlo Theater in Naples, and for whom Monsieur de Lucheux was busy negotiating an engagement at the Paris Opera. The Marquise was too proud to demand an explanation about that subject by letter. It would have been too easy to deny everything from a distance. She didn't even want to appear to know that she had been completely forgotten. He didn't write; she didn't write, and she waited.

Finally, however, among the letters forwarded to her each morning from Paris to Crôsne, she found one of those dispatches that, by the splendor of its seal, already testified as to its official origin. The notation *Par Ordonnance* indicated that it had been delivered by one of the riders working at the disposition of each ministerial department. She recognized the handwriting of Monsieur de Lucheux on that legal document. The care he had taken to use that method seemed to announce an important revelation, and, in fact, following some excuses about his long silence, explained by a pretended indisposition which had had serious side effects, the Count appraised her know of the existence of the Secret Bureau, a State secret that they had decided to confide to him, and the importance of which he didn't need to emphasize. Then, he added that Lefebvre was one of the men employed for that surveillance.

"Oh!" exclaimed Madame de Camembert, "that's how it was done then!"

And for the rest of the day, she remained thoughtful and preoccupied.

The next day, she was the prey of the same mental agitation, often carried into a monologue. The third day, she said to her old husband:

"Dear, I'm going to Paris tomorrow and I will perhaps dine with the little Vicountess. So, don't wait for me after six o'clock."

"Go, dear love," said the Marquis. "In any case, be sure to tell the Priest to not miss coming here to get his revenge; the the day before yesterday, if you recall, I won three games."

"Really," said the Marquise, "you're on the way to becoming as good as Philidor[33] and Monsieur de La Bourdonnaye."[34]

"That's saying a lot, but it's true, I'm making progress."

The Marquise went back up to her bedroom, where she wrote a note that she took the trouble to take herself to the post, when going to the village of Crôsne to visit her poor.

The next day, late in the evening, the waiters of an inn in Very were surprised to see a little stooped old lady with a gold pommel-head cane, wearing the classic costume of the dowager—that is to say, hooped petticoats, and a jupe aurore bodice with stripes—get out of a carriage. She also wore beauty patches and her powdered hair was covered with black crepe on a shepherdess hat tilted coquettishly over her ear.

"A private room!" she asked, in a cracked voice, but it was noticed that she had the habit of commanding in a lordly and sharp manner.

"Is Madame la Duchesse alone?" asked the waiter, who knew his role, and had gone immediately to pick up a title from the highest on the ladder.

"Marquise, young man," she replied, correcting him. "If you will, please, you can lay out two place settings. I am ex-

---

[33] François-André-Danican Philidor (1726-1795), prolific composer of operas as well as champion chess-player of his time. He once played Benjamin Franklin.

[34] Louis-Charles Mahé de La Bourdonnaye (1795-1840), possibly the strongest chess master in the early 19th century.

pecting my nephew. You will prepare for us: Champagne, truffles, the best you have. I will leave the menu up to you."

"Madame la Marquise honors me."

"And when my nephew comes, a big man with a moustache and graying hair, have someone bring him here. He will ask for a table, and then arrange it so everything will be on the table at the same time. We will change our plates ourselves. Does the door have a lock?"

"Yes, Madame la Marquise."

"Well, then, go, my child, and tell the cook to distinguish himself."

The waiter left, laughing, and after several comings and goings, the supper was laid out on the table.

"Everything is ready, Madame la Marquise, he said, "and when Monsieur your nephew arrives..."

"Chill a second bottle of champagne," said the old woman, daubing her nostrils with a yellowish tobacco that she took from a magnificent gold box with intricate designs.

At the same time the wine was ordered, the nephew arrived.

"Good evening, you wicked thing," said the dowager. "Now," she added, speaking to the waiter, "shut the door after you, and don't even think about eavesdropping. I will be watching, and God help you if I catch you at it!"

When the aunt and the nephew were alone, "Commandant," Madame de Camembert said to Lefebvre, "how do you like my disguise?"

"Ravishing, and if I hadn't been told in advance, I would never have recognized you."

"That's because, among other little talents, I have that of acting. On receiving my note, you weren't afraid of some kind of trap?"

"A trap, here? That was hardly probable, and then, you wicked thing, you were careful to reassure me with your postscript: *There won't be any armchair there.*"

"No, but, you villain, if you don't behave, there's my cane."

The Marquise had said that sentence with her comedian's voice, then, in her natural voice, she added:

"Now, let's eat; I'm dying of hunger."

"Ah! My little witch," Lefebvre asked, "in what you're serving me, are you sure there's no poison? Because I think you are capable of anything."

"On the contrary, I need you to listen to me wide awake. We have to deal with some serious subjects. And the bizarre disguise that I decked myself in to guarantee my incognito ought to make you understand the gravity of the matter."

"That's amusing," Lefebvre said, looking around him. "Then this place is definitely used for some important business! Why, some months ago, I dined here in a very important circumstance in my life."

"Was that your recruitment into the Secret Bureau?" the Marquise asked.

Lefebvre turned purple.

"The Secret Bureau?" he asked. "What do you mean by that?"

"That if you have my secrets, my dear Commandant, I am also up to date on yours. But you don't need to worry. I don't wish to use that... quite the contrary."

"But, I assure you, Madame, that I don't understand you at all."

"Come now, don't act childish; you should have thought that, before deciding on the business of today, I would have made certain of my information. You are employed by the secret office of the postal service. You unseal letters, and that's how the one with which you caused me such great trouble came into your hands."

"But if that were true, Madame la Marquise, do you think it would be very prudent of you to know it? You must have heard of the story of the *Man in the Iron Mask.*"

"Commandant," continued the Marquise, ignoring that last remark, "you have shown some attraction for me, am I right?"

"I would be a great liar if I said I was over it."

"Well! Then a great warrior like you must know the story of Madame de Coëtquen with Monsieur de Turenne.[35] It's worth that of the *Man in the Iron Mask.*"

"I can't recall it at the moment. Tell me some of it."

"Louis XIV," the Marquise continued, "had confided an important State secret to Monsieur de Turenne. Madame de Coëtquen wanted to know it. Turenne was in love with her, and he revealed the secret to her."

"In love, in love!" replied Lefebvre. "If he was like me, on half pay, he was a great fool."

"Well! To get to the heart of the matter," continued Madame de Camembert, "some drastic actions are sometimes necessary."

"First of all," asked the Commandant, returning to the military metaphors, "let me ask you: is there a vacancy in the ranks?"

"Yes. I have broken off with Monsieur de Lucheux."

"Let's drink to his health!" Lefebvre said happily, touching his glass with that of the Marquise.

"But there is another difficulty," Madame de Camembert continued. " I want to be Queen of France, nothing but that."

"The Devil! And can I do something about that?"

"Everything, if you don't hide anything from me. For example, how did my letter to Monsieur de Lucheux come into your possession?"

"That was very simple. Suppose that all the letters addressed to one person were considered worthy of attention; not one would reach its destination without being read."

"And why Monsieur de Lucheux rather than someone else? All of them couldn't be read."

------

[35] Henri de La Tour d'Auvergne, Vicomte de Turenne (1611-1675), French Marshal and the most illustrious member of the La Tour d'Auvergne family. His military exploits over his five-decade career earned him a reputation as one of the greatest generals in modern history.

"Because everything that has anything to do, near or far, with the Pavilion Marsan is carefully monitored, by order of the Minister of Police; and since your friend is Brigadier of the Guards of the King's brother…"

"I understand. Aside from politics, you must know a great deal about other things. Are letters addressed to women also read?"

"Assuredly. They aren't more privileged than any other people."

"Excellent! My dear, you see, I want to know everything *curious* or *interesting*, as the public newspaper criers say. I've been told that, in the past, they prepared a summary of all the correspondence read for Louis XV. Am I not worth more than Louis XV, who doesn't even have his tomb at Saint-Denis?"[36]

"You are worth more to me, my dear beautiful lady, than all the kings of the earth, but only when you're nice, and you aren't always so; for example, when you come at people with a pistol in your hand."

"Did I press the trigger?" the Marquise asked, laughing.

"No, but I wouldn't like to find myself in that position very often."

"You are wrong, because you were superb in that position. If I ever want to listen to your flattery, your impassivity in that encounter would be a memory that would argue strongly in your favor.

"So, you are sending me back again to the *calendes grecques*[37]?"

---

[36] Somewhat incorrect. After his death on 10 May 1774, Louis XV's body was taken to Saint-Denis. The body was dug up by the French Revolution on 16 October 1793 and partially destroyed. The bones were eventually found and reinterred in the Basilica's ossuary in 1817.

[37] The calends was a feature of the Roman calendar, but it was not included in the Greek calendar. Consequently, to postpone something *ad Kalendas Graecas* was a colloquial expression for postponing something forever.

"We're here this evening to talk about business. Will you promise to tell me everything?"

"Yes, if you promise to use my information with reserve and discretion."

"Do you think me so stupid as to want to kill the goose that laid the golden egg? So, it's agreed, our bargain is done!"

And she held out her beautiful hand to Lefebvre.

"Is that the last good-bye that you are giving me?" the amorous Commandant asked.

"An aunt could hardly do anything more for her nephew here, but you know the way to the chalet. That will be our meeting place during the summer."

That said, the Marquise rose and rang loudly for the waiter.

"The bill," she said, "and call me a carriage."

Lefebvre wanted to pay for the meal, but the Marquise didn't permit him to do so, saying that she intended to play her role as Aunt Aurora right to the end.

"Can I at least know the day of my first visit to the Crôsne pavilion?"

"The day after tomorrow, at eleven o'clock sharp, Monsieur Ferlut can present his bill," the Marquise replied, smiling.

XI. The Neighbors

Monsieur de Lucheux's negotiation to bring to Paris that lovely dancer who had had such a popular opening in San-Carlo wasn't crowned with success, and after several months, called back to his service as Brigadier of the Guards, he showed himself toward Madame de Camembert, more tender and eager to please than ever. He hadn't hidden from himself the possibility of a somewhat difficult task. The tepid warmness and the rarity of his letters hadn't gone unnoticed, and blaming that forgetful attitude on his health was becoming embarrassing, since the fatigues of the voyage had only turned his body into appalling good health. Thus, he thought he should increase his explanations: if his sojourn outside of France had been of such long duration, that was because, after the sacrifice of the cruel separation was over, he had thought it prudent to get all the benefits of a somewhat prolonged absence. It shouldn't be understood that he had spent all that time in Naples; he would have died of boredom. Feeling an immense need to move about to distract himself, he had visited the Abruzzes and the two Calabrias, but considering the bad reputation of those places, where attacks by brigands are frequent, in order not to worry those who loved him, he hadn't told anyone about those excursions during which, in addition, it was physically impossible for him to send her news.

"Well, well! Are those brigands, in fact, so terrible?" Madame de Camembert asked.

Monsieur de Lucheux had the honesty to confess that nothing of that type worth recounting had happened to him.

"What about the Neapolitan theaters?"

"Oh! They're quite mediocre."

"But they say that they have remarkably good dancers there."

"Pah!" said Monsieur de Lucheux, "we have much better than that in Paris."

"Isn't it strange, then, that you, on behalf of the Opera, undertook to recruit some there!"

At that blow, Monsieur de Lucheux had to understand that his choreographic distraction had been found out. He blushed, looked embarrassed, and then tried to take an offhand and mocking tone. Then, seeing himself harshly discarded, following the procedure of those caught in the act, he fell back on his wounded dignity, spoke of jealousy, and of ridiculous suspicions.

"I don't *suspect* you, Monsieur," answered Madame de Camembert, coldly. "I am sure, and since being the rival of a woman who has her heart in her legs appears to me to be supremely ignoble, you will find it good, Monsieur, that, in the future, I won't have the pleasure of seeing you outside the presence of my husband."

Thus, dismissed from the heart and not from the house—a cruel refinement—the scorned lover vainly used every method to secure the revocation of that sentence. But his attempts at a *tête-à-tête* were declined, his letters sent back to him unopened, and the most respectful and humblest repentance treated with a disdainful coldness, that was assuredly more than he needed to let him know that the rupture was irreparable.

Like all lovers similarly cast aside, Monsieur de Lucheux felt an open and bloody wound after the lukewarm emotion of his former attachment, and the exile to which he had just been condemned; it became the major preoccupation and torment of his new life. To find out if he had a successor, to identify him, and, if need be, throw him violently out of his path, suddenly became his obsession. But in no way could the implacable Marquise admit being acquainted with Lefebvre. She surrounded herself, therefore, with such refined precautions that, despite his curiosity and even espionage, Monsieur de Lucheux couldn't verify that she was involved with someone.

With the certainty he thought he had acquired that he hadn't been replaced by someone else, his passion could do nothing but become bitter and excited. In fact, he then acquired the conviction that he had been discarded *for himself,* a notion twice as harrowing, because it meant that he had been rejected with calm and reflection. "You have stopped being worthy of me, and I have awakened from a bad dream," the woman seemed to say to him. Without the driving force of a new lover, she cast him out of her thoughts, and, in the same fashion, seemed to reclaim her virginity. To reconquer her became an obsessive challenge, because it wasn't only the heart, but the ego that was interested in success.

While Monsieur de Lucheux was still stubbornly trying to get back into the Marquise's good grace, after having been so cruelly punished for his theatrical affairs, the clauses of the secret treaty agreed on between Commandant Lefebvre and the Marquise de Camembert were being secretly carried out.

Soon, in fact, a mass of news and surprising information about various men and events were delivered, and Madame de Camembert found herself in possession of details so exact that she brought to light many secrets, she dumbfounded people by clear and direct allusions, with the most mysterious of nuances, and she seemed to hold the strings of many intrigues in her hands. As a spectator, or as the supreme director, installing herself with authority in the middle of so many comedies and tragedies, her entire existence seemed to resemble one of those opera balls which were then in vogue, revealing, naked, the harshest and most unexpected truths hidden behind a mask.

Her malicious gossip, and the terrible inquisition which she could exercise in the most intimate depths of private life, became more obvious every day. The salons where she became, at the same time, delight and terror, concerned themselves with her without a pause. She finally feared seeing her inexplicable source of information discovered. In order to throw the dumbfounded and frightened curiosity of which she felt herself the object off the track, she then had the idea of attributing it to the intervention of an agent which, at the time of our drama, was far from making the fortune which it now has.

In 1817, commerce with the supernatural was still unfrequented. There were no mediums, or turning tables, spirits who tapped on tables or floating ghosts, available to everybody at three francs for a consultation. Such transactions were only at the level of tarot card readers, and Mademoiselle Lenormand.[38] In suggesting that magnetism might well be the incomprehensible partner to explain her revelations, the brilliant Marquise, far from reducing her occult powers to proportions of common accessibility to anyone curious and to every economic level, surrounded herself with even more prestige

---

[38] Marie-Anne-Adelaide Lenormand (1772-1843), popular fortune-teller during the Revolution and Napoleonic era. She claimed to have given advice to Marat, Robespierre and Empress Josephine.

and a formidable atmosphere under which everything could be expected.

In the Spring of 1817, the so-called female magician found an opportunity to lose a little of the public attention that she was beginning to tire of, by disappearing suddenly from the Parisian landscape. Her old husband, at that time, was near his end, and the doctors prescribed the warmer climate of Southern France. So she took the sick man to Hyères, where she spent the remainder of the year with him, surrounding him with the most affectionate and tender care. She was grateful to that old man for the opulence which he had provided for her during their married life. He had married her, almost without a dowry, for her beauty and her immense musical talent, which at one time, had made her consider entering the theater. But, the more she became depraved, the more her artistic talents gave way to ardent caprices of an imaginative, diabolical kind; but it suited her to lead her life which had the appearance of having all the bourgeois virtues on the surface.

Madame de Camembert became a widow at the beginning of the year 1818, and, after having given some semblance of real conjugal sorrow—at least, what she thought was necessary—at the end of the Autumn she reappeared in the salons of Paris, where, with the help of Lefebvre, she again assumed her role as the dark angel of the shadows. That was the era when a pious intrigue had been launched to combat the all-powerful influence of the beloved minister Louis XVIII, who had the habit of calling him *my son*.[39] The conspirators had slipped a feminine influence worthy of Madame de Maintenon[40] which kept Madame de Camembert from sleeping. At least the equal in beauty and wit of the favorite, she told herself that, in the

---

[39] Rabou is referring to Élie-Louis, 1st Duke of Decazes and Glücksburg (1780-1860), leader of the liberal Doctrinaires party during the Bourbon Restoration.

[40] Allusion to Françoise d'Aubigné, Marquise de Maintenon (1635-1719), the second wife of King Louis XIV, who exercised great influence at court.

event that she found a way to get to the old King, who, in the boredom of his eternally seated life, showed, like all the princes of his race, a pronounced taste for revelations of scandalous nature, she had a chance to assume that crown of France which she had mentioned to Lefebvre as a metaphor. Now she saw an opportunity to turn this dream into a reality. Unfortunately for the success of the beautiful claimant, here is a portrait a historian of the Reformation drew of Louis XVIII, whose Montespan[41] she aspired to become:

It's a curious thing to say that under that King, a witty, but decrepit and impotent old man, women played a large role. It would be a story to collect that of all those mistresses that one day sought to aspire to the honor of belonging to the King. Here it was an artist who drew the portrait of Louis XVIII in fresh colors, with less talent than grace. There were some women, beautiful but schemers, who offered to distract the old King, and Louis XVIII, fickle as a young man, kept them only a day and always threw himself into new passions.[42]

Madame de Camembert was too dangerous a siren for her favor not to stir up the worry of the religious faction that had installed, near the crowned Anacreon,[43] another influence, all in the interest of Heaven. The taste that the flighty old monarch showed for her was not treated as one of those fanta-

---

[41] Françoise-Athénaïs de Rochechouart de Mortemart, Marquise of Montespan (1640-1707), the most celebrated mistress of Louis XIV, by whom she had seven children.

[42] Note by the Author: "History of the Restoration by a man of the administration." Rabou is likely referring to *Histoire de la Restauration et des causes qui ont amené la chute de la branche aînée des Bourbons*, Charpentier, Paris, 1841, by Jean-Baptiste Honoré Raymond Capefigue (1801-1872) who, during the ascendancy of the Bourbon, had held a post in the foreign office.

[43] Anacreon (c.582-c.485 BC), Greek lyric poet, notable for his drinking songs and hymns. Later, Greeks included him in the canonical list of nine lyric poets.

sies that were allowed to burn out by themselves, and which, ephemeral parasites, wouldn't upset the habit to which they were only a fleeting competition and scarcely worrisome.

Against the seductive Marquise, there was a coalition of all the devout and political interests whose declared representative she threatened. That undercover work, joined to the extreme mobility of affection that *Louis le Désiré* showed, would already have made her conquest difficult, if, thanks to a completely unexpected complication that suddenly came into her life, she had not ended by being drawn into a very different conflict.

Immediately after the legal settlement of her matrimonial rights put her into possession of the fortune that her old husband had left her, the Marquise had to leave her townhouse on the Rue de l'Université, which passed into the hands of a nephew of the dead man, her co-heir. She then bought that townhouse on the Rue Notre-Dame-des-Champs, which the reader has already been told about. Two reasons had made her choose that building: first of all, it was magnificent and princely, but strange rumors were attributed to that dwelling. It was said that, to deal in contraband, the Controller General, Abbé Terray,[44] capable of administering the fortune of the State, was, in addition, capable of augmenting his own by similar methods, and had created a network vast subterranean tunnels there. The Marquise's imagination, strongly turned toward adventures, was passionate about those. Next, she had calculated that, to meet her purveyor of secret information, that house, situated in a faraway area, with a vast garden, having an exit onto an isolated street, should be opportune. Lefebvre's happiness continued then to be surrounded with the most profound mystery, and since the acquisition of the new habitation, it seemed less than ever exposed to running the chance of being troubled by some unwanted gossip.

After more than eighteen months had gone by since his breakup with the Marquise, Monsieur de Lucheux had finally

---

[44] See Note 14.

obtained some lessening of his great emotional pain, and the proof was that he had, without resistance, gone along with the ideas of his aunt, the dowager Duchess, who was busy trying to get him married. But he accepted that denouement as a business matter. The Duchess having judged it proper, right up to the point where things were brought to a certain maturity, to keep the identity of the woman she had chosen for him a mystery, his unhurried curiosity had almost been inconsequential. He only knew that there was a considerable dowry at stake, and that his intended fiancée was such as to satisfy the most delicate conjugal vanity, so he waited.

However, from time to time, the wound that Madame de Camembert had left in his heart was reopened. His passion for her returned, and as love knows how to thrive on wild dreams, sometimes he asked himself if the mysterious negotiations, conducted only by his aunt, didn't have the beautiful, unmoved Marquise as their object. In fact, wasn't Madame de Camembert a widow, and, without mentioning the deposits that he had in the past put down on that marriage, wouldn't his former mistress make a very suitable match?

One evening, taken with the plausibility of that idea more than ever, suffering one of the excesses of amorous nostalgia to which the inconsolable regret of his exile often subjected him, he had the fantasy to go wander around the dwelling, to speak like the Romantics, *where she whom he adored breathed.* After having, for some time, given profound plaintive and melancholy attention to the façade of the townhouse from the street, he was inspired to go and continue his sad watch from the garden side. It was one of those splendid clear nights where the Moon cast great shadows on a space inundated with light, yet with little islands of obscurity so intense that the eye couldn't distinguish anything.

Lost in one of those shadowy accidents, Monsieur de Lucheux was considering a little door which opened from the garden onto the street where he stood. He then remembered a similar door in the Crôsne park, a key of which had once been entrusted to him a long time ago. While his memory carried him back to the happy past, in the street where he was alone and almost invisible, he saw a man who, while whistling a tune from the fifes of the Imperial Guard, was walking rapidly toward the door. Arrived there, he nimbly inserted a key into the lock, opened it, closed it again, and disappeared.

"But that's Lefebvre!" the man in love said to himself. He now reproached himself for not having run into the night to ascertain the visitor's identity. But once on the trail of the mystery, Monsieur de Lucheux, was not long in getting to the bottom of it. There was nothing clearer than the chain of events in that monstrous liaison! The Marquise gave herself to that man so that he would deliver her the secrets which he uncovered each day in the letters that he opened. And could that not explain that prodigious talent to know everything that he, himself, in a thousand other ways, had stupidly sought to explain? It was evident that the woman had made a bargain with an ignoble incubus to which, as a payment for his information, she abandoned herself in the shadows.

However, the Count had to be sure. The same door that had given an entry to his odious rival had also to be used for his exit. To stay there, lying in wait, perhaps an entire cold night this late in the season, was worth obtaining proof! When it was a matter of satisfying himself, his jealousy, the most furious of all the passions, Monsieur de Lucheux ignored such difficulties! The unhappy man was not spared one hour and, after having racked up a world of violent and frenetic thoughts that would furnish the material for twenty dramas and two or three poems, when dawn was about to break, he finally saw the door open again and Lefebvre appeared to him in the most indisputable of realities.

The Brigadier of the Guards had total liberty to stay in his observation post and not be seen. To show himself to that man was to put himself in a standoff. A volley of blows was the only denouement possible, but Monsieur de Lucheux didn't even have a cane with him, and would have been alone against a strong, stocky man, well built to defend himself. To ask him for an explanation could only turn into a fist fight.

"It's with more refined methods of revenge," the dethroned lover exclaimed to himself, "that miserable man, and most of all, his infamous accomplice, must pay for the night of agony that they have just caused me to spend."

We don't mean to imply that, between Lefebvre and the woman to whom he delivered the secrets which his functions made him the depository, were so innocent that nothing justified which Monsieur de Lucheux's furious jealousy, but, that time at least, his anger was misdirected. Here's how his rival's night had been employed. After having gone across the garden of the townhouse, Lefebvre had walked up a servant's staircase leading to the lingerie and other service rooms, which, on that side of the house, were located near the Marquise's bedroom. It was probably half past midnight when he arrived in the sanctuary where he was expected.

"Come in!" Madame de Camembert said, on seeing him. "I'm dying with fear, and since I knew you were coming, I didn't dare awaken any of my servants."

"Why is that?" asked Lefebvre. "You aren't by nature a coward."

"Listen!" Madame de Camembert continued. "The noise is louder at night."

Lefebvre listened and he heard perfectly distinctly long blows struck at equal intervals, communicating a dull vibration to the floor and to all the objects in the apartment. The sound seemed to be that of subterranean demolition work.

"That sound," Lefebvre said, "seems to be coming from this side of your oratory."

"Exactly," said the Marquise. "That's the entry of that tunnel I discovered by accident and that we visited together some days ago."

"What the Devil!" said the Commandant, "You should have had that entry walled up as I advised you."

"What good would that have done? Those trying to pierce that solid rock wall, where we stopped in our exploration, wouldn't have been stopped by a mere plaster and wood

obstacle that would have seemed sufficient to secure my bedroom."

"Then, we have to tell it like it is. You were persuaded
this tunnel led somewhere, and as you like strange things..."

"Well, was I wrong?" the Marquise asked quickly.

"Probably not, but if your tunnel communicates with a
cave full of bandits or a counterfeit workshop—those are not
nice neighbors!"

"Come now!" said Madame de Camembert, "it may
simply be a wine merchant who is having his cellar worked
on."

"At this hour?" exclaimed Lefebvre. "More likely, it
might be an army of street vendors preparing their wares for
the next day."

"Well! We don't know, do we?" said the Marquise,
shrugging.

She opened the drawer of a piece of furniture where she
took out the box of pistols that we have seen figure in an earlier encounter.

"Take this. Load them. You recognize them?"

"Perfectly, but what do you want me to do?"

"To go and investigate if there is any danger, instead of
waiting here."

"But that makes no sense," said the Commandant. "If
we're dealing with criminals, by going to look for them in that
tunnel, we will find them in their element, completely ready to
do us harm. Instead, when they see themselves facing alert
people in an inhabited house, they might be persuaded to run."

"Are you afraid?" asked the Marquise. "If so, I'll go
down alone."

"What a stubborn woman you are!" said Lefebvre, load-
ing the pistols.

When those were ready, he took one in each hand. When
he saw Madame de Camembert, picking up a torch, starting to
walk in front of him to light the way, he said jokingly:

"To the rear guard, please, my Colonel!"

And he went in front of her.

Through a door, decorated with a carved devil's mask hidden by a layer of paint, they went into a corridor, then down a stairway of about twenty steps before finding themselves in a long, vaulted passageway. At its end, the sound of the mysterious work left no doubt about the precise location of their target.

Approaching a breach in the wall that he struck with the butt of one of the pistols, Lefebvre shouted:

"Hey, friends! What the Devil are you doing, knocking down walls at such an hour?"

"Good evening, neighbors!" responded a high-pitched voice that one would have thought was the voice of a woman. "We'll be with you in a moment."

"But we are not at all charmed to make your acquaintance in this way," Lefebvre answered. "This is not the way to introduce oneself in society."

Lefebvre couldn't hear the answer. Some loose gravel caused several stones to fall and come rolling to his feet. He only had time to jump backward to avoid being struck. The breach that had just been opened showed the continuation of the passage, brightly lit by a torch. At the opening of the wall, there appeared a wrinkled face, that, to tell the truth, was sexless and crowned by a forest of gray hair. After a rapid glance, that same flute-like feminine voice that had already been heard, said:

"I didn't make a mistake. It really is to the Marquise de Camembert that I have the honor to offer my respects."

"Your way of offering your respects is far from ordinary, to say the least," replied the Marquise, laughing.

"We're going to enlarge the opening a little," the little old man answered. "Then I will have the honor of introducing to you your humble servant the Marquis de Lupiano, and his friend, the Comte de Montalvi."

"The Marquis de Lupiano," Madame de Camembert answered, "that rich foreigner who caused so much excitement with all his eccentricities?"

"Himself, wanting to get in rapport with a woman who is equally talked about a great deal, he thought he shouldn't arrive to meet her by the beaten path..."

"This type of introduction is, in fact, as new as it is gallant."

"Does it displease you? I won't insist on it. But now that the hardest part is done, wouldn't it be cruel to force me to put off an interview that I have passionately desired?"

"So be it, my friendly neighbor, since you have begun, finish making yourself a passageway. I am going to wait for you in my apartment."

That said, the Marquise snuffed out the candle she was carrying and said loudly to Lefebvre:

"Come!"

"You understand, my dear Commandant," she said, as soon as they had returned to her bedroom, "I don't want to take the trouble to show you to that unusual man who is going to come in here. That would be to tell him a little too clearly what you are to me."

"But he has seen me."

"Yes, but he didn't pay much attention to you and you could pass for a trusted valet that all my friends know I have, and whom I had accompany me when going to look into the invasion that I heard myself threatened with."

"Who is that Marquis de Lupiano?"

"A very unusual man. There have been very many questions about him for some time in Parisian society. I am, in fact, charmed to meet him. Fate has willed that, until now, we have never encountered each other."

"But I'm not at all charmed," said Lefebvre.

"Come now!" said the Marquise. "Didn't you notice the timber of his voice?"

And she said a word into Lefebvre's ear.

"What! Is that true?"

"Yes, and that's one of those thousand and one bizarre things about him. But, as I still don't find it proper to receive him in my bedroom, you're going to act your role of valet by going to light the candles in the little salon and light the fire already laid in the fireplace. When I enter with those gentlemen, you will leave respectfully, and I will say to you, 'That will be all, Etienne.' After that, I give you permission to listen behind the door, like the jealous villain that you are, and if, by any chance, I need your help, you will come in."

This schedule was followed in every detail. The Marquise went to receive the visiting strangers at the door of her oratory and, by a side exit to that room, without passing into her bedroom, she conducted them into the little salon, where Lefebvre had finished arranging everything when they entered.

The conversation, which he was authorized to overhear, lasted a long time and his patience was put to a rather tough test, because the distance was too great from the fireplace near which those talking were seated to the door behind which he was hidden, for him to understand anything but some disconnected words.

The Marquis de Lupiano and the Comte de Montalvi, two of our former acquaintances, having taken leave through their hole in the wall, Lefebvre seemed to believe he had the right to be consoled for his long and useless action as a co-listener. But the Marquise was too occupied with the great horizons that her conference with the bizarre person who had just revealed himself seemed to have opened up to her, to be consoling. That produced a lovers' quarrel that lasted until the time had come for Lefebvre to leave. And as he had expressed his discontent in less and less measured terms, he was impolitely kicked out.

We ask, did Monsieur de Lucheux have very many reasons to hold so much against him? Never had a love rendezvous passed so chastely.

XII. A Marriage for Money

Released from his lookout post, Monsieur de Lucheux went home to bed. He had been there hardly two hours, trying vainly to sleep, when his Aunt asked for him. If Lefebvre had known the old Duchesse de Lucheux, he would have realized that she had been the model for Madame de Camembert's disguise the evening of their supper at the inn in Very. She was a little stooped woman having the voice of her infirmity, commanding, brusque, and horribly infatuated with the privilege of her birth.

"My handsome nephew," she said, "I have spoken to you about a marriage, and I didn't want to tell you what people we were dealing with, before everything had been arranged. When one has done so much to make one's common, at least, before going through with it, you have to be sure of the result."

"But, my good aunt, with you, one is hardly exposed to bad company."

"Oh, yes, you are. Financiers are like garbage, but, after all, when they are needed, one has to use them! Even the great Louis XIV himself didn't hesitate to be polite to Samuel Bernard[45] when he wanted to say a word to his millions."

"Then, it's into the financial world that you're thinking of marrying me?"

"Yes, my boy, because, you see, you shouldn't have any illusions. I have no more than forty thousand *livres* of income to leave to you."

"Come on, auntie! Don't talk about a future that is still so far away—God willing!"

"On the contrary, I'm talking about it because you have a great name to uphold, and it takes a deep purse to provide for the honor of our house. Today, we are living with 100,000 *livres* of annual income, but I've been forced to sell a portion of our assets. And we can't make any more debts! All those suppliers and tradesmen will want to be paid. There's no hope to come from the Court. What can the great families expect of

---

[45] Samuel Bernard (1651-1739), financier who was ennobled by Louis XIV in 1699, and made Comte de Coubert by Louis XV in 1725.

a Jacobin King? There is, then, no longer anything but the maltote[46] to which we can turn."

"Who, then, is the Croesus[47] whose daughter I must marry?"

"I had thought of Madame de Camembert—a wealthy widow, a beautiful name! But I don't know what you did to her, because she can't stand you. And, just between us, despite her great airs of religiosity, I suspect she is basically a little *Voltairienne*.[48] She may be acceptable in her behavior, but I don't believe she is at all so in her ideas."

"Yes; my opinion is that there would be more than one objection one could make to that choice."

"Isn't that true! So it is your opinion, too? Well, mine is to marry you to wealth, so I said to myself, one day: what about Martin Lambert, my banker? That's a good prospect. He has shovelfuls of money and although he likes to act the Republican, his wife is always enraged to be called only *Madame*. He once introduced to me to his only daughter, a little girl who, on my word, allowed herself to be very pretty and to whom he will give a million in dowry. I therefore got things started, and had only one word to say to make the mother reverse herself, with nothing but the thought of allying herself to our noble family. I thought we were on the point of coming to terms when we ran up against the most stupid blockage."

"And what was that?" asked Monsieur de Lucheux.

"Oh! Nothing important, my love. The little girl is already in love."

"But, auntie, that's an obstacle that could be serious."

---

[46] Extraordinary taxes raised to pay for extraordinary expenses, such as war.

[47] Croesus (595 BC–c.546 BC), last king of Lydia renowned for his wealth, who reigned from 560 BC until his defeat by the Persian king Cyrus the Great in 546 BC.

[48] After Voltaire, who had very liberal views on marriage, religion and society, for which he was imprisoned and banished.

"Forget about that! Would Martin Lambert give his daughter to a mere secretary?"

"I don't say that he is giving her to him, but what if she insists on it?"

"That's because the boy lives under the same roof, where he has been allowed to get a foothold, because, it appears that he also writes speeches for her father in the Chambre des Députés. The little girl, who has him within reach, has amused herself to take that first inclination of a schoolgirl, which never amounts to anything, as a proof of love."

"Be careful, auntie. Sometimes those first impressions have great repercussions in the future."

"Come now! A man like you shouldn't be afraid of a little nothing who is something in the household only because he can write! It's only a question of introducing you, so as to put that little fellow to flight, that I have made you come into the situation before I had arranged it. I ask you, when one can be called Comtesse de Lucheux, why would one choose instead to be called Madame Lefebvre?"

"Lefebvre!" exclaimed Monsieur de Lucheux. "What family is that young man from?"

"As you might think, I informed myself. His mother sells lingerie; his sister has married a factory worker; and his father is an officer on half-pay. Everything there is of the worst reputation. But Lambert keeps the little boy at hand because he is his ghost-writer for their gambling den of Deputés, he seems ready to sacrifice his daughter to him. He gives as a reason that the father had rendered him a great service. But the fact is that he doesn't have the least intention of carrying through with that marriage. The truth is that he has put it off for more than two years. And from the time that I put you in the ranks, he isn't made uncomfortable, except to find an honest way to take back his word."

"That, auntie, I can help you give it to him," said Monsieur de Lucheux, carried away by jealousy.

"Tell me a little about that," the Duchesse asked.

Monsieur de Lucheux then recounted how he had been told of the secret position that Commandant Lefebvre occupied within the Postal System, and how he had been advised to not duel with him. Excited as a young girl, the old Duchesse immediately rang to ask for her carriage.

"But, auntie," Monsieur de Lucheux remarked, "this is a State Secret. We should be discreet."

"A State Secret!" replied the dowager. "What do State Secrets mean to me"?

"I think it may be sufficient for that young man to find himself in concurrence with me, and we should think twice before inflicting upon him the consequences of his father's infamy."

"I'll make sure you're not connected with the confidence that I'm going to share with her father. It's marvelous that I didn't know about it before, that they have reestablished that malicious system of the *Ancien Régime. Par Dieu*! They didn't begin to look into letters just today. Something rather similar happened to me under Monsieur de Maurepas.[49] Well! He really had a good idea, that poor Monsieur Lambert, to want to give his daughter to a man who tears open seals!"

"In fact," Monsieur de Lucheux ended by telling himself, since with each evil deed, passion finds a way to salve one's conscience, "a right-thinking man owes it to himself to prevent a scoundrel from carrying such dishonor into a family."

There is nothing truer, but to be accepted as moral, such a service would have to be disinterested!

XIII. A Squeezed Lemon

We will later tell how, in the encounter of the Marquis de Lupiano with Madame de Camembert, there was nothing for-

---

[49] Jean-Frédéric Phélypeaux, Comte de Maurepas (1701-1781), French statesman who held at various times the positions of chamberlain of the royal household, minister of the marine, and director of the secret service.

tuitous, and how despite his Romanesque appearance, a simple explanation can be given for it.

At this moment, to lead the story of Commandant Lefebvre to its conclusion, it is important to state that, by some natural affinity, which probably hasn't escaped the reader, feeling both energetic and passionate toward the unexpected and the bizarre, Lupiano and the Marquise were quick to understand each other. Confidence between them was neither slow to mature, nor long in creating a close relationship. The proof of their rapid and cordial understanding was that, four days later, when Lefebvre again saw the Marquise, he found Lupiano already privy to all their secrets. Sent away harshly, the Commandant had returned the following night. But, after entering the garden of the townhouse with the key he had been given, and which he had not been asked to return, as one does to a chamberlain relieved of his duties, when he tried to enter by means of the servants' stairway, the door was outrageously closed.

Rather brutal by nature, he then tried to make some noise, counting on the fear of a scandal to have the door open for him. But the only thing that opened was a window from which a pistol was fired. All the inhabitants of the townhouse were on their feet, and to avoid being taken for a thief, the unhappy Commandant had only enough time to escape by the door that had just given him access. Then he was forced to respectfully ask for a rendezvous in writing, and when he added that he had to speak to the Marquise about *serious and pressing matters,* that phrase, as we are going to see, was heartfelt. It was not a question for him of saving his amorous ego.

"You're choosing your time badly to be so disobliging to me," he said to Madame de Camembert. "I'm a lost man. Look at the letter I received!"

And on a small pedestal table, near which the Marquise was seated, he threw that letter, going himself a little further away, taking a seat in a bergère,[50] where all his attitude showed the most profound discouragement.

Madame de Camembert unfolded the paper which had been put with that rudeness under her rather disdainful eyes, and she read what follows:

Monsieur:

When you receive this letter, I will have left France. I said good-bye this morning to my mother and my sister without telling them of my plan. I am taking leave of you at a distance, as is proper between people who couldn't see each other again without cruel explanations.

Yesterday evening, Monsieur Lambert asked me to come into his study. "My dear Alfred," he said to me. "I have not ceased for a moment being perfectly happy with your services. I intended as a recompense for them to give you my daughter, whom you love and who would have accepted you with pleasure as her husband. But after what I have learned, that is no longer possible. Your father has an infamous job; he is employed at the Secret Bureau where letters are unsealed, and it was by that means that he found the way to render me an important service, that I would have wished to be able to recompense. But at least, I will testify my gratitude to him by assuring him that the secret is inviolable.

"My daughter," Monsieur Lambert added, "is going to be married. Her hand has been asked by the heir of a great name. I would have preferred you as a son-in-law, but I now have no reason to decline this honorable request. Until the moment when my daughter leaves my house, to follow her husband, it would probably appear to you, as it does to me, proper that you leave. Nothing is easier to accomplish by means of a mission which I now intend to give you. In a few months, you can come back to us, because I don't intend to deprive myself of your precious collaboration. But on leaving,

---

[50] A French armchair with a wide, deep seat and upholstered sides, made from about 1725.

I expect a favor from you; that by a note written to my daughter, you will assume for yourself the breakup that your father's situation has forced upon us. Not wanting to tell the poor child the true cause, which must remain between us, it is necessary that my change of will be not in her eyes a caprice of paternal authority, against which, she might perhaps revolt."

"In an hour, Monsieur," I said, "I will have left your house, and in two days, before taking sail for America, a country with a future and liberty, where I have often thought of going to search for adventure, I will be certain to send a letter to Mademoiselle your daughter fulfilling the conditions that you desire."

"But, my dear friend," Monsieur Lambert answered, "it is not necessary for you to go so far. The sugar beet industry will soon be debated in the Chamber. I can then, rationally, send my secretary to study that question in Northern France."

"No, Monsieur," I answered. "I will leave my country, where I don't wish to bear a stained name."

"That would be," he answered, "to take the thing very tragically. The mistakes are personal; I guarantee you that the secret of your father's occupation will be well guarded. Why separate ourselves? You are useful to me and I can do a great deal for your future."

Seeing me unshakeable in my intention, Monsieur Lambert then said to me:

"Well, then, go, my dear boy, but America is a long way away and you aren't rich. Let me at least pay for your voyage." As he thought I was about to refuse, he promptly added: "I know that you don't want to be in my debt. But I have done nothing for you except pay you a meager salary. I was thinking that other services might make up for that. There is, right now, in Le Havre, a ship leaving for New Granada.[51] *I know*

---

[51] The Republic of New Granada was a centralist republic consisting primarily of present-day Colombia and Panama with smaller portions of today's Nicaragua, Costa Rica, Ecuador, Venezuela, Peru, and Brazil. It was created after the dissolu-

the Captain. Let me give you a letter for him. He will give you every imaginable consideration, and nothing will keep you from going to join the great movement for independence which, under the auspices of the famous Simon Bolivar,[52] promises to take that part of Central America away from the bigoted Spanish domination."

That horizon tempted me, Monsieur, and in the hopes that it could tempt you also, accepting the offer of Monsieur Lambert, I leave to wait for you. Your bravery, that has never been doubted, your great experience of war can render precious services to the cause of liberty, and in the shadow of its triumphant flag, the father that I have lost, the son that you no longer have, can in this way respect and love each other as they did in the past.

Alfred

When she had finished the letter, the Marquise asked:

"Do you know the way in which Monsieur Lambert was informed of your situation?"

"No," replied Lefebvre. "To make him decide to give his daughter in marriage to my son, I committed for his profit one of those indiscretions of which I often made myself guilty to merit your good graces. From one and the other, I have found the same gratitude."

Without answering that attempt at an explanation, Madame de Camembert said:

"Well, I can tell you who the informant was. Here, read this…" and at the same time, she gave Lefebvre a letter that

---

tion in 1830 of Gran Colombia, with the secession of Ecuador and Venezuela.

[52] Simón José Antonio de la Santísima Trinidad de Bolívar y Palacios (1783-1830), Venezuelan military and political leader who played a leading role in the establishment of Venezuela, Bolivia, Colombia, Ecuador, Peru, and Panama as sovereign states, independent of Spanish rule.

she had gone to take out of her secretary. That letter was from Monsieur de Lucheux. He had written to the Marquise:

Dear forgetful one,

I am no longer astonished like the Recluse [53] *of the Vicomte d'Arlincourt. You see everything, know everything, hear everything. Last night, I surprised the lovable enchanter, whose power you borrow, entering your townhouse. I don't need to tell you that, with that discovery, I feel myself very reassured. I know fewer secrets than you do, but I know one that is worth its weight in gold, since, consoling me for our breakup, it gives me the assurance that your poison would never spread over my life. Goodbye, dear Madame Lefebvre. Please forget me as I forget you.*

Comte de Lucheux

"Then," Lefebvre said, "you are supposing that your former lover, as revenge...?"

"Oh! The interest is less noble," countered the Marquise. "I know through his aunt that a marriage has been arranged for him with Mademoiselle Lambert. That will let you understand that he used a method he had at hand to push your son aside."

"This time," Lefebvre exclaimed, rising, "that's too much. Using the pretext of my functions, he refused to duel with me, but there is still a way to force that man to accept me as an adversary. I will slap him in the face in a public place,

---

[53] Note from the Author: "A novel then in vogue." Charles-Victor Prévot, Vicomte d'Arlincourt (1788-1856) was a French novelist, whose popularity in the 1820s gained him the title of "Prince of the Romantics," rivaling that of Victor Hugo. *Le Solitaire* [The Recluse], a gothic novel, was published in 1821. It achieved an extraordinary celebrity; in the space of a few months, the book was reprinted a dozen times, translated into ten languages, and became the basis for seven operas and twice as many dramatic adaptations, numerous songs, parodies, paintings and lithographs.

and if, after that, he still declines the encounter, let him make his will, the scoundrel, because as God is my witness, I will kill him."

"That's a concern," replied the Marquise with a sinister smile, "that, according to all appearances, with which you will be spared. Someone else will take care of him."

"Who then would think of stealing my revenge?"

"The man you saw here the other night. He's a brave knight who doesn't let a woman be insulted without punishment. You could do nothing for him, but I showed him that insolent letter and he will take care of the matter."

"But to give him that letter to read was to tell him about our relationship—the secret of my occupation. How imprudent to open ourselves to an unknown person..."

"An unknown person? We may never have seen each other before, but across space and time, we were reaching out to each other. We understood each other from the first second we met. Our friendship seems to date from four days ago; in reality, it dates from a thousand years ago. We must have known each other formerly in the land of souls."

"Because of that, I'm no longer astonished at your having forced me to ask to see you in writing."

"He, my lover?" the Marquise exclaimed, shrugging. "Not at all! Didn't I tell you that his senses were dead. Haven't you seen what kind of man he is? Say, rather, that I am his daughter. I could be by age, as I am by will."

At that moment, a sharp and commanding knock was heard at the door of the oratory which led to the tunnels.

"Listen! Here he is. He's come to give me an accounting of what he's done with Monsieur de Lucheux."

Then, as if to show to Lefebvre how little she was concerned whether that interview was or not to his taste, she added:

"Would you be kind enough to do me the favor of going and opening the door?"

Lefebvre took a torch and, a few seconds later, returned with the Marquis de Lupiano, who was wearing his arm in a sling.

Going to the Marquise, he took her hand, on which he gallantly deposited a kiss, and said:

"It is done my lady now. You have been served. Pyrrhus gives up his faithless life to God. [54]

I will not answer you as Hermione," the Marquise answered. *"Why murder him? What did he do? What right? Who told you tot?* But I see that you yourself are wounded?"

"Oh, it's nothing," replied Lupiano. "Caused by my own carelessness. His shot grazed my arm, but mine hit him right in the heart. He died without suffering."

"And you aren't afraid of having to account for that unfortunate duel?" the Marquise asked.

"Me, having to account for it? The thing happened at three o'clock in Montmartre in a place where we were hardly hidden, in the presence of four honorable witnesses who had arranged everything. Yesterday in the Champs-Élysées where I was horseback-riding, that gentleman looked at me as if I were some sort of curious beast. I told him very calmly and softly that his way of looking at me was insolent and one thing led to another. We came to the point of exchanging cards and so forth. Why do you think the authorities may have to do with all that?"

"Commandant Lefebvre," the Marquise then said, "that I have the honor of introducing to you."

"Charmed to make your acquaintance," replied the Marquis. "Please forgive me for having interfered in your busi-

---

[54] They're both quoting from Jean Racine's play *Andromaque*, Act V, Scene III (1667). At the climax, provoked by Hermione's desperation, Pyrrhus, the son of Achilles, is murdered by Orestes' men in a mad rage; this only serves to deepen Hermione's despair. She takes her own life by the side of Pyrrhus and Orestes goes mad.

ness, but that Monsieur de Lucheux had put you in a situation that you would have had trouble making go away."

"Perhaps," Lefebvre said.

"I don't agree. Prejudice was in his favor and unless you wanted to have trouble with the law, he wouldn't have decided to fight you."

"No extremity would have made me recoil."

"Then I congratulate myself even more so for having stolen your rightful revenge, since I have reasons to believe that, at this moment, it is particularly necessary that you should avoid drawing attention to yourself."

"What is there in my case that's so particular?"

"It's because Madame hasn't perhaps used your indiscretions with all the necessary *discretion* and the Secret Bureau is beginning to suspect that there is a daily displacement of the inviolable secrets to the advantage of our dear Marquise, which for the guilty one is a matter of life or death. From that point, dear Commandant, for them to discover that you are the unfaithful employee, you understand, is only a short step, and even though Monsieur de Lucheux's mouth has now been padlocked, he might have had the unfortunate pleasure of talking."

"But, Marquis!" exclaimed the Marquise, "you make me tremble. The mystery of my rapport with Monsieur is only held by a thread."

"It's exactly because that danger preoccupied me that I sent to see the man called Saint-Rambert, who is today at the head of the Secret Bureau, and whom I discovered that I knew rather well in the past. I made him talk, and he is positively on his way to identifying you Commandant, as the thief of all the secrets that have been stolen from them. As for the person you delivered them to, our dear Marquise, he's still looking, but it seems to me he has already decided to use some very severe forms of justice, following the precedents of their code of discipline. The past examples of the Secret Bureau's discipline, you must understand, Monsieur, are not all reassuring."

"Dear Monsieur," said Madame de Camembert, speaking to Lefebvre, "I don't see any other solutions; your safety and my reputation are equally at stake here. You must follow the actions of Monsieur your son."

"You are talking very casually, Marquise, about breaking, at the first panic, all the ties which keep me here."

"But balanced against your comfort, the concern for my consideration and my future, does that count for nothing?"

"But that security, that you were talking to me about a while ago, I am ready to sacrifice it for you."

"My good Monsieur," said Lupiano, "please allow me to say that you are speaking like a man in love; in other words, without a great deal of thought. The chances of being identified are not the same between Madame and you. Madame is already under suspicion, while you are not yet so. But the day that you become compromised, she will be too. And let's not even talk about the terrible misfortune of stigmatizing the life of a beloved woman. Would you be any less separated if they lock you up in some prison? I, who am talking to you, spent several years in the dungeons of Vincennes, and I can tell you that it would have been rather difficult for a lover to come and visit me there."

"That is obvious," said Madame de Camembert, "and Monsieur's stubbornness is only egotism, at the same time brutal and stupid."

"If you loved me, Madame," Lefebvre said, "you would think otherwise."

"And who told you that I ever loved you!' the Marquise exclaimed with great disdain.

"That's true," said Lefebvre. "Between us there were only the two sides of a shameful bargain."

"Come now," said Lupiano, "in such a serious situation, a lover's quarrel is as ridiculous as it is misplaced. When I spoke to you of a prison, Monsieur, I told you the nicest part. Do you know a little about Saint-Rambert, your honored director?"

"Not much good," Lefebvre responded. "If I can judge by the scoundrel who is his right-hand man, and by whom I was recruited for that prison which I joined the Bureau."

"This Saint-Rambert, Monsieur, I know him well, because I almost had him hanged once, because he was the leader of a band of criminals known as *Les Chauffeurs*.[55] I'll let you wonder if he would bargain about your life, in case the good administration of his 'prison,' as you call it, seemed to him to be compromised."

"Well!" said Lefebvre, walking excitedly around the room, "then let him take my life! He couldn't do me a greater favor."

While Lefebvre's back was turned, Lupiano gave the Marquise a signal to indicate to her that things had to be handled with gentleness and soothing words. Too intelligent to misunderstand what was being asked of her, she approached Lefebvre in her most feline way and said:

"My love, forgive me for the ugly words that have escaped me. You know that I love you, and I must love you, because what kind of woman would I be if, between us, as you said, there had been only a bargain."

"Well, if you love me, you wouldn't talk to me about a separation."

"So be it then. Let's take all the chances; you, to cause me to lose my reputation, and I, to be the cause of your death, because there is no way to delude ourselves. You yourself know how critical the situation is. Just a moment ago, on your arrival, giving me that letter from your son to read, didn't you cry out: *I am lost!*"

"Undoubtedly, from the point of view of honor, when I learned that my son knew of my odious occupation. Do you have a right to reproach me for it?"

'My love, I have never claimed to have but the most perfect respect for your character. But while taking advantage of the position you had taken, do you believe that I have never

---

[55] See Book 1, Part I, Chapter VI.

secretly deplored it? After thirty years of honorable services rendered to your country, when the Emperor himself, your idol, placed on your chest the medal of honor, was it your proper place to be associated with men like those which the Marquis described just a moment ago?"

"I have already thought twenty times about ending my life," responded Lefebvre, "and without the flowers that your love threw over my infamy..."

"Well! A way of rehabilitation is now offered to you. Your son wrote to ask you to go with him in the cause of American independence. When so many other reasons suit you, take that heroic goal, without hesitating because of a woman!"

"But when that woman is you..."

"You will find that woman again. The Emperor was unjust to you. He left you to vegetate in the lower ranks, when others, who weren't nearly worth as much as you are, became Maréchals. But in the war where you can go and take part, you have every chance to gain the highest fortune. Bolivar certainly doesn't have near him a great number of officers like you, who have served in all the campaigns of the Empire."

"Bolivar!" Lupiano said quickly. "When I left France in 1814 with Montalvi, he was the one I went to join. For more than two years, I was his Chief-of-Staff, and when concern for my health forced me to return to Europe, we were heart-broken to leave each other. If, for his son, or for himself, Commandant Lefebvre wants a letter of recommendation, I can assure him that they would be very welcome."

"You see, my love, how this is all providential. You may write me some day to have me come and be crowned the queen of some American kingdom."

"As for that, no," said Lupiano. "They establish only republics there."

"So, Monsieur le Marquis, you helped Simon Bolivar?" asked Lefebvre, with astonishment. "Who would have thought it with your very frail appearance?"

"As a corsair, Monsieur, under the tricolored flag, in the seas of India, where the English, I beg you to believe it, still remember my name. And Napoleon, speaking to me in person, offered me a commission in the Imperial Navy ."

"Which you accepted," Lefebvre said with admiration.

"No, that I refused. That's why he sent me to Vincennes. He was a little despotic, your great man."

"Ah!" said Lefebvre, "he lost because of that."

"Yes," said Lupiano, "and for his not making peace so stubbornly. War for him was a mistress that he could never make up his mind to leave; a great lesson to study, my dear Commandant."

"Very well," said Lefebvre, strongly shaken in his resistance, "give me twenty-four hours to think about it."

"If you hadn't asked for them, Commandant, I would have advised you to take them. Great decisions mustn't be made on the spur of the moment."

There was nothing more to be said about the matter.

"Marquis," said Madame de Camembert, "do you have on you that flask of *L'esprit de Borneo* that you let me sniff the other day? This discussion has upset me. I find myself very near becoming sick."

"Of course I do," Lupiano said quickly, taking from his pocket a flask of colorless liquid.

He poured several drops of it on the Marquise's handkerchief. She carried it to her nostrils, breathing deeply. It produced an effect totally contrary to the one that should have been expected. The sick woman's eyes became fixed and glazed and, after a few seconds, leaving the handkerchief in the hands of the Marquis, who hurried to take from her, she fell into a swoon that was rather frightening.

"Oh! *Mon Dieu!*" exclaimed Lefebvre "She's completely unconscious."

"Let her alone," said Lupiano, opposing any intervention from Lefebvre. "That's the effect of the medicine. She'll come to herself in a moment."

In fact, the Marquise quickly recovered the uses of her senses.

"Are you better?" asked Lefebvre, who held out his hand.

"Yes, my love; it has passed. I feel the Marquis saved me from a terrible nervous crisis. So, gentlemen, good evening! I'm going to call my maid and go to bed."

"Commandant," said Lupiano, "I would like to see you again. Please give me your address."

"No, I have bachelor's accommodations; if you will allow it, I will come to your townhouse."

"Until tomorrow, then," said the Marquis," without coming to see Madame, because like you, but less fortunate, I must not see her here except as smuggled goods. I will give you her news as I get them."

After having said that, he was the first to leave using the tunnels. Some instants later, Lefebvre, after having given the Marquise a kiss on the forehead, went down the servants' stairway that led to the garden.

A quarter of an hour after his departure, the Marquise hadn't rung for her maid, and she had not gone to bed. The Marquis de Lupiano suddenly appeared in her bedroom.

"What torture," she said on seeing him, "to have to poison oneself to be delivered from that odious man! Ah! I hope he has come here for the last time, and that from tomorrow forward, you will deliver me from him."

"Thanks to the means I suggested to you, to treat him gently, your liberation, it seems to me, is now on the right path. I came to see that the anesthesia wasn't too violent. You breathed too deeply. You know that after a few minutes, it means death!"

"I was using it like a person who wants to have a tranquil night and to get rid of someone she despises."

"All right! I see that there doesn't seem to be any ill effects, so I can let you go to bed," said Lupiano, kissing the Marquise's hand, saying: "To the first day of your liberty!"

The duel in which Monsieur de Lucheux had succumbed had enormous repercussions. The curiosity that, twenty years before, Monsieur de Lupiano had excited in London, under the name of Marquis de Samaniego, was at that point, in the Parisian world, carried to its highest paroxysm, but it must be added that, in becoming overly excited, it changed character noticeably.

After the more or less amused comments, of which the strange Marquis had been the object, followed attention a great deal more measured in its expression; we almost said *respectful attention.* For it must be recognized, the better part of the glory and the renown of conquerors is made up by the number of men who died serving their ambition; there is always a kind of fearful respect for the killers of men. That sensation must be derived from the great respect that we have for life; every man, who, in one way or another, disposes of those of his kind, a murderer, a hangman, and finally the duelist, are always sure of not going unnoticed.

Lefebvre seemed to have escaped that common impression. He had been present at so many massacres himself, doing his part of it, that a little blood on a man's hands didn't astonish him very much. What's more, when he had seen the Marquis' face through the breach broken through the underground wall, that apparition had seemed to him to be that of an

---

[56] Montyon Prizes are a series of prizes awarded annually by the French Academy of Sciences and the Académie française. They were originally endowed by the French benefactor Baron de Montyon. The endowed prizes were as follows: (i) Making an industrial process less unhealthy, (ii) Perfecting of any technical improvement in a mechanical process, (iii) Book which during the year rendered the greatest service to humanity and (iv) The *prix de vertu* for the most courageous act on the part of a poor Frenchman. The latter is the one being referenced here.

old concierge putting is head through the little window panes of his lodge. The later confidence of Madame de Camembert wasn't such as to modify his derisive opinion of the person that he had immediately formed.

However, during their second encounter, when Lupiano showed himself to him, his head encircled with a bloody halo still warm from the execution he had just performed, thus avenged of the man who had successively struck him in his dearest affections, the Commandant, like everyone, felt himself submitting to that ascendancy, sometimes violent, sometimes persuasive, that the dark enigma of the Marquis was in the habit of exercising over everyone who approached him.

Then, when they saw each other again, Madame de Camembert's friend didn't have any trouble finishing his work. With the most serious fears that he knew how to inspire in Lefebvre concerning the possible consequences of his epistolary indiscretions; by the high hopes he had laid out before him in case the Commandant chose to serve the cause of the Columbian insurrection, and finally, by the eloquent ability that he used to reignite in the old soldier both his instincts of honor and his memories of military glory, Lefebvre finally decided to go and join his son in America.

There remained, however, the question of good-byes. Lefebvre couldn't decide to leave without having seen, one last time, the lady of his thoughts. On the other hand, Madame de Camembert had never seen in him anything but someone to supply her with up-to-date confidential information, and since she could foresee new spaces that her friendship with the Marquis de Lupiano might open up in her life, she made it a matter of ego to end cleanly and abruptly with that disagreeable used instrument. That seemed to her both vengeance and rehabilitation. When the usefulness of his cooperation had ceased, it seemed to her that their previous relationship had had the character of some kind of prostitution of her person, and that idea revolted her.

Somewhat burdened with reconciling two opposite wills, Lupiano got out of his difficulty by seeing Monsieur de Saint-

Rambert, a.k.a. Dulac, a.k.a. Rempailleux, with whom he had effectively reestablished a relationship, and he had not been slow in making him his humble servant, as it will be ultimately explained.

On receiving a threatening letter from his Director in which he was told that his disloyalty had been discovered, and that the next day he would have to appear before the gentlemen of the Secret Bureau assembled as a law court to examine and sanction his conduct, Lefebvre understood that a longer stay in Paris would expose him to some real danger.

Taking advantage then of the offer of a valid passport that had been taken care of by Lupiano, and quickly putting in order his last preparations for departure, he went to Belleville to say good-bye to his family. He caused them some worry when he told them of the preceding determination by Alfred, and his own to follow him without delay.

Madame Lefebvre, who had for a long time carried her canteen when following the Imperial armies, was not dismayed at the idea of going to test the fortunes of war in the New World, and she insisted strongly that she wanted to leave with her husband. But Lefebvre didn't welcome her conjugal devotion, and thanks to a charming little granddaughter that Amanda had brought into the world a little less than a year after her marriage, they all made the woman see reason. It remained settled that Lefebvre would depart alone. He had only to promise that he would give them news of himself frequently and not chat too closely with cannon shells and bullets.

That separation accomplished, Lefebvre went back to Paris, and, before going back to see the Marquis, with whom he was supposed to dine before his departure, set for ten o'clock that evening, he walked down one of the most populated streets of the Saint-Denis neighborhood to see a leather merchant, from whom he had ordered a toiletry set, that was supposed to be delivered to him that evening.

The house where the Commandant had business was one of those hives divided into an infinite number of cubicles which each sheltered a business and a family. In those sorts of houses, a passkey, which each of the renters had, dispensed with the formality of a concierge. Lefebvre therefore had some difficulty finding the lodging of the leather worker where he had come only once, in the evening, having been taken there by someone else. Taking a chance, he knocked at a door that he thought he recognized. It was distinguished from the neighboring doors by having the luxury of a doormat.

After he had knocked twice, the second time rather forcefully, the door opened half way; but the woman who came to open it not only closed it very quickly, but, what's more, he heard the sound of a lock in the interior being closed immediately, indicating either that Lefebvre's face hadn't appeared reassuring, or that it had awakened a bad memory.

The Commandant could explain that reception better than we can, because in the face of the woman in the half-opened door, he had had the time to recognize Herminie Daliron.

He remained an instant to consider whether he should knock again, but while hesitating, he heard the voice of a child crying; he realized that any insistence from him would be useless. Not having escaped any of the misfortunes foreseen in her letter of good-bye, Herminie could feel, for the man she had to consider their architect, only aversion and contempt. So, having come for another purpose, Lefebvre thought that some information might be obtained from the worker he had come to see. The Commandant, having paid for and picked up his purchase, asked in an apparently indifferent voice:

"Who is that woman whose door I had mistaken for yours? Who closed it in my face as if I had come to murder her?"

"On the floor below?"

"No, on the floor above; a woman whose face is pock-marked from small pox."

"Ah, yes!" said the worker's wife. "Madame Smith. That's very simple. This isn't the hour when she is available."

"What do you mean, *when she is available*?" Lefebvre asked. "What does she do?"

"Well! She has a lot of jobs," the charitable neighbor answered. "Linen maid, milliner… She's a woman with a lot of strings to her bow."

"You say that as if that were something to think about," the Commandant remarked.

"Not at all! There is no one more regular in her habits. Every evening, at precisely ten o'clock, you hear her come downstairs. She's like a clock."

"Come now," said the leather merchant. "You're talking too much! Leave that unfortunate woman alone; she's never hurt anybody. On the contrary, it's not all of you other honest women who would have sat up three nights in a row with that poor sick old woman upstairs in her garret, and who, after she'd passed, would have buried her with your own hands."

"Parbleu! All of you husbands would be happy if we left our housekeeping chores to take on the work of a nurse!"

"But if these evening outings are regular," Lefebvre asked, "what does that mean to you?"

"That she likes company, because you almost never see her come back alone."

"How can you allow such a woman in your house?"

"What does that have to do with us? There's never any scandal in her apartment, while in many of the households around us, there is fighting. During the day, there is not a soul in her apartment. In the evening, if she goes out to sin, it is only with well-behaved people, and it is not by vice. She is a woman with responsibilities."

"Yes," said Lefebvre, "it seemed to me that I heard a child."

"The child, first of all, but after that, she has a brother who is already of some age and that she is having brought up in a private school. Could a working woman earn enough for all that by her work alone?"

"If you will allow me, my dear fellow," said Lefebvre, "the motives may be respectable, but the method is a little shocking and dangerous."

"But that's how men are!" said the leather worker's wife, "completely indulgent for those creatures. What's more, if they're not watched, that one may well turn into a home wrecker, mark my words!"

"Come now," said the leather worker, shrugging, "she thinks well of us."

"Yes, but she acts important as if ordinary leather work doesn't impress her, that woman who only dotes on the Good Lord."

"Do you mean to say that she is devout?" asked Lefebvre, who found that the leather worker's wife wasn't being very coherent in her wicked gossip.

"What? Yes! You can believe that she goes to Mass every day. I myself have seen her more than once in the church on Sunday. You should see her saintly 'holier than thou' airs."

"That's rather unusual," remarked Lefebvre.

"As for me," said the leather worker, "I see this as proof that she is not settled in her evil ways, and I believe that she won't be slow to leave them, because I have seen a young lady having a very respectable appearance come and visit her several times. I believe she was a lady from Charity."

"Or another type like her, or maybe a marriage-maker from the *XIIIème*,[57]" said the leather merchant's wife with that

---

[57] 13th *arrondissement*. Until 1860, Paris had only twelve *arrondissements* (districts) and it was fashionable to say, for unwed couples living together, that they had been married in the 13th, as a way of saying that they hadn't been properly married. At the time of the expansion of Paris, the initial plan provided that the new 13th *arrondissement* would be what is today the 16th, but the influential inhabitants of Auteuil and Passy, two of the communes newly annexed, did not want this scandalous label to be applied to their residences, not to mention all the superstitions surrounding the number 13. The

ferocity of evil thoughts, which is remarkable in a woman of the people, when she has the good fortune to be irreproachable.

"Be quiet," said the merchant impatiently, "if you think that with all your wicked gossip, you are giving a good idea of yourself to Monsieur."

"At least, I can hold my head high," the housewife answered proudly.

"It's obvious," said Lefebvre, preparing to leave, "that honest women need a spokesperson, but one should also have a little pity for those other unfortunate women."

After having taken his leave, as he was going down the stairway, the Commandant crossed a woman who looked both very elegant and very distinguished. Magnificent blonde hair arranged in spirals in the English fashion, which hadn't yet arrived in France, fell on her shoulders and gave her the appearance of a foreigner.

Lefebvre thought that the beautiful blonde could be the charitable lady whom he had just heard talked about. He halted to see which door she was going to. He verified that it was, in fact, at Herminie's apartment that the newcomer stopped. Without having let any emotions show, Lefebvre was terribly tortured by remorse about the frightful details he had just gathered. His conscience laid bare to him the terrible sequence of events to which the unfortunate Herminie had succumbed, and he could not hide from himself, in his imagination, that odious slope that led right back to him.

He had the patience to wait three quarters of an hour in the street for the woman he had encountered on the stairway to come down. He approached her as she was leaving, his hat in his hand, respectfully, just before she was getting into a rented carriage that had been waiting for her.

---

numbering of the districts was consequently changed to the one we know today. With eight new districts added soon afterward, the expression fell into disuse.

As in the past, he started by claiming to be a member of Herminie's family. He then explained that, having learned of the girl's distress, he had come with the intention of offering her some help. But before going to her apartment, he had gotten some information from the neighborhood. That information was distressing. What was he to make of it? It was to verify its veracity that he had taken the liberty to stop a person as distinguished as she in the street.

The lady answered, with a rather pronounced English accent, that, in fact, Herminie was on a rather shameful path. In order not face crushing expenses, she had let herself be drawn into rather ugly and regrettable things. But far from being lost without redemption, she only looked forward to a time when she would have provided for the fate of her two children, as she called them, in order to enter the Refuge as a *Repentant Daughter*.[58]

"Unfortunately, the Lady of Charity added, "to take from her the burden of her brother and her child would require a rather large sum. The resources of our Order are rather limited, and we can't use them all to help only one unfortunate person, however exceptional and worthy she might be. How-

---

[58] The Order of Our Lady of Charity, also known as Order of Our Lady of Charity of the Refuge, is a Roman Catholic monastic order, founded in 1641 by Saint John Eudes, in Caen, France. Moved by pity for prostitutes, Father John at first attempted to house them under the care of good and pious women. One of these women, Madeleine Lamy, persuaded him that more was needed. Three Visitation nuns came to his aid temporarily, and, in 1641, a house was opened at Caen under the title of Refuge of Our Lady of Charity. Other ladies joined them, and, in 1651, the Bishop of Bayeux gave the institute his approbation. In 1664, a Bull of approbation was obtained from Pope Alexander VII. That same year a house was opened at Rennes, and the institute began to spread. When the French Revolution broke out there were already seven communities of the order in France.

ever, the poor lost sheep that has gone astray still has some savings, and waiting until we can take her out of what I will call her virtuous quagmire, I see her from time to time so as to help her keep her good intentions, that fortunately have not disappeared."

Lefebvre then explained that, about to take a very long voyage, he couldn't do anything very helpful toward the salvation of the sinner. However, he could contribute a modest offering of 500 francs that he would send to the domicile of the person he was talking to, if she would be kind enough to accept it, because he was leaving Paris that same evening.

The Lady of Charity gave her address: Madame de Saint-Rambert, Rue du Colisée.

On hearing that name, Lefebvre didn't want to ask if she was related to Monsieur de Saint-Rambert, the director of the Secret Bureau. As for himself, he refused to give his real name and passed himself off as a benefactor who wanted to remain anonymous. In reality, he was a debtor paying a small amount down in reparation for all the evil he had caused.

XV. Another Side of Lupiano

When he arrived at the apartment of the Marquis de Lupiano, Lefebvre was still suffering from the sad revelation that he had discovered. To drown his sorrow, he drank a lot of the quality wines which Lupiano who, to quote the song, *had a cellarful,* offered him. But the more he drank, the more he cried. His country, his family, his friends that he had to leave, became each in turn the object of so many elegies. Most of all, he didn't run dry about the behavior of Madame de Camembert who had refused him the consolation of saying good-bye to him before his departure. He never stopped repeating that his heart would be eternally wounded.

The Marquis tried to console him by swearing that the lady's indisposition, the beginning of which he had seen, had become worse to the point of making it impossible for her, his beautiful love, to see him. Then, in an abrupt about-face that it is not unusual to encounter in a man whose reason is beginning to be obscured by the fumes of alcohol, Lefebvre exclaimed:

"I don't care anything about your Marquise; you can take her for your mistress, since something seems to be simmering between you two. We won't cut each other's throats for her; she's a real icicle, a rock-hard Berezina.[59] If I stayed in Paris, I'm the one who would have ditched her. I just found someone from the past, and what a woman she was! Oh, how I loved her! And to say," he continued, crying, "that it was my fault that all those bad things happened to her! I'm a scoundrel, Marquis, a worthless man, and you are right to send me to leave my bones in the Americas, in Caracas, in Venezuela,[60] and all other countries of the devil, which would have been only a mouthful for Napoleon, if he ever had had the idea of going there..."

Questioned out of curiosity about the nature of the wrongs he had caused to that woman from his past, which he was reproaching himself about, and whose memory moved him to tears, Lefebvre didn't hesitate to recount, in the greatest details, all his history with Herminie Daliron, including their last encounter. With his unusual turn of mind, the Marquis couldn't avoid taking an interest in the strange creature whose life story he had been told.

"Commandant," he said, "your trust will not be wasted. Tomorrow I will concern myself with that poor girl. If she is the woman that you say she is, all her troubles are over. You

---

[59] The Battle of Berezina took place from 26 to 29 November 1812, between the French army of Napoleon, retreating after his invasion of Russia and crossing the Berezina (near Borisov, Belarus), and the Russian armies. It ended with a mixed outcome. The French suffered very heavy losses but still managed to cross the river. Since then the word has been used in French as a synonym for disaster.

[60] A departure from Bolivia being previously mentioned.

know that I am rich, and it is perfectly easy, without troubling myself, to create a future for her and her children."

"Ah! Marquis!" Lefebvre exclaimed, getting up and going to embrace Lupiano, "What a weight you would be lifting off my shoulders! That's well-placed charity! Here," he added, rummaging in his pockets to find a roll of gold coins, "I promised 500 francs to Madame de Saint-Rambert. Would you give them to her at the same time?"

"Keep your money," Lupiano replied. "You don't have too much, and, on the contrary, you would have done well to have accepted what I offered you."

"Never!" replied the Commandant, taking a drunken theatrical pose. "Lefebvre has been known to have faults, but as for being cheap, I'm incapable of it! So, take my 500 francs, or I'll throw them out the window."

"No. If you don't put them back in your pocket, I will do nothing for Mademoiselle Daliron. That's a new obligation you will have toward her."

"You devilish Marquis!" Lefebvre shouted. "But, fine! It will be as you wish, because you are the stronger. But see here, my little man, as you are treating me, that's how it's necessary to treat that Marquise de Camembert; with a strong hand, I tell you. Otherwise, if you let her do to you what she did to me, put her claws into you one time, you're finished!"

When Lefebvre had begun to show a great deal of emotion, the Marquis had taken care to send the servants away. And we already know on what a different footing of intimacy he was with the man from Genoa we knew as the Prince de Bevillacqua, also called Comte de Montalvi, the former head of the French National Lottery, who had sold his wife's daughter to a flesh dealer.

To cut short the growing excitement of his guest, the Marquis addressed Bevillacqua:

"Montalvi," he said, "we mustn't let the good Commandant miss the hour of his coach. Do me the favor of telling someone to put him on it. We are going to see him embarked."

A quarter of an hour later, after warm embraces shared with the two friends who had brought him there, swearing many promises to exchange news, Lefebvre was bundled into the coach leaving for Le Havre. Once installed, he soon fell asleep, which allows us to take leave of him.

The next day, in the afternoon, Lupiano went to the townhouse on the Rue du Colisée, where we have already seen Kitty Ketch meet Dulac, a.k.a. Rempailleux, before, and how she had become his wife under the name of Madame de Saint-Rambert. Several carriages were assembled in the courtyard where the Marquis stepped down. Greeted at the bottom of the steps by a servant, the splendor of Lupiano's carriage having made him rush to meet him, he asked if Madame de Saint-Rambert was receiving callers.

"I am very afraid," he was answered, "that Madame cannot see Monsieur. She is at this moment in conference with the council members of her works."

"What works?" Lupiano asked.

"The works of Notre Dame du Bon Secours, of which Madame is treasurer.

"Well! As it happens, I want to talk to your mistress regarding something that is precisely connected to that work. Here is my card. Take it to her."

By disclosing his identity, the Marquis was, in fact, decreasing his chances of being seen. Some time ago, in London, Kitty Ketch had seen the Marquis de Samaniego at the house of aunt, Mistress Aston, the owner of *The Bottle and Magpie*. And she knew from her husband, who had recently renewed his acquaintance with the Marquis, that Samaniego and Lupiano were one and the same. She therefore knew that if she appeared before him, she might be recognized and she had no desire to meet with someone who knew her shady past so well.

However, since for a great number of reasons, which will soon be known, the Marquis was for her a man to be handled carefully. So, while using the pretext of her charitable occupation to hide herself, she asked a gallant Duke, who had con-

verted her to Catholicism,[61] and had lifted her to the high rank she presently occupied, to please go and meet the inopportune visitor. The Duke was, at that moment, with her as part of the aristocratic reunion of the men and women who made up the Administrative Council of the works of Notre Dame du Bon Secours, with which the Marquis had just said he had business.

If the name Lupiano hadn't had a very happy effect on Madame the Treasurer, it must be added that he wouldn't have found a more welcoming reception from the reunion. Since his duel with Monsieur de Lucheux, his notoriety among the higher social classes had undoubtedly increased. But we must also say that it was the notoriety of a dangerous man, that of kind of tiger and blood-drinker, so that when the Duke went out at Madame de Saint-Rambert's request, it was with one voice that all the women present urged caution, moderation and prudence, as if he was Saint George leaving to fight the dragon.

The Duke, who laughed at all that, began by explaining to the Marquis how Madame de Saint-Rambert was busy with giving a report on the financial situation of the *works,* and had found it impossible to come and meet him, and as she, at the time, had been told it was a business matter and not purely a social one that had brought the Marquis, then it as felt that she could be conveniently replaced by another one of the members of the Council.

"May I know," Lupiano asked, "to whom I have the honor of speaking?"

The Duke gave his name and title.

"Far from complaining about the substitution," the Marquis said courteously, "on the contrary, I'm happy about it. I wanted to speak to Madame the Treasurer about a woman placed in a very unusual situation, and that matter wouldn't

---

[61] See Volume 3, pages 263-264. For some reason, Rabou never provided the name of that "gallant Duke."

have been easy for me to describe in depth, if I had to speak to a woman."

"Who is the woman you are talking about?" asked the Duke. "If she is a charge of the Association, I am as well informed as anyone about everything regarding her."

"It's a matter, if I am well informed," explained the Marquis, "of a kind of moral phenomenon—a girl who has fallen into the last degree of degradation, and yet having done so with the pretext, or excuse, of the most generous and honorable intentions. She calls herself Madame Schmitt, and lives on the Rue Neuve-Saint-Denis."[62]

"Very good," said the Duke. "I know who you mean. She's a girl who was recommended to us by Monsieur the Curé of Saint-Leu, who is her Confessor, and as you stated it very well, she's a true moral phenomenon, who has come to the attention of our Society more than once. Basically, despite the depth of her fall, there is every reason to believe that she has very good sentiments. But in a certain way, having to do with her religious opinions, her head is the theater of a disorder, which, at times, we despair of being able to repair."

"You astonish me. She was presented to me as having followed all the practices of a truly devout person."

"Without a doubt, she is a very pious person, but she has a rebellious piety, exalted and nourished, it appears, by reading books on mysticism, so much so than she has become perfectly indifferent to religious perfection, and the scandalous abandon of herself in which she continues. She doesn't intend to end it until she is assured of the survival of the two children who are her first concern.

---

[62] A street in the 2nd and 3rd arrondissement, historically known as a haven of prostitution. It started an an old road that ran along the ramparts of the enclosure of Charles V; it was then called Rue des Deux-Portes, then became the Rue Neuve-Saint-Denis in 1655 and took its current name of Rue Blondel by decree in 1864.

"But, then," said Lupiano, jokingly, "she would be worse than being a lost woman; she would be a heretic filled with that famous Quietism Doctrine[63] that started such an ardent quarrel between Bossuet[64] and Fénelon."[65]

"Do you think, in fact," the Duke replied, without noticing the Marquis' irony, "that the ideas of Madame Guyon [66]go so far as to imply such depravity?"

"Certainly, Monsieur," said the Marquis. "Before I found myself set on a somewhat different path, and such as you now see me, I studied theology. I am perfectly familiar with the doctrine of Quietism, and, according to me, that doctrine so hotly pursued by Louis XIV is only a mixed renewal of that long heresy of the Gnostics[67] that, under infinitely varied

---

[63] A set of Christian beliefs that rose in popularity in France, Italy, and Spain during the late 1670s and 1680s, associated with the writings of Miguel de Molinos (and subsequently François Malaval and Madame Guyon), which were condemned as heresy by Pope Innocent XI in 1687. Quietism elevated contemplation over meditation, intellectual stillness over vocal prayer, and interior passivity over pious action to achieve a sinless state and union with the Christian Godhead.

[64] Jacques-Bénigne Bossuet (1627-1704), bishop and theologian, renowned for his sermons, considered one of the most brilliant orators of all time. Court preacher to Louis XIV, he was a strong advocate of political absolutism and the divine right of kings.

[65] François de Salignac de la Mothe-Fénelon (1651-1715), Roman Catholic archbishop, theologian, poet and writer, remembered mostly for his *Adventures of Telemachus* (1699).

[66] Jeanne-Marie Bouvier de la Motte-Guyon (1648-1717), mystic accused of advocating Quietism, although she never called herself a Quietist. She was imprisoned from 1695 to 1703 after publishing the book, *A Short and Very Easy Method of Prayer*.

[67] Followers of Gnosticism, a variety of ancient religious ideas and systems, originating in Jewish-Christian milieus in the

forms was, right up to the 6th century, the despair of the Church. Between the sectarians of that heresy, the *Pneumatics,*[68] or *Perfects,*[69] professed aloud the opinion that, when they had arrived at an intimate union with God, they could indulge themselves in all material penchants without, for all that, soiling in any way their souls, that were already detached and independent of the body."

The Duke listened in admiration to that killer of men, whom the ladies had feared for him to encounter, who proved himself to be a theologian perfectly familiar with the thorniest and the most heated religious questions. However, having every reason to believe that his interview with the Marquis had some interest more positive than that of research concerning the opinions that Madame Schmitt might profess in matters of faith, he was interested in finding in what ways their *works* might be helpful to that woman.

"Well," continued the Marquis, "there I am very far off the topic. I have heard it said that, when that unfortunate woman finally secures the means of existence of her brother and her child, she has decided to retire into a convent of the Repentant Daughters. And as the *works* has, without a doubt, a

---

first and second century AD. The Gnostics believed that the material world was created by an emanation of the highest God, trapping the Divine spark within the human body. This Divine spark could be liberated by gnosis.

[68] The *Pneumatics* ("spirituals" from Greek word for spirit) were, in Gnosticism, the highest order of humans. A pneumatic saw itself as escaping the doom of the material world via the transcendent knowledge of the Divine Spark within its soul.

[69] *Perfect* was the name given to a monk of the medieval Christian religious movement of southern France and northern Italy commonly referred to as the Cathars. The *Perfecti* were expected to follow a lifestyle of extreme austerity and renunciation of the world. By that virtue they were recognized as trans-material (i.e. spiritualized) angels by their followers.

great number of other similarly needy persons, not finding herself able to fulfill the conditions that she requires for her transformation, I have come to put into the hands of Madame the Treasurer the amount of money that would be thought to be necessary in order to deliver that worthy woman."

"But, Monsieur," the Duke exclaimed, "have you considered that it's a matter of a considerable sacrifice—to take financial charge of the existence of two children!"

"Ah!" the Marquis said nonchalantly, "it's only a matter of sixty thousand francs; that should make up two incomes of 1500 livres each, which seems to me perfectly sufficient to take care of the immediate worldly needs of the two subjects, who would then be expected to getting on in life as they would like."

"Sixty thousand francs, Monsieur—that's quite a sum, and although the *works* has, amongst its members, many rich and generous persons, I don't know any who are in a position to gladly take on such an engagement."

"That is precisely why I have come," said the Marquis. "I can do that, and I am in the habit of doing so when the occasion presents itself. I have even thought that, for Madame Schmitt's entry into a religious community, an additional sum might be necessary and I have foreseen that. But your revelations about the interior state of that unfortunate woman has somewhat modified my intentions. First of all, is it certain that, with the independence of her religious convictions, she would persevere in submitting herself to the discipline of a religious community; also, and that seems even more doubtful to me, would there be a convent that would consent to give asylum to a subject thus stained with heresy?"

"As for her idea of taking the veil, I believe she will persevere, because that idea of hers is tied to her extreme devotion. Just the other day, she was saying to Madame de Saint-Rambert: 'After the extremities due to the need to provide for the needs of my two children, I wouldn't know how to live any longer in a world that would judge me according to their mundane ideas. To be the mother of my son, and the sister of my brother, without casting on them the stain that I carry, I must disappear. After my honor, my death is still necessary to complete my work. I would willingly kill myself, but I am not sure that that action would find grace before God. The convent, a living suicide, takes care of everything at the same time. In the eyes of men, it would be my ultimate expiation.'"

"But, Monsieur le Duc," Lupiano said quickly, "don't you realize that a woman who speaks in such a way is an exceptional being? Truly, you give me the idea to get her away from any clerical influence. I myself know from experience, from having practiced it, what religious life is like, and in my opinion, it is too narrow to house a will and a character with the strength and the magnitude that must be recognized in Madame Schmitt."

"We are all in agreement, Monsieur le Marquis, that we are not dealing with a common person. That was particularly the opinion of Monsieur the Curé of Saint-Leu and it's because of that, despite the shameful state to which that woman has knowingly descended, that we haven't stopped being concerned about her. But if she reenters worldly life, I ask you, what would you do about it?"

"Well, there may be a number of mundane interests with which she could be reattached."

"I fear you are mistaken. You are, without a doubt, talking about an unhappy love affair, which was the beginning of all of Madame Schmitt's mistakes, which might be repaired. But Madame de Saint-Rambert knows that, on that subject, her mind is made up. From the day she fell to the depths of her shame, between the man that she loved and herself, she raised an impassable barrier. 'I would rather die than to see him again!' she exclaimed on one occasion. 'Only God is high enough from the things of the Earth to comprehend and glorify my infamy!'"

"Let her then go into a convent, and may God see that in the one she enters, she does not carry the moral perturbation that Madame Guyon threw into Saint-Cyr."

"First of all, Monsieur the Curé of Saint-Leu, whom she loves and honors, will continue to be her confessor, and he will oversee that peril. After that, at the Repentant Daughters, devotion is not as sophisticated as at Saint-Cyr. They are occupied a great deal more with manual labor than with religious subtleties."

"At your risk, Monsieur le Duc," the Marquis de Lupiano said. "Now, could you get me some paper, a pen and some ink?"

While a servant, immediately rung for, went to get what the Marquis asked:

"What sum do you think is necessary for the religious marriage of our protégée?"

"For the Order which she seems to have decided on, ten thousand francs would constitute a magnificent dowry."

"That's what I thought also," said Lupiano.

And he got down to writing.

When he had scratched a few lines, he gave the paper back to the Duke, who read what follows:

To my banker: Monsieur Martin Lambert.

On my order, please remit the sum of seventy thousand francs taken from my account into the hands of Madame Schmitt, residing on Rue Neuve Saint-Denis, for a liquidation of an estate which she inherited in the Dutch Island of Borneo that I carried out on her behalf.

Paris, 30 November 1818.

Marquis de Lupiano

After the Duke had finished reading, the Marquis added:

"You see, Monsieur, that it is important to me that Madame Schmitt go and collect the money in person from my banker, and you will please forgive me if don't ask Madame the Treasurer to go and collect him on her behalf. In any event, I like to believe the *works* will be consulted about its use. My motive here is not mistrust. I am perhaps still more curious than charitable, and I admit that, by doing things this way, I'm challenging our protégée to see if, confronted to that little fortune coming to her, nothing will change in her resolutions. As for Madame de Saint-Rambert, I have a favor to ask, that is for her to go and cash a postal order of 10,000 francs that I'm going to add to the other 70,000 francs for the benefit of the *works*. I believe that there should be some recompense for the valuable service performed by your organization as well."

The Duke was effusive in his gratitude for the unexpected gift.

"I don't believe, Monsieur le Duc," said Lupiano, "that I have bought at too high a price the honor of making your acquaintance."

As he was going to get back into his carriage, there was a prolonged exchange of politeness between Madame de Saint-Rambert's envoy and the Marquis de Lupiano, the former wanting to accompany the latter right to the steps of his coach, and the latter making every effort not to be accompanied.

When the Duke went back into the drawing room, where the Council was still assembled, he was asked on several sides:

"So? What did that man want?"

"That man," the Duke answered, "among many other strange things of which he wouldn't be suspected of, behaves like a monk; talks about theology like Monseigneur of Persepolis [70] and signs checks for eighty thousand francs to his banker as we give two *sous* to a blind man on leaving the Church of Saint Thomas Aquinas."

"That's astonishing," exclaimed the old Princess de G***, "a miscreant who brings a dead man with him into drawing rooms. Don't you see that he's a sorcerer, who should

---

[70] Likely Monseigneur Martha, Bishop of Persepolis, a powerful figure at the archiepiscopal palace and a genial propagandist who devoted himself to increasing the subscriptions for the basilica of the Sacred Heart.

have already been denounced to the officials and to those Messieurs du Châtelet!"[71]"

XVI. The Champ d'Asile

The exclamation of the old Princess de G*** dealt with a new eccentricity, one that the Marquis de Lupiano had recently thrown into the stream of incessant curiosity of which it pleased him to be the object.

A long time ago, in the Prologue to this story, we recounted the story of *The Girl with the Death's Head,* a dark and burlesque creation, designed to divert political preoccupations[72] just like the story of the *Piqueurs* [73] or of the *Rain of Silver* in the Rue Montesquieu,[74] both of which must have originated in the minds of the Police.

That stunt, the success of which had been considerable, was too much to the taste of Marquis, whose mind liked those sorts of escapade, for him not to have felt the need to include it in the number of shadowy mystifications that he spent his life recreating.

Setting himself the task of giving a body to that undertaker's joke, he had been seen introducing as his daughter, who had recently rejoined him in Paris, a woman, with a re-

---

[71] A former stronghold in Paris with courts, police, and prisons on the site of the Place du Châtelet.

[72] See Volume 1, page 52 seq.

[73] In the second half of 1819, a number of young girls complained, perhaps hysterically, that they had been wounded on public roads by sharp instruments which some unknown jokers had used to sting their backside. The Police investigated but found nothing.

[74] In August 1819, in another case of public hysteria, people started to believe it rained silver at the corner of the rue Montesquieu and rue Croix-des-Petits-Champs in the 1st district of Paris; the police had to be called to keep the peace. Vidocq mentioned this strange incident in his *Memoirs*.

markably well-made figure, but who habitually wore a wax mask over her face. Far from dissimulating the nature of the hideous infirmity that the mask had been made to cover, Lupiano took it upon himself to give a very plausible explanation. In the remainder of the story, he went so far as to give that girl, the plaything of such a horrible caprice of nature, a fabulous dowry offered to the first suitor who could look on her without fainting. Lupiano, without circulating the story himself, did nothing to stop its propagation. Because of that, several visitors presented themselves at his townhouse and asked to meet the rich heiress.

The Swiss doorman was ordered to greet them politely. Immediately introduced to the Marquis, and according to his mood of the day, they were sometimes received with deceitful encouragement, that ended in some grotesque conclusion, and sometimes they saw themselves harshly shown out again in order not to complicate with more ridicule a campaign set up to appeal to the credulous. Among these burlesques matrimonial attempts, we will recount one in all its details.

The rather biting and dramatic way in which it began will enlighten us about the projects of that extraordinary man who, after having been the Marquis de Samaniego in London, the merchant Salvador Arbib in Livorno, the Marquis de Saint-Faust, twice, in Paris, was now the Marquis de Lupiano, his fourth and latest incarnation.

One afternoon, to pick up things a little further on, Madame de Camembert, seated in front of an attractive dressing table decorated in Belgium lace, was in the hands of a lady's maid who had just finished arranging her magnificent blonde hair.

"Victoria," said the Marquise, "look and see what that little red stain that I have on my shoulder is."

"Perhaps Madame was bitten by some insect?"

"No, if it was that, the mark would have gone away; it's been there for several days. It even seems to me that, in rubbing my finger over it, it is a little swollen. See for yourself."

"I don't feel anything, Madame, and the bite is hardly visible."

"You reassure me," said the Marquise, too much in love with her own beauty not to be affected by the least tear in it, which this threatened to be.

She had just stood up, throwing off her dressing gown, when that old servant she trusted that we know about, entered her bedroom carrying, on a silver plate, a visiting card that had just been given to her. It was that of someone asking for an audience with her.

"What is that?" The Marquise asked disdainfully, after having read: "*Lelouard, Wholesale Food Supplies.*"

"I don't know, Madame; it's a gentleman who looks very presentable."

"You should have said that I wasn't at home! If I must now receive bakers!"

"I didn't exactly say that Madame was here. I said that I would go and check. But he is a well-dressed man. He even sports several decorations."

"All right, let him in into the drawing room," the Marquise said, shrugging. "I will join him in a moment."

For the noble Madame de Camembert, a wholesaler of foods was a baker. She could also have said a butcher, or even better a *riz-pain-sel (rice, bread, salt)*, if she had known the disdainful and technical term, which was the usual name, in the army, given to the agents who supplied the commissaries of Napoleon's Grand Army. Despite the negative esteem in which those who provided such staples were held, above all by the Emperor, who used them, but didn't like them, it must be said that they were the true financiers of the era. The speculation that is frequent today in industrial enterprises was, at the time of the Empire, on the side of the suppliers to the army. The Ouvards, the Seguins, the Vanderberghes,[75] and finally

---

[75] A discussion of these suppliers and their contributions can be found in *Le Service des Vivres dans les Armées du Premier*

François-Honoré Dubignon, whose tragic end we have already recounted, have left their names in history as the great suppliers of food to the armies.

Drawn by the fortunes to be made by following in their footsteps, many men with good backgrounds and abilities applied for service in their enterprises. Making a great deal of money, leading a life of luxury, and often having the opportunity to open their purse, not only to French officers, that in reprisal for having been nicknamed *Rice-Bread-Salt,* they called the *Epaulettes*, but also to foreign generals who fought on our side, the employees of the suppliers, while lacking respect, nevertheless were in good standing with everyone with whom they dealt. They affected military airs, and often displayed ribbons of various colors in their jacket lapels. Those came from the little princes, our allies, and were their way of cheap recompense as payment for the services rendered to them, or to their armies.

At the beginning of our long story, Monsieur Lelouard, the man who Madame de Camembert was ready to receive with such bad grace, had been seen, it will probably be remembered, accompanying Georgiana, the so-called "Bloodied Girl," to Bordeaux.[76] In his function as a purveyor of supplies to the armies, he could have reaped nice benefits; he was a man of rare intelligence, with the integrity of deep pockets, the easiest way of furthering his fortune. But he was vain, loved an elegant existence, gold, a good table, gambling, women; in a word, everything that makes the wildest dreams possible. The fall of the Empire, to which he was ardently attached, because, he said, it was a time that one could get ahead in business, had found him in a somewhat compromising situation. And at the moment when, for the second time, he's going to come back on stage, we scarcely know the extremities to

---

Empire - 1804-1815 by Alain Pigeard & Jean Tulard, University of Paris-Sorbonne, Doctorate's Thesis, 1995 -World Cat.

[76] See Volume 1, p. 60 seq.

which the embarrassment of his finances may have forced him.

On arriving in the room where she was expected, Madame de Camembert saw, leaning on the fireplace, where he was warming his feet, holding them to the fire one after the other, a tall man, with a thin and angular face, with graying hair cut in the *malcontent fashion*, wearing a blue coat buttoned right up to his chin. It was, in fact, decorated with a ribbon of several colors, but the *Legion d'Honneur* was not included.

Coming forward with ease to the Marquise, who had not invited him to sit down, he said:

"Madame, I am here under the auspices of a man that you honored with some goodwill, Commandant Lefebvre. I left him about six weeks ago in America."

"Commandant Lefebvre?" asked Madame de Camembert, putting an expression her face of someone trying to recall. "I don't think I know him."

"You astonish me. He has never had any other name; he was the head of a Battalion in the former army and served in the 122nd line."

"That's very possible, but I don't recall anyone by that name among my acquaintances, neither in France nor in America."

"That is strange. Is it really to Madame la Marquise de Camembert that I have the honor to speaking?"

"Yes."

"And there aren't two ladies named de Camembert in Paris?"

"Not that I am know of."

"Of course," said the wholesaler, with an evidently gallant intention. "There couldn't be two like you."

But that courtesy didn't appear to the taste of the fiery Marquise.

"Frankly, Monsieur," she said dryly, as Monsieur Lelouard began to look for something in the pocket of his coat, "whether or not there are two of us is irrelevant. I have the honor of repeating to you that I do not know a Monsieur Lefebvre."

That sentence was pronounced in a firm tone that seemed to dismiss the one to whom it was addressed.

"Nevertheless, here is a letter that certainly carries the address of Madame la Marquise de Camembert, Rue Notre-Dame-des-Champs," said the supplier, glancing at the sealed envelope that he was at that moment holding in his hand.

"You are bringing a letter?" the Marquise asked.

"Yes, Madame, and my visit had no other purpose than to bring it to you."

"Then give it to me," the Marquise said.

"No, that wouldn't be proper. Since the man who had the honor of writing to you is completely unknown to you, there must have been a mistake."

"You will allow me, Monsieur, to say that I find it unusual that you might want to keep a letter that is so clearly addressed to me, notwithstanding my absence of relations with its author."

"But it would also be very unusual for a person who is a complete stranger to you to correspond with you."

"That happens every day. Some people whom one does not know may have an occasion to write to you."

"Without a doubt, but when people who entrust you with a letter tell you to put it only in the hands of the person to whom it is addressed; that they know intimately that person, and that they even claim that you will be received by that person with all kinds of respect and politeness, when nothing that they have told you comes to pass, it is obvious that there has been some kind of mistake. In that case, a smart representative can do nothing more in this matter but present his excuses and leave."

At that, Monsieur Lelouard bowed and started toward the door.

"Just like that, Monsieur," said Madame de Camembert with emotion, "your intention, that you just stated, is to keep that letter with you."

"Yes, Madame. I am above all accountable to Commandant Lefebvre, who gave it to me."

"All right, Monsieur. I will find out how to force you to give it to me."

Lelouard didn't answer except with a respectful bow of his head and went out.

The evening of the same day, at about eleven o'clock, as he was returning to the furnished room where he was registered, he found in the office of the establishment a gentleman dressed all in black who announced in a rather mysterious way that he needed to speak to him.

"Well, Monsieur," Lelouard said, "I'm listening."

"No, let's go up to your room, please."

"May I observe that this is not a proper hour to enter into a secret conference with a person one doesn't have the honor of knowing."

The mysterious person partially opened his coat showing his official badge.

"I am," he said, "the Commissioner of Police from the Luxembourg district."

Lelouard had no other objections to make and, a moment later, he received in his bedroom the officer of the police who explained that Madame la Marquise de Camembert, one of the most outstanding people in the city, had asked him to come to her house in order for her to complain about a procedure, that in fact she had some trouble understanding. The story of the letter, explained from the complainant's point of view, the magistrate added that he would be happy to act as a peacemaker. He had hoped that Monsieur Lelouard wouldn't hesitate to give him the contested letter.

After having, in his turn, presented his version of the facts, Lelouard stated his intention to persist in what he called his careful reserve. He had no reason to want to compromise himself for Madame de Camembert, who had received him as a valet, not even asking him to sit down. The letter, the author of which she had several times affirmed that she did not know, was in his hands. It would remain there until further instructions from Commandant Lefebvre.

Going perhaps a little too far in his role as a friendly middleman, the Magistrate replied, smiling, with a look of complicity, that women sometimes had reasons not to admit knowing certain people; that perhaps, in a first moment of surprise, the Marquise had used an ill-considered statement, that she had then felt she had to support. He again asked Monsieur Lelouard to be willing to comply with her request, to bring to a close a ridiculous affair.

Lelouard's answer was that the Commissioner had gone much further than he in seeming to accept certain suppositions, that, as far as he was concerned, he had never believed possible. But, once again, Madame de Camembert had behaved in the most disobliging way. Therefore, in the interest of peace, here was what seemed possible to him. He would have the honor to presenting himself again the next day at the Marquise' house, to again put at her disposition the letter that he had been asked to deliver. She would probably, this time, admit to knowing who it came from. Only on that condition would he release the epistle, the subject of this debate.

"But, Monsieur," the Police Commissioner said, "that doesn't arrange anything. Madame de Camembert can't be humiliated in that way."

"I am sorry. I have told you what I can do."

"Monsieur, upon my authority as a Magistrate, I will take that letter from your hands."

"And I will give it to you upon upon presentation of a warrant from the King's Procureur that you will do me the honor of fetching."

"A warrant that I will have in less than an hour."

"During that hour," the wholesaler said, "that letter will have left my hands. Let's see if we can find a better arrangement," Lelouard proposed," and deal with things in a friendlier way. What Madame the Marquise wants is not to have that piece of paper, coming to her from a person to whom she is indifferent, since she doesn't know him, fall into strange hands. Her real interest is that the letter, the contents of which worry her, no longer be left to my discretion. As you can see, Commissioner, the seal is still intact. In your presence, I'm going to place the letter inside an envelope, put the address of the person for whom I am the agent on it, and, if you will take the trouble of accompanying me, I am going to deposit it into the mail box of the main post office. That way, you will not suppose that I have found any way of appropriating its secrets."

The Magistrate argued a little against that solution, but as he saw his authority misdirected, he finally agreed. After having accompanied the intractable agent to the mail box on the Rue Jean-Jacques Rousseau, a little before midnight, wanting to prove his zeal, despite the late hour, he went to give the Marquise a report.

At the moment that he was permitted the rare honor of penetrating right into the Marquise's bedroom, where, to tell the truth, she had been waiting with some anxiety, she had hurried to hide someone in her oratory.

After the Commissioner had explained the relative success of his ambassadorship, Madame de Camembert seemed only partly satisfied. On the side of her ego, she had suffered a total failure, but after all, what was done was done. She cut short all the apologetic explanations which the Magistrate seemed to want to go into, and, after having cleverly sent him away, very little satisfied himself, she hurried to recall the person she had hidden, who was no other than, as one might have guessed, the Marquis de Lupiano.

"Damn!" he said ironically on entering, "you have, my dear child, handled that situation very nicely, and your intervention of the Police Commissioner was something fortunately devised."

"What do you expect?" she replied with some bitterness. "I lost my head at the first word. If I had had you at hand to give me advice, things would have turned out differently."

"Well, yes, but because of our plans for the future, we have agreed that, vis-à-vis everyone, we should pretend not to know each other, you cannot have me constantly at your beck and call. It will be necessary to remain calm and to consider things twice before having the police intervene in our affairs again. I have told you often that they are basically a compromising instrument that I have spent my life making fun of, and every time that they come to grips with a clever man, they will meet with the same lack of success. Now, Monsieur the baker, as you call him, is a rather insolent person who didn't get at you in an essential way, but he is also an adversary who must be taken into account."

"Oh! He will pay for his insolence!" the Marquise exclaimed.

"The truly fatherly weakness that I feel disposed to show toward your smallest fantasies would certainly cause me to second you in your projects of revenge, but in order for such a vengeance to be satisfactory, it must be carried out by one's own hands without calling in the Police. What's more, it takes time and thought."

"Yes, and with all that time and thought, a letter that may vomit up who knows what most compromising secrets is floating around in society."

"Don't act so feminine, my dear, and let's not get excited. That letter will not float around in society, because I have written a note to Saint-Rambert. He will intercept it and send it to me in the morning. If Lefebvre chatted with the impertinent man, that's a misfortune he will warn us about. But the possession of that letter that torments you so much will not make any difference. If, on the contrary, Lefebvre has been a discreet lover, our man, by putting his message in the mail, has put it out of the way of having anything about you discovered. We already have then a beautiful result with which you can sleep peacefully tonight."

"Be careful, Marquis," Madame de Camembert replied, "his slap is still too warm on my cheek, and if you delay chastising that man, you will lose much of my esteem."

"La! La! My Beautiful One, I am not gunpowder to be used to pulverize your enemies on command. You should be mindful that in an affair that concerns you, I don't intervene without remaining behind the scenes. We must deal with things indirectly, and then, I repeat, this enemy doesn't seem to me easy to deal with. In his behavior I find a little of myself, which doesn't say that we won't finally get the best of him."

"Three days, Marquis, that's all the delay I will give you!"

"Well! That's something to be taken under advisement."

On that, Lupiano took his leave and left through the tunnel.

The next day, in the morning, he was alone in his office, holding in his hand the famous letter, the original of which Saint-Rambert had sent him. In Madame de Camembert's life there could be nothing hidden from him. He had just finished reading Lefebvre's amorous epistle, which he had taken it upon himself to unseal. By reading it, he had acquired the proof that, in no way, had the exiled Commandant confided anything of importance to Monsieur Lelouard, who had been warmly recommended, but nothing more, to the Marquise so that she could help him, by her reputation, in the settlement of the matter of arrears that the Minister of War owed him. Armed with that assurance, Lupiano already felt himself more at ease for the attack, when a card was brought to him.

"Ah! It's Heaven that sends that to me," he exclaimed, on reading it: *Lelouard, Wholesale Food Supplies*. In fact," he added, "Lefebvre himself would also likely have sent a letter to me."

It's not necessary to go and hunt the prey that enters the trap voluntarily. When Monsieur Lelouard, as soon as he was announced, said that he was coming on behalf of Lefebvre, not going into his former relationship with the Commandant, Lupiano said:

"Ah! That good Commandant Lefebvre! I am delighted to have news of him. How is he?"

"A letter that I have the honor, Monsieur, to be charged with giving you, will show you that he has undergone many great misfortunes."

"How's that? What misfortune has befallen him?"

"First, he lost his son, due to yellow fever, almost at the moment he disembarked. The poor young man died in my arms, despite all our efforts to save him."

"Ah! That's sad," said the Marquis, unsealing the letter given to him.

"May I?" he asked before beginning to read.

After he had read the letter he continued:

"In fact, that poor man appears terribly struck by the death of his son, whom they say was a boy of great promise, and to the fact the he feels he somewhat contributed to that sad end. He wrote some truly dreadful things. But tell me, Monsieur, why is that letter dated from Texas, the Island of Galveston? I thought Lefebvre was in South America, in New Grenada, with Bolivar, to whom I gave him a letter of recommendation."

"In fact, that's where I met him. But the death of his son made him detest the country, and then he and I gave way to a decision that you will understand. Rumors had come to us about a colony of French refugees, dispersed in different parts of the United States, that was going to be founded in Texas. We wanted, then, to be reunited with our former army comrades, so we took sail for Galveston Island, the place chosen for the gathering."[77]

---

[77] The *Champ d'Asile* (Field of Asylum) colony was a short-lived settlement founded in Texas by the Lallemand brothers in January 1818 by 20 Bonapartist veterans. Land was offered to the settlers on March 3, 1817, after a vote by Congress. The colony was to bring some military men for protection, but concentrate on agricultural work, cultivating grapes and olives. On December 17, 1817, the settlers, included about a hundred veterans from the *Grande armée*, sailed from Philadelphia for Galveston, where they arrived on January 14.

"The newspapers," said Lupiano, "actually mentioned that colony, to which they gave the name *Champ d'Asile*, but I'm very much afraid, it struck me like that Shakespeare play, *much ado about nothing*."

"That's also my impression," replied Lelouard. "Sometimes it's whispered that it was used to restoring the Mexican Crown[78] to be given to Joseph-Napoleon, who has gone, as you know, to America. Sometimes it's described as just a simple agricultural colony, and given that fact, there are magnificent projects made on paper. Among the colonies already assembled, there is a former regicide from the Convention named Hulet, who, in his quality as an ex-legislator, has taken charge of drawing up a constitution before anything else."

"Ah! Hulet is there?" the Marquis asked quickly.

"You are acquainted with him?" Lelouard asked.

Lallemand and the other colonists convened in New Orleans, and on March 10 left for Galveston. They sailed up the Trinity River to Atascosito where they built two small forts. Mexican governor Antonio María Martínez, having heard about this expedition, sent his own troops to San Marcos, wary of an attack. The colony was abandoned shortly afterwards. Also see Volume 3, Note 137, page 267 for the Hulet connection.

[78] The reader will recall that Napoleon III set up Prince Ferdinand Maximilian of Austria (1832-1867), the younger brother of the Austrian Emperor, to become Emperor of Mexico, that was at that time ruled by President, Benito Juárez. Maximilian and his wife, Carlotta, arrived in Mexico in April 1864. He was captured and executed by the forces of Juárez in 1867. His wife, Carlotta, then in Europe, became insane on hearing of his death. Joseph-Napoleon Bonaparte (1768-1844), Napoleon's elder brother, became King of Naples and Sicily (1806-1808), then King of Spain (1808-1813). He lived in the United States during the period 1817-1832. Allegedly, some Mexican revolutionaries offered to crown him Emperor of Mexico in 1820, but he declined. Joseph eventually returned to Europe, where he died in Florence, Italy.

"Oh! Very much so. He's a rather villainous man."

"In any case," Lelouard answered, "he's a great dreamer, and instead of founding republics, he would do better to think of the health of his daughter, a very interesting young girl who doesn't have two years to live if he doesn't manage to take her back to Europe. What's more, Utopian politics aside, you can imagine, Monsieur le Marquis, what that troop of men is like, brought together from the four winds of the Earth, embittered by privations and regret for their native land. Among them no question is brought up that doesn't set them at odds with each other. Before my departure, there were already two or three duels. That turbulent debris from the Empire knows nothing but the saber to settle all difficulties."

"Ah! Well!" Lupiano said. "Then the colony doesn't have a leader?"

"Oh, yes, it does. There is General Lallemand, a brave military man who fought in the war with honor, but I don't think him cut out for his mission as a colonizer.[79] After he had been asked many times, he at last decided on a short appear-

---

[79] François Antoine Charles Lallemand (1774-1839), French general who served under Napoleon. After the Emperor was defeated and exiled the first time, he joined the army of Louis XVIII. In 1815, he and his brother Henri tried to lead a rebellion against the Bourbons, but were arrested. When Napoleon returned from Elba, he released them and gave them both commands in the Imperial Guard. After the Battle of Waterloo, Lallemand accompanied Napoleon to Rochefort, where Napoleon surrendered. Lallemand tried to follow Napoleon into exile but the British refused that and imprisoned him in Malta for two months before he escaped. Lallemand and other Bonapartist officers were condemned to death in absentia. The brothers were not included in the later amnesties. Lallemand then went to the United States and tried to found a colony in Texas. After Louis-Philippe restored the old imperial military grades after the July Revolution of 1830, Lallemand returned to France and was asked to serve as governor of Corsica.

ance on Galveston Island. Then, probably not very flattered by the elements of the colonization he found united, he left for Philadelphia, promising to come back in forty days with provisions, money, weapons, agricultural materials, because those assembled lack everything in general. I am persuaded that he had enough of the enterprise and that he won't come back. As for me, still having some resources, when I saw him get on his way, I also left with my department. I wanted to take Lefebvre with me. He, like me, despite the fervor of his Bonapartist opinions, hadn't been included in any proscription list and could very easily return to Europe. I wasn't able to get him to pull up stakes. The poor devil is full of illusions. He shares the money he has brought with a great number of former acquaintances whom he has found there. After that is gone, God knows what will become of him!"

"But," Lupiano said, "there's a subscription set up to help the colony, at the bankers Gros, Davillier & Cie.[80] *La Minerve* and other liberal newspapers are supporting that affair with all their strength."

"Well, yes. I've also picked up a brochure that's sold at the Lavocat Bookstore to help the subscription. Everything in it is magnificent. But having seen things first hand, I judge them to be very dark. Among the journalists that I wanted to enlighten, and who exploit the *Champ d'Asile* as a method of opposition to the government, I am considered a pessimist"

"I subscribed for a sum of 6,000 francs," said the Marquis, "and if I am duped by a mirage, the good intention is still there."

---

[80] Gros, Davillier & Cie., located at 15 Boulevard Poissonnière, in Paris. See John Porter Hollis, *The Early Period of Reconstruction in South Carolina*. A Manifesto written by Lallemand about the colony was published in the newspaper, *La Minerve*, a liberal newspaper. A public subscription was set up by the newspaper, remained open for a year, but collected less than 1,000 francs.

"You have certainly done a good thing, Marquis. I was in the office of the newspaper you sent your contribution to, at the moment that Monsieur de... Montalvi, I believe? One of your friends came on your behalf. I guarantee you that your name had an effect. They talked about your contribution for two hours."

"They said unpleasant things?" the Marquis asked.

"Not at all! Strong and extraordinary things."

"Well? What did they say?"

"They talked about your duel with Monsieur de Lucheux, and a girl whom you helped enter a convent, of the rare beauty of your carriages, of your enormous fortune, of Mademoiselle your daughter, and of the superb dowry that you are giving to make up for the imperfection that itself was discussed."

"Et cetera, et cetera," the Marquis said, continuing to laugh. "But, to shift to a more interesting subject, let's talk about you. Commandant Lefebvre, in his letter, praised your frank, decided, energetic character. He talked about your rare business ability. I am then not astonished with his decision to introduce you to me as a man somewhat on bad terms with Fortune. The amusing and the mediocre are his usual favorites."

"It's true," replied Lelouard. "Because of the fall of the Empire, my financial horizon has become a little obscured."

"Well then, let's see! What can I do for you? I, who do so many extraordinary things."

"Monsieur le Marquis, it seems to me that there should be some great things going on on the stock exchange that should be looked into. The War Indemnity, stipulated to be paid to the Holy Alliance, has created a crisis, and..."

At that moment, a visitor was announced.

"Monsieur" said Lupiano to Lelouard, in showing him out, "I am sorry not to be able to talk longer with you, but we will continue this conversation at our next opportunity, won't we? Or, if an invitation with so short a notice doesn't seem incongruous to you, would you do me the honor to come and dine with me and some friends I am getting together this evening? I will introduce you to my daughter, whose *imperfections* are only too real, the one whom they were discussing in front of you the other day. But you will see that she has wit and better things. I hope that her conversation will please you. As for her nose that is unfortunately too short, just between us, I'm making it longer with twenty thousand louis."

"That's a nice extension," said the wholesaler.

"All right then! Shall we say, this evening at six o'clock?"

"Certainly. Until this evening, since you wish to do me that honor."

Who would have said, with a reception so cordial in appearance, that the revenge of Madame de Camembert was still on its way?

XVII. The Girl with the Death's Head

That evening, on entering the Marquis' drawing room, where all the other expected guests had already assembled before he arrived, Lelouard noticed, in the corner of the fireplace, a woman whose form seemed ravishing to him, and to whom Lupiano quickly introduced to him.

But when he found himself face to face with that seductive beauty, it was with a kind of dismay that he discovered, without warning, that instead of the attractive face promised by the rest of the person, he saw a face of colored wax, like the ones hairdressers and the sellers of corsets set out to advertize their wares. However, something more repulsive appeared in that parody of life which he had just beheld. Instead of the beautiful glass eyes and the fabulously long eyelashes of the figures in showroom windows, the deformity of the beautiful heiress, enveloped in wax, was pierced in the manner of antique masks, by two holes which showed her strong, shining eyes, and, in the place of the opening for her mouth, a kind of grimace from which escaped a cavernous voice that seemed to evoke a ventriloquist.

The rest of the gathering seemed equally strange to Lelouard. One would have said that they had blown in from the four corners of the earth. Beside the fuzzy head of a gigantesque Brazilian answering to the name Hernandez, the towhead blonde hair of a Russian Major formed the sharpest contrast. The English and Spanish types were also represented. In the middle of a group composed of a Hindu, an American, and a third individual in whom could be seen all the characteristics of the Javanese, and another oriental fellow originally from Malaysia, there was a Frenchman holding forth who was called "Doctor" by everyone. Finally, in his fine crimson wool robe and his Astrakhan hat, there was an Armenian, courting Lupiano, his daughter, and he Comte de Montalvi, a favorite of the household. In total, this cosmopolitan assemblage was comprised of twelve guests.

Carefully dressed, some of the guests seemed uncomfortable in their outfits, as if unused to wearing them. What's more, to look at them closely, in their physiognomies, they constituted a kind of sensitive clavier where the note of all the human passions seemed ready to vibrate under the slightest pressure. It was rather improbable that, among those nationalities gathered together from so many different points of the globe, communication and sympathy could be carried to a high degree of intimacy. The cold and almost silent atmosphere in the room was, without a doubt, the result.

After a while, the French doors of the drawing room opened and a maître d'hôtel came to announce dinner. To his great astonishment, Lelouard, treated as the most important person in the room, saw himself invited by Lupiano to give his hand to his daughter, for the custom was then not to offer one's arm to a woman to conduct her to the table, but one's hand. *Gentlemen, a hand for the ladies!* is still a standard of the manners of the petite bourgeoisie as sketched so naturally in the happy tableaux of Paul de Koch.[81]

On taking Mademoiselle de Lupiano's hand, Lelouard was surprised to feel, through the glove, the warm circulation of life. The glacial contact of death would have seemed less unexpected from that type of spectre. In addition, he was going to have her as the unpleasant dinner companion during the whole meal. On his plate there was a hand-written card assigning him the place of honor to the right of the daughter of the house. One must say, however, that suddenly transported in the middle of splendors of a truly Oriental luxury, Lelouard wasn't long in feeling his thoughts take a less frightening turn. There was nothing as magical as the aspect of the dome-shaped dining room where the dinner was served. Thus, like so many mirrors, the white stucco panels with which the walls were covered, reflected the brightness of the candelabras and the fairy lights. As if in the middle of summer, although it was mid-February, through the full white satin drapes embroidered with gold, the open windows looked out on the scene of a greenhouse filled with the most exotic and rare plants. A delightful series of lights had been strung through their leaves and that winter garden produced scents so cleverly combined and so penetratingly sweet that their combination could be compared to a suave concert of perfume.

The table was shining with crystal and silver, especially the most fantastic forms of Indian silverware; there was not one dish served that Lelouard could have identified by name, but also not one which its fine smell didn't announce in advance, and sported the most appetizing appearance. Finally, a last sumptuousness was that, behind the seat of each guest was a servant with a copper complexion, dressed in a white muslin turban with a red cashmere scarf around his neck.

---

[81] Charles Paul de Knock (1793-1871), French writer, the son a Dutch banker guillotined during the Revolution. He wrote over 100 novels dealing with middle-class Parisian life.

Drawn by this royal splendor to give to the Amphitryon[82] something above his title of Marquis, the wholesale merchant said to Lupiano:

"Your Lordship has undoubtedly lived in India, from which you transported here its customs?

"*His Lordship*," the Marquis replied, with humor, "has done something better than live there. He was born there, as was his daughter. We are both the subjects of the Princess of Sirdanah, the famous *Begum Sumru,*[83] and I even had the honor to be her Prime Minister for many years."

---

[82] Theban general in Ancient Greece who accidentally killed his father-in-law, Electryon, king of Mycenae. He later married his daughter Alcmene, gave birth to two twin sons, Ipicles and Heracles (Hercules). *Amphitryon* was the title of a lost tragedy of Sophocles, and another by the Roman playwright Plautus (254-184 BC). It was still performed during the Middle Ages, and staged regularly during the Renaissance. It inspired several other theatrical works including three Spanish plays, two Italian plays, and a Portuguese play. In 1636, Jean Rotrou (1609-1650) translated Plautus' play into *Les Deux Sosies*, which inspired Molière's *Amphitryon* (1668), which contained the line "The true Amphitryon is the Amphitryon who gives dinner." (Act III, sc. v.); thus the name Amphitryon has come to be used in the sense of a generous entertainer, a good host.

[83] Joanna Nobilis Sombre (c.1753-1836), known as Begum Sumru (née Farzana Zeb un-Nissa), started her career as a dancing girl in 18th century India, and eventually became the ruler of Sardhana, a small principality near Meerut. She was the head of a mercenary army, inherited from her European husband, Walter Reinhardt Sombre. This army consisted of Europeans and Indians. She is also regarded as the only Catholic ruler in India. Begum Sumru died immensely rich. Her inheritance was assessed as approximately 55.5 million gold marks in 1923 and 18 billion deutsch marks in 1953.

However famous the *Begum Sumru* might be, Lelouard had never heard of her, but he didn't make the mistake that we have seen committed by a young member of the House of Lords when, the first time he was in London, Lupiano had brought into his juggling act the Indian illustration that he had just used.[84] Instead of asking who that famous Princess he didn't know was, he said:

"After the Russian campaign, if it had turned out better, it would have been a simple matter for the Emperor to lead us to the conquest of India. After the samples that I have had here of the magnificence of that country, it seems to me doubly regretful that Napoleon wasn't able to follow up on this project."

"Napoleon! What a great man!" said the Brazilian Hernandez, swallowing a glass of Madera.

That was the only sentence that left his mouth during the dinner.

"Were you part of that memorable campaign, Monsieur?" exclaimed Mademoiselle de Lupiano at the same moment.

"I had that cruel honor."

From that point on, questioned with breathless curiosity, Lelouard had the sweet necessity of recounting everything personal for him in the great drama, the memory of which he had the good fortune to evoke. A notable part of the dinner was then occupied by the story of the doings and adventures of the wholesale supplier without his having the least bit taken advantage of the curiosity of his listeners. They, on the contrary, seemed to take turns questioning him and encouraged him to multiply explanations in most minute details.

At the end, he appeared a god to Mademoiselle de Lupiano when he told her that he had often seen the Emperor and that the Emperor had even spoken to him. He was careful not to add that it was a day when the great hero had found the

---

[84] See Volume 1, p. 290.

bread of the troops to be of detestable quality and had told him he was a scoundrel and threatened to have him shot.

However, charmed with his success as a story-teller, Lelouard was, little by little, reconciled to the spectral girl, whom he finally found really interesting. Then, after having the merit to be such a good listener, Mademoiselle de Lupiano, in her turn, began to speak. In the chat that had become general, she began to reveal the graces and treasures of her mind that her father had earlier announced as a natural compensation for her horrible infirmity. Not eating, she only intermittently carried to her lips, with a hand of dazzling whiteness, a golden incised goblet with an elongated pouring lip that allowed her to sip some swallows of Cyprus wine. Better than any other guest, Mademoiselle de Lupiano was able to hold her own in the conversation. She made remarks so excellent, her sentences were so sharp and so picturesque, her chosen words so accurate, like so many sudden explosions, following each other so effervescent and so happy, that one would have said it was a show of fireworks brought out in Lelouard's honor. As for the merchant, his mind was dazzled by the flares and the scintillating arabesques which never stopped bursting out in front of him.

They were almost ready to leave the table when the Russian Major said to Lupiano:

"Marquis, you have just given us a dinner without equal, but there is one of us who will have to pay dearly for it."

"How's that?" the host asked.

"Will you please count your guests?"

"In fact," exclaimed Lupiano, after having done that, glancing around the table, "there are thirteen of us! Montalvi, how is it that you didn't notice that when making out the list of those invited?"

"This morning, we were only twelve, but you found it convenient to invite someone else."

"At least, you should have told me about that."

"I didn't even think about it," the man from Genoa answered. "I find that superstition ridiculous."

"But you know that, for me, thirteen has always been a fatal number."

"I am very sorry," Lelouard said, "to have been the one to cause this misunderstanding, although to tell the truth, Marquis, with a mind as independent as yours, I have trouble understanding the importance you attach to it."

"On the contrary. What has happened to us, Monsieur," Lupiano replied, "seems to me very worthy of attention. And for nothing in the world, would I remain under this unknown menace. Each of you know what he should do, Gentlemen," he added with authority. "You must find the place card that was put on your plate."

Each guest searched and could present the card on which his name was written. Having his servant give him a silver platter, the Marquis, after having deposited his own place card, passed it to the neighbor on his left, who did the same.

"But, father," Mademoiselle de Lupiano then said, "please let me point out to you that you are going to cruelly blame a single head for a vague possibility that is equally divided among us."

"Are you afraid?" the Marquis sharply asked.

"Me, afraid?" the young girl shrugged. "Am I not, as my maid tells me, the ultimate child of misfortune?"

"Then let the process finish. The one who will not see this year finish will at least be able to put his affairs in order."

The platter finished circulating around the table, and each guest, without the respect for humanity allowing any exterior sign of what he might be feeling, did as the Marquis had requested. When the platter came back to him, and after he had counted the cards and found the number correct, the Marquis carefully mixed them up.

"Here," he said, presenting that kind of funereal lotto to the beautiful white hand of his daughter, in order for her to draw the name of the chosen one.

"Yes," she said, "that honor should come back to me."

And, without hesitating, she picked a place card that she then gave to her father. He unfolded it slowly and then his lips opened in a smile.

"Messieurs," he said. "Thank God, I am the one designated by fate."

And placing the open place card on the plate from which he had taken it, he had it make the rounds of the table. After it had come back into his hands, he added:

"At least, my hospitality will not have been fatal to anyone. My dear guests, , it seems to me that to offer you my life at dessert, that's to do things rather well."

As everyone protested, and among other things, mocked the prediction, the Russian Major invited himself to return on the day of its anniversary.

"My dear Major," Lupiano replied, "the certificate of longevity that you award me resembles those hopeful words that still delude philosophers on the morning of their death. But what is written is written."

On that, he rose, giving the sign to leave the table and added enthusiastically:

"While we're waiting, Messieurs, let's go have coffee."

When they had gone into the drawing room, while Lelouard savored the most authentic and the most delicious *moka* in a marvelous cup from Japan, Lupiano asked:

"Well, what do you think about my poor child?"

"She has more than spirit, she is the genius of conversation," Lelouard answered.

"Yes, isn't she droll? And it seems to me, therefore, that with fifteen or sixteen hundred thousand francs, I should be able to find her a husband in Paris."

"Ah! Monsieur le Marquis!" said the purveyor of wholesale goods. "How can you let that ridiculous gossip get about that shows you as willing to throw such a distinguished person at the head of the first man who comes along?"

"What do you expect? Can I keep fools from being fools? After all, I can't act too proudly."

"Come now," said Lelouard, "under our beautiful Restoration, where the nobility needs to remake its fortunes, tomorrow, if your heart told you to, you could have a duke or a peer for son-in-law. A while ago, at the stock exchange, the marriage of one of the greatest names in France with a rather ugly girl but from a family of substantial means was big news. And that girl, without a mind and without a figure, had only a million as her dowry."

"Speaking of the stock exchange," said the Marquis, taking Lelouard under the arm to lead him to a sofa, where he had him sit down, "let's return to our conversation of this morning. You told me that you thought that the crisis now in Paris could be fruitfully exploited?"

"Yes, but nothing should be tried with less than a hundred thousand francs in capital."

"Pah!" said Lupiano, "that's not even a business deal; and two, three, even four hundred thousand francs wouldn't be a problem for me. But everything considered, in the short time that I have left to live, would it be worth the trouble to create this additional worry for myself?"

"Oh! Marquis!" exclaimed Lelouard, "that idea of your impending death can't be taken seriously!"

"You are mistaken. I believe myself very positively condemned, and if I am talking to you at this moment about where to invest my capital, it's less with the thought of making a profit than with the subject of our previous conservation in mind. I am frightened of the trouble that, after me, my poor daughter, for whom communication with the outside world is difficult, might encounter in the administration of her interests. And a man who finds himself in my path, and who, it seems to me, could be an energetic and informed administrator for her, I don't hide it from you, every other consideration apart, is the kind of son-in-law that I would like."

At that moment, the cords of a piano, majestically struck, cut short that beginning of confidences.

"That's my daughter," Lupiano said, interrupting himself, "whom these gentlemen have asked to sing. You're going to see that she will acquit herself quite well."

After some competent preludes, which showed a talent above the ordinary, the heiress played some romances by Romagnesi,[85] a composer then in fashion, and—something to note—her tomb-like tone then took on a dramatic expression which moved one right to the very soul.

At the first notes of a new song that she had just begun, the Marquis exclaimed:

"No, I beg of you, not that one!"

But the virtuoso didn't pay attention to the paternal warning. However, after a few measures, her voice, altering, turned into tears. At the same moment she left the piano and the drawing room precipitously. While Lupiano was rushing after her, Montalvi explained to Lelouard:

"It's a ballad which has something to do with her situation. She always wants to sing it and can't finish it without crying."

"So much talent, intelligence, sensitivity," said Lelouard, seriously, "but is her deformity as bad as it's been reported publicly?"

Montalvi simply made a desperate gesture, as if to say that the reality was greater than what public gossip had claimed.

"It was nothing," said Lupiano, who had just returned. "Her tears gave her relief. I beg your pardon, Monsieur," he continued, addressing Lelouard, "for having thus exhibited our family wounds. We appear to be like beggars who try to get attention by demonstrating their infirmities."

"Please believe, Monsieur le Marquis, that I am greatly touched by all that I see here."

"No," said Lupiano, "that's ridiculous. We have to use the right word." Then in a casual tone, like a man who wants

---

[85] Antoine Joseph Michel Romagnesi (1781-1850), French composer, music publisher and music theorician.

to remember his duties as master of the household before everything, he added: "Messieurs, why don't we have ourselves a game of bouillotte?"[86]

Before and after the musical incident, the drawing room was almost empty. Only Montalvi, Lelouard and the man they called the Doctor had remained.

"Marquis," said the Doctor, "there are only four of us; there won't be anyone to take his place if someone leaves; let's play piquet[87] instead; besides that's your usual game every evening."

"How does that seem to you?" Lupiano asked the merchant.

"I like piquet; I would gladly play that."

He could have said that he played it with frenzy, and Lupiano had guessed the passion for gambling in him, just by the enthusiasm he had shown for financial speculation during their recent conversation. In addition, his work as a food supplier was already a presumption in favor of that vice. In the army, those who furnished ammunition and food were in the habit of risking fabulous sums on one card.

At the end of several hands, the Marquis had lost a dozen louis.

"I'm not your equal," he said to Lelouard, "but rest easy, you're going to have someone better to compete with you.

---

[86] 18th-century French gambling card game of the Revolution based on Brelan, very popular during the 19th century in France and again for some years from 1830. It was also popular in America. The game is regarded as one of the games that influenced the open-card stud variation in poker.

[87] Early 16th-century trick-taking card game for two players. Piquet is played with a 32-card deck, normally referred to as a piquet deck. The deck comprises the 7s through to 10s, the face cards, and the aces in each suit, and can be created by removing all 2–6 values from a 52-card poker deck. Each game consists of a match of six deals. The player scoring the most points wins.

Monsieur de Montalvi is an accomplished player. For years, he played the Genoa lottery. The evening before the day when, reduced to dire financial straits, he was going to blow out his brains, it was the bank that he broke."

Montalvi took the place of Lupiano, who remained to chat with the Doctor. Lelouard was equally lucky against his new adversary, and soon had won twenty-five louis.

"Monsieur," said the man from Genoa, "we will leave it there, if you will. I thought myself a skilled player, but one can't hold out against you."

"Well, Messieurs," said the Doctor, approaching the table where Lelouard was still seated, "how did you do?"

"Doctor," Montalvi answered, "he beat me fair and square."

"What! A player of your ability! Ah! Well! I must join in then," said the Doctor. "I'm only a weak player, but perhaps, I will have some luck, since the masters have been beaten."

Seeing that a third game was beginning, Lupiano said:

"Messieurs, I'm going to leave you. I'm going to see how my daughter has recovered from her emotion."

Montalvi took a place beside the Doctor, who first won a hand. The two following hands went to Lelouard because of his superiority in the game or because of his lucky star.

"Have you any objections to higher stakes?" asked the Doctor, seemingly excited.

"It's up to you," replied Lelouard.

Twenty-five louis from each player were then placed on the table. The Doctor took them all in a few hands. As they were going to begin another hand, Montalvi asked:

"Monsieur Lelouard, what can I serve you? Ice cream, sherbet, a glass of sherry? Nothing makes one thirstier than gambling, especially when the game is exciting."

"Anything you would like," said Lelouard.

"As a military man, you perhaps also smoke?"

The question was asked with so much good will that Lelouard didn't take it as malice.

"Yes," he answered, "a pipe, from time to time."

"Well, I'm going to have you smoke some tobacco like you have never before tasted."

Shortly afterward, a servant that Montalvi had rung for, came in with a bottle of sherry and three long jasmine pipes that he filled with a tobacco yellow as gold.

"You are right," Lelouard said, after he had inhaled several puffs. "That's better than that mouth-burner that's commonly called the *corporal*."

"I will have some pounds of it sent to you," Montalvi said, pouring him a glass of sherry.

"Excellent," said Lelouard, enjoying it. "Everything here is perfection itself."

"Yes," the man from Genoa answered sadly, "except for the poor daughter of our friend. Beautiful body, mind, talented, adorable sweetness of character, she has everything... except a face that can be shown."

"In such a sorry state that you believe her to be unmarriageable?"

"I am far from saying that, because I would be the first to do it, if I were free. I wouldn't have to be asked very long to include myself in the ranks of her suitors."

"The same goes for me," said the Doctor. "What about you, Monsieur?" he added, speaking to Lelouard. "Are you married?"

"I? No."

"You have, perhaps," said Montalvi, "some situation more enduring than the official ties?"

"When did we, followers of the Empire, ever have the opportunity to commit ourselves to anyone, anywhere?"

The conversation didn't go any further. The pipes were finished.

"Shall we start again?" said the Doctor.

The game began again and soon the mood became fierce. It was midnight. Lelouard, in the middle of various kinds of luck, found that he had won fifteen thousand francs. But bad luck, which didn't let up, followed. And at about one o'clock in the morning, the Doctor, getting up, told him that he owed him, on his word, the sum of a thousand louis. When Lelouard asked for a new and last hand, Montalvi said:

"If I were at my own house, I wouldn't refuse what you asked for, but the Marquis will be unhappy with what is happening, and will certainly reproach me for having let things go so far. The candles are at their end. I won't allow myself to have them replaced."

Lelouard took down the address of the man to whom he owed money.

"Monsieur," he said, on leaving him, "I will have the honor to give you news of me tomorrow, in the morning."

XVIII. A Son-in-law under contract

Lelouard left with more bad temper than with real worry. While gambling, the sherry had gone to his head. He was not aware at that time of the extent of his monetary trouble.

The next day, when he awoke, it was a different matter. Already low on money, the relative enormity of the sum he had to pay in twenty-four hours put him in a cruel emotional state. His first thought, in common with all losing gamblers, was to ask himself if he hadn't been duped. He himself was not a stranger to the *art of dealing cards,* not that he ever used it—that had been a study he had wanted to undertake in order to protect himself, if need be, from the cleverness of the card sharks. Yet, nothing in the play of his adversary had seemed suspicious to him, to a point when it would have been necessary to stop playing, He had to acknowledge that everything had gone on in the most natural way, and that he had had a streak of bad luck against him. He had stubbornly continued to play and had lost, that was all.

Nevertheless, however that might be, he had to pay, and looking into his finances, Lelouard found that he only had at most of fifty louis, a sum absolutely necessary for him to go on living for several months. He believed that he had the right to some rather significant arrears from the government, but he himself, in presenting a letter of recommendation from

Lefebvre to a woman he had been told had some credit, had indicated that those resources might be far away and uncertain. Who, in fact, knew the delays and disappointments that could be expected when settling a debt with the State, always a fastidious debtor, and always having, to a certain point, creditors at its mercy?

At the moment, the wholesale food supplier could not doubt the approaching and favorable resolution of that affair, and it was in that sense that he spoke to five or six friends whom he visited in the morning in order to borrow against that guarantee. But only 500 francs, that is to say a drop of water in a bucket, was all he could gather. The only door open to him was that of an artist, a renowned sculptor, who, while waiting to receive a large sum of money from the government for a commission, could reasonably be counted on for a loan of 20,000 francs.

"At the moment," that true friend answered, "I can only lend you a thousand *écus* that I earned from making a bust that I delivered yesterday. It was that of a Faubourg Saint-Germain aristocrat, a Monsieur de Lucheux, who got himself killed in a duel some months ago by the Marquis de Lupiano, whom you have probably heard about."

"Indeed! It was at his house, yesterday evening, that I lost the sum that today I don't have."

"Well, my dear fellow, take these three thousand francs. I didn't get them without some trouble. However much sorrow she felt at the death of her nephew, the old Duchess, who ordered his bust from me, bargained with me more than a bonnet merchant on the Rue St-Denis would have."

Lelouard took advantage of the generous devotion of the sculptor, but he still lacked 15,000 francs. Returned to his lodgings for lunch, he was lost in thought about the ways, more or less desperate, to which he might have recourse to come up with that sum, when, to his great displeasure, he saw his creditor, the Doctor, come in.

"Monsieur," the Doctor immediately said, "I beg you not to take my visit in the wrong way. I haven't come to put a knife to your throat, quite the contrary!"

Vain, as all debtors, and particularly insolvent debtors, Lelouard hastened to respond that he certainly hoped to be able to pay his debt during the day, or at least within a very short while.

"It's not a matter of that," the Doctor answered. "I have just come from Lupiano, whose usual doctor I am. I wanted to check that the nervous crisis his daughter had had last night didn't have any harmful after-effects. He made a terrible scene, telling me that I had transformed his house into a gambling den, that I didn't need to ever come back—in short, everything that Montalvi had predicted."

"I must thank him for the interest he takes in my misadventure, but a thousand louis, that's not the death of a man. I have been in a great number of other battles. During the Polish campaign, you should have seen the gambles the general section took!"

"Lupiano," the Doctor continued, "isn't a man to let himself be easily understood, but I am as clever as he, and in the circumstance, I saw very well where the issue wounded him."

"What do you mean?" Lelouard asked, curious.

"Yesterday evening, after dinner, you talked a rather long time with him?"

"Yes," Lelouard replied.

"You talked about business, money, speculations?"

"That's true; he understands those questions rather well."

"Yes, but you understand them still better than he does, because from what he told Montalvi, you impressed him very much."

"*Mon Dieu!*" Lelouard said modestly. "I pointed out to him an opportunity to make some money at the stock exchange and he, in fact, seemed to be impressed with my little exposé."

"Well, that's it," said the Doctor.

"What do you mean, *that's it*?" replied the wholesale food supplier.

"He has seen in you a man he could usefully employ in the enormous speculations that are usual for him, and I have upset his projects."

"But in what way?"

"I must tell you first of all that Lupiano can't stand gamblers. He says that they're the kind of men that can't be relied on in any way. Naturally, in believing he had discovered in you that inclination, he abandoned his idea of making you his representative at the stock exchange and in the financial world. But there was also another thought with respect to your cleverness in business, a more personal thought, a double investment, if I may express myself in that way, and his intentions, although rather hidden, didn't escape me."

"What do you suspect that intention was?" asked Lelouard.

That mode of confidence by insinuation was well made to overexcite his curiosity.

"Last night, do you think that the scene at the end of the dinner was comedy acted out?" asked the Doctor.

"My word, I don't know what to say about that, but it seems to me hardly believable that anyone could have faith in such a superstition."

"Well! I can guarantee you that Lupiano has the most real and conscientious devotion to that superstition. He is now convinced that he has scarcely a year to live, and given that, the future of his daughter does preoccupy him greatly."

"That's possible, because he mentioned something about it to me."

"So, you see!"

"Then do you suppose that he has some matrimonial plans that would involve me? To tell the truth, certain words in our conversation seemed to me to imply it. But the thing was so unlikely that I didn't hold on to that fleeting thought."

"For anyone who understands the Marquis' business, nothing, on the contrary, is less unbelievable than his desire to assure himself of the cooperation of a new person, intelligent and capable. His fortune is princely. Having shares in all the banks and the banking establishments in the world—only yesterday he had at his table some of their directors or representatives—Paris is the only place where he hasn't yet planted his speculator flag. And when a man comes to him with views and thoughts on the financial situation of this Great Modern Babylon,[88] where he has already begun his operations, when, most of all, preoccupied with the thought of impending death, he may fear that he doesn't have enough time, and by his sudden disappearance, the interests of his only heir would find themselves in inextricable, complicated trouble, would you doubt that he could have the idea of connecting himself to that providential man who has just fallen into his hands?"

"But," objected Lelouard, "I thought you just said that our unfortunate game of piquet was enough to drive me out of his thoughts?"

"You have to be put back there, in his mind, and that is exactly what I have come to talk to you about."

"But by what means?"

"As simple as two and two make four," replied the Doctor. "It hinges upon what Lupiano considers a gambler—just think about it. A gambler is not the man who loses a mere 20,000 francs in one evening. What is 20,000 francs to Lupiano, who is accustomed to moving millions around? A gambler, in his opinion, is a man who gambles beyond what he possesses, or with someone else's money, or that which he doesn't have.

"I understand that," Lelouard said.

"By seeing you lose those thousand louis, the Marquis, according to what Montalvi told me, since you were presented to him as being in a momentarily difficult position, must naturally have believed that you had that passion for gambling, a dominating influence, which could lead to anything."

---

[88] Paris.

"But," Lelouard exclaimed, "that would be taking things the wrong way."

"What does that matter to you, if I have the means to rectify that false opinion? In half an hour, when I go tell Lupiano that you have paid me cash on the spot, his point of view will change completely. You will no longer be a man having a bad flaw, having risked beyond your means. Better than that, you are a man who pays his debts straightforwardly, giving an excellent idea of his credit. And your worth, in the Marquis' opinion, will increase accordingly."

"Your rehabilitation plan is excellent, but I have not paid you, and I am not even sure, right now, that I am able to give you anything beyond a down payment."

"I know very well that you haven't paid me, and I don't care anything about your down payment. The important thing is that, for Lupiano to be told that you have settled your debt, right to the last penny. As for me, that goes without saying, a little later, you may use the dowry to repay..."

"The dowry, the dowry!" said Lelouard, interrupting. "That's marvelous, but I am not married yet, and I don't even know if I want to be. I must admit to you, that deformity that makes that poor young woman the prey of the first man who comes along, leaves me a little taken aback."

"Listen," the Doctor said mysteriously, "when I help people, above all, I help myself—I don't use any subtleties and I just admitted it to you very candidly. But at this moment, the twenty thousand francs that you owe me would be very welcome."

"That's quite understandable," replied Lelouard. "Not everyone has the Marquis' fortune."

"That said, when I get it into my head to be useful to help someone, I don't do things halfway. And to cut short your hesitations, which are very natural, I'm going to confide a great secret to you."

"Which you can believe will be in sure hands."

"Far from being a monster," said the Doctor, lowering his voice, "Mademoiselle de Lupiano, who has to take off her mask for me, is just simply an angel of beauty."

"But then, how do you explain that hideous masquerade?"

"Wait. You must first understand that Lupiano is the fiercest deceiver that you could ever meet, and that, with a very particular taste, he adores gravediggers' jokes."

"Yes, that's what I've heard."

"That's not all. Horribly vain, he would not admit the weak side of his daughter."

"But, in that beautiful heiress, there is then a weak side?"

"Do you know of anything perfect under the Heavens?"

"No, but I would like to know..."

"*Mon Dieu*! It's something far less serious than you think: Mademoiselle Lupiano has simply been struck by a malady that you have perhaps heard talked about, and that we call *catalepsy*."

"Isn't that a nervous affliction that causes one to be struck motionless, remaining immobile in the position where one was at its onset?"

"Precisely! But it's a malady more frightening and more unusual than it is dangerous. There are almost no examples where it has caused death, and, with care, an appropriate regimen, and often just time, it ends perfectly well."

"If that's what it is, I don't see anything that should stop us."

"Only," the Doctor continued, "that affliction has had a unpleasant consequence for the poor girl. To tell you everything, a valet that Lupiano had in his service had fallen madly in love with her. One day, he came upon her in that cataleptic state and then he, well... But the miserable wretch was killed afterward by Lupiano who blew his head off with a pistol."

"Hum!" said Lelouard.

"But," the Doctor continued "there remains fifteen or sixteen hundred thousand francs of dowry, plus reasonable expectations of more in the future, the intelligence and talent that you already know, a beauty that is in nothing inferior to them. As for the secret that I have just confided to you, since the event happened in India, it is known only by three persons: her father, Montalvi and I!"

Believing he should answer, the purveyor of army supplies, responded:

"Well! Doctor, that's something to think about."

"Undoubtedly, and I suppose that, if to the advantages that I have just been enumerated, one could add the virginity of eleven million virgins, it wouldn't be entirely impossible for you to make up your mind."

"Come on!" Lelouard replied to that ironic comment, "we don't really know for sure if the Marquis has thought of me as a potential son-in-law, and we're just discussing suppositions."

"I guarantee you that the Marquis has thought of you, in the event that you would authorize me to tell him that you have settled with me..."

"In any case," Lelouard said, smiling, "I don't see how I could oppose that officious lie."

"Pardon me, but nothing would be easier. You only have to forbid me to speak. I would certainly do nothing without your agreement."

"Well," said Lelouard, who, like a woman at the end of defending her virtue, wants only to add a little ceremony to her surrendering, "we can always give it a try."

As he finished that sentence, a boy from the hotel where he was staying came to tell him that a man with a face like soot and dressed in a bizarre costume was at the reception below carrying a letter addressed to him. He wouldn't give that letter to anyone else, and, what's more, he seemed to be deaf and dumb. When he had been motioned to go upstairs, he seemed not to understand and remained in place like a soldier at attention.

"That's the Marquis' Hindu servant," said the Doctor. "He is, in fact, deaf and dumb, and because of that, defiant as a devil. You had better go down and see him, and to be done with it."

When Lelouard appeared on the stairwell, the Hindu rushed to meet him, but instead of giving him the letter he had been told to deliver, he made a sign to him to go back up, and that he was going to follow him.

Back in his room, where he no longer found the Doctor, Lelouard finally came in possession of the following letter from Lupiano:

Monsieur

I learned that my drawing room was made into a gambling den, and that the friendly hospitality that I thought I was offering you was transformed into a veritable trap for you. To repair that injury done to my household, as much as I can, I send to you, enclosed, a draft for the sum of twenty thousand francs. You will send me a receipt for such a payment when it seems convenient to you. It will serve to acquit one of those debts for which there is no procrastination possible, and that you might perhaps have trouble settling in the time limit desired.

Please believe me to be, with all my consideration,
Your very devoted,

Marquis de Lupiano.

While Lelouard was reading that note, the Hindu had spread out on the table twenty bills of one thousand francs, and, after having rapidly counted them twice, he bowed and left.

The Doctor reappeared. Not wanting to be seen, he had moved into a neighboring room.

"You understand," he said, "for the success of our little intrigue, I must not be seen by any of Lupiano's servants, who would tell him of my presence here with you. Well! What did he write you, our dear Marquis?"

"Here," said Lelouard, handing him the letter.

"Ah! I now understand," said the Doctor, laughing, "why that poor devil didn't want to come up. Carrying that money, he was afraid to venture up into a trap, or to be directed to the wrong person. He has been told that he should beware of thieves in Paris. But you see," he continued, "how things work out miraculously! There is your debt paid, and it certainly would be agreeable to me to profit by Lupiano's munificence. But I will certainly not do that; that would be the ruin our little agreement. Instead of picking up the pile of money, you're going, right now, to take it back to the Marquis, telling him that you have been rather fortunate to free yourself of your debt using your own resources. From that point on, I will no longer need to intervene. I am sure that, completely reassured about you, he's going to offer you his daughter—and her dowry. Go quickly. I'll wait for you here in order to know the results more quickly."

A half hour later, Lelouard was at the townhouse of the Marquis de Lupiano, who seemed surprised on being told that his financial assistance was not needed, since the Doctor had already paid.

"Then why did Commandant Lefebvre tell me that you were in a difficult financial situation?"

"Certainly, I don't have very much cash lying about, but I have arrears due from the government for much more than the sum I lost. With that guarantee, I saw some friends open their purses to me."

"That's different, and I'm spared a beautiful sermon that I had promised myself to preach to you. To lose money that one has, that's the least of things; but if, as I had first thought, you had wagered beyond your resources, while making it a point of honor to help you, I would have, I confess to you, taken a rather mediocre opinion of your moral state."

That said, he took the sum Lelouard had brought back to him, made no overture, spoke of several insignificant things, and ended by asking permission to leave him, using as a pretext a pressing business matter.

Back in his own lodgings, Lelouard showed himself rather astonished at the negative results of his visit.

"That doesn't astonish me the least in the world," said the Doctor. "We wanted to do without the intermediary; that was a mistake. Lupiano is a great deal too proud to go beyond what he insinuated to you yesterday."

"But he stayed a thousand leagues from that. He didn't even speak to me about the business of the stock market. He talked to me about tiger hunts as they're practiced in India."

"Yes," said the Doctor, "that's a ruse, against which you have to proceed with caution, but let me act. I'm going to see him and ask the question to him straight out."

"You won't find him; he was going out."

"I'll see him sometime during the day. As for you, stay here until dinner time. In a few hours, at the latest, I will be back with news."

Lelouard spent those few hours in real anxiety. It's so true that a way of making us want things that we were the least sure of wanting, is to place them out of reach and to let us get to them with some difficulty. At about five o'clock in the evening, the army foods supplier received another note from the Marquis, who invited him, if he had nothing else to do, to come and have dinner with him, adding that he had something serious to discuss with him.

That dinner that Lelouard made certain to attend was less splendid that the one of the evening before. The guests were only Montalvi and the Doctor, who did not attempt to talk to him privately. As for Mademoiselle de Lupiano, she did not appear and gave as an excuse, that could be seen as a favorable sign, that she was slightly indisposed.

During almost the entire dinner, the Marquis talked about the female sacred Hindu dancers and other unusual things in India, but not a word about the serious discussion. After coffee, he left the drawing room and was absent for almost a half hour. During that time, the Doctor said to Lelouard:

"I would gladly offer you a return match, but that can't be thought about here."

"Certainly not," said Montalvi, "and if I wanted to fall out with the Marquis forever, I would only have to ring for someone to set up a gambling table."

Finally, Lupiano reappeared and took Lelouard into a corner.

"Monsieur," he said abruptly, "I know by way of the Doctor that you would have no repugnance in becoming my son-in-law."

"Yes, I indicated as much to your friend."

"I must tell you that, yesterday evening," the Marquis continued, "I would have been charmed with that notion, but this morning, when I wrote you, I had pushed aside with disdain. Finally, after having seen you during the day, it began to smile on me again."

"I see," said Lelouard, who was beginning to be impatient with all those circumlocutions.

"Well, Monsieur, I find more than one difficulty in our mutual desire."

"Which ones?" Lelouard asked.

"First of all, there is the matter of religion; my daughter practices the Cult of Brahma and there is no hope of your converting her to Catholicism."

"Ah! If that's all, a good Voltairian like me can't be stopped by that consideration."

"Excellent!" said Lupiano. "You are like me a free thinker; but what, most of all, makes me hesitate is the fear of not seeing my daughter happy. That terrible infirmity, when you see her face to face..."

"*Mon Dieu*! Monsieur le Marquis, the importance that you attach to such and such facial deformity is perhaps exaggerated. At my age, a man is most of all impressed by moral character, and, on that chapter, I was able to judge your daughter for myself. I never encountered any deception in her. As for myself, I am neither handsome, nor young, and I would rather expect to see Mademoiselle your daughter bargain about her consent."

"The notion of her consent must not disturb you. In India, we marry our daughters without consulting them, and there has never been an example where the will of the father was not carried out. What's more, with the somewhat oriental imagination of my daughter, a man who not only has seen the Emperor, but has *spoken* to him, can only be a very suitable husband."

"Then, I don't see what other obstacles your very watchful eye could encounter."

"Well," said Lupiano, "since you insist, there is really nothing that prevents me from accepting your word and giving you mine. However, you will allow, before a certain and definite conclusion, on an irrevocable and mutually agreed upon delay that is part of the customs of my country. In India, as in some European countries, a marriage must be preceded by engagement ceremonies. Materially, the parties are always free to cancel their agreement during that period, but morally, especially for the woman, the engagement has a certain importance. Thus, after that important formality, you will be allowed to see your fiancée every day in tête-à-tête, which is usual. As for myself, in advance of the dowry, as is customary, I will pay you one-fiftieth of the total sum, that is to say, a hundred thousand francs, which, in case of a broken engagement, will remain in your possession. You understand that, from our side, the thought of a rupture is not likely."

"And on my part, my dear Marquis, please believe that there will be no hesitation, nor any going backward."

"I hope so, but I don't know about that," Lupiano replied. "Before such monstrosity, nature can sometimes revolt."

"When the moment comes," the merchant replied, "I am sure not to lack indulgence, recalling that which I needed myself and was willingly given me."

Well then," the Marquis asked, "when will the engagement ceremonies begin?"

"I leave you to fix the date, but wouldn't it be proper to arrange a preliminary encounter between Mademoiselle your daughter and..."

"No, that's not according to our customs. Let's see, does tomorrow suit you?"

Lelouard was somewhat stupefied at the short period of the delay and in the way in which he responded:

"So be it, tomorrow it is!'

Some of his surprise was visible, so the Marquis said:

"I see that the speed with which I have dealt with this matter astonishes you, but understand, my dear future son-in-law, that I never proceed in any other way. When I make a decision, it's made, and if the business cannot be taken care in an hour, and drags on twenty minutes more, I leave. We have known each other for two days; is there something that would make it impossible for you to become my daughter's fiancé?"

"Nothing, without a doubt," Lelouard said.

"Then, except for your consent, that is what will happen."

"Until tomorrow, then," said the future son-in-law.

"Tomorrow at three o'clock," Lupiano confirmed, rising. "The Brahmin that I have in my household will prepare everything for the ceremony. No act, no paper, will need to be furnished for the occasion. Think about it until noon; if by that time, you haven't let me know that you've changed your mind, the meeting will take place as planned."

During the conversation between the father-in-law and the son-in-law, the Doctor and Montalvi had left the drawing room. Lelouard then left alone; he didn't need to think further about it. His decision was made.

XIX. M. de Pourceaugnac and
the Commandatore's Statue

The next day, as three o'clock struck, Lelouard arrived at the townhouse of the Marquis de Lupiano. Several carriages, stationed in the courtyard, made him think that the ceremony would not take place just in the presence of the family and a few witnesses.

In fact, he was taken to a vast drawing room that was not the one in which he had been introduced two evenings before. There, he found the guests of the first evening dinner and he had to receive their felicitations. At the far end of the room a Pagoda had been erected, a kind of altar on which the representations of innumerable Indian divinities had been arranged in rows in an amphitheater. Those figurines in gold-plated copper, clothed in silk cloaks, blue or light rose, resembled a collection of marionettes in repose. In front of the Pagoda, on a white cotton rug worked with a silver silk designs, two seats covered with the same material had been positioned, before a small round table in rosewood, where a lamp not yet lighted, covered almost all the surface.

Shortly after Lelouard's arrival, Lupiano appeared, giving his hand to his daughter. Wearing a dress of rippling muslin, she was walking, her head covered with a white veil. She went to sit down on a prepared seat to the left of the table in the Pagoda.

After having cordially shaken the hand of his future son-in-law, the Marquis said to him in a low voice:

"Go take a seat beside your fiancée."

Then, as Lelouard had already taken some steps in the direction indicated, Lupiano stopped him:

"Wait! You can't walk in your shoes on the rug that is a consecrated object. We are fastidious in the Brahman religion."

On a sign by the Marquis, a Hindu servant approached and conducted Lelouard into a neighboring room. An instant afterward, Lelouard reappeared wearing a pair of yellow oriental slippers that contrasted sharply with the rest of his black suit in a way that as rather unusual. During that short absence, a string of candles planted around the Pagoda had already been lit, and between the table and that illumination a Brahman and his assistant had taken their places.

Standing, dressed in a white robe and belt, his head covered with a gigantic turban of the same color, that man, whose voluminous head dress and a kind of mustache made of vermillion red, made a rather burlesque figure. He stood ready to pronounce the engagement ceremonies. He began by mumbling some words in a language that could have been Sanskrit, but that resembled greatly that which Covielle spoke in *Le Bourgeois Gentilhomme.*[89] He pushed a table into the space left empty between the two fiancés, and lit the lamp, which created enormous shadows fed by the alcohol in the wine that soon looked like a bowl of punch in flame.

Elevating the pitch of his voice considerably, making it move through shrill inflections that went, without transition, from sharp to deep, low-pitched, he would have continued to remain unintelligible to Lelouard if, coming to place himself beside his son-in-law, Lupiano had not explained to him, in a very low voice, that the fire illuminated between the two, when joined as a couple, signified the strength of the sentiments that must animate the two spouses. The Brahman then approached the fiancé and the fiancée, threw some grains of rice over their heads, accompanying that dry sprinkling with a spoken commentary.

"The rice," Lupiano, continuing his role as interpreter, "means the fruitfulness hoped for in the marriage."

Finally, the Brahman spread out a green veil between the two, something that was explained by the Marquis as being the

------

[89] Molière's comedy (1670) in which Monsieur Jourdain, a bourgeois who has inherited his father's wealth and despises his middle class background, imitates the aristocracy, wishing be taken for one of them. Sadly, he is comically gullible and easily taken advantage of. He wants his daughter, Lucille, to marry a member of the aristocracy, but she is in love with Cléante, a member of the bourgeoisie. When Monsieur Jourdain cannot be shown that he is making a fool of himself, Cléante, helped by his valet Covielle, dresses up as the Sultan of Turkey and his valet, pretending to be a Turkish holy man, marries them, speaking a pidgin dialect which he passes off as Turkish, thus persuading Monsieur Jourdain that he has been promoted to the nobility.

symbol of the pleasures promised to their union, but also as an injunction not to indulge in them before their marriage, during the time between the day of the engagement and that of the marriage ceremony.

When the priest lifted the veil, the sound of instruments was heard in an adjoining room; the French doors opened with the air of a march, which someone knowledgeable in music would immediately have recognized as being by Lully. The Hindu servants that Lelouard had seen at the dinner two evenings before entered as a procession, marching two by two. When twelve had filed out, a person dressed all in black appeared following them, gravely carrying in his hands the instrument, today out of fashion, that so mercilessly injures Monsieur de Pourceaugnac at the Théatre Français.[90]

Seeing that, beginning to suspect some carnival farce, Lelouard suddenly stood up.

"What does this buffoonery mean?" he asked the Marquis.

"It means," Lupiano answered gravely, taking out of his pocket a billfold gorged with bank notes, "that you don't know that ablutions pay a great role in our religion, which requires that you wash away all your impurities. Before counting out to you the hundred thousand francs of the dowry agreed on in advance, I must ask you to pass into the room next to this one where the armed man that you see there will..."

---

[90] A clyster syringe. *Monsieur de Pourceaugnac* is a three-act comédie-ballet by Molière, first presented on 6 October 1669 before the court of Louis XIV at the Château of Chambord. The music was composed by Jean-Baptiste Lully, who took a role himself on stage in the première, portraying a doctor in the dance of the enemas. Monsieur de Pourceaugnac is betrothed to Julie, the daughter of Oronte. Unbeknownst to him, she is in love with the young and handsome Éraste and has no desire to wed Pourceaugnac. In order to avoid the marriage, Julie and Éraste solicit the help of Sbrigani who uses his guile to help the young couple through a series of clever deceits.

"Monsieur," said the wholesale supplier, "I will willingly go along with a joke, but on the condition that it doesn't go beyond certain limits."

"What do you mean, a joke!" said Lupiano. "It's a question, my dear Monsieur, of a symbolic and hygienic rite that has nothing more extraordinary about it than all the other ceremonies that you practice. Prepared with water from the Ganges, our sacred river, that emollient, composed according to a traditional formula, will endow you with the highest degree of sainthood."

"Let's leave it there, Monsieur," exclaimed Lelouard. "This is without a doubt one of those comedies which you make a habit of."

"A comedy?" said the Marquis. "One that would cost me a hundred thousand francs!"

"Your bank notes," replied the wholesale supplier, "are probably as genuine as the cards used in your drawing room."

"Monsieur!" the Doctor shouted, "you are insulting me!"

"Yes, Monsieur, I am! This ignoble farce has been mostly prepared by your efforts and you will answer me for it."

"With all my heart, Monsieur le Fiancé, but you will please, first of all, settle with me for the twenty thousand francs that you still owe me. I am not so stupid as to blow off the head of one of my creditors."

"What, Monsieur!" the Marquis said with animation. "You have not settled that debt of honor when I offered you a way to do it? Then, was your generosity a comedy? From that, I must take as true that other infamy I was told about you this morning. The hypocrite who, by refusing to dip into my purse, only intended to draw more ample blood, is very capable of stealing a woman's letters."

In face of that pretended discovery that put the behavior of Madame de Camembert in the mystification so patiently carried on for three days, a great movement of indignation appeared among the witnesses of the scene. Nevertheless, Lelouard stood his ground.

"All this," he said, "as I can now very well see, was a plot! Monsieur le Marquis," he added with dignity, "you can have me murdered, since you are twenty against one, but you won't manage to make me look ridiculous."

"Murder you!" Lupiano replied, "Only if I had been stupid enough to take you for my son-in-law! But now, it's possible for you to leave, and the sooner, the better. Go, Monsieur, pick up your shoes! What's more, I authorize you to recount what happened here, where you were welcomed cordially. Public opinion will judge us."

Lelouard hastened to take advantage of the liberty just given to him, and from that moment on, for more than six months, no one heard anything more about him in Paris.

In the month of December, toward the end of 1819, Lupiano ostensibly got in contact with Madame de Camembert, acquiring her townhouse; it was also at that time that the Marquise announced publicly her intention to retire from the world and to go bury the remains of her life in the Convent of the Sacred Heart in Turin.

Once in possession of that building, Lupiano, after having it sumptuously furnished, wanted to have a house-warming party, and, as he never did anything like anyone else, here is how he went about it:

His hope was that the elegant society of Paris would be received in the drawing rooms the day he opened them, without his having invited anyone, since he was a bachelor and knew himself accused of a type of notoriety too equivocal for any lady of society to consent to accept his invitation. As a consequence, the following advertisement appeared the same day in all the Paris newspapers, and it was repeated in several provincial newspapers and abroad:

A man with whom public attention has been preoccupied for some time, Monsieur le Marquis de Lupiano, has just bought from Madame la Marquise de Camembert the beautiful townhouse that she previously occupied on the Rue Notre-

Dame-des-Champs. After having completely remodeled the interior, the new owner had the fortunate idea to turn the somewhat indiscreet curiosity that his person, as well as that of his dwelling, has not ceased being the object, to the profit of the poor.

Thus on December 6, Saint-Nicolas's Day, he will inaugurate his splendid habitation by giving a grand masked ball, where he intends the incognito of the mask to be rigorously respected. His intention is not to send any invitations, but, in order to conserve to that reunion the character of elegance and distinction which must be its primary charm, one where everyone will be in agreement in saying that the preparations were magnificent, the entry ticket, to be purchased at the door, shall be fixed at the sum of one hundred francs.

An employee of the office of the Mayor of the XIème Arrondissement will be in charge of the collection, which will be his responsibility, and which will be immediately donated to Charity, without any deductions for the expenses of the ball, which Monsieur de Lupiano intends to pay himself.

N. B. Any person not masked will be rigorously refused entrance, and the master of the house himself will give the example of his submission to that rule.

The last statement of that advertisement, which was talked about as can well be imagined, was such as to assure success, because with the master of the house either not present or in disguise, the townhouse that day would become a sort of public place, where there was no longer any reason for anyone to hesitate to present himself. The entry fee rather high, but it became a guarantee against the danger of a mixed social group, so difficult to avoid in subscription and charity balls.

The question remained, had the host, in himself and in the magnificence and unusualness that could be expected of him, sufficient strength to draw a crowd. Now, in that respect, Lupiano was sure of his facts, and the calculation was easy. Between pretty young girls of loose morals, who at that time were called *lorettes*, rich foreigners, women and men of the high society who were just curious, those having an intrigue to unfold who would take advantage of the convenience of the mask, young men and other adventure seekers, thinking that, in such circumstances, making the conquest of some adorable young things would be inevitable, Paris could easily produce 300 persons. At 100 francs a ticket, the expected profit for the poor would therefore be 30,000 francs.

When the evening of the reception arrived, the first hours appeared to leave the receipts below the calculations of the *Impresario*. So many stories had been told about the deceptive habits of the Marquis that many people had asked themselves if, by going to knock on the door of his townhouse, they wouldn't have the annoyance to find it closed. Others had of-fered to bet that very few people would answer the advertise-ment, and to pay a hundred francs to walk around in deserted drawing rooms wasn't anything attractive. So, before starting on their way, the prudent sent someone to reconnoiter the place. But, when they came back to tell them that there were not enough police to take care of the lines of carriages; that splendid lighting made the street where the Marquis' town-house was situated seem like a house on fire; that in the court-yard, entirely covered by a tent and provided with rugs, there was a deluge of shrubs, flowers, and lights, those who had been waiting hastened to go take part in those magnificent things.

Thus, the first estimation of the money taken in was ex-ceeded by a great deal. In the night of December 6th, the townhouse of Abbé Terray, vast enough to contain a large crowd, was visited by about 500 persons, bringing the final take to almost 50,000 francs.

Even this figure was to be exceeded, because, with the permission of the authorities, always accommodating when it was a question of enlarging the purse of the poor, the Marquis had established in one of the drawing rooms, a Pharaoh

Bank,[91] a gambling game today somewhat out of fashion, but because it often played a part in the stories of novelists, it appealed strongly to the imagination of the crowd. Now, in taking care of that bank, or having it taken care of, Lupiano was careful to acquaint the Mayor with the probable take of the game, because the economics of the game are calculated so as to multiply chance in favor of the bank.

The grandiose apartments in the purest Louis XV style, carefully renovated, consoled the eye after the frightful furnishings of the Imperial period. Everywhere there was gold, damask, Chinese satin, brocade, lamps and brocatelle, bronze originals, delightful models of clocks, chandeliers, candelabra and torches, some master tableaux, jardinières filled with rare plants, Chinese bric-à-brac, ceilings by Boucher,[92] Lemoine,[93] Vanloo,[94] Fragonard,[95] all admirably restored, some Watteau[96]

---

[91] Pharaoh, or Farobank, is a late 17th-century French gambling card game. It is descended from basset, and belongs to the lansquenet and Monte Bank family of games due to the use of a banker and several players. Winning or losing occurs when cards turned up by the banker match those already exposed. It is not a direct relative of poker, but faro was often just as popular, due to its fast action, easy-to-learn rules, and better odds than most games of chance. The game of faro is played with only one deck of cards and admits any number of players.

[92] François Boucher (1703-1770), painter, draftsman, etcher, who painted classical themes.

[93] Jacques-Antoine-Marie Lemoine (1751-1824), artist, who painted classical themes.

[94] Charles-André van Loo (1705-1765), from a family of well-known French painters.

[95] Jean-Honoré Fragonard (1732-1806), painter and printmaker.

[96] Jean-Antoine Watteau (1684-1791), brilliant draftsman, who painted architecture, landscape scenery, and famous characters from Italian comedies.

above the door, rugs with Turkish, Persian, Indian designs, an orchestra that could make paralytics dance, brilliant lighting, and a profusion of refreshments, that was what made up the material part of the party.

As for its moral content, it was less animated than severe. Few people had risked wearing full-blown costumes and dominoes[97] in all colors formed the background of the crowd. One wondered what was under these impassive figures and those pierced masks, under which shone eyes like so many carbuncles. Where everyone was searching, everyone wanted to recognize someone, or be recognized, there was too much preoccupation to have time for extraneous and widespread gaiety. A masked ball is less a dancing reunion than a thinking one. Behind each word, as behind each borrowed face, there perhaps hid someone that one wanted to see, and in that guess work, in the effort made by the mind, was naturally found some disappointment on the side of the pleasure of the senses.

There is no other reason for the reputation of boredom and sadness that was finally attributed to that lost institution that was called the Opera Ball. In our time, in the same place, all of that has been changed, and one is supposed to amuse oneself. That is to say, we have replaced intimate chats, clever fencing with the language, the exciting search for the unknown person, by the wildest dances, the rut of the common man, the drunken dock worker, and the boisterous behavior of every kind of prostitute. Where is progress then? It is only that matter having snatched the baton of Musard[98] has thrown spirit out of the door.

---

[97] In the 1800s a long, wide black cloak with wide sleeves decorated with color somewhere on the robe.

[98] Philippe Musard (1792-1859), composer popularly nicknamed "Napoleon Musard, Lord of Quadrillles and Galops," quadrilles being very animated dances, and the word "galops" indicating the steps of a dance resembling that of the gait of a horse.

At about midnight, a small man, wearing a fire-colored domino, was seated at the Pharaoh Bank. At the somewhat commanding petulance of his movements when he dealt the cards, and at the thinness of his voice, letting fall at intervals the sacramental words: "Make your bet, Mesdames et Messieurs," many thought they had recognized the master of the house. There was then a crowd around the game table, and a tall man, also dressed in a red domino costume, had some trouble making his way through the crowd to reach the dealer, to whom he whispered some words in his ear.

The game finished, the banker rose, announcing that the session would be restart again a little later. Moving into a corner with the Domino who had come to speak to him:

"So, my dear Montalvi, you're saying that a man is walking about, dressed all in white, like the statue of the Commandatore in *Don Giovanni*?"[99]

"Yes, Marquis, but I repeat, instead of having a fantasy face, his plaster mask resembles in a terrifying way the face of Monsieur de Lucheux, as pale as I saw him when he fell, killed by your hand. You can understand the scandal and the commentaries."

"Let's go see that," said Lupiano, without any reaction. "There must be some insolent prank."

After having gone through several rooms without finding the object of their search, the two friends came to the great drawing room, where there was dancing, The orchestra sud-

---

[99] *Don Giovanni* is a 1665 play by Molière and a 1787 opera by Wolfgang Amadeus Mozart with a libretto by Lorenzo Da Ponte. Both are based on the legends of Don Juan, a fictional libertine and seducer. The first written version of that legend was written by Tirso de Molina in Spain around 1630. They all involve the eponymous protagonist killing the father of a girl he has seduced, eventually concluding with the famous last supper scene, whereby Don Juan invites the statue of the father to dinner. The ending depends on which version of the legend one is reading.

denly stopped playing. There was great movement in the crowd and two red Dominoes, before whom the crowd moved aside, rapidly carried out a woman in an Albanaise costume who had just fainted.

If, in the middle of the excitement caused by that accident, some observer had paid attention to anything other than the event itself, at the end of several minutes, roughly opening up an empty space, nine or ten red Dominoes had come from various directions to form a group around Montalvi and the Marquis; that kind of group couldn't remain unnoticed for very long.

"Montalvi!" Lupiano then quickly said, "tell these imbeciles to separate. No danger threatens us."

Then, going to one of the zealous assistants, the first one he reached, he asked him in a low voice:

"What is it, Major? What happened to the Marquise?"

"It was the man dressed like a statue who approached her from behind to speak to her during a quadrille. At first, she listened to him peacefully, then she suddenly collapsed and the Doctor, helped by the Major, only had enough time to detach her mask under the pretext of giving her some air."

"That Commandatore who made such a scandal," said Lupiano, "where is he so I can speak to him?"

As the Marquis was glancing around him, he saw, coming to meet him, the object he was searching for, and, despite his impassive nature, he felt a little shiver run down his back finding himself face to face with the pale image of the man whom he had killed the year before. However, his emotion only lasted a moment. He walked to the phantom and said:

"Monsieur, I'd like a word, please, in private."

The masked man bowed his head gravely, as did the statue of the Commandatore in the Mozart opera, and he followed the Marquis into a room that had not been invaded by the preparations for the party. As they were both entering, they were joined by Montalvi and Hernandez, who, in a low voice, gave the good news about the Marquise.

With that backing, Lupiano found himself in a position to carry out everything he would mete out to the insolent trouble-maker.

"Monsieur," said the Marquis, "a *masque* has its freedoms, and I shall respect them by not asking you to take off your mask, as strange as it might be. However, as master of this house, I must act somewhat as the police concerning what takes place here. You will permit me to ask you what words you said to make the woman to whom you spoke faint."

"When I spoke to Madame la Marquise de Camembert, whom I was able to recognize," replied the unknown man, "acting in the spirit of my character, I could not but speak to her of what had happened between us."

"What do you mean, *what had happened between you*? What was there anything in particular between the Marquise and the man whose resemblance you have taken?"

"You are mistaking me for someone else, Monsieur le Marquis. I am, if you will—and please remember that—a personage from the world beyond this one. As such, the most secret circumstances of others' lives are known to me."

"Speak more clearly," exclaimed Lupiano. "I'm not here to continue a farce in bad taste, but to obtain clear explanations which I can very well compel you to give, if you force me to."

"Oh! As far as a farce in bad taste is concerned, you can, Monsieur, give me pointers. I don't know of any more odious and more miserable than that which was arranged by you several months ago against a man of honor without his having done anything to merit it."

"Who are you talking about?" the Marquis said quickly. "In my life I have duped many fools."

"I want to talk to you about a poor supplier of wholesale staples named Lelouard, who came to you with a letter from Commandant Lefebvre. He had one also for Madame la Marquise de Camembert, and in both houses, he found the same eagerness to be hospitable."

"Are you then the same Monsieur Lelouard who stole letters and didn't pay his gambling debts?"

"No, Monsieur, and unless, against all the rules observed by honest people, you force me to take off my mask in your house, where I have paid to walk about under such form as suits me, I will continue to be Monsieur de Lucheux."

"Well, then, I will ask Monsieur de Lucheux what right does he have, in this *fête*, the rules of which he is hiding behind, to insult a woman?"

"And what, Monsieur, do you think an unfortunate dead man could have talked about to Madame de Camembert if it wasn't the thing that weighed the most on his heart—to tell her what exceptional kindness she demonstrated by having him killed by you."

"Monsieur, be careful!" the Marquis exclaimed. "Your words are becoming very serious."

"Such was not the impression of our amiable friend, because she listened very calmly to my reproaches, and it was only then I talked to her about a discoloration that she had on her neck, letting her know its danger, that she fainted under her emotion."

For a moment, Lupiano lost the mocking composure that ordinarily never abandoned him. But becoming once more in command of himself, he sought to ascertain to what extreme his secrets had been divulgated:

"You are saying, Monsieur," he continued with a tone of innocence, "that I killed Monsieur de Lucheux to please Madame de Camembert? But at that time, I had just arrived in Paris and the person you mention wasn't even known to me by sight."

"You mean to say that she wasn't acquainted with you in the day time, since at night, using a secret tunnel opening into her oratory, you took the trouble to take her the still warm and agreeable news of my death."

"Now I know who you are!" said Lupiano. "You're Commandant Lefebvre!"

"Do you think so, Monsieur? Lefebvre was heavy and short. Me, I am tall and lean! Commandant Lefebvre! Would Heaven make that he could be here, instead of on a vessel that my phantom eyes see setting sail at this very moment for the far-away island of Madagascar."

"Then," said the Marquis, pushed to the end of his patience, "you insist on being Monsieur de Lucheux?"

"Yes, Monsieur, and truly so! I would be annoyed not to be Monsieur de Lucheux, because you must agree that I revenge myself a little by intriguing you."

"Well, my dear Monsieur de Lucheux, it seems I didn't kill you... enough. With your permission, we're going to do the same operation again."

"Be careful, Marquis de Lupiano. Don Juan only killed the Commandatore once, and during their second encounter, the lesson he received was very unpleasant."

"Montalvi," Lupiano said, "do me the favor of going to find my pistols in the drawing room."

After the man from Genoa had left, the unknown man asked:

"A duel here, between these four walls?"

"The room is a good fifteen feet long. If each of us stand at an angle..."

"So be it, Monsieur. Dare I inquire about the health of Mademoiselle, your daughter, who is somehow one of us, people from beyond the grave?

"She is marvelously well," the Marquis answered.

"I first mistook Madame de Camembert for her; because they are both blonde, the same height, and are wearing the same costume."

"He knows everything!" Hernandez said in a low voice to Lupiano, who was walking up and down the room impatiently.

"Yes," the Marquis responded, "but we're going to see just how he will hold out right up to the end of the challenge."

At that moment, Montalvi returned.

"You load the weapons yourself," Lupiano said to his adversary. "You have no witnesses."

The statue of Monsieur de Lucheux loaded the weapons like a man taking care of a chore, without giving the least indication of emotion. Once the weapons ready, he chose one and went calmly to take his place at an angle of the room.

"Fire, Monsieur!" Lupiano shouted to him.

"Not at all, Monsieur. I came to trouble your ball. You are the insulted party. It is up to you to fire first."

"You must know from experience that I rarely happen to miss my man."

"It doesn't matter, Monsieur. I will not begin. Even being from the other world, I still know how to behave."

"My word, Messieurs," said the Marquis, addressing the man from Genoa and the Brazilian, "if this isn't the moment of our thirteenth guest, I would be very mistaken."

Then addressing his opponent, he said:

"Monsieur, your self-possession goes to my heart. You are a brave man as I like them, especially when they are people of intelligence. Give me your hand, I beg you, and after that, your face, if you will."

"With such gracious manners, you can ask anything from me," the phantom said, detaching his mask, then rummaging in his leotards. "Lelouard, wholesaler of food supplies, at your service. And here is twenty thousand francs that you will kindly give to the Doctor."

"We will talk about that later," Lupiano said. "My dear friends," he added, speaking to Montalvi and Hernandez, "go back to the ballroom and tell our friends that everything is taken care of. You, Montalvi, will you please take my place at the Pharaoh Bank. And you, Monsieur Hernandez, please be kind enough to have some pipes, sherry, and refreshments sent to us. I must first talk with Monsieur, and from all appearances, our conversation will be long."

PART II. THE RED BROTHERHOOD [100]

I. As a Kind of Preface

Like a snake that swallows its tail, after an immense circuit, our narrative, as our readers have perhaps notices, seeks to connect the mysteries and incomprehensible events which have served as its point of departure, to the place where we have arrived today.

Four murders, committed in Paris during the year 1819, surrounded by dramatic and romanesque circumstances, could create the belief in a kind of tribunal of *Francs-Juges*.[101]. Those uncatchable and invisible phantoms worked outside the law, taking upon themselves the right to dispense high and low justice for crimes that came to their attention, and remained unknown from public condemnation.

The Marquis de Lupiano, for a time suspected of being the head of that bloody organization, had proved his innocence with that mocking and ironic serenity, which we have seen him display, when threatened by the police of every country,

---

[100] The original outline added: "or Saint-Helena" to the title.

[101] The Vehmic courts, or *Vehmgericht*, a vigilante tribunal system of Westphalia active during the later Middle Ages, based on a fraternal organization of lay judges called "free judges." Proceedings were often secret, leading to the alternative titles of "secret courts" or "silent courts." The peak of activity of these courts was during the 14th to 16th centuries, with scattered evidence establishing their continued existence during the 17th and 18th centuries. They were finally abolished by order of Jérôme Bonaparte, king of Westphalia, in 1811. See Volume 2, pages 77 seq.

and even in the presence of Napoleon himself[102]. Such was established the doorway of the vast labyrinth through which the reader's curiosity has been walking for a long time. Today there are no more secrets in that cloudy atmosphere in which our story was born; the moment has come to clear away the clouds.

Moving from unheard-of misfortunes of which we will soon tell the extent and character, to the most somber misanthropy and the most terrifying skepticism, cultivating with rare perseverance and an unusual fecundity of imagination the detestable thoughts of evil, the man who, today, calls himself the Marquis de Lupiano had, for a long time, done nothing but work in a vacuum.

What purpose, in fact, did the famous *Sleepers' Club* that, in London, had conducted him to Newgate Prison, and the society of the *Brothers of Death*, that had brought him nothing but a stay in Charenton,[103] and the long funereal cackle making up the occupation of his entire life, serve, if not, at most, to hold at bay his eternal need for agitation, and to sow around him terror and astonishment, equally sterile?

In the two organizations he had previously founded, his claim was to have elevated suicide to the state of a religion where, by means of an atrocious lottery, the self-immolation of human victims was carried out. But never, in that lottery, had he earned the right for himself to end an existence which weighed heavily on him. Like another Ahasverus,[104] weary of living, yet unable to die, each time that his sinister creations were destroyed, he had thrown himself sometimes into the life of a corsair, sometimes into those immense wanderings where contraband, printing counterfeit money, and other unlawful occupations had finally put him in possession of a fabulous fortune.

---

[102] See Volume 2, pages 31 seq.

[103] Lunatics' asylum founded in 1645 by the Brothers of Charity; the Marquis de Sade was interned there.

[104] The Wandering Jew.

Made stronger by the power of gold, he only found himself more to be pitied, because in proportion to the power of every user, the tendency to want more only increases.

In that way, the captivity that Napoleon had inflicted on him could be considered a blessing, in the sense that it finally created an obstacle on the path of that fierce determination that carried him breathlessly across dreams and aspirations to the Infinite. In the Vincennes dungeon, he had been, if one can speak this way, *forced to sit down,* to gather his thoughts, and what's more, in the person of the Prince Bevillacqua—the man we now know as Comte de Montalvi—he had met a friend.

Let's be clear about that—with the composition of his mind and his character, Lupiano couldn't really be anyone's friend. He was one of those souls without a peer, who must go through life alone. But the man from Genoa, his companion in captivity, had become an admirer, a confident, a blind follower. He spoke his thoughts aloud before that man, to bring them to complete maturity and to control their value. To sum up, it seemed to the Marquis that he had gained a third arm the day that it had been agreed between Bevillacqua and him that they should be united together, and that henceforth they would never leave each other's company.

Having spent a great deal of time in secret societies, it was at first on the side of politics that the man from Genoa had tried to turn the destructive instincts and the appetite for moral anarchy that he has found so strongly developed in Lupiano. At first, Lupiano had seemed disposed to follow him in that path. He was indignant about that fashion of European gendarmerie that, following the Imperial despotism, seemed to constitute the Sovereigns of the North and almost immediately after the release from Vincennes, obliged by his unfortunate duel with General de Chandeville [105] to leave Paris and France, it was toward Germany, where there was then a great excitement about liberal ideas, that he directed his steps.

---

[105] See Volume 3, pages 170 seq.

But that excursion to the other side of the Rhine had ended in great disappointment for him. In the *Deutscher Bund*,[106] the *Burschenschaft*,[107] the *Arminia*[108] and the *Black Knights*,[109] he had encountered nothing but empty and mystic professors, noisy students, swallowers of tankards of beer, some ambi-

---

[106] The German Confederation was an association of 39 German states in Central Europe, created by the Congress of Vienna in 1815 to coordinate the economies of separate German-speaking countries and to replace the former Holy Roman Empire, which had been dissolved in 1806. Most historians have judged the Confederation to have been weak and ineffective, as well as an obstacle to the creation of a German nation-state. The Confederation collapsed due to the rivalry between the Kingdom of Prussia and the Austrian Empire.

[107] One of the traditional student fraternities founded in the 19th century inspired by liberal and nationalistic ideas. It was significantly involved in the March Revolution and the unification of Germany. After the formation of the German Empire in 1871, they faced a crisis, as their main political objective had been realized.

[108] The Catholic Students Society Arminia was one of Germany's oldest Catholic male student societies. It was founded on 6 November 1863 at the University of Bonn. The name was chosen in reference to Arminius, the chief of the Cherusci who drove the Romans out of Germany and thus became a symbol of the not yet unified fatherland. In 1865 Arminia, among four other Catholic corporations, became the founder of the *Kartellverband katholischer deutscher Studentenvereine* (KV), Germany's second oldest umbrella organization of Catholic male student societies.

[109] An ancient German body of knights whose existence is traced back as far as the time of King Arthur, and who, in the absence of a strict and impartial administration of justice, had banded together to help the oppressed, aid the distressed and correct wrongs done. Their device was, "Charity, Generosity, Justice."

tious people, a great number of fools, and shifty informers. For wanting to put a little order into the ideas of the German democrats, and to make the Teutonic transcendent verbosity which had deafened him pass into the domain of action, he had finally ended by being mistaken for a Russian agent. Disgusted with these powerless conspiracies without a future, he decided to go to Hamburg, and from there, embark for South America.

Leaving the country at the moment when Napoleon's return from the Island of Elba [110] was again putting in question everything that the abdication of 1814 had seemed to decide, Lupiano went to assist Simon Bolivar in New Grenada, and, for some time, as he had confided to Lefebvre, he had served as Chief of Staff beside the hero of the Colombian Insurrection. But he grew tired of that war, the end of which one could not predict, and, still accompanied by the man from Genoa, he returned to Europe, however with a notable increase in his fortune, calculated at that time to be in the neighborhood of fifty million.

His sojourn in Germany had been sterile. Passing into Westphalia, he had spent some time in Dortmund, formerly the principal seat of the famous *Vehmic Courts*. In that city's library, he had discovered the ancient rules of that bloody justice brought together under the title *Dortmund Code*. In reading them, he had concocted the idea of an association which was to have as a mission, to search out and punish the thousand and one crimes that had remained unknown and escaped the chastisements of official justice.

Counting on the fact that in Paris, the Great Whore, better than any other place in the world, he would get an abundant harvest of those anonymous misdeeds, it was there that the Marquis de Lupiano settle, while his friend Bevillacqua took the name Montalvi, toward the end of 1818. He had come

---

[110] The Hundred Days marked the period between Napoleon's return from exile on the island of Elba to Paris on 20 March 1815 and the second restoration of King Louis XVIII on 8 July 1815 (actually 110 days).

to give a shape to his idea. A famous novelist[111] appeared to have gotten wind of the Marquis' idea, and, under the title *History of the Thirteen,* in three short episodes, where unfortunately the progression of the interest appeared to be somewhat decreasing, he had seemed to want to show the work the *Red Brotherhood,* the origins of the name of which remained unknown to him. But in some ways, the famous storyteller was well informed. He was rather close to the truth in this passage from his preface:

There was then in Paris, thirteen brothers who formed a group disregarding all of society and finding themselves together one evening like conspirators, not hiding any thought from one another, they used, turn by turn, a fortune like that of

---

[111] Honoré de Balzac (1799-1850). *L'Histoire des Treize* (1833-39) are three short novels concerned in part with the activities of a rich, powerful, sinister and unscrupulous secret society. While the deeds of The Thirteen remain frequently in the background, the individual stories are concerned with exploring various forms of desire. A tragic love story, *Ferragus* depicts a marriage destroyed by suspicion, revelations and misunderstanding. *The Duchess de Langeais* explores the anguish that results when a society coquette tries to seduce a heroic ex-soldier, while *The Girl with the Golden Eyes* offers a frank consideration of desire and sexuality. The director of the prestigious *Revue de Paris*, Rabou was Balzac's friend and published his novels in his magazine. Their mutual trust was such that Balzac entrusted him with the task of completing some of his unfinished novels after his death. Rabou uses Balzac's stories here both as a point of departure for his own story, and as a criticism of Balzac's work. For his critical aside, Rabou jumps from 1819, the time of his story at this point, to the time of the composition of *Le Cabinet Noir*, sometime before its first publication in 1848.

the Old Man of the Mountain,[112] having their feet in all the drawing rooms, their hands in all the safes, their shoulders in the street, their heads near ears, and making everything serve their caprices without scruples.[113]

---

[112] Nickname given to Rashid ad-Dïn Sinän (1132/1135-1192), legendary Grand Master of the Assassins and a central figure in the 3rd Crusade.

[113] Rabou misquotes Balzac, whose foreword is actually much more detailed: *In the Paris of the Empire there were found Thirteen men equally impressed with the same idea, equally endowed with energy enough to keep them true to it, while among themselves they were loyal enough to keep faith even when their interests seemed to clash. They were strong enough to set themselves above all laws; bold enough to shrink from no enterprise; and lucky enough to succeed in nearly everything that they undertook. So profoundly politic were they, that they could dissemble the tie which bound them together. They ran the greatest risks, and kept their failures to themselves. Fear never entered into their calculations; not one of them had trembled before princes, before the executioner's axe, before innocence. They had taken each other as they were, regardless of social prejudices. Criminals they doubtless were, yet none the less were they all remarkable for some one of the virtues which go to the making of great men, and their numbers were filled up only from among picked recruits. Finally, that nothing should be lacking to complete the dark, mysterious romance of their history, nobody to this day knows who they were. The Thirteen once realized all the wildest ideas conjured up by tales of the occult powers of a Manfred, a Faust, or a Melmoth; and to-day the band is broken up or, at any rate, dispersed. Its members have quietly returned beneath the yoke of the Civil Code; much as Morgan, the Achilles of piracy, gave up buccaneering to be a peaceable planter; and, untroubled by qualms of conscience, sat himself down by the fireside to dispose of blood-stained booty acquired by the red light of blazing towns.*

Monsieur de Balzac was still truthful when he showed that red was the costume of dark societies and when he noted the disbanding of their sinister society at around the time of Napoleon's death. But he shows himself less informed in claiming that the Red Brotherhood did not have a leader,[114] and that only chance brought about their dispersion.

He also states that he knew almost little about the intimate secrets of the association. He forgot to speak about an extremely powerful lever that it had outside its own resources. Once that lever was suppressed, its existence became hardly believable, and without it, it could no longer exist or function. Finally, in presenting Lupiano's twelve *tools* as so many unknown poets, so many Manfreds,[115] Fausts,[116] and Melmoths,[117] driven by the taste for *Asiatic pleasures* and by the horror of the platitudes of vulgar existence, the author of the *Human Comedy* manages to leave the real to approach with full sails the shores of fantasy.

From that point, faithful to his poetic writing so dear to ladies, given over to the incessant domination of those feminine interests to which he has sacrificed so much in his books, he becomes contemptuous of what he calls the stories of tunnels and cadavers, and instead of bloody dramas and novels full of terror which his readers must be waiting for, he is careful to invent, as he says, gentle adventures where the woman is

---

[114] Somewhat untrue, since Balzac writes: *The aforesaid leader was still an apparently young man with fair hair and blue eyes, and a soft, thin voice which might seem to indicate a feminine temperament. His face was pale, his ways mysterious. He chatted pleasantly, and told me that he was only just turned forty. He might have belonged to any one of the upper classes. The name which he gave was probably assumed, and no one answering to his description was known in society. Who is he, do you ask? No one knows.*

[115] Poem (1816-17) by George Gordon, Lord Byron.

[116] Rabou must have had in mind Goethe's work (1829).

[117] Gothic novel (1820) by Charles Maturin.

radiant with beauty and virtue or where members of the stock exchange are the heroes.[118]

This, one must understand, is the true novel of the Red Brotherhood, barely looked into previously, their story having been made insipid. To use a fashionable word, their real story is here in all its rawness and crudity.

Not only did the Red Brotherhood have a leader, they had a dictator, and that dictator was that pale sickly man with an almost ridiculous appearance who has revealed himself to us under many diverse identities before, until he incarnated himself in the personage of the Marquis de Lupiano.

Later the reader will recognize that it was not a matter of chance but a very sovereign and thought-out act of his will that, shortly after the death of Napoleon on the island of Saint-Helena, he dispersed and annihilated the elements of the organization that he had formed. In that organization, there were not twelve poets. What he would have made of them, only the Good Lord might know! But here was a man of genius and superior will power who had not drawn his ideas of revolt against the social order either from the frenzied need of suffering, or from the vulgarities of existence. That man, that desperate man, that bloodied mocker, was Lupiano, who, believing that he had an account to settle with the horrible mockery of his destiny, had made for himself so many playthings with the laws of society and of justice, merely in order to escape confrontation with his thoughts.

---

[118] Balzac writes: *When a writer has a true story to tell, he should scorn to turn it into a sort of puzzle toy, after the manner of those novelists who take their reader for a walk through one cavern after another to show him a dried-up corpse at the end of the fourth volume, and inform him, by way of conclusion, that he has been frightened all along by a door hidden somewhere or other behind some tapestry; or a dead body, left by inadvertence, under the floor.*

As for the *Condottieri* [119] that he employed, they were all men of action, terrible rogues, for the most part, since, before coming back to France, Lupiano had taken care to skim them off from almost all the jails in the universe.

He had hired these men, gave them a meager existence, ordered them to appear not to know each other, and by the ascendance of his genius, the strong discipline with which he had bent them to his will, the solidarity he had created, giving them all the same opportunities, he had generated a true feeling of union and common devotion. He had made a single bundle from their separate wills, so coherent and docile that the Superior of a monastery wouldn't have been more religiously obeyed. But beyond all those elements of strength, the Marquis felt himself in possession of incommensurable power when, by way of Madame de Camembert, he had found himself in possession of all the secrets of the Secret Bureau. The way in which he had begun his intimacy with that lady is already known to the reader. It remains now to show that, despite its strangeness, their first encounter came about very naturally; that as always, Lupiano hadn't asked anything of chance, and with that precious conquest, he had brought it about with complete and entire premeditation.

II. The Court of France

It was the name given in 1819 to a kind of modern-day Court of Miracles[120] located on the exterior boulevard, between the barriers of d'Enfer and of Mont-Parnasse.

---

[119] Leaders of the professional military free companies (or mercenaries) contracted by the Italian city-states and the Papacy from the late Middle Ages and throughout the Renaissance.

[120] Slum district of Paris where beggars lived and from which they entered the wealthier sections of Paris to beg as cripples, blind, or maimed. When they returned to their hovels, they became "miraculously" healed.

Formed of vast irregular constructions, it held the remains of a farm, the outside wall of which, erected in 1787, had enclosed the outbuildings within the city limits. That unpaved enclosure, encumbered with piles of gravel, manure, and garbage, was closed on the boulevard side by an unsightly carriage door surrounded by two wooden posts and a palisade made of ship's planks holding up a collapsed wall for two-thirds of its length. A hauling enterprise that had not prospered had followed the farm. Then, to take advantage of those buildings whose dilapidation and abandon threatened them with near destruction, the owner, by making numerous interior improvements, such as workshops, sheds, and small house accommodations, had adapted them to the needs of the poor and worker population.

His tenants were a renter of carriages, a laundress, who, at the same time, served as the concierge for the little colony, a nursemaid, a Cartwright, and other artisans of diverse nature: organ grinders, an animal trainer, acrobats, professional beggars, and even some convicts wanted by the law.

One fine morning, hiding behind the name of a third party, Lupiano had come to acquire that unusual property, and after having turned out the peaceful households and workers, which could have become an obstacle to this place becoming the general quarters of his mysterious operations, he replaced them with some of his associates to create the semblance of diverse industries. There also he stored material and equipment necessary for his various projects. Thus, he had procured some old rebuilt rental carriages and turned them, in the language of thieves, into what was called then hackney cabs. Identified with a fictitious license number, but having the honest appearance of vehicles registered with the police, they could, in the evening, be used for some suspicious job without there being any way to find them again. The Marquis's foresight even went so far as building fake hearses that he held in reserve either for one of his mortuary mystifications or, if needed, for clandestine burials.

Better informed than Madame de Camembert because, when she had bought the former Terray townhouse, she had had only a vague understanding of its subterranean connections, the Marquis de Lupiano, when he had become the proprietor of the Court of France, knew with certain knowledge that, under the hovels and buildings that he was going to populate with his associates, extended vast caves and tunnels, including one with a vaulted passage that reached the townhouse on the Rue Notre-Dame-des-Champs. When the two proprietors came to an agreement, nothing was easier than to connect the two buildings with such different aspects and value with a passage that had been closed for many years.

When Lupiano was thinking about being able to say that there would soon be no longer a wall between the Court of France and the Camembert townhouse, was precisely the time when the Marquise was making the most noise in the Parisian salons with her dreaded malicious gossip and that universal knowledge of others' lives that most folks were not far from attributing to a supernatural explanation. That townhouse, having its official entry in Paris, was to be of inestimable value to the Red Brotherhood, giving them a secret entry *extra muros*. It would have come even more strongly to the attention of the Marquis because of its then-owner, Madame de Camembert. In a woman so beautiful, rich, intelligent, coldly wicked, having the reputation of taking pleasure in dark things, and having the habit of procuring for herself rare insights right into the most inaccessible recesses of private life, it was impossible for Lupiano to not anticipate an interesting personality to study, perhaps even a desirable colleague to procure.

He felt himself drawn to that woman, and could easily have met her in society, become acquainted with her, and then recruit her into his schemes. But for the future and the usefulness of their alliance, to remain strangers to each other in the eyes of the outside world was infinitely more convenient. Seemingly working in isolation, at different points, their two clandestine powers could cover a great deal more horizon. Separately, they would be better able to throw off the curious interested in learning about them off their scent. In addition, if, in the terrible liberties that Lupiano was proposing to take with the social order, he experienced some serious failure, the Marquise would remain outside the scope of his misfortunes. Instead of having to defend herself as his accomplice, she could still serve very effectively the interests of the Brotherhood in peril. In addition, the natural aversion of the Marquis for the beaten paths, and the unusual pleasure that he experienced in astonishing and strongly striking imaginations, were well known. That explained his strange way of introduction to the Marquise, whom he had correctly judged when he thought that form of melodramatic appearance would be welcomed by her. From that point on, the mode of nocturnal communication between then continued for some time. Soon, the student having surpassed all the hopes of her master, they had no secrets from each other, and the two knew each other to the depth.

When Lupiano knew the price at which the Marquise had bought the indiscretions of Lefebvre, he claimed that, even in ridding her of that demanding and inconvenient informer, he could still maintain the intelligence established with the Secret Bureau, understanding the value of the lucrative business which he had just discovered. Not only did he claim to exploit it for himself, but he also claimed to do so on a larger scale and with much more results.

The head of the Secret Bureau was in a position to be differently informed than Lefebvre, who was only a simple employee. The name of the man currently in charge, Monsieur de Saint-Rambert, had been given to the Marquis by Madame de Camembert as being a man of very approachable integrity. Lupiano had at first presented himself to Saint-Rambert with the intention of putting down all the money necessary to purchase that integrity. But, when, in the person of this high-ranking and secret civil servant he had recognized Rempailleux, the former leader of the *Chauffeurs* and the Invisibles,[121] who, later, under the name of Dulac, had joined the

---

[121] See Volume 1, pages 149 seq.

Sleepers' Club, but had refused to be the *brother who must die,* a clause to which all the members of their association had submitted under their charter, and instead had gone to denounce the association to the English Police,[122] the negotiations found themselves unusually simplified.

Partly by fear of the indiscretions and the brutalities of the terrible Marquis, by whom, for one hour he remembered having been within minutes of hanging, and partly by the addition of an income of sixty million francs offered to him over and above his appointment as Director of the Secret Bureau, Saint-Rambert had promised to deliver to Lupiano all the secrets of which his functions made him the depository. It remained agreed that the Marquis would be careful that no use of such secrets would be made that could be traced to his revelations.

When she found out that the mysterious power that she had for a long time possessed had thus been transferred to the Marquis, Madame de Camembert was all the more eager to follow the fortune of the extraordinary man who had revealed himself to her. With surprising virility, she had wanted to be associated without reserve to all his projects and to all his luck, even if, according to her, she had occupied the *thirteenth chair* in the association that still remained to be filled.

But, Lupiano only wanted her in his murderous brotherhood as an honorary member, or a foreign associate, and to bring about a complete liberty in their relations, he had begun by inventing the farce of the *Girl with the Death's Head.* The self-assurance and the cleverness that the Marquise had put into playing that personage assuredly had nothing unbelievable about it, if one will recall the manner in which she got disentangled from Lefebvre.

Somewhat later, to tie more tightly her life with that of the Marquis, whom she had come to call her venerated father, she pretended to sell her townhouse to him, and play the comedy of retiring in the Convent of the Sacred-Heart in Turin,

---

[122] See Volume 1, pages 328 seq.

while secretly staying in Paris under that macabre disguise. She was now free to become completely absorbed into her new family, and to espouse its morals, lifestyle, ideas, and interests.

However, it must be said that, during the episode during which she became was annoyed with Lelouard, she showed herself regrettably female. Her insistence on being right and in revenging herself for what it pleased her to call a terrible affront, by practicing a cruel hoax on the merchant, might perhaps have ended by causing the Brotherhood serious trouble if Lupiano—as it remains for us to tell—hadn't managed to make the threatening Statue of the Commandatore one of his most active and intelligent agents.

The day of his masked ball, we left the Marquis in a *tête-à-tête* with Lelouard. Recognizing in all of that man's actions, as he had previously told Madame de Camembert, an energy and a strength of invention that he himself wouldn't have disavowed, he had decided to initiate him into all the mysteries of his shady enterprise. Bringing up the matter frankly, he said:

"Monsieur, I must ask you to take back the 20,000 francs which you have just given me for the Doctor. They were not won from you honestly."

"You astonish me," Lelouard responded. "I don't think I'm easy to dupe, and I watched closely my adversary's play..."

"To catch him cheating," Lupiano interrupted. "And you would have, if he hadn't been one of the cleverest of prestidigitators. But I surround myself only with first-class virtuosos of every kind. In addition, you were able to see with what art everything was carried out to bring you right to the denouement of the comedy, from which you have just taken your revenge very cleverly."

"Then you will admit, Monsieur le Marquis that in my turn I have finally intrigued you a little?"

"To the point that I have the greatest curiosity to learn how you have been able to prepare this interesting vengeance."

"*Mon Dieu*! Nothing was simpler. The day after the day the Doctor had taken me in so well, I went to a sculptor friend to ask him to open his purse to me. He had just finished a bust of Monsieur de Lucheux, made from a plaster mold of the face of the dead man. You understand that, from the same mold, I could obtain a frighteningly real mask."

"Very good! But the part that the Marquise played in the death of Monsieur de Lucheux, who told you that?"

"After having been exemplarily discreet about his relationship with Madame de Camembert, Lefebvre admitted everything to me when he found she didn't even deign to remember his name.

"Then he has returned, that excellent Commandant Lefebvre?"

"The poor man! On the contrary, he is on his way to Madagascar, where he is probably going to find other deceptions after those of the *Champ d'Asile*, but before his departure, I was able to talk to him at some length."

"Here?" Lupiano asked.

"Oh, no, Monsieur le Marquis. In Texas, where I've come from."

"What! You undertook that voyage just to get that information from him?"

"Exactly. Wouldn't you have done the same?"

"Well, yes; but except for you and I, I hardly know any man capable of going so far to get information"

"On leaving you," Lelouard continued, "I was desperate, the victim of one of the most humiliating jokes. Under the burden of a debt that didn't allow me to get revenge for that detestable trick, I was prey to a furious desire for vengeance. In thinking about it deeply, I persuaded myself that between Lefebvre and Madame de Camembert, there must have been something more than what he had told me. You yourself, Marquis, had excited my curiosity to the highest degree, and it wasn't difficult to see that, around you, if one managed to put himself in a not respectable situation, there was something to glean. To write to Lefebvre would not have been very conclusive. To be sure of getting all the truth from him, I had to talk to him in person. Thanks to my friend the Sculptor, and to a business man to whom I sold my arrears from the State at a discount, I had, and well beyond that, the sum necessary for my trip. Then, being in possession of your secrets and those of Madame de Camembert, I had been back about a week when the advertisement of your masked ball gave me the idea to put into operation, under this disguise, the precious discoveries that I have reported."

"You are far from knowing all of my secrets," Lupiano replied, "but you are, nonetheless, a man of resolution and unusual perspicacity; and instead of merely gleaning, it is up to you to harvest until your hands are full around me. But before I open myself to you without reservations, there is one last curiosity. What did you say to Madame de Camembert to cause her to faint? She isn't a woman to be easily intimidated. And, under her mask, how could you be sure you were speaking to her?"

"It was precisely talking to her about the small mark on her shoulder that helped me to recognize her, and I was able to frighten her to the point of making her lose consciousness. But I must give her justice: when I accused her of having been the cause of the death of Monsieur de Lucheux, she didn't blink."

"But that mark," Lupiano asked. "What is so unusual about it?"

"Monsieur," the wholesaler said, "the first time that I went to see Madame Camembert, I noticed that she had a little bright red stain on her shoulder, that could have been taken for an insect bite. Certainly, during our first encounter, if she had received me as I had a right to expect, instead of sending me away so rudely, I would have called her attention to the danger that threatened her rare beauty.

"What!" said Lupiano. "You believe that something so little apparent that even I didn't even notice it, could be a sign of something serious?"

"I am speaking, Marquis," Lelouard answered, "from my personal experience. Ten years ago, something of the same nature appeared on one of my arms. I didn't pay any attention to it, just like Madame Camembert. It grew larger, became swollen, and when I finally spoke to my doctor about it, he recognized what they called a *tissu érectile,* a kind of subcutaneous fungus, capable of taking on enormous dimensions.[123] I got rid of it only with a bloody operation which left a large scar."

"The Devil!" Lupiano said. "A scar on the shoulder of a pretty woman—that's a thought that would made the most courageous faint."

"The danger is not yet great," Lelouard said, "but in about six months, that mark that I noticed, because there is no better observer of a pathological case than the one who himself has gone through it, appears to me to have made some notable progress, and if the Doctor is as clever a medical practitioner as he is a clever piquet player, you would do well, my dear Marquis, to place her in his hands."

"Yes, certainly," said Lupiano. "It will be taken care of. The dear Marquise is our joy and pride, and something that might spoil her beauty would become a cause for mourning, a calamity for everyone of us."

It isn't necessary to reproduce here the content of the confidences into which Lupiano entered almost immediately with the new recruit. These two men were evidently made to understand each other, and the next day, with the enrollment of Lelouard, the thirteenth seat in the Red Brotherhood, until then still vacant, couldn't have been more usefully filled.

During the month of January 1820, that is to say, some months after Lelouard's recruitment, and after he had, in many other occasions, justified the high opinion that the Marquis

---

[123] Rabou is confusing erectile tissues with what looks like a mycosis, or fungal infection of the skin. *Tinea versicolor,* for example, is caused by a fungus that lives in the skin and produces spots that are either lighter than the skin or a reddish brown.

had had of his resolution and mental resources, Lupiano saw him enter one day with a letter in his hand.

"What is that?" the Marquis asked.

"A letter from Lefebvre, who writes to me from Madagascar. The good man, without knowing it, gives us more than one piece of precious information! Read it!"

My dear friend, Lefebvre wrote, *I didn't make a bad move in coming here, and, almost on arriving I found my niche. King Radama-Manijaka, the head of the powerful Hovas tribe, who finally conquered the entire island of Madagascar, likes Europeans very much, and most of all, as they told me in Texas, he is passionate about a former companion in arms of Napoleon.*

As soon as I disembarked, I was introduced to a man from Malta, a former surgeon in the Republican army, and, like us, very enthusiastic about the Emperor. With his ability in surgery and other talents, he has so well ingratiated himself with the King of the Hovas that he is today First Minister and and has even married a cousin of the Queen.

Through him, I became straight away a General in the army that the King would like to organize after the European fashion. There is even a possibility of my becoming Minister of War, seeing that the native who is presently holding that post understands about as much about war as the old beasts of emigrants who, in France, at the present time, are routinely made generals and colonels.

But my nomination must be handled from a distance, because in that mahogany court of the King of the Hovas, there are as many intrigues, and perhaps even more, than in European courts—only here, those things play out with the knife or, better still, with tanguin, *a kind of local poison used to put criminals to death. That's their own version of the guillotine, but it's also very nicely used in society. However, I can't be slow in getting that portfolio. My friend, the man from Malta, wants the thing done before his departure for France, where he is soon to go in order to negotiate a treaty of friendship and commerce with your cowardly government.*

He's a strange fellow, that man, who was here and has supported me so well. Although we have both been around quite a bit, his life is filled with even more events than yours or mine. We are a great resource for each other in the middle of all these savages. We have become very tight, and he has shared all his adventures with me. It is strange how fate sometimes brings people together! For at one time, he was also employed by that infamous Secret Bureau, to which I owe all my misfortune! And they were so gentle and fatherly towards him that, because of some small misdeeds committed during the exercise of his functions, they delivered him to the English to be hanged! It's true that, under the Emperor, the English had already asked for his return, claiming that he had been the cause for the sinking of several of their vessels, causing major losses in both lives and goods. But the Emperor hadn't wanted to give them that pleasure, and it took the Restoration to engage in such base actions.

However, as that devil of a man always takes care of himself, and doesn't leave it to someone else, just as he was about to be hanged, he informed the Lord of the Treasury about a counterfeiting operation involving the Bank of England, by means of which his sentence was commuted to deportation to Botany Bay. [124]

From there, he found a way to escape and arrived in Madagascar, where knowing, as they say, both God and the

---

[124] See Volume 3, page 255. Somehow, Rabou was planning to write about Matiphous' adventures in Australia, as indicated in his original outline, since there should have been a section entitled "Botany Bay" between those entitled "Britannicus the Black" and "Commandant Lefebvre" in Volume 3, but never did. As was the custom of the times, it is entirely possible that this was the result of editorial interference, Rabou being asked to cut short this plot thread that might have proved unpopular with the readers.

Devil, he immediately met a former friend whom he encountered there to guide him. When I say "friend," that depends on the circumstances. In a foreign country, there is no rank and grade, and one should not disdain anyone's help. That friend was a Negro that he once had in his service in France. Since he had returned to his native land, that man had arrived just in time to provide introductions and serve as his interpreter.

And I learned yet another evil deed perpetrated by that abominable office of letter-openers! That poor African devil, by following an employee of that villainous place, was on the verge of discovering the entry into the Secret Bureau, so what did those scoundrels do? They framed him up and, to stop him from talking, they sent him to prison. The unfortunate man still doesn't know why he spent several years in jail, since if Matiphous (that's the name of my man from Malta) was willing to talk frankly to me about having been employed by that shady operation, naturally he didn't want to share the same confidence with that black man whom he has hired again in his service as his intendant, since he is now highly placed. He said further that this is a secret that shouldn't be spread around, expecting that, if the Hovas become more civilized, it might perhaps become useful to set up a little Secret Bureau in Madagascar. Power changes men's minds so much that it convinces them to find good what they have otherwise condemned in another country.

As far as the French Secret Bureau is concerned, Matiphous is planning to do something better than merely blame it. Once he's in Paris, he proposes, using his position as Special Envoy, which will make him untouchable, to stage a confrontation with his former colleagues, and as he won't lack funds, he will pay, if he has to, journalists who, moderately financed, will write whatever one wishes, to expose very loudly the turpitudes which he witnessed and which he will call to their attention.

He will certainly contact you because when he leaves, I will give him a letter for you. If you can help him in his fight against the letter openers, I will say frankly, my dear friend, that you will oblige me enough.

As for the famous Marquis de Lupiano, when I described to Matiphous the affair that forced me to leave France, he believes he knows him. He says he is a very dangerous man who, in fact, deceives indiscriminately and, it would seem, changes his name as he does his shirt. But what's more, he assassinates and poisons for the least thing and must be approached with caution because he always has a band of brigands in his pay. Profit by this information, and if you still want to get revenge, wait until Matiphous, who knows that person well, arrives to give you a hand.

As I mentioned, it won't be long before he arrives. He has already chartered a ship that is setting sail for Bordeaux. He has retained it just for himself, because he is bringing with him his Malgache wife, who wanted to go on the voyage, and he has a very large retinue that is part of his entourage, among whom, oddly enough, is Britannicus, the native I told you about above.

One very big question is, once I'm Minister, should I ask my wife to join here? She could come to me on the same ship as Matiphous when he returns. I like the thought of having her with me, feeling really much affection for her, but here is the problem: at her age, she still carries the ridiculous notion of being jealous. There are pretty women here, in shades more or less dark, who don't ask anything better than to help me pass the time, so her being here would give rise to endless scenes. However, I will decide before Matiphous' departure, and if he is to bring her back with him, I will charge you, my dear friend, with getting them in touch with each other so that she can be ready to leave when he returns.

With this, I shake your hand and ask you to believe forever in the old affection of your devoted friend,
The Division General,

Lefebvre

"That's very good," Lupiano said, after finishing his reading. "To teach Monsieur Lefebvre to mind his own business, we will send him Madame his wife. As for Monsieur Matiphous, who does in fact know me, and with whom Montalvi and I, have more than one old account to settle, we are going to see about snatching him on the way. That Maltese, what does he think he's doing! To upset the Secret Bureau, the most beautiful jewel in our crown!"

III. The Return of the Bloodied Girl[125]

Several days after receiving that letter, Lupiano visited the Doctor's office. The Doctor, although one of the most active amongst the Marquis' associates, had, in the interest of the Brotherhood, kept a numerous and highly placed clientele, which he had previously gathered. A doctor is spontaneously initiated into so many secrets without counting the thousand hidden things he has to look into.

"Doctor," the Marquis said upon entering, "I have come to ask you for a consultation."

"What's wrong with you?" the Doctor answered. "You don't appear to me to be very ill."

"On the contrary, I come rather to ask your advice on an extraordinary matter."

"I'm listening, Marquis. I am certainly the man to cure you of your problem."

"You know," Lupiano replied, "what has been agreed on? That we will send to Bordeaux, before Monsieur Matiphous arrives, a siren instructed to bring him back to us, his feet and wrists tied together."

"Yes, and that siren is our dear Marquise, and Montalvi would be accompanying her."

"I have changed all that."

"Why?"

---

[125] For this chapter, the reader might want to reread Volume I, Prologue, Chapter IV.

"First of all, in thinking it over, I told myself that it is impossible that, in a great city like Bordeaux, Madame de Camembert wouldn't be recognized by someone. Then, I found that, for some time now, she's been on unusually friendly terms with Montalvi, and a *tête-à-tête* of two or three weeks might bring to fruition those amorous feelings..."

"Are you jealous?" the doctor asked.

"No, thank God! I don't behave that youthfully. The Marquise is a woman whose mind and resolute character I admire, but her type of beauty is not one of those that can turn my head. Only, in the middle of a business as serious as ours, I don't like to have to deal with two lovers and their affairs. You know as well as I do the possible consequences. I have then decided that, in the place of the Marquise, I will find some other enchantress."

"To unearth one as valuable as her won't be easy."

"Oh! I know, Doctor, that you also have a weakness for her. I am somewhat informed about what happens in my business, and the other day you were seen placing a respectful kiss on her white shoulders."

"Your Hindu is a stupid spy," the Doctor quickly replied. "I had just taken off the bandage of caustic potassium over the little wound that I had made on her shoulder to get rid of the dangerous fungus that Lelouard had pointed out. It was doing well. When I announced a complete cure to her and that there would be no scar, she exclaimed effusively. '*My good, my excellent Doctor! I want to kiss you!*' I then brushed my lips across the place I had just cleansed. I could have done that in your presence, and indeed in front of the whole universe, without anyone thinking there had been any harm in it. Those are little medical liberties to which the slightest importance shouldn't be attached."

"Nevertheless," the Marquis continued, "as irresistible as your beautiful sick woman might be, I have got it into my head to find someone to replace her. Just today, as I was walking with Montalvi across the Panorama Passage when fate made me put my hand on the one I was looking for."

"And what was that triumphant beauty doing outside?"

"At the moment when we were passing, she was leaving the shop of a toilette merchant named Madame Constantin."

"A bad origin," said the Doctor. "Some kept girl."

"Precisely," Lupiano replied. "One with the magnificent and copious attractions which must speak to the senses of Monsieur the Malgache Envoy in a different way than the grand air and the somewhat disdainful elegance of the Marquise. Just imagine, my dear fellow, someone marvelous to find, some very unusual individual, for the role we have for her to play. Information obtained from the second-hand dealer says that's a creature who carries misfortune with her; all her lovers have ended in a violent death, and that happened so often that she has come to have the rather significant nickname of the *Bloodied Girl*."

"Georgiana!" exclaimed the Doctor, who moved about easily in the world of the courtesans. "I only know that one."

"Well, well! What do you know about her?"

"She is, in fact, remarkably beautiful, but she hasn't been heard from for some time. I thought she had disappeared from the Paris horizon."

"I think it was because, as it seems, terror has made a wide void around her. Having myself gone to her domicile, I found her in a poor little apartment at the back of a courtyard, Rue Roquépine. There, just as I arrived, a bailiff was busy collecting her meager furnishings. Everything in her apartment showed misfortune. She has come to the last degree of abandon. So, you can't imagine how providential I appeared to her!"

"So you have hired her? That's marvelous, and I think that Monsieur Matiphous only has to appear on the scene to be caught like a fish. But what was that extraordinary matter that you came to talk to me about?"

"That matter, Doctor, is Mademoiselle Georgiana herself. Would you believe that I'm afraid that I've fallen in love with her?"

"You, Marquis?" responded the Doctor with an imperceptible smile.

"Yes, my dear fellow, me. I'm sixty-two-years-old. For a long time, women haven't meant much to me, so I am totally astonished at what I feel. Has Nature willed that between certain organisms there may be irresistible affinities? What is certain is that, for a long time, no woman has attracted me as that woman has. It seems as if there are treasures of happiness in store for me there. Is that a deceptive instinct? Should I give in to it? Or must I fight that attraction as being a vain and dangerous?

"Marquis," the medical doctor said, "you make a habit of playing with every danger. You should be careful. That girl's influence is something serious. Set free in Paris about 1811 by Mirza Babba, the Persian Ambassador, who was causing so much excitement at that time,[126] by the beginning of 1814 she had already counted four victims: a very young man named Alexis Vandel..."

"Vandel, the son of the former Director of the Secret Bureau?[127]" Lupiano quickly interrupted.

"Yes," the Doctor said.

"Well! I love her just for that, that good Georgiana. The father of that young man was one of my mortal enemies. Without knowing it, she has worked toward my vengeance."

"Very good, but to this first murder, you must add that of the famous merchant, François-Honoré Dubignon; that of Colonel Saint-Clair; that of General Comte de Chandeville, killed in a duel with a Russian..."

"Not true, if you please," Lupiano quickly replied. "The Comte de Chandeville was indeed supposed to fight his duel with a foreign officer, but before they encountered each other, I picked a quarrel with him and I had the advantage of dispatching him in the Vincennes Woods with a pistol shot. That old beau had, by way of parentheses, a somewhat unsteady

---

[126] See Volume 2, pages 130 seq.
[127] See Volume 2, pages 211 seq.

hand. His ball, after having gone through my hat, went on to find Montalvi's wife in the bushes, and stretched her out dead." [128]

"Montalvi's wife!" the Doctor exclaimed with astonishment. "Then Georgiana would be our friend's daughter. He recognized that the unfortunate woman struck by the General's stray bullet, whose autopsy I made, was the mother of a young girl taken away from her in her infancy, and who was none other than your Bloodied Girl. At the Opera, she thought she recognized the Russian Major who had been her ravisher. The duel with the Conte de Chandeville resulted from that. The poor mother ran to the dueling field to find out the truth when the shot meant for you hit her."

"I don't know anything about all that," Lupiano responded. "The evening of my duel with the Comte, accompanied by Montalvi, who was my witness, I was in a hurry to leave Paris. We had scarcely left the Vincennes dungeon and didn't think it prudent to wait to see how the police would consider that massacre."

"But that wasn't all," the Doctor added. "That evening, the Russian committed suicide, so that foreigner, the Comte de Chandeville, and her mother, made up the mortuary tally of that fatal girl for just one day."

"Oh! My God!" Lupiano said. "What a story!"

"To that it has to be added that, just when the Comte was on the dueling field on her behalf, she had herself taken away by a rich Englishman to London. There, she wasn't slow in becoming a widow. Back in Paris, she had still some more success with the undertaker, but by then I had lost track of her."

"We must again modify our program," Lupiano said, without pausing at all those discouraging details. "I cannot send Montalvi to accompany her."

---

[128] For the story of that duel, see Volume 3, pages 176 seq.

"It's sure," the Doctor said, "that a father sent to conduct his daughter where you are going to send her, would be playing an unusual role."

"It's not that," replied the Marquis. "Georgiana is not Montalvi's daughter; he is only her step-father. Her mother had an affair before their marriage. He had assumed the paternity of that child, but he hated having her in his house, so when she reached the age of five or six, he started to think about getting rid of her, and ended up selling her in Livorno to a man who supplied harems."

"But… Our friend is a monster, then! That idea is hellish," the Doctor exclaimed.

"Pah! He did much worse to his wife, whom he thought he had something to complain about. One of these days I'll tell you about his vengeance *with Genoa sauce,* and you will see that, compared to that terrible righter of wrongs, we are but little saints. And just because of that, I don't want to put the poor girl into his hands. Who knows if his still fierce hatred would cause him to do something bad to her."

"Or even," said the Doctor, smiling at a horrible supposition, "that he wouldn't be tempted by a charming ragout of a quasi-incest. In case your tender and vague desires become reality, that would become a throat-cutting obstacle between you and him."

"Doctor," Lupiano said with some solemnity, "I renew my question: Do you believe that certain women have the ability to affect us in an unusual way, so much so that where death seems to have occurred, suddenly life is revived again?"

"Without a doubt, that is possible. There are some people exhalations of whom seem to have with our nature what I would call an unexplainable congruity. The Germans have some unusual ideas on that subject. They claim that each individual looks for the other half of himself that has gone astray into the other sex, and that perfect happiness is in the union of those parts coming together as a whole person. I admit, however, that Georgiana is not exactly the complement I would have desired for you."

"Come dine with me this evening, Doctor," Lupiano said, rising. "You will see her. In a few hours she should be installed into one of the apartments in my townhouse. Perhaps by studying her a little, you will judge her less severely."

"Oh! I have known her for a long time," the Doctor said, "She's a true odalisque,[129] a pure-blooded courtesan, not only in mentality but in heart."

"But magnificently beautiful," replied Lupiano with excitement.

"And you want to send her to that Matiphous to seduce him! Be careful, Marquis, that is not a girl who does things half-way. You may next find that she has too religiously accomplished her mission."

"I haven't said anything yet to her about her mission," the Marquis replied. "Still, come; we will talk again about all this. And if we have to look for some other woman, Paris is big; we will find one."

IV. Chaste Suzanne

On entering the drawing room where, at the Lupiano townhouse, people usually gathered before dinner, the Doctor found neither Montalvi nor Madame de Camembert, who were the habitual dinner guests. Walking with large steps around the room, Lupiano's customary attitude showed extreme preoccupation.

"What have you done," the Doctor asked, "with the Count and the Marquise?"

"Don't talk to me about them," Lupiano replied. "You see me in a virtual civil war. Madame de Camembert finds herself insulted because I thought of bringing Georgiana here, as if I could have that girl leave from her own place, so that everyone knew where I was sending her. As for Monsieur de

---

[129] An odalisque was a chambermaid or a female attendant in a Turkish seraglio, particularly the court ladies in the household of the Ottoman sultan.

Montalvi, he doesn't understand why everyone doesn't admire his method of putting children into the slavery of harems, and because I made him understand that it would perhaps be inconvenient for him to encounter his earlier victim, by whom he could be recognized, just as she recognized the Russian Major, he became furious and left."

"You are right, Marquis, it's not good to introduce lovers into the business of our association."

"What lovers are you talking about?" Lupiano asked with vehemence. "Just as I was going to pick up that young lady—it had been agreed that I would send my carriage to get her at about six o'clock, and that she would come and take up her residence here—my coachman came back empty-handed. He learned from the concierge of that impertinent girl that two other gentlemen had come in a carriage to pick her up, and that she had left with them."

"Ah!" said the Doctor, "she's not an easy girl to bridle. Do you want me to go to her place and find out what that running away means?"

"I don't want anything," Lupiano replied. "I want us to sit down at the table and have dinner. Tomorrow, I'm going to bring all our people together, pay them for their services, and tell them to seek their fortune elsewhere. In two days, I will be on the way to India, where I will finish my life peacefully."

Knowing that resolutions made when irritated shouldn't be contradicted, the Doctor replied:

"That is perhaps not a bad idea. Without a great deal of usefulness, we are engaged in a dangerous game. The police could finally take it the wrong way that we are stealing its jobs. However, I want to have a clear conscience about what has happened to Mademoiselle Georgiana, and in less than a half-hour, I hope to give you a full accounting."

"But, my dear fellow, you won't find anyone at her place. I, myself, immediately paid the back wages of the chambermaid, telling her she was free, and that I was sending her mistress to Italy."

"In any case, I'm going to go see for myself," the Doctor answered.

Clairvoyant enough to see that his insistence was far from being displeasing, he jumped into a cabriolet that, for pressing matters, was always ready under one of the sheds of the townhouse.

Shortly thereafter, he reappeared in the drawing-room where Lupiano was waiting for him.

"Well!" said the Doctor, "your runaway's absence is now explained."

"How's that?" the Marquis asked with curiosity.

"You know, or perhaps you don't know, that right now the Theater of the Porte Saint-Martin is putting on, under the title of *Chaste Suzanne,* a grand Biblical ballet for which it has spent considerable money."

"What does *Chaste Suzanne* have to do with Mademoiselle Georgiana?"

"Let me tell you. What seems most of all to attract the crowd is the heroine that they propose to show in the most audacious *décolleté*. The role was intended for a remarkably beautiful actress named Mademoiselle Bégrand."[130]

"I still don't see the rapport," Lupiano said, "that this can have with what happened to me."

"On the contrary," the Doctor replied, "there's a very natural chain of events. In her quality as an officially recognized attractive woman, Mademoiselle Bégrand believes she is authorized to commit all kinds of caprices, and this afternoon, some hours before the dress rehearsal, she let it be known that she was indisposed."

"Is it with Mademoiselle Georgiana that they want to replace her?"

---

[130] Author's note: "See the newspapers of the time." Mademoiselle Bégrand was an attractive dancing girl who indeed played the lead in the not-so-chaste ballet *Chaste Suzanne* at the Theatre de la Porte Saint-Martin dressed only in a semi-transparent gown in 1826.

"Exactly. A friend of the director pointed out that the defection of Mademoiselle Bégrand threatened a mortal embarrassment, and this evening, just as our beautiful odalisque was getting ready to come to you, they came to get her to replace the delinquent one."

"But you can't improvise being an actress!"

"The role is silent and rather undemanding. It's only a question of spreading out her beautiful figure in front of the public. Besides, it's more than probable that, despite her good will, Mademoiselle Georgiana won't actually appear on the night of the opening. As soon as she felt herself near to being replaced, Mademoiselle Bégrand, as if by magic, found herself in radiantly good health."

"And that stupid woman is ready to compromise the magnificent situation I was preparing for her, in order to play, in the wings, the role of an understudy?"

"That's precisely what her maid pointed out to her. She said she had fought with all her strength the notion that Georgiana should break her word to you. But you understand, just the idea of being put in competition with one of the prettiest women in the city carried her beyond any other consideration."

"So that," Lupiano said, "at this moment, perhaps, that woman who spoke to my heart, is displaying the secret of her charms before the public."

"Oh!" the Doctor replied, "but they remain hidden under a flesh-colored garment falling below her knees. And then, this is only a dress rehearsal."

"Where," replied the Marquis, "there are almost as many people as at a first representation. Besides, couldn't one go to that dress rehearsal?"

"I believe so. I'm somewhat acquainted with the Director of the Porte-Saint-Martin, and by mentioning your name..."

"I don't want to ask for my admission as a favor," replied Lupiano, "and find myself obliged to that gentleman."

He then picked up a pen and wrote:

In the envelope, with the letter, he placed a five-hundred
franc bill, and gave it to be delivered.

"That's royally paid," said the Doctor.

"Or nothing given, if the man knows how to act. But I
would prefer that he kept the money."

After this exchange, Lelouard was announced and introduced.

"Ah! My dear fellow," Lupiano said, "you arrive like the
Messiah!"

He led him into a corner where they conferred with great
animation. After they finished talking, Lelouard quickly left
the drawing room, just as the messenger sent to the Theater
returned with the Director's response.

"You see, my friend, that he has bravely kept my money," said the Marquis, after having unsealed a fold under
which he found an entry pass. "But, we won't have enough
time to have dinner. We're going to have a biscuit with some
Madera, and we will have supper this evening when we return."

Before leaving, Lupiano called his Hindu, to whom he
gave some instructions in a low voice, and twenty minutes
later, he and the Doctor were sitting in a well-located box in
the Theater of the Porte-Saint-Martin. There, nothing remarkable happened.

"So then, Marquis, what does she look like to you?"
asked the Doctor when Georgiana came onto the stage.

"As the men of the people say," Lupiano answered,
"she's a superb woman, but my taste for her is totally extinct.
That grand publicity given to her charms had on me the effect
of cold water poured over my head. She will be excellent for

Monsieur Matiphous, to whom we will decidedly dispatch her.”

On entering the drawing room that they had left some hours before, the Doctor and Lupiano found it filled with dresses, hats, pieces of cloth, in the middle of which there was an ankle-length fur coat trimmed and lined with sable and two magnificent cashmeres from India.

“There, if I’m not mistaken, “said the Doctor, “is the wedding trousseau that you have ordered for Mademoiselle Georgiana. I very much doubt that the Director of the Porte-Saint-Martin theater could have done things as well.”

The Marquis, without answering, glanced at all that brilliant paraphernalia of ladies’ apparel. He carefully put it together in a corner of the drawing-room and, little by little, hid it behind a wall of chairs. Hearing the sound of a carriage enter the courtyard of the townhouse, he went to a window to see what guests where coming to see him at that ungodly hour.

“Ah!” he said happily. “Lelouard is decidedly a clever man.”

Georgiana, to whom Lelouard was giving his hand, appeared two minutes later.

“Finally,” said Lupiano, going to meet the newcomer, “here you are, beautiful young lady. We have truly had a great deal of trouble to get you here.”

“But, Monsieur,” Georgiana said, “by what right have you had me brought here at near midnight? You have no power over me.”

“I beg your pardon. A short time ago, you did me the honor of promising me that you would come and live in my townhouse. As a consequence, I hurried to pay the bailiff I found installed at your place. Afterward, I got in touch with your concierge, that you told me was a very worthy man who could be trusted, and after having left him money to pay the other creditors who might appear, I instructed him, with your agreement, to take care of selling the small amount of furniture that I had just kept from being seized. Finally, I paid your chambermaid, who, for more than two years, had not received any wages. It therefore seems to me that all that constitutes a serious arrangement."

"But what do you want? To be my lover? You are old. You don't seem to me to be in good health. If you happened to die, they will again say that I am the cause. That finally becomes tedious."

"Not at all, Mademoiselle; I don't at all aspire to the dangerous happiness that you are imagining. I want you to be mine, but like a beautiful statue, not anything else. For that, I had offered you a salary of twenty-five thousand francs, a vehicle, lodgings in this townhouse. You accepted it with a certain eagerness."

"Then why were you worried if I would be faithful to you?"

"Because I don't like to be ridiculed, and I don't want the public to know the extent of our liaison. I don't want to look like a deceived lover. What's more, the situation that I count on setting up between us shouldn't be in any way disagreeable to you, since you yourself told me that you have never been in love in your life."

"Well! I certainly wouldn't want to begin with you. Someone has come to offer me something that suits me better. I will give you back what you have spent for me and I ask you not to detain me any longer."

"No," said the Marquis. "I'm not someone who has just loaned you some money. I am someone who adores you, whose homages you have been very willing to accept. I'm not letting myself be deposed immediately. Do you want to know what's going to happen to you? They took you as a substitute for an actress who, like you, has caprices, and who refused to go on stage this evening. But tomorrow, she will come to put herself at the disposition of the Director. You are as beautiful, more beautiful, perhaps. However, she will be preferred to you, because she is a consummate actress, and you are not, and I know whereof I speak, for I was present just a short while ago at the rehearsal. You know nothing about the profession. Then, if the Director is generous, which I have some reasons to doubt, he will send you, for tonight's performance, a thousand-franc bill. You will spend it for perfume or on some other luxuries that you find at Madame Constantin's. At the end of forty-eight hours, you will find yourself in the same deplorable position from which I have just taken you."

"If I want to be unhappy, that's nobody's business."

"Don't say childish things, my dear love. Can you do without luxury? You would steal to have cashmere... look..." he added, briskly exhibiting the *novelty* items which he taken the trouble to hide as a surprise. "Do me the pleasure of looking at these and tell me what you think of them."

Achilles, when at the Court of King Lycomedes,[131] offered weapons, wasn't any more prompt to drop his feminine disguise.

"Ah! the beautiful shawls," exclaimed Georgiana, rushing forward. "Those are real ones, from India. Mirza Babba, my Ambassador, didn't have even one worth as much as those."

"And those hats, those dresses, that fabric from Leroy[132] and from Pradel, don't seem to me something to disdain either," Lupiano said, smiling.

---

[131] At the request of Thetis, Lycomedes, King of Scyros, concealed Achilles in female disguise among his own daughters. There, the Greek warrior had an affair with Deidamia, which resulted in the birth of Neoptolemus (Pyrrhus). As Odysseus drew Achilles out of his disguise and took him to Troy, Neoptolemus stayed with his grandfather until he too was summoned during the later stages of the Trojan War. Not existing in Homer's *Iliad*, this episode is written down in detail in a later version of the story, *The Achilleid*, by the Roman poet Statius.

[132] Louis Hippolyte Leroy (1763-1829), founder of the House of Leroy, one of the foremost fashion houses of the early 19th century First Empire Paris. He was known as the favorite fashion trader and the official fashion designer of empress Josephine de Beauharnais. He was very successful and also pro-

"All that is for me?"

"Without a doubt, my child. And you'll have to agree that is well worth the flesh-colored outfit that the Director of the Porte-Saint-Martin Theater gave you. After that, if you like the comedy, we will have you play it for us, but clothed."

"What? Do you have a theater?"

"No, it's more a matter of a drawing-room comedy. Just imagine, my charming one, that I have a friend who has gone insane. He claims that women of color are infinitely preferable to white women."

"What a peculiar taste!" said Georgiana, standing in front of a mirror, trying on a delightful rose cape that had caught her attention. "Ah! Monsieur," she added, "look how it suits me. I would have ordered it if it had flattered me more."

"It makes you ravishingly beautiful; the Leroy fashions are always admirably successful. Well! Let's return to that friend of mine. In order to cure him of his passion for black women, I have arranged that he will see you in Bordeaux, where he is soon to disembark with a cargo of black and brown creatures, whom he talks about as if they were white women."

"Ah! To leave Paris, that doesn't suit me very much. I like it only here."

"Yes, but to leave for two, or three weeks at the most, in a comfortable carriage, accompanied by a respectable man who will pass for your husband, the boredom of your sojourn would be charmed by all the pleasures you would encounter in a big city. Would that be beyond your ability?"

"Well! You see, I have been in London with a very rich Englishman. My God, how bored I was there!"

"I can well believe it, because London is a foggy city, but Bordeaux has a superb climate, and so many claims to beauty. You're going to cause a revolution there as soon as you show yourself. And then, just think of what you're going

---

vided dresses for several other royal and Princely courts in Europe during the early 19th century.

to do! To uphold the honor of the white race against those native women that they dare prefer! You will be bewitching a man who has had the effrontery to claim that not one European woman is capable of making an impression on him.

"We'll see about that!" said Georgiana, draping herself in one of her cashmeres and trying to see herself from the back in a mirror.

"Then it's all agreed," said Lupiano. "And as for that poor man, his fate is settled. But since he's a friend, to whom I wouldn't want anything bad to happen, you must remember to keep your word to me. After you have stirred his heart well, I don't want you to go beyond a certain point with him in your flirtation. Besides, that's the best way to punish him for his blasphemies and depraved taste.

At that moment the clock struck midnight; it was a rare piece containing a carillon which played several airs.

"Say, then, Monsieur the Seducer," said Georgiana, upon hearing that music, "you told me this morning that your name was Hernandez, and that you were a Brazilian businessman. I really believe that you have lied to me."

"What gave you that idea?"

"That clock—it seems to me I have seen and heard it at the townhouse of the Marquis de Lupiano."

"You have been to the Marquis de Lupiano's?"

"Yes. Last year, I went to a big masked ball for the poor, where it cost one hundred francs to enter. I now recognize this drawing-room."

"Well, well, my beautiful one, don't you like me just as much as a Marquis as you did as a Brazilian merchant?"

"Ah! So you're that Lupiano whom they say is very rich! Now I'm not so surprised that you had me kidnapped. It seems that you are a domineering type of person, and no one is strong enough to resist you."

"I'm only domineering with people who want to play games with me and break their word to me, but to those who are cooperative, and who respond to my kind overtures, there is no better companion than I."

"This trip that you want me to take, will that be soon?"

"It will be tonight, if you continue to agree with me, because the friend in question may disembark at any time, and the least delay might cause us to fail."

"But this role that I must play on the spur of the moment... I'm very tired!"

"Then, let's begin by going to supper," said Lupiano, offering his arm to the courtesan. "During that time, they will bundle up all your arsenal of toilette articles, that you will add to when in Bordeaux. Resources are abundant there, and you won't lack money. If, after supper, you feel strong enough, the horses have been ordered, and you will start on your way. Otherwise, we will wait until the morning."

Georgiana's conquest wasn't very far advanced when the supper prepared with her in mind made her come around to all of the Marquis's wishes. A table service of magnificent, exquisite wines and that demonstration of wealth to which a woman of her kind always shows herself to be sensitive wasn't slow in bringing about in her a change of disposition. Becoming suddenly talkative and communicative ,she said to the Doctor, whom she hadn't noticed before:

"But I know you.. Aren't you the Marquis' doctor?"

"With your permission, my goddess."

"Then, if anything happened to him, you would be the one to call, not me."

"Oh! The Marquis is careful, and nothing will happen to him. He knows what a dangerous woman you are, and he has certainly promised me, as he told you a while ago, that you will be only a magnificent statue for him."

"That's what we will find out when I return," Georgiana replied. "Many others have said just as much."

"But first of all, let's take care of our Monsieur in Bordeaux. You will take care, isn't that true, of giving him a good lesson?"

"Don't worry about that. That one will become mad about me!"

"I must introduce you," said Lupiano, "to the respectable man that I'm going to give you as a pretend husband. You can see him over there," he added, pointing out Lelouard. "That's the man who has a brightly colored decoration in his lapel."

"That naughty man who, when the actors entered, had me get into an ugly hackney cab, telling me that he was the Theater secretary, and that the Director had told him to take me back to my place!"

"But," said Lupiano, "if the carriage wasn't brilliant, let's agree that the horses were good."

"As for that, yes! I thought they had the bit between their teeth, and it was only in the courtyard of your townhouse that I realized the trick that had been played on me."

"Do you regret it?" the Doctor asked.

"Not at all, and on the contrary," the courtesan answered, lifting her glass gaily, "I drink to the health of Monsieur my husband."

"Now," said the Marquis, rising, "let's go drink coffee and smoke tobacco. That's a custom of the harem of Mirza Babba that we must keep."

Going back into the drawing-room, completely at ease, the courtesan went to sit on a divan, her legs crossed in the Oriental fashion, and while drinking coffee and liqueurs, she smoked a magnificent water pipe that Lupiano had brought to her. The narcotic effect of the tobacco had, without a doubt, been increased with some substances that had been carefully mixed with it, because, at first, slightly drowsy, she soon fell into deep slumber.

"So, my dear Lelouard," the Marquis then said, "you're going to get on the road with her. You see how you must deal with her, a combination of gentleness and severity, but, most of all, surround her with all the pleasures of luxury. Don't let her get too familiar with you. Take care to write to us and I leave it to you to organize how Monsieur Matiphous will be drawn into our nets."

That said, Georgiana was wrapped in a *witchoura*[133] that Lelouard had been careful to put with her other presents. Still asleep, she was taken across the townhouse garden, right to the little door that we already know about. There, an overland carriage harnessed to horses belonging to the Marquis was waiting. It was to take the travelers to the first public way station, so that just in case of some trouble with the police, the point of departure of the intrigue could not immediately be identified.

Once Georgiana was warmly settled into the carriage, with Lelouard at her side, Lupiano wished them a good trip, and they started rapidly on their way.

V. An Ode of Horace

On February 13, 1889, a *Dimanche Gras*,[134] a day that Louvel's dagger[135] has marked forever in a bloody slash in history, that immense ossuary in Paris called the Catacombs was the theater of the most extraordinary and unexpected scene.

Just imagine, in the middle of that somber and solitary empire of death, a gallery inundated with light and decorated with fresh garlands, where the flower and the leafage of the rose laurel were married to tufts of perfumed violets. A long table had been set up in that gallery. Around it, in the place of seats, some reclining couches, decorated with purple covers,

---

[133] A fur-trimmed, warm, ankle-length winter fur coat, worn in the first third of the 19th century, from approximately 1880 until 1830. From the Polish *wiczura*.

[134] Trinity Sunday, the last Sunday before Carême.

[135] On 13 February 1820, the Duke of Berry was stabbed and mortally wounded when leaving the opera house in Paris with his wife, and died the next day. The assassin was a saddle maker named Louis Pierre Louvel (1783-1820), a Bonapartist opposed to the monarchy. Louvel was arrested and guillotined on June 6.

received the gently reclining guests. To see all the serving objects, the amphoras, the Etruscan pottery, the urns, the ewers, the richly incised cups, it was impossible to misunderstand the idea of a reconstruction of the Greek and Roman civilization which the organizer of that banquet had intended.

To complete the illusion, at the high end of the table, dressed in a sleeveless tunic, to which was fastened the skin of a panther and her head crowned with roses intermingled with reeds and ivy, a woman held in her hands a harp in the form of a lyre. Inspired by the contrast of the place so proper to evoke that philosophic thought that among the ancient mingled, even in the orgy, the memory of Death, she was chanting some verses that, like the rest of the scene, one would think a free translation of that ode of Horace to *Postumus*:[136]

Who among us, in these days of feasts,
Can count on new days?
The ivy that adorns our heads
Tomorrow will grow on our tombs.

Let us say, however, that the exterior of those who listened to her did not follow to excess the imitation of antiquity. Just like the queen of the festivity, their heads were adorned with flowers and leaves, but in their long silk robes, the color of fire, surmounted by a hood thrown back, they would be taken instead for a conclave of cardinals seated at the table of some capricious courtesan.

The reader, we hope, would not misunderstand, and he has without a doubt guessed that the terrible association of the Red Brotherhood was in the process of celebrating in their own fashion the joyous solemnity of the Carnival. Now, were those people only there for the banquet, and, in any event, how had their hostess procured access to that strange place where

---

[136] Book II, Ode XIV, but the version quoted by Rabou doesn't look much like Horace's original Ode.

the feast was celebrated? Those are two questions that our story is going to answer.

As soon as had Lupiano found himself in possession of the subterranean tunnel that connected his townhouse to the *Cour de France,* he had calculated that, through that tunnel, he could easily gain access to the catacombs. Their main entry bordered on the *Barrière d'Enfer,*[137] near which the buildings of the former farm that he had acquired were also situated. Following those plans, his associates had executed the necessary work, and by means of a shaft fitted with a spiral staircase, they had reached the level of the funereal galleries. By means of a horizontal passageway, they had made an opening to the level where the human bones uniformly rested. Setting up a steel door, and continuing their industrious arrangement, those bones now hid, to the point of being almost invisible, the method of entry that the Marquis had thus created.

That conquest had remained of mediocre use to the Marquis for a long time. Once only, he had used it to prodigiously puzzle the Police by continuing, with the murder of an unfortunate guardian of the ossuary, the series of mysterious executions that he undertook in the name of his private justice. But with the reception prepared for Matiphous, it will be seen that a great role had been reserved for that terrifying place into which, at any hour of the day or night, Lupiano could have access.

---

[137] The Barrière d'Enfer (Gate of Hell) was a pair of tollhouses that once served as a gate through the Wall of the Farmers-General at the current location of the Place Denfert-Rochereau. The name comes from the Rue d'Enfer (now Rue Denfert-Rochereau). Some historians think it was thus named because it was a place of debauchery and robbery, while others believe the name comes from the Latin Via Inferior (in contrast with Rue Saint-Jacques, which was known as Via Superior), or derived from the nickname *en fer* (of iron) given to a door on the Wall of Philip II Augustus.

The morning of February 13, Lelouard, returning from Bordeaux, where he had spent about three weeks, had come to give an account to the Marquis and to announce the return of the courtesan in the evening, bringing Matiphous with her.

That same evening, dressed in the red domino costume that was the official costume of the Brotherhood, and holding in his hand a lighted torch, Lupiano, his twelve affiliates following him, had left the townhouse on the Rue Notre-Dame-des-Champs. Through the underground tunnel, in the evening, they had gone in a single file right to the door giving entry into the catacombs.

Arrived at that gloomy enclosure, they found a limited space, covered on one side by a vast red drapery descending from the top to the ground, and on the other, by a stage with a chair covered by a canopy situated on top. At the base of the stage, from left to right, twelve seats were aligned. The space in between held a table covered with a red cloth. The same color was present in all the decoration of the room, lit by a wrought iron lamp. The arrangement had the appearance of a law court.

When the twelve seats were occupied by the members, Lupiano mounted the chair and said to them:

"Brothers and friends… In a few hours, a man will appear before you. Guilty of a great number of misdeeds, he is recommended most of all to your severity by his attempt, of which we have written proof, to bring trouble into the affairs of our Brotherhood. To put him to death and to bury him obscurely in a corner of these galleries is incontestably our right, and by that, we would have provided sufficiently for our safety. But that clandestine manner would not have matched the dignity of our justice. In a short while, you will give your approval, I think, to a more maturely thought out and a little less clandestine scheme, by which we will have completed the destruction of that inconvenient man who has thrown himself in our path.

"But for now, while waiting for his hour to come, let's not forget the joyous customs of the day that unites us. A few steps from here, our excellent friend, Madame de Camembert, has been busy providing for our pleasures, and in the things she has arranged for us, you will find the usual trace of her lively and poetic imagination."

That said, Lupiano came down from the chair of his Presidency, and led the associations' members to a brightly- lit space that could be seen around the corner of a gallery. He suddenly put them in the presence of the splendid banquet where the Marquise was going to do the honors, after having set up all the details with the true patience of an archeologist and a scholar.

As the banquet was drawing to its close, a hired carriage crossed the enclosure of the *Cour de France*. Immediately, Lelouard, who had gone out several times to look for the arrival of the two lovers, told Lupiano that the game he had set to catch was caught in the trap.

"Let's let him first sit down at the table," the Marquis answered. "As for you, my charming friend," he added, addressing Madame de Camembert, "since at all costs you want to be responsible for the transportation, I believe the moment has come to set up your trap."

When he had arrived in Paris, Matiphous believed in good faith that he had abducted Lelouard's wife. And as a naïve accomplice in the betrayal for which she had been used as a tool, Georgiana remained persuaded that the confusion of being surprised in the act with a white woman was, for a man who adored African beauties, all the salt and the danger of the mystification that had been so patiently prepared for him.

As a consequence, carrying out point by point the instructions that she had received, in order to arrange for Lelouard, who couldn't get started on the road but some hours after her, to get to Paris ahead of her, she had asked her traveling companion to stop mid-way for one night of rest. Then, on her arrival, she had stopped at the house of a Madame Lacombe, a laundress, who was the concierge of the *Cour de France*. It was agreed that the lovers would find a lodging there prepared to receive them.

In order to give that arrangement more verisimilitude, Georgiana had passed off their hostess as her confident and her nurse. And on his side, believing himself to be exposed to being pursued by a furious husband, and to the jealous searches of the legitimate wife that he had abducted in Bordeaux, the envoy of King Radama had given willing credence to this well-hidden love nest that his enchantress had supposedly prepared for them.

Upon entering a pretty, tiny room, the existence of which would have been hard to suspect, under the vile shacks that concealed it, Matiphous had the agreeable surprise to discover a comfortable supper already on the table. At the same time, he was taken into a corner of the room in which he had noticed a bed where someone had taken care to turn down the quilt, and where he certainly counted on not being alone to take possession of it very soon.

Because of the fatigue caused by a trip that, at the time our story took place, lasted hardly less than five days, Georgiana had no appetite. While the man from Malta did honor alone to the cooking of Madame Lacombe, she was content drinking several cups of tea, without, however, letting herself be persuaded to go take possession of the nuptial couch in advance. For about twenty minutes, Bacchus then turned into the antechamber of Venus. Suddenly the candles, placed on the table, darted out fireworks with a crash, soon followed by almost complete obscurity. Matiphous hadn't yet had time to recover from his surprise when, by the untrustworthy light of the fire which burned in the hearth, he saw four masked men dressed in red domino costumes enter into the room. Immediately throwing themselves on him, the unknown men tied him up despite his strong resistance, and, a short time later, having completely lost the freedom of his movements, he found himself seated in front of the dreaded assemblage of the Red Brotherhood, presided over by Lupiano.

"Monsieur," the Marquis said to the prisoner, "this is not the first time we have had the pleasure of meeting. Already, in London, some ten years ago, I was on the point of having you hanged, and I was later satisfied with having a souvenir imprinted on your shoulder. You have had the madness to navigate into my waters again, and here you are, coming from Madagascar, with the intention of upsetting the Secret Bureau, of which, in addition, you were a faithful employee, and that I myself honor with my great protection. Further, you are a very immoral man who left in the lurch a charming woman of royal blood to run around the world with a person of the slightest morality that you have turned aside from her duties. All that, Monsieur, can only end badly, and I see you faced with a disagreeable denouement. Speak! What have you to say in your defense! You are before a tribunal charged with judging you."

"Since you know that I have come from Madagascar," the man from Malta answered, "you cannot be ignorant of the fact that I was sent by King Radama, whose Minister I have the honor to be, and I presented myself on the soil of France clothed with a diplomatic identity that all civilized nations have always regarded as inviolable."

"That's marvelous," replied Lupiano, "but as an ambassador who begins his mission by abducting a woman from her husband, and who harbors the preconceived idea of compromising with his indiscretions an institution that the State regards as indispensable for its security, places himself outside the boundaries of the Law, don't you think?"

"What manner of tribunal are you?" the man from Malta quickly answered. "I am familiar enough with the customs of France, where I lived for a long time, to know that no official justice functions in a place like this with this bizarre ceremony."

"Our tribunal, dear Monsieur, if you are curious to know about it, is called the tribunal of the Red Brotherhood. Its sentences are without appeal and it usually carries them out itself."

"That means that you are continuing in Paris your abominable Sleepers' Club, and that, after having led me into a trap, you now intend to murder me."

"You are mistaken, Monsieur. Not a hair will fall from your head. We will treat you as the Regent in the past treated the Spanish Ambassador, the Prince de Cellamarre, taken in the act of conspiracy. We will give you back your passport and you will forcibly return to Madagascar, from where you came."

"Why, then, all this violence against me? Why am I tied up?"

"Because in our position as an extraordinary tribunal, we have our way of proceeding. You came from Bordeaux in a first-class carriage. Now it is our intention that you return there in a humbler stagecoach, perhaps even by merchandise transport."

"Messieurs," he added, now addressing his associates, "will you show our guest the method of transport that we have prepared for him?"

Several of the brothers rose and shortly thereafter they returned and placed in front of Matiphous a huge box lined with hay and cotton, which could easily contain a seated man. Matiphous didn't give that strange object all the attention that one might have supposed; the beginning of very deep sleep had been apparent in him for several minutes.

"Monsieur, Monsieur," Lupiano shouted to him, "you're falling asleep too soon. Listen to a little of what I have yet to tell you! You see that you will be very comfortably packed in that box. In Bordeaux, when Monsieur Britannicus, to whom we have addressed the box, takes the trouble to unpack you, it isn't to be feared that he will find any damage, or any fracture."

Instead of answering, Matiphous, whose arms and legs were tied, slid his whole body out of the chair on which they had seated him. The narcotic in the wine that he had drunk at supper had probably been mingled with too strong a dose. In losing sooner than expected the feeling of the atrocious torture for which he was reserved, he took from his executioners the pleasure they had promised themselves in the cold contemplation of his moral torture.

"The fellow is lucky!" the Marquis said. "He will pass away without knowing it, from life to his demise. Let's go, Messieurs," he added. "Proceed with the inhumation."

When Matiphous had been placed in the box, on the bed of hay and cotton which lined the bottom, they were careful to put a gag in his mouth, in the unlikely case that, coming out of his lethargic sleep, he tried to call for help. Then they attached to his neck the next number in the order that the society inscribed to each of its murders so as to securely establish that it was still the same hand that had committed the act. Registered under No.5, the unfortunate man from Malta was next given a light covering of dirt borrowed from the soil of the funereal place where the sacrifice had taken place. That was an abominable refinement of cruelty by which they tried to organize a sort of portable sepulcher for him.

Finally, after having nailed shut the lid to what could very well be now called a casket, using a brush dipped in shoe polish, one of the brothers, following the custom of embalmers, took the trouble to write in big letters on the cover the words *top* and *fragile,* to show in what direction the parcel should be placed and to ask some care from those who handled it. Everything was thus completed.

"It would have been more pleasing," said Lupiano, who always did evil with terrible cleverness, "to have sent it as ordinary merchandise, but it would take at least two weeks en route, and it would be feared that a cadaverous odor coming from it might arouse suspicions. Then our consignment would be opened and wouldn't reach its intended destination. So, therefore, we will send it by way of the stage coach. Now it remains to know the transporter whom the Marquise may have found.

Shortly thereafter, the Marquise returned from her expedition, bringing with her the young student named Maisonneuve with whom the scene that he himself recounted in the Prologue took place.[138]

---

[138] See Volume 1, Pages 70 seq.

When the stupid young man was on his way with the crate, believing he was only taking part in a Carnival joke, Madame de Camembert said:

"Messieurs, I hope that you are not going to leave my dessert, which you had hardly touched when the arrival of this Monsieur was announced."

"I will join you a little later," Lupiano answered. "I must go look a little at what the "widow" is doing."

"And I," said Montalvi, "formally promised to honor with my presence the costume ball given this evening by my friend, Monsieur B*** the Notary."

"Let's go, my faithful ones," said the Marquise," addressing the other guests.

Taking the arm of the Doctor, she followed the ten other brothers and returned to the banquet hall.

On entering the bedroom where the travelers had been received on their arrival, Lupiano expected to find the companion of Matiphous asleep. He supposed that Georgiana, having eaten with the gallant, would have succumbed like him to the influence of the narcotic with which the wine on their table had been so abundantly saturated.

But far from having succumbed to sleep, she was engaged in a violent argument with the woman Lacombe. The woman, wishing to obey the instructions given her, was claiming to hold Georgiana prisoner until the order had been lifted.

"Well, Mesdames, what's going on between you?" Lupiano demanded.

"Ah! It's you, Marquis," shouted Georgiana. "And Monsieur Matiphous, what has been done with him?"

"Monsieur Matiphous? What does that matter to you? Your role with him is finished."

"Yes; but I was told it was all a joke, and I saw four men come to take him away, brutalizing him."

"However that might be, you don't need to be involved in this any longer. That man is nothing to you."

"Well, you told me that you were friends who just wanted to have a laugh at his expense, but now, when I ask you where he is, and how that joke you were planning to play on him turned out, you don't know how to answer me."

"I'm not answering you because the treatment reserved for him should be completely indifferent to you. And if you insist, I warn you, you might give me some strange ideas."

"And you as well. You make me think that you used me to cause him pain. Well, that's outrageous! That's not what we agreed on."

"I'm going to remind you about our agreement. On your return from Bordeaux, you must come and live in my town-house, where a delightful apartment awaits you, a carriage, ravishing outfits, and 25,000 francs for your small pleasures. But on your side, you must faithfully serve me without fail."

"Faithfully serve you how? Since you are afraid to be my lover."

"We will see about that later. In the meantime, didn't you promise to not entertain any amorous offers from anyone else?"

"Why on Earth should I do that! Aren't you the one who sent me to Bordeaux to have someone make love to me?"

"But you were not supposed to respond to that attempt."

"Playing with fire, you often get burned."

"So, you fell in love instead of causing it?"

"I certainly caused it, I ask you to believe that."

"So are you in love with that man?"

"There is no need to be in love to not want to be the cause of something bad happening to him."

"You didn't answer me. You spent one night on the road?"

"Of course, since it was Monsieur Lelouard's orders."

"And that night, you spent it alone?"

"Monsieur Lelouard told me that it was absolutely neces-sary for me to stop at Poitiers or at Tours. Monsieur Matiphous didn't want to, saying that we would be followed too closely."

"Then, you kindly devoted yourself to make your travel-ing companion act according to Monsieur Lelouard's orders?"

"Ah! I find all these questions tiresome!"

"So you, who in your entire life have not known what affection was, you fell in love with the only man you had been forbidden to think of."

"Then, it's because of jealousy that you had him taken away with so much wickedness?"

"I had him taken away because he is a miserable man guilty of more crimes than there are hairs on your head."

"That's not true. He's a good and loving man who has always been very unhappy."

"Ah!" Lupiano said ironically. "He told you the story of his life?"

"What do you think anyone talks about when, for five days, one is alone in a carriage? Besides, it was very interesting, his life story. It was a novel. Like Moses, he began by being exposed, very young, to the waves, but it wasn't on a river; it was on the sea, where he was in much more danger."

"And where did that happen to him?" Lupiano quickly asked.

"In Malta."

"In Malta?" repeated the Marquis, showing a certain emotion.

"Yes, in a country where there are orange trees and knights."

"Are you sure you're not mistaken? It happened in Malta?"

"No doubt. And he is a man from a very good family, because he has the crown of a Baron tattooed on his left arm with the date 13 February 1778."

"Georgiana, my daughter!" Lupiano shouted. "If I see that with my own eyes, there will not be a queen more fortunate than you."

"Parbleu! You can certainly see it. It's written in rather visible letters."

At that moment Montalvi entered.

"Marquis," he said with excitement, "I need your advice. A while ago as I entered the drawing rooms of Monsieur

B***, the notary, and who did I find there but that imbecile that the Marquise brought to us! Instead of going to the stage coach for Bordeaux, he had the disastrous idea to present himself at the ball with the crate."

"Ah! Your news is providential!" Lupiano exclaimed. "Go immediately to our brothers, take three of them with you, and disguised as hired laborers, go to the notary's house, each of you carrying a crate on his back."

"I understand," said Montalvi. "In the middle of the the confusion that all these identical boxes will cause, we will get our hands on the *good one*."

"Yes, yes, that's really it! Run! You must succeed, because you can't imagine the importance of this! Or, rather no; I'll go with you."

Then, after having taken several steps, he came back to Georgiana like a man beside himself.

"My dear," he said to her, taking her head between his two hands and kissing her with effusion, "I understand now why I was attracted to you. You have in your hands my happiness for the rest of my life."

Then he dashed out the door, followed by Montalvi.

"Well, well! What's wrong with him?" Georgiana, completely surprised, asked herself. "You'd think the man is no longer in his right mind!"

VI. *The Green Snake*

Despite all the diligence and the ability in the world, more than an hour passed before Montalvi returned from the home of the notary B***. The more someone is dominated by a moral impression, the more the notion of the passage of time is wiped out. It could be said that, during that terrible hour, given over to all the tortures of doubt and the wait, Lupiano expiated the thirty years he had filled with the bloody orgies of his satanic conceptions and his desperate fight against the social order.

It is understood that, in the man for whom he had set up a terrible end, Providence had just revealed to him a son lost to him for a long time, and whose death, he believed, had been one of the great sorrows of his past life.

But what if that son was not returned to him alive! If Heaven, to punish him, had willed that the luxury of cruelty in which he had taken pleasure would be crowned with its probable denouement: the murder of the one who could have become the consolation of his old age. What, then, would be his remorse and what terrible regrets he had prepared for himself. So, wasn't that anxiety a spectacle to draw tears from that man of iron in the presence of the unknown that, for a few more instants, separated him from the truth.

If the recovery of the box succeeded, once that first success obtained, would there still be time to react against the hellish multiplicity of chances of destruction amassed on that head that had suddenly become so precious and so dear to him? Sometimes, his expression gloomy, trying to give himself the appearance of patient resignation, he stayed in one spot; at another moment, he got up quickly and approached Georgiana and the Doctor who, with some of the brothers, were waiting, like him, in one of the drawing-rooms of his town house. To the courtesan, he asked if she was very sure of the date that she had recalled to him; to the Doctor, if there was some depth to his art to draw on; with the associates, he discussed the obstacles that Montalvi was likely to encounter on his expedition. After having himself told to satiety that the man from Genoa and the brothers who seconded him were not men to let themselves be stopped by any difficulty, he walked around the apartment with big steps, and then went to sit down again, just to get up again soon, as if that perpetual agitation could make his perpetual preoccupation weigh less heavily in that decisive hour of his life.

Finally, in the courtyard of the town house, one heard the resounding noise of a truck that Montalvi had had the idea to take from the storehouse of vehicles of every kind assembled, as is known, at the *Cour de France.* Some instants later, the doors of the salon were opened wide to give passage to the terrible *perhaps* which the four associates returned triumphantly carrying.

The crate had barely been placed on the ground when, armed with tools prepared in advance, Lupiano and some of the brothers, began work to take the nails out of the lid and, soon after, Matiphous, dead or deeply asleep, was deposited on a large divan, in reach of the cares that the Doctor was going to lavish on him. While the man of that art, after having ordered that all the clothes be taken off the subject, listened attentively his chest to ascertain his heartbeats, the Marquis, a candle in his hand, searched avidly for the date and the Baron's crown that would constitute proof of the parental relationship of the man that he now wanted to snatch from death. But, at first, nothing appeared to him.

There was more than one reason for his disappointment. His search was too breathless and too summary for the marks that, forty-two years before, had not been stamped very deeply on his son's arm to strike his eyes immediately. Next, it must be noted that, having become a citizen of Madagascar, Matiphous had adopted the fashion of his country of adoption, where tattooing is very much honored and serves at the same time to confirm social hierarchy. He had so much more willingly submitted to that practice because, thanks to it, he had found the way to make disappear that note of infamy that, in London, had been impressed upon his shoulder by the order of Lupiano, his eternal persecutor.

The flesh given over to his fantasy, the artist in Madagascar had sketched the figure of a serpent, being born at the base of the loins and crossing the chest in all its breadth, after having been rolled over the shoulder, where it absorbed the famous letters T. P. coming back to dart a flaming tongue, the color of blood, over the right pectoral muscles. Executed with great art and stained with a nuance of golden green, that tattoo drew the eye to that spot, so that everything close to it paled by comparison and remained obscure.

"Georgiana, you infamous deceiver!" Lupiano cried out. "That inscription, I don't see it!"

Thus called out, the courtesan, seated in a corner, decided to confront the body that, until then, she had carefully avoided to examine.

"See, Monsieur!" she said, pointing with her finger to the spot where he should look. "You claim to love him, but now, that poor unfortunate man, you don't know how to recognize him, either with your eyes or with your heart."

"Georgiana! My angel, my beloved, Oh! Yes! You're right: *13 February 1778*, and here's the crown of my arms!" the Marquis then cried out.

He threw himself into the arms of the woman that he had abused a moment before.

"Yes, but what if you have killed him?" responded the courtesan, receiving his hug coldly.

"Be quiet, you viper!" replied Lupiano.

And running to the Doctor, he asked:

"He's sleeping, isn't he?"

"Silence!" answered the Doctor, who, on his knees near the victim, continued to place his ear on his chest, still searching to recognize if an appearance of life persisted in the region of the heart.

"It seems to me," he said, standing up," that I can perceive some faint heartbeat."

"He is saved!" exclaimed Lupiano, grasping the Doctor's arm with force.

"I won't answer for anything yet," he replied.

Then, addressing Georgiana:

"My child," he continued, "kneel down near the sick man, put yourself mouth to mouth and force air into his lungs, but very little at a time, and in a very measured fashion, because, otherwise, we run the risk of bringing about some tear in the pulmonary vessels."

Ecstatic about that practice, where he saw something more than a mere physical maneuver, Lupiano cried out:

"Oh! Yes! They love each other, and her breath must surely bring him back to life."

While with an ardor that can only be imagined, Georgiana gave Matiphous the same care that resembled the one that, twenty years before, he himself had given to Broughton to save him from hanging, the Doctor sprinkled strong, cold vinegar water all over the patient's his body.

Soon, a long sigh escaped from Matiphous' lips, confirming the hope for his return to life.

"This time, Doctor, the victory is ours!" the Marquis quickly said.

"I don't know anything about that yet," replied the Doctor. "The asphyxia could have been brought on by just the effect of the narcotic. He ingested such a strong dose! We are now dealing with one of the most dangerous types of comas."

"Damn your scientific terms!" Lupiano said. "A coma, what's that?"

"Sleep, often followed by death, since you want to be told things." Then, speaking to the brothers present, he added: "Messieurs, have two of you hold him under the arms and try to make him walk!"

That prescription filled, nothing in the sick man testified to the least sensibility or the faculty of locomotion. He remained, in the hands of those holding him erect, an entirely inert mass, his face covered with deadly paleness and his pupils horribly dilated, which gave his eyes, that had remained open, a frightful strangeness.

"Put him back on the divan," said the Doctor, recognizing the futility of the means of stimulus to which he had just resorted. "I see, by the state of his pulse, that we are facing a stroke. There's no delaying blood-letting."

While the preparations for the operation were rapidly done, Lupiano asked:

"Where are Madame de Camembert and our other Brothers?"

And that curiosity shouldn't be taken for a diversion to be used to conquer his mortal anxiety. His question expressed that feeling of indignation in which the passive attitude of someone indifferent fills us when faced with harrowing sorrow.

"The Marquise," one of the associates present answered, "claims that all the care will be useless, and some of the messieurs remained at the table with her, to keep her company."

"I will remember that stoicism," Lupiano angrily said.

And as he approached the sick man, a jet of blood that Georgiana courageously caught in a cuvette, brought his attention back to the question of life or death that was being debated.

"Blood is flowing out well," the Doctor remarked. "That's a good sign."

"Oh! We will save him!" exclaimed the Marquis. "Is there not Providence in all this?"

"You must not be too hasty to hope," answered the Doctor, busying bandaging the wound. "The effect of the bloodletting can't be produced immediately. Now have some lemons and some coffee brought in."

"I'm going to get them myself," said Lupiano, who couldn't remain in one place and was only too happy to descend to that servile task, when it was a question of his son's life.

He returned shortly thereafter with what the Doctor had asked for.

"Monsieur, Monsieur," Georgiana said, running to face him. "He moved and spoke a little; the Doctor says that now there is some hope."

"Take everything I'm holding, my daughter," said the Marquis. "I feel my legs about to give way under me."

And, becoming horribly pale, that man, ordinarily so energetic, and which, until then, had been very strong despite the terrible incertitude, appeared about to faint under the announcement of the happy denouement, which could now be foreseen. Supported by some of his assistants, and sitting down on a chair that had been brought to him, he had soon recovered enough to say to the Doctor, whom he saw attentively near him.:

"My friend, go back to your patient. I am all right; it was only dizziness."

However, Georgiana, who had stayed near Matiphous, had managed to have him swallow some spoonfuls of coffee cut with lemon juice, and the ease with which it was swallowed seemed to the Doctor to be a new measure of a favorable conclusion.

But suddenly, the scene changed. The patient was seized with convulsions. A bluish tint covered his face; his mouth became contorted; his eyes became fixed. From his dull look and the death rattle that escaped from his chest, it seemed that he was about to expire.

"He is lost!" Montalvi said very low to those watching that sad spectacle with him.

Drawn by the movement that this new incident had caused, Lupiano stood upright in front of that bed of sorrow, witnessing, speechless, the ruin of all his hopes. In a few minutes, he seemed to have aged ten years.

"Massage! Massage! Let everyone do that!" exclaimed the Doctor.

Several hands rubbed flannel pads soaked with vinegar vigorously over all parts of the body, fighting the coldness of death which the extremities threatened to extend to the center of life. Less than a quarter of an hour after the beginning of that battle, warmth returned to the skin, the pulse became more normal and more distinct. Soon, some drops of sweat appeared on the patient's forehead and, a moment later, more sweat appeared. Seeing that, the Doctor exclaimed

"He's saved, and I'll answer for him."

Two big tears rolled down the Marquis' cheeks. Then, seeming to awaken from a dream, he said:

"Down on your knees Messieurs! Let us thank Providence together for the benediction that it has chosen to bestow in the life of your leader."

The men to whom that sentiment was addressed looked at each other with astonishment that, if well analyzed, would have been translated as: *Happiness has turned the head of the poor man who certainly seems to have become mad.*

However, dominated by the control that, on every occasion, Lupiano knew how to impose on those near him, the men present followed his example and bent their knees. Then, with a loud and profoundly emotional voice, the Marquis repeated:

"My God, you have tested me cruelly. I revolted against your power and against your justice. Now, you send me joy. I will not be ungrateful and forget such a great gift, and henceforth, I will use the last days of my life to bless and glorify you."

"Amen!" said a voice in a burlesque tone.

Everyone turned around, and saw Madame de Camembert, followed by the Brothers who had remained eating with her, coming in, somewhat the worse for wine, disturbing with her inopportune gaiety the solemnity of the scene in the middle of which she had inserted herself.

"Don't blaspheme, woman!" exclaimed Lupiano, rising.

And taking the Marquise by the hand, he led her in front of the bed where, from moment to moment, Matiphous showed more confirmation of the victory won valiantly over death.

"You see that man?" he said. "He's my son. God has just given him back to me, and you don't want me to thank Him?"

"Let's rejoice, all right!" she said. "I certainly wish to, but I don't like these pious antics."

"Go away, you heartless creature," Lupiano answered. "A while ago you came too late, and now you come too soon."

"In fact," responded the Marquise," you remind me that I have an account to settle with that silly student who followed his instructions backward."

"That's futile," said the Marquis.

"Come now," said the Marquise, "the insult is personal and no power on earth will keep me from getting even with him."

"Remember that at least I forbid you to get revenge in a bloody way."

"Don't worry, Papa," said the Marquise insolently. "That you have become a saint will be remembered. Monsieur Maisonneuve will be chastised in a fitting manner, but gently. I have my plans."

And she left.

"Now," said the Doctor, "let's transport our strapping fellow to a hot bath where there is nothing more to do but let him stew in his own juices. I wouldn't give him but twelve hours to feel better than anyone here."

VII. The Disbanding of the Brotherhood

The Doctor's prediction wasn't entirely accurate. The morning of the next day, Matiphous still remained in a great state of prostration that could only be explained by the terrible shock he had undergone. In that weakened and listless situation, any emotions could be dangerous for him. Therefore, neither Lupiano, nor Georgiana, were permitted to communicate with him. In addition, he himself didn't show any great hurry to be aware of the place or circumstances in which he had awakened. His extreme exhaustion and vague and incomplete memory of the danger he had escaped, had left him rather indifferent to the explanations that might have been given to him. The luxury and the attentive cares with which he saw himself surrounded were sufficient to demonstrate that he was in kindly and friendly hands. For the moment, just as asked of him, he didn't worry any further.

The same day, the burlesque revenge that Madame de Camembert was going to pull down on the student Maisonneuve, brought about, at the Lupiano townhouse, the descent of justice that was described in our Prologue.[139] It has been shown how the Marquise managed to derail the suspicions of the magistrates, and how, in presenting Georgiana to

---

[139] See Volume 1, Pages 88 seq.

them in the place of Madame de Camembert, who was supposedly in Turin, it put an end at the same time to the long mystification of *The Girl with the Death's Head.*

The completely providential event with which he had just been favored caused a profound moral revolution in the Marquis de Lupiano. He decided to end the conspiracy in which he had invested so much of himself. The dissolution of the Red Brotherhood was the first sign that he intended to make a better use of his enormous riches and his powerful faculties. But he was chained to his detestable past by multiple ties that couldn't be undone without some agony of indecision. That was one more reason that, with that rapidity of determination that was natural to him in everything, he proceeded without delay to disband his army of evil. Obliged to delay his first encounter with his son, the cares that he was going to take for the dispersal of his accomplices also helped him to circumvent his impatience and served as a distraction.

His first order of business concerned Madame de Camembert. Going to her apartment as soon as it was a proper hour to do so, he said:

"Dear Madame, you showed yourself yesterday very lukewarm both to my happiness and the cruel concern which assaulted me almost at the same moment. And following that, it pleased you to describe in a rather unpleasant manner the burst of gratitude that such celestial goodness brought forth in me."

"The words just slipped out," Madame de Camembert replied. "But also, Marquis, your transitions are of such brusqueness and of an unexpected..."

"Which doesn't rule out anything as to their firmness, since it's with a formal and immovable position that I have come to announce the most ridiculously virtuous dispositions."

"Ah! Really?" said the Marquise with a very marked nuance of irony.

"Yes," Lupiano replied seriously. "I will no longer continue to direct the detestable association of which I was the tie and I will put all my efforts into bringing about its complete dissolution."

"That's a misfortune for humanity, because, after all, to clean up after the law and punish crimes which have escaped its attention was both exemplary and meritorious."

"It was a usurpation of public power, and I have decided to renounce it, which puts me under the obligation to put an end to our situation."

"With me and all those who had followed the fortune of your idea."

"With you, first of all, dear Madame. So, this townhouse, of which I am ostensibly the owner, but which in reality has never ceased to belong to you, I am hereby restoring to you. My intention is to no longer reside here."

"You realize that I am not chasing you away and that to leave it is your own decision."

"Now I am not alone. I have a son, and I can almost say a daughter. Since there a few weeks ago, the idea that Georgiana might live under the same roof with you seemed somehow insulting and monstrous to you, you can understand that it cannot be my thought to impose on you such a guest."

"In fact," the Marquise said bitterly, "Mademoiselle Georgiana seems to be received like the rising sun now!"

"I owe her too much," Lupiano answered "that everywhere and always, in the degree that it suits her, she shall always be for me Queen and Mistress. This, in my household, that I must therefore begin by setting it up. Also, why would I continue to be an inconvenient guest for you? The particular convenience that your house presented for the conduct of our enterprise, was, to tell the truth, my only excuse. But today, that scheme is abandoned…"

"You have only to fall out with your accomplices," Madame de Camembert quickly interrupted, "who, after all, are only useless and inconvenient instruments."

"As for the subordinates," Lupiano answered, "I intend to assure their means of existence, and I hope not to leave them on bad terms. As for the masters, I would be happy to see them follow my example and enter the narrower pathway that I have resolved to walk. But will they imitate me? That is the question. When one has ceased agreeing on the manner of living one's life with others, intimacy becomes difficult."

"And what tells you that I cannot, like you, turn to asceticism?" replied the Marquise. "Is your devotion of the kind that that damns the world before even knowing if they deserve it?"

"If, in fact, dear Madame, my example touches you, here, it seems to me, is what you should do: get over the small humiliation of not persisting in your pretended religious vocation, return from Turin; take your place again in society and occupy once more the distinguished position that you had before knowing me; and, since you are a young widow and very pretty, in order not to need a protector, in your place, I would remarry."

"And why not? I wonder if he would want me, that cherished child who fell to you from Heaven. In that way, we would be but one happy family."

"Oh! You wouldn't want to be competing with Mademoiselle Georgiana. You could find someone a great deal better than my son, a kind of adventurer like me. For example, a choice that I would suggest is Monsieur de Montalvi."

"Why Monsieur de Montalvi?" asked the Marquise turning red. "Has it ever seemed to you that I paid any attention to him?"

"No," said Lupiano. "I know, on the contrary, that you were rather desperate to make the trip to Bordeaux with him in *tête à tête*. But since I know all about his terrible behavior with his first wife, in passing, I warn you against the prospect. The isolation in which he is going to find himself will make him nothing short of the impossible."

"Ah! So Monsieur de Montalvi, your virtual aide-de-camp, will also be ostracized, and you don't hope to succeed putting on him your whitewash of virtue?"

"To bring about transformations like the one that you have witnessed takes some great event overwhelming one's life."

"Well! If you have found a son again, can't one say that Monsieur de Montalvi has found a daughter again?"

"Yes, but a daughter whose life has been blackened by him, and whom he couldn't think of encountering again."

"Decidedly, Mademoiselle Georgiana will be, for each of us, somewhat of a stumbling block. But let's talk of something else; how is Monsieur Matiphous doing this morning?"

"He is very weak, and the Doctor says, without having any serious fear, that should not see anyone, which forces me to ask you again for your hospitality for today."

"Come now, you must be joking Marquis! Do you need to leave here that brusquely? You have an enormous amount of moving to do, and it will take weeks, with all the diligence possible, before you are installed somewhere else."

"What amount of moving? But I have nothing to take away from here."

"What! What about the huge and sumptuous furnishings that you have stacked up here?"

"They will remain here—if you will have them."

"But I can't! The value of the contents goes beyond what contains them. I don't accept such munificence from a hand that has become so lukewarm to shake mine."

"All right, Marquise," said Lupiano, rising, "we will talk again about all that. The Capuchin[140], I hope, will persuade you to return to goodness, and you won't hold it against him to have awakened you from a bad dream."

Thereupon, they separated rather coldly.

A quarter of an hour later, Montalvi, Lelouard, and the Doctor were together in Lupiano's office.

---

[140] The Order of Friars Minor Capuchin is an order of friars within the Catholic Church, among the chief offshoots of the Franciscans. They took their name from their habit and hood the color of burnt umber.

"Messieurs," he said to them, "a moment ago, I announced to Madame de Camembert that I am resolved to break with my turbulent past, and that I renounce the honor of being your leader. India, which has always attracted me, will probably be the last stop in my old age. But, before we separate, we must talk about our respective interests..."

"But," said Montalvi, "why that separation? Our liaison between us two began before that enterprise that you don't find convenient to continue."

"My dear Montalvi," the Marquis answered, "I believe that you are far less disposed than our two friends present here to become my companion in the somewhat bucolic existence that I intend to live on the banks of the Ganges. There, I will be a rich nabob busy improving some great estate that I plan to buy. A man of action like yourself would have difficulty being happy in the calm and uniformity of such a life, and that is without even taking into consideration the daily contacts between you and another person, who has no great reason to pride herself on the way you treated her."

"Ah! Very well!" the man from Genoa exclaimed. "I am sacrificed to Mademoiselle Georgiana."

"My friend," Lupiano answered, "I owe to that girl the single moment of happiness that, for more than forty years, has entered my life. If, therefore, that arrangement suits her, she will never again leave me. But I intend to place you at the head of a great banking institution that I will set up with several millions in capital, with our friend Monsieur Lelouard, in whom I have recognized a great understanding of business. If you will transfer to that sphere the activity and intelligent energy that you have, until now, put into enterprises that were either useless or regrettable, in a few years, you will have restored your fortune, and nothing will prevent you from recovering your name and your title of Prince de Bevillacqua."

"I don't want anything from you," replied Montalvi. "You have broken in a few minutes a close relationship of fifteen years!"

"This is your first reaction," replied the Marquis. "To persuade to reach a different decision, I'm counting on Lelouard, who, I'm sure, will not resist making use of my capital."

"Without a doubt," the former wholesale food supplier answered, "but on the condition that you don't stay a stranger to your creation, in which you will retain an interest, and you will not refuse us either the help of your advice, or that of your friendship."

"That goes without saying," Lupiano answered. "But the assistance of Montalvi, the former financier who, for so many years, sustained that brilliant duel with the Genoa lottery, would be a great deal more useful, and it is with extreme regret that I would see him remain deaf to our common requests. As for the Doctor, I would be happy if he would be willing to accompany us to India. However, if it costs him too much to become an expatriate, I would beg him to accept a pension of 30,000 francs, that would allow him to *play* at medicine as a distraction."

"I will go to India," said the Doctor. "That's a country that I have always wanted to visit."

"Thank you!" said the Marquis, shaking his hand. "After this, I must see to the future of our other associates. I will gather them this evening, and I will announce that each one of them, if they haven't gotten into trouble with the law, will be able to withdraw from Montalvi, Lelouard & Company an annual retirement income of 10,000 francs. With that, each man can live honorably. And I like to believe that their future thus assured, these honest men will lose the taste for the dangerous activities and the adventurous existence of which they have shown themselves, at least until now, all too fond."

"And what if one of them," the man from Genoa remarked, "found it more beneficial to deliver the notorious Marquis de Lupiano into the hands of the law?"

"I doubt," responded the Marquis, "that that thought will come to any of them. They would understand that I would then have a case for legitimate defense, and on that ground, I have seen to it that I shouldn't be toyed with."

"Marquis," Montalvi replied, "you have said what you would like, but that is still a miserable end: *desinit in piscem mulier formosa superne*."[141]

"Thanks to Madame de Camembert's pleasantries," Lupiano replied, "I believe that we we were exposed, this morning, to a much more miserable ending. The law was positively on our tracks, and without my presence of mind, everything would have been discovered. That's enough of tempting Fate. And, because of the happiness that it has sent me, it has paid me in advance. I don't want to bargain with it. Now, Messieurs, I leave you. I must go and look at a new dwelling several leagues from Paris that I have in mind. You, Lelouard, for your part, go look for a townhouse in which to install your bank offices. As for my dear Doctor, he will top the debt that I owe him if, from now until I return, which won't be before nightfall, he could arrange it so that our patient is in a state to see me."

"I will try to do that," the Doctor answered.

Lupiano then went to to Evry-sur-Seine, where he intended to visit the Chateau de Petit-Bourg that the newspaper advertisements had listed for rent fully furnished.

In the evening, when he reappeared at the townhouse on the Rue Notre-Dame-des-Champs, not only was Matiphous on his feet, but the resuscitated man had been brought up to date on all that that he should know by Georgiana and the Doctor. The father and the son had then only to embrace, and both of them, after the enormous turmoil with which their existences had been filled, could now consider themselves as having arrived at a safe harbor.

---

[141] Loosely translated: a woman with a fully formed upper body, but with a mermaid's tail. Referenced in literature, it usually means that projects begun with hope ends in great disappointment.

The former associates that Lupiano had called his subordinates, and to whom he intended to give an individual income of ten thousand francs, received that communication with a great lack of excitement. To consider the matter more closely, excluding Montalvi, Lelouard, and the Doctor, who had already been provided for, there remained nine parties entitled to receive money; that it to say, the Marquis had put a strain on his fortune with an annual sacrifice of ninety thousand francs.

"We will lose by that," one of the would-be pensioners said then he was told that the payment of said that pension would be conditional upon a certain regularity of conduct that would be required of them. It was obvious, in fact, that the troubled waters and the turbulent and disorderly life from which the Marquis was trying to remove them was much better suited to their habits and instincts. However, thanks to the domination that Lupiano held over them, there was no apparent resistance, and, most of all, no threats to make him change his mind. The profound displeasure and silent irritation that his sudden retreat had created in his entourage would be revealed to him from another direction.

Several hours after the explanations that he had had with Madame de Camembert, she, as well as Montalvi, left the townhouse, where all three had lived together.

In the evening, when he had returned from his trip to Evry-sur-Seine, Lupiano saw himself greeted by the news of that double desertion. But the next morning, the attitude of the two malcontents had taken on a more hostile character, far more obvious.

A Bailiff, all dressed in black, presented himself on behalf of Madame de Camembert, carrying a legal injunction, ordering the Marquis: *to vacate the property which had been transferred to him only on the basis of a verbal and provisional sale, and in any event subject to repurchase.* In addition, the injunction ordered the *said Marquis,* to remove all the furnishings that belonged to him within a week, *at the latest.*

So, they had responded to his generous intentions through the voice of a bailiff. And in the circumstance, the use of that kind of officer who, ordinarily, is dispatched against a recalcitrant debtor of bad faith, served only to emphasize the disdainful refusal of the truly princely offer he had made.

The unfriendliness that the two were taking the trouble to show him didn't stop there. The same day, a newspaper, the editor of which, to his knowledge, Montalvi knew, published the following article:

According to all appearances, a magnificent sale of furnishings should, in some days, be called to the attention of elegant society. After having been in one of the most famous religious houses in Italy for more than a year, Madame de Camembert has returned to Paris. Her intention is to live again in her beautiful townhouse on the Rue Notre-Dame-des-Champs which she had conditionally sold to the Marquis de Lupiano, but is now reclaiming. As a result, it is likely that the famous foreigner will dismantle his household with an auction of all the magnificent furnishings previously stored in the rich dwelling, which he is going to be obliged to leave, as he finds himself about to depart from Paris, having terminated the delicate business that had brought him to France. He now intends to return to India, where serious family complications urgently require his presence. The amateurs of curiosities and objects d'art objects are hereby informed.

It is useless to remark on the perfidious cleverness of that announcement. Everything in there was calculated to wound the Marquis' ego, as well as incidentally taking care of announcing Madame de Camembert's re-entry into the Parisian salons. Not only did they shout his affairs out the window, but they completely altered his thoughts and intentions. By using the words *serious family complications,* they made a bitter and jealous allusion to his relationship with Matiphous and Georgiana, which could give rise to a thousand gossips.

Thus, the arrangements formerly planned by the Marquis were immediately modified. Responding with irritation to the newspaper that had published the notice, he wrote:

Monsieur,

You have been wholly misinformed in announcing that I plan to soon sell all the furnishings presently stored in the townhouse which I had provisionally acquired during the pious and edifying retreat of Madame the Marquise de Camembert in Italy. All the furnishings that she may want to keep are to be left for her use. On her refusal, they will be transported to the Marais, to the townhouse of M. Lamoignon, which I have leased for several years. This is also to tell you, Monsieur, that I am not precipitously leaving Paris, to which I was not drawn because of any type of business. The secluded neighborhood where I have chosen to establish my new domicile will equally inform you of my strong desire to see the public as little informed as possible of the small incidents that constitute my private life.

I have the honor to be, etc...

It can be seen from that letter that not only was Lupiano not leaving for India, but that he had even renounced the idea of retiring some leagues from Paris as he had, at first, intended to do, having in mind to hide during the time necessary to prepare for his actual departure. Now having but one thought, that of buttressing his denial, he intended, in less than a week, to be installed in the new townhouse which he had leased.

Three days later, his move had been accomplished; and another three days later, surrounded with upholsterers and workmen of all types, he had managed to put his new apartments in a state ready for him to move in. In the interval, he had still found time to take care of other matters equally important to him.

Foreseeing in the type of rebellion that Montalvi and the Marquise had staged against him, an intention to continue the dangerous association that he had just dissolved, he employed some trusted domestics to fill in the underground tunnel that connected the Camembert townhouse to the catacombs and the *Cour de France*. Then, to be done with that shameful property, which had the appearance of never being anything but a bandit's lair, he had arranged, the same day, for all the tenants to leave, using one of those expedient procedures familiar to him, i.e.: he had ordered his men to set fire to it. Rendered prodigiously combustible by their dilapidation, the shacks that he wanted to make disappear had been consumed in a few hours, without any vestiges remaining.

All his affairs thus put in order, Lupiano one morning left for Versailles, where, during the confusion of his move, he had sent Matiphous and Georgiana to spend their honeymoon. After having had lunch with them, he spoke of taking them back to Paris. While the former odalisque proceeded to get dressed, an operation habitually always long and complicated, the Marquis suggested a walk in the part to Matiphous. There, bringing up a subject that never ceased preoccupying him, he said:

"Let's talk a little about Georgiana; are you sure of the feelings you have for her?"

"I love her with all my soul," Matiphous responded. "In addition to being a charming girl, don't I owe her my life?

"For that," the Marquis answered, "she has equally all my affection. However, neither for you nor for me is she absolutely the wife we would have desired. Her past is... She has probably touched on something about it?"

"She has told me all about her life, as I have told her about mine. And both of us, it seems, have been more unfortunate than guilty."

"So you know that, as a certain woman that Brantôme[142] talks about in his life of the *Dames Galantes,* she sacrifices all her lovers to an end more or less disastrous?"

"Only the lovers whom she didn't love, but, in reality, I am her first love; so you see that, on the contrary, she saved me from a terrible death."

"Supposing that you have effectively broken the spell, I like to believe, however, that your gratitude will not go so far as making her your wife?"

"My word! Until now, I haven't thought so far ahead. Returned, as the poets say, from the gates of death, I'm letting myself live."

"Without caring about another serious and legitimate union?"

"Oh! Legitimate," Matiphous interrupted. "Perhaps not in Madagascar, where, may it please God, I will never again set foot. In fact, I'm going to write to my native half that she can begin her journey back to her country and at the same time I will give her all the money and notes that I have collected."

"But in letting her know that you are in Paris, you may be giving her the idea of coming here to join you and reclaim her rights?"

"What rights? In Madagascar, our marriage ceremony consisted in slaughtering a bull. My so-called wife and I dipped our left hands in a dish that held its blood, raised our right hands and pronounced the following oath: *I swear before*

---

[142] Pierre de Bourdielle, Seigneur de Brantôme (c.1540-1614), a.k.a. Abbé de Brantôme, soldier, historian, writer. His *Memoirs* give a picture of the general court-life of the time. There is hardly an *homme illustre* or a *dame galante* in his gallery of portraits who is not engaged in some kind of sexual immorality; yet the whole is narrated with the most complete unconsciousness that there is anything objectionable in their conduct. His life was the subject of the historical drama film *Dames galantes* (1990) that focused on his relations with women. The lead role was played by Richard Bohringer.

the Sun, the God of the world, to love and protect the one that I today accept as my companion and not to leave her, unless I deem it necessary, until after two rice harvests have followed our union. Now, in Madagascar, rice is harvested twice a year, so I was then committed, at the most, for only a year."

"Then everything is for the best in your new love. And I see that I, alone, played the role of trouble-maker."

"You, Monsieur? How is that?"

"It is not allowed, in the customs of the country we are living in, that a father should receive the mistress of his son under his roof. Because of that, not wanting to be separated from either you or Georgiana, I talked about retiring to India. There, our past, to all of us, would be unknown. Besides, the local customs are less prudish and straight-laced."

"To speak frankly," Matiphous replied, "I don't regret a great deal that your project of emigration was frustrated. After several years of exile among savages, I have a real need not to deprive myself. As for Georgiana, she wouldn't know how to live outside Paris."

"So be it, but she will have to live here alone, since with the hostile curiosity of which I am presently the object, her presence in my house would cause too much scandal. What's more, everything has already been already arranged. I have bought her, in the Chaussée-d'Antin, a little townhouse that I had very comfortably furnished. You will see it at your convenience, and nothing will prevent her, from time to time, to bring me the joy of her presence."

"Well, father, it seems to me that everything is reconciled thanks to your generous arrangements."

"Yes, but, up until now, Georgiana hasn't shown herself to be a kind of Lucrezia[143], and in the great liberty that we are

---

[143] Lucrezia Borgia (1480-1519), daughter of Pope Alexander VI and Vannozza dei Cattanei. Her brothers included Cesare, Giovanni, and Gioffre Borgia. Her family arranged several marriages for her that advanced their own political position. Rumors about her and her family cast Lucrezia as a *femme*

going to give her, what if the desire for some distractions should come to her?"

"Then that would mean that she has stopped loving me. And that's one of the misfortunes that one always ends by one consoling oneself."

"Very well," said Lupiano. "I see that you love her wisely. I was afraid that you would hesitate between her and me, but your philosophy reassures me, and we can go tell her about our arrangements to which, I also believe, she will willingly resign herself."

Two hours after that conversation, Lupiano's carriage, which had brought from Versailles what he called his two *beautiful turtledoves,* stopped on the Rue Saint-Lazare in front of a small townhouse, built between a courtyard and garden where a concierge, with all the appearance of a servant from a fashionable household, hurried to open the door. In the vestibule, paved with colored marble, there stood a footman wearing modest, but in good taste, livery.

After having gone through a suite of apartments furnished with rare care, coming to a bedroom, a masterpiece of comfort and elegance, Georgiana was surprised to see her lady's maid, who had been let go the evening of her departure for Bordeaux. Lupiano had taken the care to have her found and brought back, because he knew that her service pleased her. The house was visited in all its details, including a washroom where the richness and the clever distribution would have crowned a housekeeper with happiness.

"Let's go see the outbuildings," said the Marquis.

An English coachman, assisted by his groom, reigned and governed there. With respectful dignity, he showed the visitors three thoroughbred horses, a saddlery admirably maintained, and two fast and elegant vehicles, a carriage and a *demie-fortune*[144], as it was then called.

---

fatale, a role in which she has been portrayed in many artworks, novels and films.

[144] A carriage drawn by one horse.

They then returned to the drawing-room:

"My dear child," said Lupiano, "the house we have set up for you supposes that its proprietor has a fortune of some thirty thousand livres of income. Here's a contract that assures you forty thousand, but as you are not economy incarnate, and as we want to see you always sheltered from need, I tell you in advance that, in those forty thousand francs of income, there are fifteen thousand that are untouchable, and that you can only withdraw annually. You are now going to live here in entire independence, that unfailing faithfulness that you promised, but didn't quite keep; however, I like to believe I can hope that you will grant it to the man you have chosen?"

"Yes, because I love him," the courtesan said quickly.

"Then, I leave him to you," said Lupiano, rising. "Only remember that he doesn't not just belong to you alone and that I claim a good part of him."

"Will you come to see me sometime?" Georgiana asked caressingly.

"No, that would not be any more proper than to lodge you in my house, but from time to time, Gregorio will bring you discreetly to my house, where I will always be happy to receive you."

Conducted to his carriage by the two lovers, the Marquis reminded his son that he expected him at the dinner hour.

Lupiano had not been mistaken; Montalvi and Madame de Camembert intended to continue his work, and, for that purpose, a reunion of all the former Red Brothers had taken place at the townhouse which the Marquise had repossessed. But Lelouard and the Doctor, who had attended the convocation only with the firm desire to make it useless, had no trouble demonstrating that this attempt was but a fanciful dream and that it could have no serious consequences.

While they were far from seeing in Montalvi, who posed himself as a worthy successor to the Marquis, the necessary abilities for that role, they certainly didn't wish to contest his abilities and limited themselves to remarking that Lupiano's immense fortune had been the moving force of the enterprise.

Now that that power had become lacking, nothing was possible. Madame de Camembert offered to contribute to the work all the resources that she had, but they objected that the 60,000 francs of revenue that constituted the total sum of her fortune would be absorbed just by the pension stipulated with Dulac, a.k.a. Rempailleux, to whom Lupiano paid that sum annually in order to obtain communications from the Secret Bureau. So, what could she do for the association?

Obliged to go into the path of abuses and thefts, instead of remaining hidden avengers and audacious supplements to official justice, the Red Brotherhood would no longer be anything but a band of criminals living from day to day off the product of its work, and what results could be expected from such a bloody harvest where uncertain results would have to be shared between so many hands? Extremely sensitive to that consideration of daily bread, and having only a very relative faith in the management of Montalvi and Madame de Camembert, the men that Lelouard and the Doctor were addressing had easily understood that it was in their interest not to fall out with the Marquis, and that the best thing for them to do at the moment was to be content with the means of existence that he had promised them. Therefore, they separated without deciding anything, and what Lupiano had set free remained definitively set free.

In learning about that ridiculous failure, the Marquis felt more pity than anger, and pretending to ignore what had happened, he convinced the two objectors to commit to come with Lelouard and the Doctor to inaugurate the possession of his new dwelling—what was called having a housewarming party. It was that dinner that Matiphous was told he had to attend.

At the beginning, although Lupiano had indicated, by his invitation, that he had kept no grudged about the rebellion, a little embarrassment and coldness was apparent among his guests who, after some reflection, had all answered his invitation. The wine and the good food having their usual effect, the dinner ended by being very joyful. On requests from every direction, even Montalvi decided to accept, in partnership with

Lelouard, the direction of the future banking house that the Marquis wanted to set up for them, and which was soon to begin its operations. All clouds cleared away, everyone separated with all the appearances of the best relationships, and it was agreed that, some days later, Madame de Camembert would, in her turn, invite all those united at that moment at her table.

When the father and the son were finally alone Lupiano said:

"My son, that trust that you have in Georgiana, can I not hope to have it myself? You must understand that I have some curiosity to know the events in your life."

"You know some of them," the man from Malta replied, "and I'm afraid that the rest will not always seem very exemplary to you."

"After your confession," Lupiano replied, "I certainly plan on giving you mine, and we must equally promise reciprocal indulgence, since your birth was, for you and for me, the beginning of a long series of misfortunes, which may be our excuse."

"So be it," said Matiphous.

And with the most absolute frankness he recounted all the adventures which the reader has already been told.

When he got to the famous scene that had taken place at the Sleepers' Club, Lupiano said:

"It is greatly to be regretted that, at that moment, the English police came between us, because, evidently, in that first encounter, the voice of blood spoke to me. Don't you remember that, in the presence of that courageous contempt for death, I made an affectionate move toward you?"

"Although I felt some hatred for you," replied Matiphous, "I wasn't also without feeling some attraction. But the hour of our coming together again hadn't yet come."

He then continued his story right up to the retrieval of the strongbox at the young painter's studio, where Dulac, a.k.a. Rempailleux, had stored it.[145]

"And that strongbox," Lupiano asked, "what became of it?"

"Probably, it is still in the place where I hid it."

"Well," said the Marquis, "we will put your conscience at rest by sending the treasure that you have conserved for them back to the heirs in America. Everything considered," he added when Matiphous had finished speaking, "thrown into the middle of such circumstances, who was more without fault than you? I would very much like not to have to make more painful confessions to you, but it is too late today to undertake the long story of my adventures. Tomorrow, you will know everything."

IX. The Marquis' Confession

The next day, the Marquis de Lupiano began tackling the story of his life:

"I was born," he said, "at the end of 1737 in the Electorate of Hanover.[146] Greatly preoccupied with the enlargement of his house, my father, the Baron of Kormer, of whom I was the only offspring, had, since my infancy, carefully arranged for me to marry a rich heiress. Toward the age of

---

[145] See Volume 3, Pages 183 seq.

[146] The Electorate of Brunswick-Lüneburg, colloquially known as the Electorate of Hanover, was established in 1692 as the ninth Electorate of the Holy Roman Empire and formally approved in 1708. It was ruled by the House of Hanover, a cadet branch of the House of Welf. With the ascension of its prince-elector as King of Great Britain in 1714, it became ruled in personal union with Great Britain. Merged into the Napoleonic Kingdom of Westphalia in 1807, it was re-established as the Kingdom of Hanover in 1814, with the personal union with the British crown lasting until 1837.

eighteen, I received the order to find the paternal choice agreeable, and to prepare myself for a marriage which, I was told, should not be put off, since all the social conventions had been met.

"I had more than one reason to see things differently; first of all, my extreme youth; next, my future, in whom nothing seemed pleasant except the dowry; then, a perfectly beautiful and intelligent cousin, who had been left an orphan and had been brought up with me under my mother's care. Less accommodating to the ideas of her husband, she would have seen our union with pleasure. And I must add that the sentiment which drew me toward Carlotta, the companion of my childhood, found her heart a warm echo.

"My father's explosion of disappointment at the first sign of resistance—something that he hadn't even thought possible!—was terrible. Accustomed, in the least matters, to be despotic, the Baron persuaded himself that, with threats, some violence, he could easily counter what he called my foolish pretentions. But he had come up against a strong personality and a will of steel that his harsh and lordly procedures could only deeply exasperate. Condemned to remain in my bedroom and threatened with seeing my cousin sent away from the household which, for many years, had been her only refuge, I came to an extreme resolution, that of furtively leaving the paternal roof. A loan that it was possible for me to cash in, from a rather large legacy left directly to me by my grandmother, made it possible for me to carry out my plan.

"For some time, I traveled without my father manifesting a strong opposition to my residing in foreign countries. He was hoping that absence and a greater experience of life would cut short a love that was an obstacle to him. One day, he thought he had delivered the last blow to my passion by letting me know that my cousin was eagerly getting ready for a marriage that he had arranged for her.

"Instead of softening my will, that news, which, furthermore, had nothing real about it, only made me take a desperate resolution. The protection of the *Grand Bailli*,[147] head of the *German Tongue*, offered me an easy access to the Order of Malta.[148] I announced my intention of taking vows. That decision was relatively agreeable to my father, because in committing myself to celibacy, I raised between myself and the woman he stubbornly refused to give me for a wife a barrier that could never be crossed. It's true that, at the same time, it made our name die with me. But the Baron had obtained at least a negative victory for his paternal authority, of which he was, above all, jealous. He gave his consent more quickly than I would have thought to the commitment that I spoke of mak-

---

[147] The *Grand Bailli* was a dignitary of the Order of St. John of Jerusalem, created in 1428. A *Tongue* was an administrative division of the Knights Hospitaller (also known as the Order of St. John of Jerusalem) between 1319 and 1798. The term referred to a rough ethno-linguistic division of the geographical distribution of the Order's members and possessions. Each *Tongue* was subdivided into Priories or Grand Priories, Bailiwicks and *Commanderies*. There were initially seven *Tongues*: Provence, Italy, England, Spain, France, Auvergne, and Germany. The German Tongue dated back to 1182 with the creation of the great priory of Bohemia. With the transition to the Protestant religion in 1538, the German Tongue's importance was reduced since the Order of St. John of Jerusalem could only include Roman Catholics. Originally, the German *Tongue*'s *Grand Bailli* was in charge of keeping the castle of St. Peter in Bodrum. The *Grands Baillis* were always from Upper Germany, which often presented problems of comprehension due to their language, High German, and their lack of understanding of Latin languages.

[148] The Sovereign Military Hospitaller Order of Saint John of Jerusalem of Rhodes and of Malta, also known as the Order of Malta, is a Roman Catholic lay religious order traditionally of military and chivalrous nature. It was founded as the Knights Hospitaller circa 1099 in Jerusalem, making it the world's oldest surviving chivalric order.

ing, and which, besides, he counted on making me renounce one day.

"After having honorably *made my caravans*, that is to say, make several sea journeys on the galleys of the Order,[149] I came to Malta where I took my vows and came in possession of all my rights as a knight and began to lead, at Valletta, the capital city of the island and headquarters of the Order,[150] a life that idleness and the knights of my age didn't always make very edifying. In various pleasures, I found forgetfulness of the love, henceforth hopeless, that, until then, I had never stopping thinking about. But without a taste for superficial and passing attachments, it wasn't long before I became engaged in a serious adventure which was to decide the whole future of my life. Passionately in love with a young nun, I managed to find a way into her convent. After I had made her fall in love with me, I arranged several nocturnal meetings, but she soon told me with horror that she had to hide one of those situations that bothers even a woman in secular life, and which was an affront to the vows we had both taken.

------

[149] Desirous to provide for the well-manning of their galleys, the Order demanded that all the knights and servants of arms should be obliged to *make* four *caravans* in person on board the galleys of the Order, before being knighted.

[150] The building of a city on the Sciberras Peninsula of Malta had been proposed by the Order of Saint John as early as 1524. Back then, the only building on the peninsula was a small watchtower dedicated to Erasmus of Formia, which had been built in 1488. In 1552, the watchtower was demolished and the larger Fort Saint Elmo was built in its place. In the Great Siege of 1565, Fort Saint Elmo fell to the Ottomans, but the Order eventually won the siege with the help of Sicilian reinforcements. The victorious Grand Master, Jean de Valette, immediately set out to build a new fortified city to fortify the Order's position in Malta. The city took his name and was called La Valletta.

"An elopement was then our only resource. Unfortunately, if it was easy to get out of the convent, we still had to leave the island, and enormous difficulties would be encountered in the flight that we were planning. While time passed, with us planning all kinds of projects impossible to carry out, I received the order to leave for an expedition, a cruel complication that, however, didn't take away all hope of salvation. My absence couldn't be, at the most, but for several months. The size and disposition of the monastic dress of the woman I was forced to leave gave her great chances of being able to disguise her condition.

"At the time of my return, the outcome so feared had become imminent, but nothing about our secret seemed to have been suspected. Having more money at that time than before my departure, I found myself more easily in a position to organize everything for our impending flight. The night that it was to take place, with a ladder, I had gotten into the garden of the convent, situated a short distance from a creek where a boat and two rowers were waiting for us. For more than two hours, I endured mortal anxiety about a delay that I couldn't explain, when the nun who had facilitated our meetings came to tell me that, probably following her extreme emotion, my lover, just at the moment when she was ready to come join me, had been surprised by birth pangs.

"She then told me that, despite that terrible blow, nothing was completely lost. The birth, although without the help of a doctor, fortunately, had taken place without incidents, and, according to all appearances, before the end of the night, making an effort, the mother of my child would be in a condition to follow me. But to give her strength and courage, my presence was needed, and everything had been arranged so that, without any danger of surprise, I could be taken to her cell.

"I had no reason to distrust a woman who, for us, had always shown herself to be diligent and faithful, and besides, was this a moment to rely on being careful? I therefore followed the woman leading me. She soon brought me to the young mother, who, on seeing me enter, said to me with great emotion:

" 'It is a son, my beloved!'

"And she joyfully showed him to me. A little later, I asked the woman who had given birth if she felt strong enough to get up and follow me, since the night was already far advanced, and moments were precious.

" 'My sister,' she answered, 'has gone to see if everything is quiet in the convent. But, while waiting for her to return, couldn't you put some mark on our baby so that, one day, it could serve to identify him. Who knows if he will not be taken from us.'

"Agreeing with that idea, I hastily, with a needle, as I had often seen sailors do, tattooed on the left arm of the infant the crown of my arms and the date *13 February 1778*. Then, I rubbed the powder from one of my pistols that I had taken care to bring with me into the design, while it was still fresh, rendering it permanent, and sowing the consolation and the happiness that, forty-two years later, I would reap."

"It was a true inspiration from Providence," said Matiphous.

"Or at least," Lupiano continued, "a luminous prevision of maternal love, because I had scarcely finished the operation that the other nun returned with a frightened air.

" 'Everything is lost!' she cried. 'The Abbess knows all! She is coming in this direction.'

" 'Flee, my love, and carry away our son,' my mistress said.

"I didn't even have time to think about what I should do. The door of the cell suddenly opened, giving entry to the Mother Superior. Four men wearing masks accompanied her. And at their head, his face covered, walked a somber person I recognized by his costume from having seen him elsewhere, as the high dignitary who, at Malta, in the name of the Court of Rome, exercised the fearful functions of Grand Inquisitor of the Faith. Badly disposed toward our Order, with whom he had had violent arguments, that man was reputed to be wicked and cruel. In the religious houses over which he had control, it was known that even the most minor faults were punished with merciless severity.

" 'Miserable one,' said the Abbess to the nun, 'how could you believe that your sin would remain hidden? For more than six months, I was told everything by the woman that you thought you had enlisted to your side. I was watching you. Give me the product of your debauchery!'

"And she snatched the infant from her hands.

"As for me, on the order of the Inquisitor, I was attacked by those henchmen, who didn't give me time to use my weapons, and I soon succumbed under their number. I was dragged into a room, whose windows, fitted with strong iron bars, opened onto the sea. A door covered with plaques of metal, and solidly locked on the outside, almost immediately closed on me. For nine days I remained confined in that prison. The man who brought me my food, which was served in abundance and with a certain care, was the only human being that showed himself to me. It was impossible to obtain a word from him, no more than from a guard who was watching incessantly behind my door being careful every hour to open it to reassure himself that I hadn't begun some work in view of preparing my evasion.

"As my captivity was prolonged, something strange happened to me. Day by day, I felt myself getting weaker, a loss of energy that, at first, I attributed to lack of exercise and the influence of my mental suffering, but toward the eighth day, my condition had become so complete, my head so cruelly weakened, and I felt such a decay and such weakness in my whole body, that I began to wonder if in the food served to me some substance that caused that delirium hadn't been mixed. I wondered if, in that form, one of those slow poisons that the Italians call *ad tempus* hadn't been administered to me. In the morning of the tenth day, suddenly seeing the victim of my imprudent love enter my prison, I would have believed in some clemency from our torturers, but I knew that monastic vengeances are pitiless. In that unhoped for and so unlikely reunion, I saw instead the threat of some new wickedness.

"I was not mistaken; I hardly had time to ask my unhappy love if she knew anything about the fate of our child than I heard the guard shout from the half-opened door of the room in which we were locked:

" 'Look a little distance out at sea; you will see something curious and interesting.'

"Our eyes looked in the direction pointed out to us. You can imagine our agony and our shock when we saw on the waves a cradle in the form of a canoe in which reposed a sleeping infant. The sea was calm and the precious cargo they had just confided to it, sent further out by a little breeze, didn't seem in any imminent danger, but with the first big wave... Carried away by that thought, I threw myself furiously against the window bars, hoping that, in the extreme excitement of my despair, I would find the strength to break them. When I saw that I could do nothing in that way, I ran to the door against which I wasted no less useless strength. I called to the guard that I knew was in range of hearing, sometimes with prayers, sometimes with threats. When that man didn't answer, I went back to the window where I could measure an enormous distance, carried away by a breath of fresh wind, that, minute by minute, the frail embarkation had traveled.

"Glued to the bars, no longer living except by what she saw, the mother, the opposite of my great and loud despair, was a spectacle of passive sadness, whose explosion seemed to have been delayed until the moment when the object to which her whole being remained stuck, as if glued to it, had finished vanishing in the mist of the horizon. Other eyes were, without a doubt, also watching the moment which would mark the end of the torture to which a terrible refinement of cruelty had condemned us. As soon as the black dot, anxiously followed a long time by our eyes, ceased to be visible, the henchmen entered my prison and told us that it was time for us to separate. I tried to defend the unfortunate one for whom I could foresee a terrible future. But, in my weakened condition, against four strong adversaries accustomed to that sort of expedition, what could I do? I was brought to the ground in an instant, while they took away the one I would never again see. I was then taken before the fierce inquisitor who said to me:

" 'Monsieur, you ought to have paid with your life for the affront that you were not afraid to make to this pious house. Fortunately for you, the Holy Inquisition has a gentler way to punish you. Among the papers of a man it had to punish, many years ago, it found a formula for a strong mixture that, for the debauched of your types, while letting them live, could alter in an irreversible way the virility that is for them the only instrument of their most shameful perversions. While at the same time telling you that the punishment is complete, you won't have, in the future anything to envy Abélard and Origen.[151] Go! You won't sin anymore.'

"Following that odious parody of the words addressed by the Savior to the adulterous woman, my bonds were untied, and I was taken out of the convent; I remained master of my actions. My first concern was to look for the men whom I had paid to take me off the island. They were honest men who had believed I was dead, and who greeted my return with joy. Taking possession once more of all I had placed in their boat, they worked several days with me exploring the area around the island without our being able to discover any trace of my infant whom I had to believe was buried in the waves.

"The poison, however, had made terrible ravages in me: on the exterior, I was to that point so transformed that when I

---

[151] Two teachers and philosophers who were distracted by their virility. Pierre Abélard (1079-1142), a medieval French scholastic philosopher and theologian, had an illicit love affair with his student Héloise. Both lovers took vows of celibacy and entered monastic life. Adamantius Origen (c.184-c.253 AD), an Alexandrian philosopher, one of the most influential figures in early Christian theology, apologetics, and asceticism, voluntary castrated himself when his virility compromised his research and writing.

saw the Grand Master of the Order in order to denounce the odious treatment inflicted on me, he could scarcely recognize me. He assured me that I was right about the monstrosity inflicted on me; but he gave me little hope for my lover. She was a prey given to the implacable, all-powerful monastic jurisdiction, and against that force, doubled with that of the Inquisition, he scarcely felt himself able to prevail.

"Judging by the terrible changes that, hour by hour, were taking place in me, since my life was broken and lost, I had spontaneously the idea of going to find shelter in a cloister, even if the Grand Master hadn't told me about a Spanish Franciscan, who, like Brother Cosme in France,[152] had made a European reputation by his prodigious cures.

"Determined to go consult that knowledgeable man, I thought that, if he found me irreparably affected, I would enter his order. At the end of some weeks, he had decided that his art was powerless to neutralize the effects of the poison I had ingested every day in little doses in all that I had drunk and eaten during the time of my imprisonment. I then wrote to my friends and to family in such a way as to make them believe I was about to commit, and, at the same time, I took the habit of a novice in the Franciscan Brothers of Malaga.

" Do what I'm doing, *age quod agis*, has always been my motto in the diverse and multiple phases of my existence. Engaged in monastic life, I had, at first, the sincere desire to accomplice all my duties. As soon the poison had finished its work of localized destruction, and let the rest of my organism recover energy and strength, I gave myself ardently to the study of theological matters with the hope that those matters would open the way to higher ranks in the Order, and later into

---

[152] Jean Baseilhac, a.k.a. Brother Cosme (1703-1781), French surgeon and lithotomist, who practiced medicine in Paris and was attached to the Hotel-Dieu. He already enjoyed a great reputation when he took the cloth in 1729. He founded at his own expense a hospital for the poor, where he practiced in person.

that of the dignities of the Church. Knowledge, joined to the regularity of the routine, had the merit of becoming easy for me, and would not have, in fact, been lacking in pushing my fortune further, if the spectacle of the always petty, and sometimes hideous, passions that polluted the atmosphere in the cloisters had not soon made all my fervor vanish.

"Under the feeling of disgust that the surroundings in which I was condemned to live finally inspired in me, little by little, there developed in me an immense need both for some change of action, and, something frightful to say, the outside world, to which I felt myself violently recalled. I could only foresee it through a thought of hatred. It seemed to me that I had the right to demand an accounting from one and all for that part of happiness of which the fanaticism of a man had dispossessed me. Envy remained my only passion and gnawed at my heart. The appetite for blood and destruction had finally substituted themselves for the loving and generous instincts of which my nature had been made at another period.

"Like those spirits of darkness that their fall had turned into the mortal enemies of God and of men, in blasphemy and the cult of evil, I searched for a bitter consolation, and when I experienced only emptiness, it was toward death that I was drawn, as the supreme remedy for my shame and my regrets. Then, however, on the side of will and intelligence, being endowed with energy and intelligence still powerful, I told myself that there would always be time to end it someday. When I had arrived at the perfect atheism, I would be firmly convinced that organized matter and a life without a tomorrow would be all I had to give back to the elements.

"In the middle of theses perplexities, a great disaster struck the monastery that I was still hesitating to leave. Situated on an isolated plateau, a short distance from Malaga, the house of the Franciscans was attacked by pirates, who overcame a resistance of which I had made myself the chief, and looting and fire soon made it a complete ruin. Having become a prisoner of the pirates, I found myself attracted to their life of combat and adventures, and the courage I had shown in the fight where I had held out against them earned their esteem, so I became part of their pavilion. After some time, an election put me at their head. Later, I served under the command of the famous Paul Jones.[153] I then went on into the Indian Ocean, where I became the terror of the English. On seeing up close the tyranny that they exercised over the Hindu populations, I conceived a mortal hatred for them and lost no opportunity to demonstrate it.

"Enriched by captures without number, most of the time achieved under the French flag, I had to make myself forgotten for some time. There was a price on my head and, by the order of the East India Company,[154] two frigates of the Royal Navy had received the order to relentlessly pursue the schooner that I commanded. The battle was too unequal, so I demilitarized my ship, and, to occupy my leisure, hidden under a false identity, I risked going into Calcutta. One day, the prospectus of a famous London charlatan fell into my hands.

"Author of a book with the ridiculous title, *Megalanthropogenese*, or *The Art of Procreating Great Men*,[155] its author, Doctor Graham, advertized that, by means

---

[153] Rabou probably meant John Paul Jones (born John Paul) (1747-1792), the US' first naval commander during the Revolutionary War. His actions in British waters during the Revolution earned him an international reputation for piracy which persisted for some time.

[154] The East India Company was a British joint-stock company formed on 31 December 1600. At the height of British rule in India, it had a private army of about 260,000 and ruled large areas of India, until 1858, when the British Crown assumed direct control. It was eventually dissolved in 1874.

[155] As strange as it might seem, this was a real (pseudo-)science popular in France and Germany at the start of the 19th century; it is , mentioned (amongst other places) in *The Spirit of the Public Journals for 1802*, Vol. 6, p. 81, by Charles Molloy Westmacott (1803). However, the Dr. Graham of the story seems completely fictitious.

of an appropriate treatment, and, above all, the miracles of his incomparable *celestial bed,* he could to revitalize the most faded and asleep virility. It appeared to me amusing, while verifying the efficacy of that bizarre medicine, to run the risk by going right to seat of British power—the very people who had offered a reward of two hundred thousand francs to the vessel that would capture me.

"I arrived in London with magnificent following, and hastened to put myself in the hands of Doctor Graham. By the payment of two hundred pounds sterling, I spent two nights in his famous *celestial bed*, where perfumed fumigations and the sounds of delightful music changed nothing in my condition. After that, my apparent femininity gave rise to suspicions that were only too justified, more than ever, by a curious and frivolous world, whose attention I had unwittingly drawn to me. I had to suffer several humiliating blows. It was then, dear Gregorio, that, because of the rage and despair into which several successive indignities had thrown me, I gave way to the fabulous eccentricities and atrocious vengeances of which you were the witness and the confidant."

"And also," Matiphous added, "somewhat the victim, even thought, as you noted yesterday, our two hearts were very near to speaking to each other."

"Yes," the Marquis replied, "but the Customs Board had pitted us one against the other creating hostility that prolonged the misunderstanding for a long time afterward. Then, after again taking up the fight against the English, and after having given myself the distraction of an immense wandering overland that made me comparable to the Wandering Jew, eight years later, I finally arrived at Livorno under the name and the dress of an Armenian merchant.[156] Your name, that I found mingled with a sad melodrama, was one of the reasons that made me decide to inflict it the most painful denouement."

---

[156] Salvador Arbib.

"Then," said Matiphous, "the three bodies found in the cave in Venezzia...?"[157]

"That was my work," Lupiano answered. "During the short empire that I had created for myself during that strange episode, Fauntleroy, accompanied by Hans Krafft, the engraver, and Christiana, your fiancée, came to me to ask me for an asylum against the pursuits of the law. That man who, in London, had so profoundly wounded me in the most vulnerable side of my ego, dared to offer himself to me as the one who had continued my hostilities against the Bank of England. He told how, having made Hans Krafft his instrument, he took revenge on you by overturning your projects of marriage. I then had, with the daughter of the artist, a long confidential talk. From that, I found that she still felt a deep attachment towards you, but at the same time, the complicity of her father with the counterfeiter Fauntleroy had spread a feeling of bitterness and shame over all the future of her life, which led to thoughts of suicide.

"On encouraging that dark state of mind, in addition to the fact that I was in my role as a satanic spirit, I broke in your hands that beautiful idol whose possession I envied you, punished that insolent Fauntleroy, and silently undid the existence of that white-haired child, that, it could hardly be doubted, was on the road to meet her end by the hand of the hangman.

"Poor Christiana," said Matiphous, regretfully.

"When I put an infallible poison in her hands, I was sure," Lupiano continued, "of the use she would make of it, because she had a manly soul. She divided it into three parts: one for the tempter, one for the old man, whose habits of laziness and innocent disorder had, little by little, led him to crime, and the third for herself! With the theatrical pomp that I had the pleasure to lay out for their funerals, I showed an act of defiance to the Imperial Government. Then, and, in my usual way, having henceforth an account to settle with that all-powerful power before whom all Europe trembled, it was in

---

[157] See Volume 3, Pages 137 seq.

Paris, in the heart of its domination, that I hurried to make my next domicile.

"There, under the name *Brothers of Death,* I continued the operations of *The Sleepers' Club.* Then I went on a new campaign in the vicinity of the Ile-de-France. Returning to Paris, I found the author of all my misfortunes across my path. Hidden under the false name of Vandel, Hulet, my evil genius, the Inquisitor of the Faith, had now become Inquisitor of Correspondence. Distilling drop by drop my revenge on that man and his family, I was on the way to making him pay dearly for the crime he had committed in Malta, when a letter intercepted in the post, put Napoleon in the path of that monstrous organization which had escaped the attention of his vigilant and notorious police, and was operating only a few steps away from him.

"There was an encounter between the Emperor and I.[158] He wanted me to account for the death of one of the officers of his guard that the Charter of our Association had chosen for suicide. I did not bend either under seductions or threats from my dreadful interlocutor, but I was ruined, and, during the rest of his reign, the dungeon at Vincennes condemned me to powerlessness and inaction.

"Taking part in the following events of my life, Georgiana and the Doctor were able to tell you how, again free, I was led to conceive the idea of the *Red Brotherhood* that was the pathway by which Providence drew us toward each other."

"Yes," said Matiphous, "and its ways can't be admired too much."

"And bless them as well," continued Lupiano, "because by finding you again, I have banished from my heart all regret and bitterness. From now on, I want to be good, and Hulet himself is included in the general amnesty that I have decreed.

"Oh! Hulet," the man from Malta said, "I don't consider his debt paid. He has twice made an attempt on my life, and if I ever get my hands on him..."

---

[158] See Volume 2, Pages 31 seq.

"Come now, don't be difficult," the Marquis said, "don't go looking for bad business. Henceforth we can have a nice and calm life. Therefore, let's let the past sleep."

X. The Autopsy of the Strongbox

In talking about a possible encounter with Hulet, Matiphous couldn't know how probable that encounter was. During the year 1819, Hulet, the regicide of the Convention,[159] had decided to petition for the revocation of his exile. He used as an excuse for that humiliating action, the state of his health and that of his daughter, Helena. Made to suffer greatly by the voyage and the American climate, the sick girl, in the opinion of the doctors, had no chance of recovery unless she could have the beneficent influence of her native air.

In 1819, under the Ministry of Decazes,[160] there was a leaning toward the ideas of unity and forgiving; hence, the request of the banished man had been easily approved. It was at the moment that Lupiano had just come to lease the Lamoignon townhouse. Hulet, who had returned to France, had been living, for some months, with his family in his former apartment on the Rue Barbette, that he had found vacant. Thus, both living in the neighborhood of the Marais,[161] those

---

[159] The National Convention was the first government of the French Revolution, following the two-year National Constituent Assembly and the one-year Legislative Assembly. Created after the great insurrection of 10 August 1792, it was the first French government organized as a republic, abandoning the monarchy altogether. The Convention sat as a single-chamber assembly from 20 September 1792 to 26 October 1795.

[160] Élie-Louis, 1st Duke of Decazes and Glücksburg (1780-1860), leader of the liberal Doctrinaires party during the Bourbon Restoration.

[161] i.e.: The Marsh. Historic district of Paris, hosting many outstanding buildings, spread across parts of the 3rd and 4th *arrondissements*.

two men, between whom there was an abyss of hatred, were scarcely separated by a distance of some streets.

Like that of Lupiano, the life of the former director of the Secret Bureau had been cruelly tested. But at the moment when his exile had ended, happiness and consolation seemed also to dawn over his life. After the sad failure of that *Champ d'Asile* colony, of which he had entertained the notion of becoming its legislator, Hulet had gone to live in New York. There, he had met a young American who had shown a great desire to be a guest in his home. Being nicely provided for with respect to his fortune, the young man was entirely free of his actions and wishes, since he was still in mourning for his mother, whom he had just lost, and who had been a widow for several years.

His regular visits to the Hulet family had soon turned into a proposal of marriage with regard to his daughter, Helena. In order to behave like an honest man, Hulet had spoken of a secret that he was not permitted to reveal, but that could render that marriage undesirable.

"Is it something dishonorable?" the young American had asked.

"As a matter of absolute morality," answered Hulet, who considered the functions of a letter-opener in this way, "I can hold my head high; but I must lower it before someone prejudiced against certain functions of the State."

"Very well; I don't need to know any more," had replied the young man.

In addition to him being very much in love with Helena, in the United States, people are seldom stopped by our matrimonial delicacies. In that country, above all, when he is rich, a man persuades himself that, in throwing on his conjugal mantle over his future spouse, she will have consideration and a respected future. As for the matter of Helena's consent, it had been quickly settled by the loveable qualities of the future husband, his air of distinction, and, most of all, by the perfume of gentle sadness that permeated all his being. That perfume is known, even when it is watered down, to capture the imagination of young girls But how can true melancholy not be believed when the recent loss of a mother and mourning dress are there to justify it?

The marriage was then decided. Nevertheless, Helena's health formed an obstacle to its taking place immediately. It was then agreed that it should take place in France, as soon as the fiancée had regained, at the contact of her native soil, some weight and her youthful body. Included in the Hulet household on the basis of being her *fiancé* that only death could release from his engagement, not only had the young American made the voyage, but, living in communal life with his adopted parents, he ate at the same table and lodged under the same roof.

While in that surreptitious way, the web of fate was tightening between the former Inquisitor of Malta and his two victims, some unexpected contact took place when, one morning, Matiphous asked father:

"What about my strong box? What aren't you talking to me about it anymore?"

"But, first of all, where is it?" asked Lupiano.

"In the Champs-Elysées," replied the man from Malta, "at the foot of a tree where a blind man has been playing his clarinet for years. The poor man! Just today, I saw him exercising his functions, never knowing that he has a fortune buried under his feet."

"Well then, tonight," the Marquis said, "we will go practice the *extraction* of the treasure. The weather is conveniently rainy, and we will have more chance not to be bothered by curious people."

In fact, the next night, under a sky pouring down water, father and son went to visit the place where, for almost six years, the strongbox had been buried, and it was found exactly where Matiphous had deposited it. Thanks to a layer of bichlorate of mercury, with which he had taken care to coat it, the humid ground had done almost no harm to it, and well before daylight, it had been transported to Lupiano's domicile in a satisfactory state of conservation.

Matiphous had had it in his hands for some time without having been able to discover the secret of the method by which it could be safely opened. But Lupiano had lived with a good number of criminals, and he was familiar with many of the practices of their art. He solved the problem in a flash.

In gold, bank bills and jewelry, the strongbox, once inventoried, contained valuables that could be estimated at a sum of eight hundred thousand francs. In addition, it also enclosed some papers, notably a sealed letter, the one its owner had written under the very eyes of Rempailleux, a moment before killing himself with a pistol shot.

The address inscribed on was: *Mrs. Augusta Bedloe, Harlem (New York)*. Lupiano respected the seal, but he glanced at some of the other letters. Those were open. The American had received them from his wife during a long sojourn that he had made in Paris. From the tone in which they were written, it didn't seem as if his prolonged absence had been taken in complete patience. Without exactly knowing the disorder into which he had been drawn by his frenetic taste for gambling and women, that had finally driven him to suicide, Mistress Bedloe, suspected that her husband's life had not been very exemplary, and she complained strongly about the abandon in which he had left her.

It is very strange, she said to him in one of the conjugal lamentations she regularly addressed to him once a month, *that in your stubborn residence in Paris, you have not been able to procure any information about the Vandels, with whom we had the misfortune to spend one night a Orgères.*

"Orgères! Vandel!" exclaimed Matiphous, to whom Lupiano had read aloud that passage. "That has the Hulet stench from a league away. Is it by way of New York that we will pick up the trail of that miserable man?"

The crime that we then committed through the intermediary of that chief of brigands, Lupiano continued to read, *weighs more heavily than ever on my conscience. It is in vain that we have surrounded with happiness the life of the child that we stole, and in the unlikely case that he should, after our death, not be recognized as our son, it will be useless for us, by means of a will, to make sure that he inherits all our fortune. I am not less racked by remorse, and my last moments will not be tranquil if we do not manage to give him back to his family. I have been very careful, since we have discovered nothing on that subject, not to let him suspect anything. He certainly loves me in a way that gives me the illusion of true motherhood; but Heaven hasn't permitted that that stolen happiness to be without bitterness for me. One of His ways of punishing me is, perhaps, that coldness you have taken toward me, and that has kept you for years away from your home, using the liberty that you have created for yourself, God knows for what.*

At least, the kind of divorce set up between us will serve as reparation for the sin we committed. In the past, you were gallant for me, even to the point of stealing infants; now you quarrel with me even for the right to live with you. But then, can't you therefore use some of those hours that you are making me spend in tears to find the trail of that family into which we have carried desolation?

If you manage to get some news of the father or the mother, it would be enough to show them this little gold heart found on the shoulders of their little Victor when the chief of the Chauffeurs had him delivered to us, to prove to them that it is really their son whom we are returning to them. I feel tears in my eyes in thinking of the happiness that his mother will then experience.

I beg you, my love, for that interest that touches my tranquility, in this life and in the other, busy yourself a little more seriously than you have until now. To find the Vandels has been your pretext for that unfortunate voyage to France where the state of my health did not let me follow you. Be an honest man and at least do the thing for which you left me. I can't hide it from you; my condition is far from getting better because of my remorse and all the other worries you give me. Hurry then, if you want to discover something in sufficient time, because however slow you still are to return and to bring

*me news, I don't dare reassure you that you will find the one
that in the past was your well-beloved,*

Augusta Bedloe

"So," Lupiano said, on finishing his reading, "Hulet also lost his child. I was more avenged than I thought."

"And by the hands," Matiphous replied, "of that excellent Rempailleux that you wanted hanged in London. I heard that story of the kidnapped infant from Britannicus in prison, before whom the current director of the Secret Bureau bragged about it, but I didn't suspect, as they commonly say, that it was a piece so well carried out."

"My dear Gregorio," said the Marquis, "I don't hold a grudge as you do. Happiness has taught me clemency, and today, if I knew where to find our former enemy, I would hurry, it seems to me, to transmit to him the information that has fallen into our hand. What's more, Hulet is perhaps closer to his son than he figured, since Lelouard found the poor man in the *Champ d'Asile* in the company of a great number of other French refugees, and they say that most of them, after the breakup of the colony, stayed in the United States."

"Well, let him stay there," Matiphous answered, "because as God is God, if he ever again crosses my path, we will vie with one another."

"I don't like to hear you talk that way," said Lupiano. "Always hating, is that a way of life?"

"When he has told me what he did with my mother," Matiphous replied, "I will see if I should tell him what was done with his son."

"That's only a specious pretext for an implacable resentment. Hulet remains, in every way, a stranger to the fate of your mother. I forgot, in the rapid telling of my own story, to tell you her final story. Shortly after my departure from Malta, on the formal complaint from the Grand Master of the Order, our persecutor was recalled to Rome, and, with a long reclusion at the Château Saint-Ange, he atoned for the abuse of power of which he was guilty.

313

"In the meantime, your mother remained in rigorous captivity, but when Malta was captured by Bonaparte, the convents were opened, and she recovered her liberty. She did not want to take advantage of it, and of herself, she then went to seek asylum in Parlermo, in a house of her order, where she rose to the rank of Abbess. Vainly, at a time already far away, I tried to see her again. I didn't manage to be received by her, but three years ago, I learned that, after penitential austerities, she had become the moral support of her community. She died there, peacefully, in an odor of sanctity. "

"But what about me?" exclaimed Matiphous excitedly. "What did the miserable man do to me, weighing down my life from my birth? Because of him, on Gozzo Island, I became an assassin; and in London, the valet of the hangman; and in Paris, a secret opener of letters; and later, a thief, because it was by a theft that I appropriated that strongbox that you're looking at—and you still wish me to forgive that man?"

"What you're calling a theft, was, on the contrary, an act of preservation, since, without you, the ignoble Rempailleux would have succeeded in his attempt. Today, we know where to find Mistress Augusta Bedloe. We're going to let her know that we hold, at her disposition, the strongbox of her late husband, and if she is no longer alive, her heirs will receive it."

"Yes, Hulet the son, right? And I'll have worn myself out to secure an inheritance of eight hundred thousand francs for him!"

"Would you prefer to keep them? Understand that in our existence, what is past is past. The instant of our reunion starts a new era for us. Unfortunately, so far, we have been cruel; but now, wickedness would be no excuse, and as the most sublime prayers says, if we want God to pardon us, we must first pardon those who have offended us."

Thereupon, Lupiano closed the strongbox. He thought that, by having Lelouard write to Lefebvre, through him, they could find out where Hulet had gone after the refugees from Galveston Island had separated.

XI. The Portrait

As has just been seen, that moral rejuvenation that paternity had brought to the Marquis, had not been brought about in Gregorio Matiphous. More ardent, because he was still in the strength of age and passions, in the middle of his misfortunes, not having had, like his father, the compensation of complete power that Lupiano had possessed even to satiety, he was drawn to enjoy, to a kind of frenzy, all the pleasures that the immense fortune of the Marquis now put at his disposal. Mediterranean, by way of his mother, as well as by the sky under which he was born, to the number of the sweeter joys of life, he included vengeance.

However, it wasn't in looking for his enemies that he spent the first moments of his new existence. Although while waiting for an encounter with Hulet, he had at hand three objects of his ardent hatred: Rempailleux, Kitty Ketch, and the Secret Bureau, as well as other, more agreeable cares that seemed to occupy him.

Now Comte de Lupiano, since his father had the title of Marquis, he pleased himself by having his calling card ornamented with his aristocratic qualifications. Spending all the money necessary for the satisfaction of his least fantasies, he took Georgiana to theaters and other public places in carriages of which the good taste and magnificence made a sensation and were commented on in the newspapers.

During that time, the Lelouard-Montalvi & Company bank had begun to function, and, thanks to the Marquis's capital by which it was backed, it was in a position to offer a loan to the government of that time. Raised by that operation to a higher financial status that, ordinarily, the most fortunate and the cleverest can reach only after an apprenticeship of several years, they made enormous profits, and the reflection of that prosperity extended even to Matiphous; he became one of the most fashionable men of the moment.

Georgiana then ran some risk of seeing herself replaced, because every woman of the theater and dangerous sirens started chasing after that new millionaire who, reaping what others had sown for him, had the leisure, at the same time as the power, to entertain his most expensive follies. But too little time had passed for satiety to have made him available to any of the schemes of which he was the object. In his eyes, the so-called *Bloodied Girl,* whose fatal influence he seemed to have conjured away, was incomparably more seductive than any of those good will offers. So, not content with possessing the original, one day he was seen asking about what painter he should chose to give the care of reproducing on canvas a beauty he didn't admit had a rival.

A man who was then in vogue for portraits was Adolphe Levillain, that young artist about whom his stay in the prison and his romanesque marriage to Madame de Pringy,[162] had contributed at least as much as his talent to surround him with an immense halo of celebrity. No society woman would then consent to the painted by any other hand but his, first of all, out of curiosity to see at close hand a man to whom such extraordinarily things had happened; then, since Levillain had become rich through his marriage, he had the means to be very expensive, and besides, his portraits were very life-like and remarkable by their elegance and their distinction.

The first time Matiphous heard pronounced the name of the man for whom he had been the cause of all his misfortunes, he wondered if it would be wise and prudent of him to voluntarily seek to meet such a man to whom he owed such a large debt. But money had turned the head of our newly-enriched man, and he wouldn't admit that any obstacles could be put in the path of any of his desires.

"Bah!" he said, "six years more on my head; my complexion tanned by the Madagascar sun; a client who doesn't bargain, and who, instead of the common name of Deschamps, has become Monsieur le Comte de Lupiano, under all that,

---

[162] See Volume 3, Pages 198 seq.

how could my identity be guessed? That Adolphe Levillain has never seen me, and, at the most, there would be only his wife who would have some chance of recognizing in me the man of the past, since she once paid me a half-hour visit, and, she would have to be in her husband's studio when I was there."

By virtue of this reasoning, Matiphous, the same day, went to the artist's studio and asked him if he would paint for him the portrait of *the prettiest woman in Paris.* At the moment the man from Malta entered Adolphe Levillain's studio, the painter was busy putting the last touches, without the presence of the model, to a woman's portrait that he was to deliver the following day.

"Interesting and distinguished figure," said Matiphous, glancing at the artist's work, "but there is something in it of suffering and sickly."

"Yes," the painter answered. "That is a young girl whose health has been rather seriously compromised. I told her fiancé, because she has been married since yesterday, that perhaps it would be better to wait for the painting until she was fully recovered. But he answered that he wanted to have the portrait of his wife such as she was at the time of their meeting. Later," he added, "you will paint her in all her brilliance. Americans, like the British, often have eccentric ideas, this Victor Bedloe certainly has the means to indulge his fantasies."

"Victor Bedloe?" Matiphous asked quickly.

"Yes, a rich landowner from New York."

"The girl that he is marrying, would it be indiscreet to ask you her name?"

"Not in the least in the world. She's a French girl, Mademoiselle Helena Vandel."

"Vandel! You're very sure that's the name of his wife?"

"Perfectly sure. Do you know that family?"

"I've heard it spoken about," the man from Malta replied in the most indifferent tone that he could take. "Monsieur Vandel, her father, was, I believe, a regicide from the National Convention who was exiled to the United States."

"I don't know anything about his political past, but he has just returned from America; the marriage was arranged there."

"And he lives in Paris today?"

"Yes," the painter answered, "he lives in the Marais, Rue Barbette, in an old parliamentary townhouse that has an unbelievable history. While I was dining there yesterday, I thought for a moment that I was transported back to the 16th century, in the middle of one of those former upper middle-class families distinguished by the gravity of their lifestyle. The mother, dressed entirely in black, seemed monastic; the father, with his long white hair that made him look like a patriarch; the future son-in-law in full mourning dress for his own mother, who passed away a short time ago, looked like a Quaker or a Protestant minister; and finally the daughter, who had the suffering and melancholy appearance that you see here. All that seemed to me to represent rather well a household during the time of the League [163] or Saint-Bartholomew. [164]"

"And the marriage, you say, was yesterday?"

---

[163] The Catholic League of France or Holy League was a major participant in the French Wars of Religion. Formed by Henry I, Duke of Guise, in 1576, the League intended the eradication of Protestants—mainly Calvinists or Huguenots—out of Catholic France during the Protestant Reformation, as well as the replacement of King Henry III.

[164] The St. Bartholomew's Day massacre in 1572 was a targeted group of assassinations and a wave of Catholic mob violence, directed against the Huguenots during the French Wars of Religion. The massacre began in the night of 23-24 August 1572, the eve of the feast of Bartholomew, two days after the attempted assassination of Admiral Gaspard de Coligny, the military and political leader of the Huguenots, ordered by the king. The slaughter spread throughout Paris. Lasting several weeks, it expanded to the countryside. Modern estimates for the number of dead vary from 10,000 to 70,000.

"But only at the Town Hall. The religious marriage will take place tomorrow at the Church of the Blancs-Manteaux."

"I doubt that it will turn out well," said Matiphous. "The poor woman has a sickness of the lungs, or I don't know it. But, to come back to the reason for my visit, when can you give us a sitting?"

"Oh! Not before three months; I have other commitments until them."

"Then I will take my turn at that time," said Matiphous, giving his card to the artist, "and you will allow me, won't you, to come sometimes to remind me to your memory?"

He then took his leave rather quickly. He thought that an immense horizon of vengeance had just opened up to his thoughts of revenge. In that American, bearing the name Bedloe and the first name Victor, having property in New York, wasn't it natural to see in him the young child kidnapped at Orgères, who had become the putative son and the heir of his ravishers?

But if that supposition was justified, a horrible misfortune would then have stealthily befallen the Hulet household. Just as the stamp of fatality had marked ancient families, an atrocious crime would have taken place, and the brother would become the husband of the sister!

What to do with that discovery, and most of all, how to to verify its accuracy, were the two ideas that came to mind to Matiphous while the painter was talking to him. To give him time to think about them at his ease, it was understandable that he would want to be alone. In going to see Bedloe, under the natural pretext of restoring to him the strongbox left by his father, he would be sure to question his identity, with all the desirable precision. But not having yet settled in his mind the manner in which he would use that disastrous revelation, Matiphous didn't find it proper contact that family yet. Besides, his instinct was rather to strike from a distance without revealing the hand that dealt the blow.

To verify the identity of the American, he had another method. He went to the Town Hall where the marriage had been performed the day before and, using the right that the law gives to everyone, he obtained a copy of the act of marriage as recorded in the official registry. After reading that document, there was no longer any doubt in the vindictive mind of the man from Malta regarding the reality of the horrible secret that had fallen into his possession. The document stated that Mr. Victor Bedloe was the son of Mr. Edgar Bedloe, a landowner in Harlem, New York, and of Mrs. Augusta Bedloe, née Templeton, both deceased, the former in Paris in 1814, and the latter in New York in 1819. And what the lie of the relationship as stated therein was that the act of marriage referenced a public document that the husband should have furnished, a birth certificate, but stated that he could not produce any.

Everything considered, after having obtained the certainty that he had been looking for, Matiphous, at least for the moment, had only to watch and let things take their course. In his horrible thoughts of hatred, his play would have been to wait for the consummation of the marriage, since until then, incest remained only a possibility on paper, and it would be only after the religious ceremony giving the spouses to each other had taken place that it would become a dreadful reality.

The next day, Matiphous had the abominable curiosity to go to the Church of the Blancs-Manteaux to be sure that the marriage had been celebrated. That parish wasn't lucky for Hulet's daughter, because it was there that, ten years before, the day of her first communion, she had undergone the cruel humiliation that Lupiano had set up, through her, for her father, to whom he was pouring out, drop by drop, the venom of his revenge so carefully planned. That time, it could be said that the serpent was hidden under the flowers. The nuptial benediction was given in the presence of a small number of friends, because Hulet continued to lead a very quiet life. But the organ, the decorated chairs, the window panes covered with velvet, the Verger in his most magnificent uniform, the bright lights, in a word, all the pomp which the Church had at its disposal for the marriage of couples that could afford the cost, were deployed in that circumstance.

However, either with a hidden instinct of the misfortune hovering over her, or by a nature essentially impressionable, and in a sick body, Helena, that day, was so horribly pale and weak, that those who attended the spectacle of the ceremony, the gossips of the neighborhood, exclaimed, saying that it was a pity to marry a girl when she looked more ready for burying!

Since he feared seeing himself exposed in his hateful intentions, Matiphous, at first, thought of not mentioning his discovery to his father, but the same evening of the day the ceremony had taken place, as they were dining together alone, the Marquis said:

"A propos, I have news of Hulet. Can you imagine that he lives almost door to door to us?"

"Really?" said Matiphous, pretending astonishment.

"Yes, this morning, as I was walking down the Rue Barbette, in a townhouse where he used to live in 1810, I saw a great fracas of carriages and coach drivers in white gloves and boutonniere. Obviously, a marriage was getting underway, so I loitered around and mingled with the neighborhood. I stopped to look at the married woman getting into a very expensive coach. And think of my astonishment! The man who was giving her his arm from the steps of the house right to the carriage, was none other than Hulet! So, I was told the rest of the story by one of the curious whom I questioned. That was his daughter that he was taking to the altar."

"Well, well… What effect did that encounter have on you?"

"It moved me more than I would have thought possible. That man who, in destroying my existence and yours, has probably forever made the happiness of such a day impossible for us, appearing to me in the midst of the holy joy of such a familial event, didn't leave me in the indulgent dispositions which I thought I would feel toward him. I still felt hatred in my heart."

"You see," said Matiphous, "there are things that can't be forgotten. After that, don't be too envious of that happy father. I, too, discovered that he was in Paris, and I know a great deal more than you about the marriage of Mademoiselle Hulet."

Asked for an explanation, the man from Malta, reassured by the confession he had just obtained from the Marquis, no longer hesitated to give him his full and entire confidence. While he, with a cruel complacency, detailed all the steps that he had taken to arrive at the certitude which he finally had in his possession, Lupiano listened with rather cold curiously.

"So," he said, "if we do not intervene, in a few hours, an irreparable misfortune, a punishment I would never have dreamed even in my most terrible fits of hatred, will have struck that man, of whom I was jealous this morning."

"But we will not intervene, I hope, father," Matiphous said quickly. "We are under no duty to do so."

"Yes," said Lupiano, "that is a punishment sent to him by the Lord. It is perhaps not up to us to put ourselves across the path of His justice."

"On the contrary, later," continued the implacable man from Malta, "we should finish our work, because expiation for such wicked men doesn't even begin until the day their ignorant happiness ceases. What's more, I've thought a great deal about it; the simplest method, at the moment, is to simply return the strongbox. It contains all that's necessary to inform him fully."

"We will talk about it later," Lupiano said casually. "What are you doing this evening?"

"I'm taking Georgiana to the Theatre Feydeau. It's an opening night."

"Well then, I think it's time for you to leave; you can drop me on the Boulevard. From there, it's only a short walk to the Rue Chantereine. I must talk with Lelouard and I don't want to miss him."

The Marquis had himself let out of Matiphous' coach at the top of the Rue de la Grange-Batelière. As soon as the carriage was out of sight, he climbed into a rented cabriolet and told the coachman to take him posthaste back to his townhouse. As soon as he had arrived there, he gave the order to hitch the horses and he had his Hindu put the famous strong-box into his carriage. He ordered the Hindu to follow him, and a few minutes later, he reached the Rue Barbette. As we have probably guessed, he wanted to hide his actions from his son.

XII. 1779 and 1824

A man who gets out of an expensive carriage is always sure of being received politely.

"Mon Dieu!" answered the servant to whom Lupiano had just asked to see Monsieur Vandel. "I doubt that Monsieur Vandel can see you now. His daughter was just married this morning and he is, at the moment, dining with his guests."

"However, I must speak to him. Tell him that it is the Marquis de Lupiano who has some matters of the most extreme urgency to communicate to him."

Lupiano was then asked to wait in a drawing-room of modest appearance, where he could hear a certain animation present at the wedding dinner which had been set up in a neighboring room.

A little later, Hulet entered from the door of the dining-room, through which one could see a table set with candelabras, splendidly served.

"You had yourself announced, Monsieur, in terms that wouldn't allow me to refuse you a short interview," he said, "but I would ask you to be brief; you have been told the circumstances which make me desire not to be kept away for long."

"It is precisely the subject of that circumstance," replied Lupiano, "that brought me here. I have to give you a communication of the greatest importance, but far from my agreeing to the conciseness that you are expecting of me, I will ask you to take me to a room less open than this one, where we can be sure that our conversation will be neither heard nor interrupted."

Hulet listened attentively, and said:

"Both of us are at an age where we do not have a taste for puzzles. Are you affirming that our interview will be as serious as you represent it, and that it could not, without inconvenience, be put off until tomorrow morning, for example? That would not be a very long delay."

"I have the honor of repeating, Monsieur, that I must speak to you at this very instant. That object," he said, pointing to the strongbox carried by the Hindu, who had accompanied him, "should already make you understand that it's not just a matter of fancy words."

More and more intrigued by Lupiano's solemn and convincing air, Hulet rang for a servant to bring light into his study, and while the Marquis was being conducted there, still followed by his servant, Hulet, with his agreement, returned to the dining-room to excuse himself before his guests for the necessity he had to slip away from their company for a little longer than he had at first supposed.

When Hulet returned to join him, the Marquis made a sign to the Hindu to put the strongbox on a table and to leave. Then, he said to Hulet:

"You are sure that no one is close enough to hear our words?"

"Perfectly sure," replied Hulet. "Please take a chair and explain yourself."

Lupiano sat down, placing himself so that the light of the lamp was directed fully to his face:

"You do not recognize me?" he asked Hulet.

"No, I don't recall ever having seen you before."

"But in the past, you were in the Religious Orders."

"Is that a question that you are asking me? For a man who just married his daughter this morning, it could seem strange."

"I am not questioning," replied Lupiano, "I'm affirming, and not only with respect to you, but also Madame Hulet, whom is, I know, a former Benedictine nun."

"Monsieur," said Hulet, rising quickly, "what are you getting at? My life has already been the object of a long persecution. Has the irksome government which, with much trouble, revoked my sentence of exile, now charged you with an investigation into the secrets of my private life?"

"At no time," responded the Marquis, stressing his words, "have I in any way belonged to any kind of police, and as far as I am concerned, I will prove to you, in a moment, that the seal of a letter has always been inviolable."

"I see. Please finish," Hulet said bitterly, understanding that here was a man who was completely informed about his past. "Because if you haven't agreed to be concise, I, for my part, haven't promised you to be entirely patient."

"A last fact to be stated is this," replied Lupiano. "In 1778, in Malta, you were the Inquisitor of the Faith, and your name was the Reverend Father Hulet."

"Eh! Monsieur, the Revolution, in which you know, without a doubt, that I also played a role, explains very well other transformations and changes of name."

"Oh! In the calmest times," replied the Marquis, "that *masquerade* is still perfectly possible. For instance, I, in 1810, under the united and orderly government of Napoleon, called myself Marquis de Saint-Faust."

"You, Monsieur? So, you would be the man who, for a long time and for no reason that I know of, has devoted all his energy in poisoning my life?"

"I was that man, and I then called myself the Marquis de Saint-Faust because, thanks to you, the name Baron de Kormer had become impossible for me to use."

"The Baron de Kormer..." repeated Hulet, like a man trying to remember.

"Yes, a young Knight of Malta, who, due your execrable fanaticism, was reduced to a condition worse than death. Do you now understand why I have always kept an eye on your career, and that all the secrets of your wretched existence are perfectly known to me."

"Today, I will admit," the ex-Inquisitor then said "that an exaggerated zeal drew me perhaps beyond the limits of decency, but since forty-two years have passed since that sin which

I committed, what expiation, therefore, do you propose to ask of me?"

"I was not the only victim then. An innocent creature was also the victim of an abominable refinement of cruelty."

"I, in fact, made a mistake," interrupted Hulet, "that of not tempering the frenetic indignation of the Abbess, a woman who thought she was empowered to use any kind of violence to avenge the insult made to her nunnery. But what she ordered to be done to the infant of whom you were the father, I didn't consent to, nor approve."

"Then rejoice with me," replied Lupiano, "because Heaven didn't allow that enormous cruelty to be successful. My son survived, and, a few weeks ago, by the most unforeseen of chances, he returned into my arms."

"You were more fortunate than I, Monsieur. A child was also was taken from me, a just punishment, perhaps, for my guilty complicity with the wrath of the Abbess. My child whom I will likely never see again."

"And yet, I have come to give him back to you!"

"You, Monsieur?" Hulet said with the greatest emotion. "Then you would be as good and forgiving as God?"

"At the least, the grace that He has shown me has not fallen on ungrateful ground. Since consolation has come to be seated at my bedside, I have forgiven my enemies, and when misfortune hovers above them, even if for a merited punishment, I rush to warn them and to save them."

"But that dear child that has been so mourned for, now so close to being returned to me, how could he be that misfortune that you would be shielding me from? Isn't it, on the contrary, an immense joy that you are making me foresee?"

"I haven't told you everything yet, and first of all, the event at Orgères... Have you explained them to yourself?"

"My child, I have every reason to believe, was stolen by a band of criminals, the *Chauffeurs*, led by a man who operated under the ignoble pseudonym of Rempailleux..."

The Marquis quickly finished:

"…Who has now become Monsieur de Saint-Rambert, and has followed in your footsteps as as Director of the Secret Bureau."

"Is that possible? A function so sensitive and important in the hands of such a man!"

"You said it yourself a while ago, revolutionary times explain all masquerades. But this is only a parenthesis, and to return to the purpose of my visit, did you suspect the reason for that crime by that man?"

"He was careful to explain his crime himself. He wrote me that he wanted to punish me for having snatched out of his claws the travelers that he was counting on robbing."

"An American and his wife who had stayed with you the preceding night, wasn't it?"

"Yes. At dusk, they'd had found themselves on the road that leads to Orgères, which was at that time a den of thieves. A storm was imminent, my house was only two steps away, how could I not offer them hospitality?"

"And you were nobly repaid. The next day, for the price of fifteen thousand livres, they bought your child."

"Could that be true?" Hulet exclaimed. "But, yes, that infamy is not improbable. They had made me a strange offer, that of adopting one of my infants. That their marriage had remained sterile was a constant source of bitterness and regrets for them."

"And the husband," Lupiano continued, "made his dear other half the gallant gift of your son that the leader of the *Chauffeurs* had agreed to procure for him. Later, a less obliging and a less tender spouse, the same man left his wife, who had returned with him and your child to their faraway country While in Paris, leaving considerable valuables locked inside in a strongbox, said to be impossible to open, he ended his life, in which his abuses of pleasure had led to satiety, by committing suicide."

"Yes, I remember," said Hulet. "That suicide got a lot of publicity. The strongbox was stolen and an employee of the

Secret Bureau which I managed even found himself compromised in that affair."

"No, no," Lupiano continued, "you are still completely mistaken about this. The real thief was, and still is, Rempailleux. The man you are accusing, and that according to your habits of violent justice, you had already condemned to death, had, on the contrary, snatched that rich prey from Rempailleux's villainous hands. And the proof that he didn't want to keep it for himself is that it sits there, today, in front of you, intact, without the least bit of the wealth it contained having been removed. What's more, with the valuables, there are also some papers…"

"And in those papers, without a doubt, you have found the trace of my child, because, otherwise, why bring that strongbox to me?"

"Indeed," Lupiano replied, pointing to the strongbox. "In there is all the information necessary for you to find your son. But that immense joy, as you called it just a moment ago, I must not hide from you, will be dearly bought."

"Why? Is it because my son, perverted by an upbringing that was not that of his family, has, in some way, forfeited his honor?"

"You still don't know the name of your erstwhile guest, that American who killed himself?"

"I was living in great seclusion, very occupied with my austere functions. From the newspapers, I learned that a rich foreigner had just shot himself with a pistol. That was one of those facts that are reported by the thousands. I didn't have any reason to look for the name of the dead man."

"But when you intervened in the matter of the employee of the *Secret Bureau* who was accused of having appropriated the American's strongbox?"

"I communicated very little with the police. There was a perpetual conflict of authority between us. I was sent a note which stated that one of my subordinates had stolen some important valuable objects, following the suicide of a foreigner, whose name they may have told me. But what struck me in that information was the manner in which the theft occurred. I have always held to the superior morality of the *Bureau* that I directed. For me, in the crime that had been denounced to me, there were two crimes: the theft and the secrets of a letter. It was the latter, most of all, in which I was interested."

"It is all very simple, in fact," Lupiano said. "Fate must have its ways, and in order for them to be accomplished, it must have wanted that name, which you will in a moment discover with horror, to remain unknown to you."

"But that name, finally, what is it?"

"Monsieur, isn't your son-in-law named Victor Bedloe?"

"Absolutely," answered Hulet, with growing anxiety.

"Well, the American whose strongbox I brought here to give to his son, was also named Bedloe, and he had no child."

"Mon Dieu! Monsieur," exclaimed the former regicide member of the National Convention with agony. "I don't suppose that, as you did in the past, you are taking pleasure in torturing me. But I am having trouble disentangling all your explanations."

That is why I used all my skills to not let you foresee where I was going, except through a cloud. The revelation that is coming to you is so frightful that, if it fell on you in a single block, it would crush you."

At that moment, there was a discreet knock at the door of Hulet's office.

"Who is it?" he asked angrily.

"Me, my dear," responded a female voice. "The bride asks me to tell you that it is wrong to leave them for such a long time like this."

"All right," the former member of the National Convention answered. "I'll be with you in an instant."

During that short talk, Lupiano had opened the strongbox.

"Here is an unopened letter written by Mr. Edgar Bedloe shortly before his suicide; and another, this one opened, from his wife, Mrs. Augusta Bedloe; plus about eight hundred thousand francs in various kinds of notes; also, a gold heart found around the neck of the child kidnapped at Orgères. When, out of my presence, because it is no longer necessary, and I don't want you believe that I came here to see the spectacle of a horrible drama, you have understood all that I am returning to you, you will see if what is most pressing for you to do now is to go and joyously celebrate that marriage."

Then, as Hulet started to show him out, the Marquis added:

"No, stay, you don't have a minute to lose. Tomorrow, if my advice and my assistance could be helpful to you, I am your neighbor. You will find me two steps from here, at the Lamoignon townhouse."

Ah!" he finally said, retracing his steps. "One more thing not to lose sight of, handle that strongbox with caution. The lock is complicated by an explosive apparatus of the most dangerous kind. I didn't have the time to detonate it. Keep it open. At another moment, when you are less emotional and less pressed for time, I will show you its secret."

XIII. The Abduction

Despite the customary gravity and the ordinarily austere aspect of his house, Hulet, the day of the marriage of his daughter, had allowed everything there to take on an air of festivity. Twelve participants were seated around the table: Hulet, his wife, his daughter and son-in-law, three countrymen of the latter, two of whom had served as witnesses; Adolphe Levillain, and Helena's doctor, who had been her witnesses; the priest who had given her the nuptial benediction; Madame Levillain, whom we have seen before in our story under the name of Madame de Pringy, and finally, someone else from back, Adelaide de la Salle, that devoted friend of Victoire de Boisbrunet, who, the day Hulet was going to the seminary of Saint-Magloire, had futilely tried to persuade them to run away together.[165]

---

[165] See Volume 1, Pages 119 seq.

Remaining unmarried, and returned from abroad with the legitimate royalty, she had contacted Madame Hulet, since she had herself arrived from America, and their former relationship was soon renewed. An emigrant and an ardent royalist, Mademoiselle de la Salle was, at first, somewhat astonished to see herself become an intimate friend of the wife of a regicide and former Convention member, a married priest; but the fast friendship that had united her to Madame Hulet in their youth, made her overlook all the discords that remained in their two existences, and, aside from some political squabbles that, from time to time, she had with Hulet, her *dear Jacobin,* as she called him, she was, in the house where we now find her, on the most familiar and affectionate footing.

In her later years, Mademoiselle de la Salle had kept that happy yet resolute character which she had showed when she first appeared to us, and the celibacy in her had not turned to bitterness; it had taken on a livelier liberty of style and speech. Certain originalities that had come with age, far from marring her loveable physiognomy, served, on the contrary, only to increase her spiciness and amusing nature. And so, she was certainly the most likeable and the most pleasant old maid that could be imagined. Notably, in that wedding dinner, where she had been one of the first to be invited, she had brought everyone to the most open and cordial gaiety, before Lupiano had come to upset everything.

When the servant who had come to announce the Marquis' visit had spoken to Hulet, like a well-trained servant, he had made the commission in a low voice, but, annoyed by the interruption, the former Convention member had asked disdainfully:

"Who is this Marquis de Lupiano?"

"Ah! He's a most extraordinary man," Adolphe Levillain said. "Paris is talking about him at the moment. He must live in your neighborhood, as we learned from a letter recently published in the newspapers."

"Isn't that the man who came, several days ago," Madame Levillain added, "to speak to you about a portrait?"

"No, that was not the Marquis; it was the Count, probably his son. He even said that he knew the family of our host."

"Me?" said Hulet. "I have never heard either of the father or of the son. But, then, with your permission, I'm going to see what's so urgent that he has to tell me. Since he is our neighbor, and he claims to know me, as inopportune as it is, there must be some good explanation."

After Hulet had left, the man whom the portraitist had described as an extraordinary personage naturally remained the subject of conversation. Each one recounted what he had been able to learn about him. They spoke about his duel with Monsieur de Lucheux, his fabulous fortune, the great masked ball that he had given as charity for the poor, the bizarre situation of his daughter, *she of the death's head,* and the peculiar adventures that queries about that strange heiress had created. The priest who had married Helena told them about the expensive sacrifice by which Herminie Daliron had been brought out of the abyss into which she had fallen. Then someone brought up the latest exploit of the personage, the fire at the *Cour de France,* an expeditious mean that he had found to clear the ground.

All in all, for a woman like Madame Hulet, living faraway from the scandals of society, the total of all the strange things that she had heard recounted about the Marquise Lupiano made him look like a rather frightening phantom. Without any encouragement from her daughter, it was then she who had gone to knock at her husband's door in order to interrupt an interview, the duration of which, instinctively, had begun to worry her. But when twenty minutes more had passed without Hulet reappearing, she became prey to such anxiety that Mr. Bedloe was about to get up to go see what that interminable conversation was about, when Hulet suddenly returned to resume his place at the table. Although he had carefully composed his expression, his wife said to him:

"Mon Dieu, my love, what did that villainous man have to say to you that kept you almost an hour, and you come back with your face all upset?"

"He had a communication to give me about things that are actually very important; you would be wrong to speak ill of him, because he has put me on the trail of a discovery which will overwhelm you with joy."

"What is that?" Madame Hulet demanded.

"We now have some chance of learning about the fate of our little Victor, who was kidnapped at Orgères."

"What! Our dear child has been found!" exclaimed the happy mother, clasping her hands.

"Found again, not yet, but greatly on the way of being so. Next, it is possible that the Marquis is going to restore to Mr. Bedloe, whose father, if I'm not mistaken, died in Paris in 1813 or 1814, about eight hundred thousand francs in various valuables, which were, at that time, diverted from the paternal inheritance."

"Ah! Well!" said Mademoiselle de la Salle, "is he a retriever dog or a sorcerer to have thus found all the missing objects?"

"Don't laugh about it, Mademoiselle!" said Adolphe Levillain. "That a man is assuredly very unusual. He owns a huge fortune, and has, very recently, funded a large banking house, which gives him connections in all parts of the world. He is therefore in a position to know an enormous number of things."

"But, what did he say about our son?" Madame Hulet asked.

"Nothing precise, only he is on the trail, and I myself verified his very precise information. As for the sum that he wants to put back into Mr. Bedloe's hands, the success is not in doubt, if we wish to help him."

"But how?" asked Mr. Bedloe, in a somewhat incredulous tone.

"Ah! In an action that will not be too much to your taste," responded Hulet. "We must, in the next half-hour, take a stagecoach together so that we can reach Orléans before dawn."

"The Devil!" said the husband. "Merely the scent of eight hundred thousand francs is not worth this upset."

"I know, my dear Monsieur," responded Hulet, "that you are very rich; but, nevertheless, eight hundred thousand francs is a large sum."

"*Parbleu*! I certainly believe that," said Mademoiselle de la Salle, "and if he wants to throw it away for himself, he must nevertheless think of his children.

Mr. Bedloe, without reacting to that malicious remark, asked:

"But, after all, what interest does that Marquis have to get mixed up in my business?"

"I don't think," Hulet answered, in an ironic tone, "that he intends to ask you for a commission. Every day, there are people who take the trouble to do something in the interest of right and justice. And besides, Monsieur de Lupiano said that he knew your father."

"All right!" the husband said, "I'll go see him tomorrow, and, while thanking him for his kindly actions, I will see, in the details that he will give me, what should be thought about his designs."

"It's true," said Hulet, "that I am not myself capable of evaluating..."

"I'm not saying that, but it's very strange that, when that money has been lost for six years, the delay to recover it can't wait one night."

"Things are what they are," responded the former member of the National Convention, "and the hazard that now intervenes in the events of our life, takes the great liberty of not doing it in a way that is totally convenient to us."

"After all, Monsieur," said the husband, "this is no one's business but mine."

"Victor!" said Helena, in a tone of reproach.

"You are mistaken, Monsieur," replied Hulet. "The business that you have with Monsieur de Lupiano is also of great importance to us. He is a bizarre and capricious man, but basically excellent. And when he sees how little importance we give to his unofficial information, I am doubtful that he will wish to continue to help us in the search for our son."

"That is obvious," said Madame Hulet, "and Victor, I can't conceive of your resistance."

"And I, Madame," responded Mr. Bedloe, "I have trouble understanding why everyone here is trying to create a disunion in my marriage. It's really a little too early."

And he threw his napkin on the table.

"My dear," said Hulet, "addressing his wife, "you see that the gentleman has given us a signal."

Madame Hulet rose from the table and was imitated by all of her guests.

During the brouhaha produced by that movement, Mademoiselle de la Salle quickly said to Helena's doctor:

"Doctor, please intervene; with a word of veto, you can still settle all that."

"I was thinking about it," the doctor replied.

And as soon as they had passed into the drawing-room, taking aside Mr. Bedloe, the doctor talked to him alone for several minutes. At the end of that short interview, the young American approached Helena affectionately,

"Are you really ill?" he asked her.

"No, but I don't find that you have been very helpful."

"You'll have to pardon me. I'm from the country of the Hurons. But the smallest of your desires will always be an order for me. Is it your opinion, then, that I should go?"

"Yes, so that we may have a chance to recover my brother, and there will be one more person here for you to love."

At that affectionate word, Mr. Bedloe carried the hand of his wife to his lips. Hulet quickly approached.

"My dear father-in-law," the husband then said, "what time have you set for our departure?"

"Not doubting your good sense and your compliance," Hulet answered, "I ordered a rented carriage more than a half-hour ago. It should be here soon."

"Do you think we will be gone a long time?"

"I hope not; however, take a few things with you."

"That will take just a moment. What kind of carriage have you ordered?"

"I ordered a fast carriage with four horses."

"Oh! No! We should take my Berline;[166] we will be a great deal more comfortable. I'm going to take care of all that."

Before leaving the drawing room, Mr. Bedloe approached Madame Hulet and took her hand.

"You're not angry with me, dear Madame?" he asked her. "My heart is better than my head."

After he had left, Mademoiselle de la Salle exclaimed:

"He's very nice, that poor boy! Because truly, you must agree, the moment is unusually chosen to make him take a long trip."

A quarter of an hour later, the horses had arrived and were hitched up. Hulet cut short as much as he could the good-byes that, without him, Mr. Bedloe would have made eternal. Soon, the sound of the carriage moving away, accompanied by a salvo of whip lashes, told that the travelers were leaving.

XIV. Blackmail and Reconciliation

The next day, following the routine of all the elegant, idle young men of the time, Gregorio Matiphous was taking his daily morning horseback ride through the Bois de Boulogne. At a pathway crossing, he was met by another horseback rider, a still very well preserved old man, who greeted him with an air of recognition. After having returned his wave in an off-handed way, without knowing very well whom he was addressing, as he turned around in order to find out, he saw the unknown man turn his horse, and, in a gallop, stop when side by side with him. At the same time, he said to him:

"Monsieur le Comte de Lupiano doesn't do me the honor of recognizing me?"

---

[166] Covered four-wheel traveling carriage with two interior seats designed about 1670 in Berlin.

"Mon Dieu," Matiphous responded, "I vaguely remember your face, but in any case, it has been a long time since we have seen each other."

"Yes," the unknown man replied. "It's been some five years. It was in Belgium, where I was then exercising functions which put me in the unfortunate necessity of deporting you back to England. Your affair, from what I learned later, didn't have disagreeable outcome. Let me congratulate you on that."

"From that summary," said the man from Malta, haughtily, "you would be Monsieur de Saint-Rambert, or to speak plainer, M. Dulac, also known as Rempailleux."

Since we know each other so well," replied the former *Chauffeur*,[167] without seeming to be offended by the tone taken with him, "you won't be startled by my hurry to warn you about a danger that you don't know about and which is threatening you."

"A danger!" Matiphous said disdainfully. "The greatest danger would be for me to continue, I think, a conversation with you which, I suspect, is useless. Please continue your ride from which I unwittingly stopped you."

At the same time, he reigned in his horse to let pass the unwelcome man that he wanted to get rid of.

"Ah! I see that you're holding a grudge," said Saint-Rambert. "That's bad, when I, on the other hand, had a right to hold one against you. After all, you stole a fortune from me."

"Yes, Monsieur, but only to remit it into the hands of its legitimate owners."

"Well! What a good deed you did there! It's easy when you've become the son of a man who counts his money by the millions! However, even that may not prevent the sword of an assassin from reaching you."

---

[167] The band of thieves once headed by Rempailleux was thus named because they held the feet of their victims to a fire to force them to reveal the hiding places of their valuables. See Volume 1.

"An assassin!" Matiphous exclaimed, in disbelief.

Because of that, he agreed to continue the conversation.

"Yes, my dear enemy, an assassin, or at least a man who has come here swearing to do something unpleasant to you. I'm speaking of Monsieur Britannicus, sent by your friendly legitimate wife whom you abandoned in Bordeaux. In her black mood, if you will allow me that play on words, she has decided to resort, I must warn you, to the most violent extremes, either personally or through the agency of another person."

"And you may have this fellow?"

"Naturally. My wife's salon having the honor to be frequented by the highest aristocracy, I am on a footing to be easily approachable. As the strongman of your Ariadne[168] had reason to believe me not disposed to regard you in the friendliest fashion, he hurried to have a chat with me."

"And how do I merit the opposite sentiment that you are now certainly trying to show yourself as having?"

"I will speak to you entirely frankly. By temperament, I don't hold a grudge. When things are over, I don't think about them anymore. Everybody has his own game and works it out in his own way. On my word, good luck to the lucky. Next, you aren't ignorant of the fact that I am a former acquaintance of your father, since in London in 1799, he had the rather amusing idea to have me hung up on nail, by your hand."

"Yes," Matiphous said, "you were in a bad position then."

"Since then, the Marquis has completely changed his opinion about me, since, about eighteen months ago, knowing that I now occupied functions where I could be of some use to him, he didn't disdain coming to me and asking for my good services."

---

[168] The daughter of Minos, King of Crete, and Pasiphae; she helped Theseus find his way out of the maze enclosing the Minotaur. She escaped with him, but he abandoned her on the isle of Naxos.

"I know that," said the man from Malta, "but he didn't ask you for them gratuitously, but with a nice income of sixty thousand francs..."

"That's exactly what I reproach him for."

"What! You're offended because he made you accept that offer?"

"I'm not saying that, but you understand that, once having made the sacrifice to accept that arrangement, I must find it unusual and a little unfriendly that he has thought it right to suddenly cut me short."

"I understand," said Matiphous. "Once you've formed a habit, it's hard to break it."

"That's very simple. You believe you can count on something; you make arrangements as a consequence; you expand your existence in a certain way; and suddenly there is a hole in your resources. It's impossible that you wouldn't be very badly affected."

"You will allow me to say this: your services were very honorably paid for during all the time when they proved necessary. When they became useless, you must also understand that they had ceased to carry the same remuneration for you."

"I understand that perfectly well, and we are in perfect agreement on this. But after all, Monsieur, your father made a certain profit from those services. The uses he made of them, I am a little doubtful about, but on that subject, I have been unfailingly discreet. Now, I find it very hard, when a man such as myself has been devoted, not curious, not gossiping, to be suddenly dismissed like a pair of old boots or a shirt with holes in it. From everything to nothing is an enormous distance. I think that the Marquis could have treated me like an officer on half-pay, something that's in fashion since the Restoration. Do you think that would have ruined him?"

"So," Matiphous said, "you wouldn't be annoyed if, using the credit that I have with my father...?"

"Well, yes, I don't find it proper to bother him directly with my request, and to get it to him, who better than you could I talk to?"

"And Monsieur Britannicus, if he has come to Paris, could one know where he is hidden?"

"Given the dangers that he might cause you, I'm sure it would please you to know that; but right now, I won't tell you where he is. After all, he is one of my former subjects, a man who has eaten the bread of adversity with me, and I wouldn't want to cause him pain. I can stop him, and if need be, even send him away from Paris, but I won't turn him over. When we have again talked about this, we will take our measures together, because, you should be careful, he's a very bad customer and has a rather venomous bite."

"Very well, Monsieur; I will tell my father what you are demanding."

"Come yourself at the Rue du Colisée to tell me the result. I will introduce you to my wife, whom you knew in the past. There is very good music and there is always a collection of charming women."

"Goodbye, then, Monsieur," answered Matiphous leaving, without accepting the invitation.

In a rather dark mood, he put his horse in a brisk trot.

"One last thing," said Monsieur de Saint-Rambert, rejoining him shortly thereafter, "I forgot to tell you to make the Marquis aware of the fact that the indiscretions I committed to his profit have been very prejudicial to me. There is a cabal that wants my job taken away from me, and they favor my Jacobin predecessor who has just returned to France. There is talk of putting him back in that place where, if those supporting him can be believed, he did a better job than I. Thus, thanks to that intrigue, from one moment to the next, I may find myself completely pushed aside."

"I will take care," said Matiphous, nudging his horse, "to add that circumstance to my plea."

And with a gallop the separation was definitive.

When he returned from his walk, Matiphous quickly told the Marquis about his encounter with Monsieur de Saint-Rambert and the conversation that followed.

"I had certainly foreseen that," said the Marquis. "The relative of King Radama wouldn't let her divorce go through without saying a word. Those Africans don't let themselves be taken advantage of so easily. But I prefer that her conjugal despair has turned to a path of direct violence. What I feared most of all was her going to the newspapers; we couldn't have avoided a deplorable scandal and leading to ridicule. Nevertheless, you must be careful. That black man has attempted to take your life once already."

"Bah!" Matiphous answered, "he is a clumsy coward. Even when he was in my service and I wasn't afraid of him, he didn't succeed."

"Agreed, but this time he's being helped by Rempailleux, who is a criminal of the most dangerous kind. In addition, no one is more perseverant than a Negro, and with the addition of the princely promises with which that woman from Madagascar must have filled his head, he can become very dangerous. You will please do me the favor, until there is a change in the situation, to never to go out anymore in the evening, except in a carriage. What's more, I will take some measures, and we will probably soon be rid of that miserable man."

"And the worthy Monsieur Rempailleux, do you intend to do something in the direction of his request?"

"Not the least in the world. What he asks is disguised extortion, and I am not in the habit of giving in to that kind of pressure. Evidently, he wanted you to understand that, knowing one of my secrets, if I didn't seal his mouth with bank notes, he would speak publicly. But I don't fear his indiscretions; he doesn't know anything for certain, and I believe he will think twice before taking on a player like me."

"However, if, as he threatened, he is relieved of his functions, then finding himself in an extreme by need..."

"We see it happen all the time in lives as agitated as ours are," said the Marquis. "There are always some loose ends that it is difficult to get rid of; that's why, you see, our departure for India must not be indefinitely put off."

When Lupiano opened that chapter, Matiphous never failed to cut the conversation short.

"Speaking of that, father, you do know that I am letting you dine alone? Georgiana has invited her doctor and some other people today. She made me promise that I would honor her banquet with my presence, and I only have time to go and get dressed."

"Until this evening, then," said the Marquis," if you don't come back too late. Me, I have some letters to write and I probably won't go out. But I caution you not to come back on foot. It's only the first days that have to be feared and it's necessary to take precautions against an ambush."

At about nine o'clock, when Lupiano was in fact busy in his study writing, a servant came to ask if he wanted to receive Monsieur Vandel. Introduced immediately, the former member of the National Convention carried under his arm a portfolio that seemed to hold a stack of voluminous papers.

"So, Monsieur?" Lupiano said to him, pushing a chair forward for him.

"Your information," responded Hulet, "was of crushing exactness, and I have come to thank you for having been able, thanks to your generous intervention, to escape a terrible misfortune suspended over my house."

"Then everything has been fixed?"

"Not yet, but we are basically saved. As soon as I was convinced, that is to say, a half-hour after your departure, I forced my son to follow me to Orléans under the pretext that, in that city, we had a chance of recovering the sum that you had already generously returned to me. I didn't need to show him the letters confirming our relationship that I didn't wish to carry with me on that journey. He took me at my word, and I left him, I believe, perfectly informed."

"How did he take your revelation?"

"With reason and happiness. What he lost on one side, he regained on the other. He was very affectionate toward me and he greatly desired to embrace his mother and his sister, but with respect to the latter, we are not without worry. She has hardly recovered from her long, lingering sickness, and she has a very impressionable nature."

"However, trading a brother for a husband, that's an exchange that one can easily accept," said Lupiano. "Your daughter has been piously brought up and, without a doubt, she hasn't let herself become prey to one of those turbulent and disorderly passions that fights against all obstacles?"

"Indeed, Monsieur. It isn't acceptance that's lacking in her, but the thought of what was on the verge of happening that might cause her some terrible physical trauma. More than one time, people been seen struck dead on realizing the extent of a danger from which they had just escaped."

"That transition has to be taken care of, adjusting her little by little to the notion that, in the end, she must accept."

"I've already started on that; even before taking my son away, I mentioned the hope that, thanks to your good offices, our lost child, her brother, might be found."

"Excellent! Madame Hulet, whom you will doubtless tell first, will be able to work effectively to prepare the way. There is a real connection between mother and daughter, which, in such a case, should prove of great use."

"I haven't yet dared speak of this to my wife," Hulet answered. "I don't believe she is capable of keeping her maternal happiness to herself. I am greatly afraid that I will have to prolong the situation longer than I would have wished."

"There are always inconveniences to that, because when a newly-married man is absent, he writes to his wife."

"Without a doubt, and that's what I have told myself, but my perplexity remains extreme. But the purpose of my visit is not just to tell you about the problems in our happiness. After all that you have done for us, I must merit your esteem. And if I cannot repair the past, I must at least try to demonstrate to you that the crime committed upon your person was not all attributable to my will."

"I have forgotten everything," Lupiano responded. "I don't see the usefulness of bringing up sad memories."

"Please hear me out," Hulet replied. "The explanations that I intend to give to you will be confirmed, if you doubt them, by a document that, in a moment, I will show you. When we met in Malta, Monsieur, I was mad. Working in a vocation of which I wanted to fulfill all the duties, I had to hold out against my ardent and vigorous nature. Terrible and relentless battles in myself perverted my moral sense. Everyone who didn't suffer alongside my own suffering became the object of my envy and furious hatred. I found you there, in possession of a happiness that was forbidden to me, and even carried by you to paternity. It offended the entire sum of the privations which I had made a vow to keep forever. Having become a kind of ferocious beast, I saw in you a prey to tear apart. Persuading myself that I was avenging an outraged Heaven for a sacrilege, when in reality I was taking revenge on you, I jumped for joy when I found in the Inquisition's archives a terrible recipe that an insane man had tried on himself—a kind of atheist and revolutionary. Glowing with the idea of punishing you in the way you had sinned, I didn't hesitate to try out my discovery on you."

"The recipe was good and effective," Lupiano said with a bitter smile. "But, once again, I don't hold it against you. You let me have time to become a father. And age would have done today what your poison did then."

"But, Monsieur, in any event, it isn't only just I that must pay the price for my satanic schemes. In me, you see the offspring of cursed family upon which has weighed, for more than two centuries, an atmosphere of fatality. On January 30, 1640, do you know what happened in London?"

"No," Lupiano said, "I don't recall that date."

"Something, Monsieur," Hulet continued, "that one hundred forty-four years later, would take place again in Paris, on January 21, 1793. And it was written that I would lend my hand to that second abomination."

"Are you talking, Monsieur, about the execution of King Charles 1st of England, and the one of King Louis XVI that the National Convention ordered?"

"Yes. It seems that history has taken pleasure to play around those two bloody dates. In 1793, on January 20, a month unhealthy for the Lord's anointed, the royal captive in the Temple prison was notified of his sentence to death, while on January 20, 1619, the trial of the second of the Stuarts began. To carry out the sentence ordered by Cromwell, an arm was needed to take the place of the executioner who had recused himself. A man who would sell his own arm was found, and that man carried the same name with which, later, I signed the death sentence of Louis XVI. Like me, he was named Hulet."

"That coincidence is indeed rather strange!" said Lupiano.

"No, Monsieur, it's only the logic of fate, and the consequences of these actions are linked one to another. Hulet, the assassin of the King, was soon punished for his crime, dying of an infamous death. Forced to go abroad, his family went to live in Hamburg, in Germany, where they became the founders of a dynasty committed to misfortune and to disastrous denouements."

"Hamburg," Lupiano said, "that place is full of memories for me."

"I know that," said Hulet, "but let me finish. For a long time, I was the head of that shadowy bureau for which honest people can only feel contempt, but do you think that I voluntarily became affiliated with it? No, Monsieur, I was only there as a link in a chain, the purpose of which was to expiate the murderous blow struck by the first of the Hulets. His eldest son, in Hamburg, became one of the founders of the first *Secret Bureau*, which have since spread throughout Europe. He then founded the one in France, which, since the time of Louis XIV, has never ceased to exist, and, like his father, he perished by a violent death. And so, from father to son, all the first-born of our family have met the most diverse and premature ends, direct consequences of the perpetuity of the functions that they filled, just like royal successions, by order of primogeniture."

"But, after all, you, Monsieur, have reached an age that leads us to believe that that terrible curse has finally ceased to apply with such terrible regularity."

"I?" Hulet replied. "My father wanted me to avoid it and in order to not become the *king of the letter-openers,* he encouraged me to take Orders. You can see how well that advice succeeded! In Malta, I was worse for you than a murderer, and in Paris, in 1814, with my own hand, I became the executioner of my eldest son."

"But that's impossible!" exclaimed Lupiano.

"Not, Monsieur, that I wanted to, but on the day of the Battle of Paris, a shot left my gun; it was a stray bullet, but because it was directed by Fate, it accurately struck my child in the temple, while, after we had valiantly fought, we were catching our breath in the Père Lachaise cemetery. I carried him on my shoulders, bleeding, from there, only to return him there again the next day."[169]

"My poor man!" exclaimed Lupiano with emotion.

"Now," continued the former member of the National Convention, "when by my regicide vote, cast despite the advice of my father, who had come to beg me not to dip my hands in royal blood, I again revived our family curse, do you believe that I am still destined to a happy and tranquil death? It's true that I am led to that necessary denouement by a very long circuit, but it is only because, on the way, I can empty the cup of all the bitterness and sadness. My father, who died on the Revolutionary scaffold; my son, my youngest child, taken soon after birth by the *Chauffeurs*; my eldest son, struck by my own bullet; and a short while ago, if you had not intervened, incest almost slipping into my house. Isn't that enough cruel stations along the length of my tragic path?"

"Consider, on the contrary," Lupiano said, "that Heaven may be appeased, since it has allowed me to arrive in time."

"However generous your warning was during our unexpected reunion, I can see, on the contrary, only the most men-

---

[169] See Volume 2, Pages 220 seq.

acing symptoms, because, separated for a long time, two branches of the same trunk now come to be rejoined to one another. Isn't that one of those frightening unusual things that foresee greater catastrophes?"

"Branches from the same trunk!" Lupiano repeated. "What do you mean?"

"Yes, because, between you and me, Monsieur, there exists a family tie. Hulet, the executioner of Charles 1st, had two sons. One of them ended as I have just told you. The other was adopted by the Kormer family, whose name he continued. He was the first of your ancestors. All of that will be explained to you in the genealogy history left by my father and that I brought to you in this portfolio. Now, don't be astonished any longer if your life, like mine, has been marked by horrible sadness, and that it was reserved to me to be your executioner. We are like the Pelopides,[170] impelled by an invisible force to tear each other apart and to spend our life between misfortune and crime."

"Once more," Lupiano answered, "I like to believe that God has finally looked on us with a more forgiving eye, since he has given me back my son; since he has permitted me to give yours back to you and to hold you back from the abyss toward which you were heading; and finally, he has substituted in our hearts a sentiment of good will and friendly interest for the strength of hatred and vengeance which ruled us before."

And at the same time, he held out his hand to Hulet, who said:

---

[170] The Pelopides are the descendants of Pelops, son of Tantalus, who was was slaughtered by his own father, cut up, boiled, and offered as a meal at a feast of the gods. His sons, Atreus and Thyestes, also excelled in cruelty and folly. Atreus murdered two or three of Thyestes's sons, and cutting them limb from limb, boiled them and served them up to Thyestes. Atreus was father of Agamemnon and Menelaus who are also called the Atrides.

"Monsieur, you make a ray of hope shine for me, and to immediately test the friendship that is beginning between us, advise me in a resolution that I am compelled to take. Today they want to give back the functions that I formerly filled with all the uprightness and honor of which I was capable. A schemer, who succeeded me, has put everything in confusion and disorder. What should I answer to the offer that the State has made to me?"

"Your instinct would be to take them back, isn't that true?"

"What made you think that was my thought?"

"That's because one hasn't been invested with great power without being nostalgic for it after one has left it. That's because men like to do again what they have done before. That's because nothing is truer than the popular dictum: *He who has drunk, will drink again.*"[171]

At that moment, there was the rolling sound of a carriage under the windows of the room where the two old men were talking.

"What's more," Lupiano said, rising and with the appearance of certain emotion, "the question you are asking me is difficult to answer. There is something good to be said for it, but also against it. Allow me to think about it. I will tell you what I think about it when I return to you the papers that you are leaving with me."

Thus dismissed, Hulet started toward the door by which he had entered.

"No, this way, please," Lupiano said to him, showing him to a door leading to a hidden staircase.

Since the Marquis was expecting no visit at that hour, the carriage must have been that of his son returning, and it was not convenient that he should encounter Hulet.

It was an admirable foresight! A few minutes later, Matiphous and Georgiana, who at Lupiano's house used only

---

[171] *Qui a bu, boira,*" equivalent to "A leopard can't change his spots."

private entries, entered through the same door through which Hulet had left.

XV. Temptation

What does life hold in store! If Georgiana's dinner guests had not left so early, she would not have asked Matiphous to take her to the Lamoignon townhouse to finish her evening. If Matiphous had not been with Georgiana, he would have gone upstairs by the main stairway and he would not have met Hulet leaving his father. If he had not encountered that man towards whom, despite the Marquis's exhortations, he still felt intense hatred, many of the events that remain to be recounted, according to all appearances, would not have happened.

Georgiana spent two hours at the house of Lupiano, whom she was accustomed to call *my uncle* and she was treated like a spoiled child there. First of all, she asked that she be made some tea. That which was one drank at the house of the Marquis was in fact of an incomparable quality. It was a kind grown in Japan, where it was reserved exclusively for the Emperor.

Near the little town of Ursi, said Monsieur de Mirbel,[172] *there is a mountain devoted entirely to its culture; that mountain which offers glorious and picturesque views, is surrounded by a deep pit so that all access to it is forbidden to men and animals. The planted areas are carefully distanced from each*

-----

[172] Charles-François Brisseau de Mirbel (1776-1854), French botanist and politician, the founder of the science of plant cytology. The plant genus *Mirbelia* is named in his honor. One wonders where Rabou found the passage he quotes here; it does not appear to be in Mirbel's *Histoire naturelle, générale et particulière de plantes* (1802-06) or in *Eléments de Physiologie Végétale et de Botanique* (1815), nor is there a town called Ursi in Japan; if he is referring to *Uva Ursi* (or Bearberry), which is a herbal tea, it has no special connection to Japan.

*other and the trees are washed or watered every day. During
the harvest, the men whose duty it is to wash them two or three
times a day, for fear of contaminating them, collect the leaves
only with hands covered by gloves. When they are properly
toasted, they are enclosed in valuable vases and carried in
great pomp to the Emperor's palace.*

It can only be imagined at what price Lupiano had procured for himself a tea so expensive and so rare. And when,
after having drunk several cups, Georgiana expressed an indiscreet wish to carry away a small supply, the Marquis answered:

"This must be for you, my beautiful one," he said, taking
the trouble to fill a box for her with his own hands.

Given to borrowing, like all like her, the courtesan
seemed to want some fantasy art objects that she noticed
among those that filled Lupiano's shelves, and he quickly offered them to her, so many, in fact, that when she left, accompanied by Matiphous, she was like a little girl on Christmas'
day, rather laughably loaded down with all she was carrying
away.

Lupiano had already gone to bed at the time Matiphous
had returned. The explanation about the encounter with Hulet
on the hidden staircase therefore had to take place the next
day.

"Was that really Monsieur Hulet?" Matiphous asked,
getting straight to the point, "whom I encountered last night?"

"Yes," answered the Marquis, "and what was your idea
in bringing Georgiana in that way?"

"But didn't you tell me that you didn't want to see her
except in the most secret way possible?"

"At that hour, she could, without impropriety, have come
up the main staircase."

"A greater reason that your visitor couldn't have done
the same."

"Believing that the sound of your carriage was announcing a visitor, it was he himself who asked me if he could slip
away without being seen. When someone like him has spent

his life in mystery and shadows, he is instinctively secret, even about insignificant things.”

“Right to guessing the existence of hidden doors and staircases,” Matiphous maliciously replied.

By that irony, Lupiano understood that his attempt to throw his son off the track hadn’t met with great success, and stung by the way Matiphous had made him feel it, he said:

“Well, my dear boy, I imagine you are not thinking of starting an investigation into the fact of the presence of that man here?”

“An investigation, no; but his visit astonished me. I don’t think that, in showing my surprise, I was doing anything improper.”

“There was nothing easier to explain,” Lupiano replied. “During the day, I returned the strongbox to him.”

“Using your own name then?”

“No, on behalf of someone who remained unnamed, but I didn’t dare use for that commission my Hindu, who is too well-known in the area. The contents of the strongbox worried Hulet, to whom I had sent a dangerous present of that type at another time. He ran after the man who had left the object at his door, and, by questioning him, he wormed out the truth from him.”

“So Hulet now knows about his daughter’s incestuous marriage?”

“No. I only sent the money and the insignificant letters to him.”

“But how did you explain to him how that strongbox came into your hands? That is, without a doubt, the question that he came to ask you.”

“He came to thank me, nothing more. Without his asking, I told him that my banking house had charged me with returning what I had sent to his son-in-law, and that it had been addressed to him by mistake. He didn’t go into the truthfulness of that explanation, which had verisimilitude, in any more depth. When you are getting eight hundred thousand francs, you look at it less closely than when it's a question of paying them."

"I certainly believe that, and it was a nice wedding present that you gave to the groom."

"Do you regret it? Aside from the fact that you don't lack money, you seemed, some time ago, to experience some remorse of conscience about that legacy."

"Pff! Everything considered, that sum doesn't belong to Hulet's son any more than it did to me. He is not the heir of these Americans whose son he isn't, and by writing to America, perhaps we might have located other relatives of theirs."

"Who would have no right to it, since, despite not having a birth certificate, Victor Hulet has in his favor a will from his pretended mother."

"However, this was a beautiful opportunity for you to take revenge on that man, when you had him there, under your thumb, and to tell him one on one of our discovery. The rest of his family, to whom, after all, I don't wish anything bad, has never known anything. Forced to keep his secret to himself, he would have undergone a real torture that would have been adequate payment for all the evil that he has done to you and me."

"My dear boy," Lupiano said, on hearing that cold and considered plan of vengeance, "I am truly sorry to find such hatred still in you. It seems to me that you misunderstand the protection with which, after long obstacles, you have been favored by Providence. When they have arrived in port, sailors no longer held it against the waves and winds by which they were almost submerged."

"Wind and waves do their job when they roar, and no accounting is demanded of them; whereas, this miserable man, sometimes dressed as a minister of peace and charity, sometimes as a kind of magistrate, has never ceased, under one guise or another, to attempt to take away our two existences. That's a crime that seems to me scandalous not to punish."

"Let justice from from Divine Providence take its course. It knows how to strike if it finds it necessary. As for me, I have asked too much of it already, and to be sure that neither you nor I will be tempted to make use of the proofs that we have in our hands, I will throw them in the fire."

"I believe that that would be something very imprudent. With that man who is always found on our path, one never knows what might happen in the future."

"So be it. But if you don't want me to disarm myself, then make me a solemn promise that Hulet will never, by you, without my consent, be told of the misfortune that happened in his family."

"I swear it," said Matiphous, "but that is an oath that costs me."

"It doesn't matter; I'm asking it as filial respect, and if it's necessary to speak plainer, I require it."

"So be it. I promise that, by me, Hulet will never know the secret that you want to hide from him. But you won't obtain pardon from me for that man. And if I could reach him without bringing into my revenge all his family, who are innocent of the evil he has done me, you wouldn't have me as an accomplice in your forbearance."

"I don't understand you, my dear boy, because, basically, you have a good heart."

"I think that I have proved that on more than one occasion, and especially to that miserable man, on the day when, I, the only one of all his crew from the *Secret Bureau,* followed his son's casket."

"Well! Then, return to those feelings. You were good when you were miserable; do you want people to think that happiness has spoiled you?"

No matter what the Marquis said to him, on leaving that conversation, Matiphous remained convinced that there was a very different explanation for Hulet's visit, and the mystery which surrounded it, one completely different from the one he had been given.

In going over the conversation he had had with his father, the latter's insistence in trying to persuade him to make no use of their discovery, and the promise required of him on that subject, Matiphous had the idea that the Marquis had not remained neutral, and that the blow ready to strike the Hulet family had been turned aside.

The way to acquire a certainty on that subject was to find out what had happened in the young household since the nuptial benediction. It seemed to Matiphous that he had a chance of gathering some information from Adolphe Levillain. He therefore went to the painter's studio on the pretext of asking him if there would be a way, as a favor, to talk about Georgiana's portrait. Once the conversation had begun, he didn't have to be very clever to obtain the insight he had come looking for, since the artist himself mentioned the Marquis, his father, calling on them in the middle of the wedding dinner to ask for an interview, worrying the entire family because of the length of his visit, then filling it with joy by the good news that he had brought, and finally, bringing to the groom the inconvenience of a brusque departure.

At that point, everything became clear for Matiphous. Not only what his father had said, but also what he had carefully hidden from him, in seeming to having gone to Lelouard's Rue de Provence offices, at the exact moment that he was, in reality, getting ready to go to Rue Barbette to spill their precious secrets. And now, the same method of dissimulation and mistrust was being used against him!

The man from Malta felt his ego deeply wounded, and he exaggerated the importance of the dissimulation and distrust so much more so because his hateful dispositions found a better place better there. It seemed to him that his honor obliged him to get the better of what he called in mind a dastardly deception, and from there, he began to work on a way to pour out his anger on Hulet, who obviously had become the Marquis' protégé—but he wisely didn't go so far as to wish it to invade the paternal domain.

Incorporating into the evil schemes that he was meditating a kind of relative integrity, in respect for the oath he had given his father, Matiphous renounced at once the idea of making use of their weapon, which, besides, had been blunted, since Hulet, once warned, must have put order into the monstrous aberration of heart of which his children had almost been the victims. Without that weapon, he was forced to search for another method of torture against the enemy against whom his fierce anger was directed. Then, in a note that was brought to him, he found that precise inspiration that he had been looking for.

Without a doubt, as a reminder to him, Rempailleux had sent him the following invitation:

Monsieur et Madame de Saint-Rambert asks Monsieur le Comte de Lupiano to do them the honor of spending the evening of Tuesday the 17th with them. There will be music.

Below that printed invitation Rempailleux had written by hand:

Please excuse this late invitation, my dear Count, delivered to you only today, but my wife, who is anxious to renew your acquaintance, has arranged for the most beautiful concert that will be given this season on this evening.
Truly yours,

Gédéon de Saint-Rambert

At another time, Matiphous would have found that invitation impertinent in every respect, but the sudden illumination that it gave him was welcome.

On that evening, he appeared in the drawing-room where, thanks to her beautiful contralto voice and the patronage of the amiable duke who had made her renounce Protestantism, Kitty Ketch hosted an excellent company, mostly men. Ordinarily, as we know, Saint-Rambert showed himself very seldom in his wife's world. But on that day, he had thought that one of his wife's reunions would be a kind of neutral ground where, without the appearance of being too impatient pressure, he could exert more pressure on Matiphous in order to obtain the response that he was waiting for.

Therefore, it was the former *Chauffeur* who, dressed in an outfit fashionable to the point of being ridiculous, presented himself to Matiphous when the latter was announced.

"My dear, you remember the Comte de Lupiano," he said to his wife, when presenting the man from Malta.

"Perfectly. Monsieur hasn't changed at all," Kitty Ketch a.k.a. Madame de Saint-Rambert answered. "However, it's been like a dozen years since we have seen each other."

"Yes," Matiphous replied. "Last in 1898 in Florence."

"I've learned with happiness, Monsieur," the virtuoso continued, "of the favorable changes that have recently taken place in your life."

That said, she left to go greet the duke, who arrived bringing with him a young, very blonde pianist who was to perform during the evening, and he introduced her.

Matiphous discovered that Kitty Ketch had gained an enormous amount of weight, and she didn't remind him at all of the young girl for whom a foolish passion had caused him to make such a prodigious sacrifice. On seeing her again, he found impertinent the self-assurance that she had gained by being someone in society. It seemed to him that the few words falling from her mouth had been uttered with an air of ridiculous protection, and that lying tone of interest when it is easy to realize that what people say to you is said purely in order to salve their own conscience. They have as little as possible interest in you, even if, basically, they are not decidedly malicious.

There were already things in that reception that were likely to bring back old sentiments of hatred in Matiphous, when an unexpected encounter brought back to his mind a sad event where the intervention of Kitty Ketch had had a disastrous effect. It restored, with all their vivacity and energy, his feelings of vengeance for events committed during from his previous life.

One will recall the proud Madame de Limeuil, the aunt of the young girl with whom Matiphous had spent some very tranquil years at the Bell Rock lighthouse. To find her at the home of Madame de Saint-Rambert would have seemed strange, if one didn't remember that she, by her conversion and by official charity, had been put into a position to edge her way into the highest aristocracy. Paris, where people don't know each other, and where all kinds of branded and adventurous existences end up, is marvelous for misunderstandings of that kind. A woman has a salon; there is good music; the society there isn't too mixed, and the household seems to be on a grand footing. The most fastidious will be duped by appearances and the thought would never enter their mind that that veneer of elegance could hide the daughter of a public executioner, who, by a bizarre mating, had joined her existence to that of a former highway robber.

Matiphous hesitated a moment before approaching that former acquaintance, then he decided to introduce himself to her, first of all because it didn't displease him to present himself under the aspect of better fortune; then, because he had a real desire to have news of Monsieur de Limeuil who, it will be remembered, entered the Order of the Lazarite Missionaries after the death of Diane de Limeuil, his beloved wife.[173]

The greeting delivered by the former Lady in Waiting was, without being very warm, at least proper. The name of the Marquis de Lupiano, which had reached her, didn't sound entirely irreproachable to her when the ex-surgeon Deschamps told her that the Comte he was the son of that suspicious and eccentric person. But, all in all, there was a halo of a great fortune and a somewhat dangerous atmosphere around that name. Matiphous's decision to reconnect with Madame de Limeuil was not followed by any disappointment. In the course of their rather prolonged conversation, he learned that Monsieur de Limeuil, after an extended sojourn in Indochina, where he had gone to carry the light of the Divine Gospel, had returned to France, and was about to leave again on another missionary journey to the Isle-Bourbon,[174] from which he

---

[173] See Volume 2, Pages 370 seq.
[174] Today, La Réunion, east of Madagascar.

would continue to another destination on the African coast, where it was thought they would have the greatest success.

Monsieur de Saint-Rambert had the good taste to not take hold of his guest too promptly in order to question him about the matter that was preoccupying him. But, as the evening was getting late, finding Matiphous close enough for a private conversation, he said to him, parodying Marlbrough's popular song [175]:

"Well, beautiful page, what news do you bring?"

"Bad ones," answered the man from Malta. "My father doesn't seem to be disposed to arrange things as you desire."

"Ah!" said Saint-Rambert in a rising tone.

"He says that you have a very nice position and what he would be ready to do for a man really in need, doesn't seem to him to be either useful or proper to do for someone who earns, at the latest information, 25,000 francs in salary."

"But did you tell him about my position being threatened by Vandel?"

"I most certainly did. So here is his idea to help you. We have known for several days that Vandel has married his daughter to a young American, who is the heir of the man from whom our famous strongbox belonged."

"Is he, by chance, the son of the dear man who committed suicide under my eyes?"

"No," said Matiphous. "I understand your idea: the strongbox we opened, my father and I, effectively told us that you started a mess which could have turned the marriage of

---

[175] *Marlbrough s'en va-t-en guerre* (Marlborough Has Left for the War), one of the most popular French folk songs about the death of John Churchill, 1st Duke of Marlborough (1650-1722), based on the false rumor of that event after the Battle of Malplaquet (1709), the bloodiest battle of the War of the Spanish Succession. It tells how Marlborough's wife, awaiting his return from battle, is given the news of her husband's death. It also tells that he was buried and that a nightingale sang over his grave.

Mademoiselle de Vandel into something quite tragic. But that's not what I mean; the child stolen with your help didn't live, and for lack of a direct heir, there's a distant cousin who stands in line to collect the eight hundred thousand francs generated by gambling and the stock market that filled the strongbox, where we found them in the company of some interesting correspondence, by which we have been so well informed."

"Eight hundred thousand francs," exclaimed Saint-Rambert, "and that's the fortune you took from me!"

"But wait," Matiphous continued, "they may not be as lost to you as you suppose."

"How's that?" the former *Chauffeur* quickly asked.

"You can be sure that neither my father not I intend to appropriate that sum."

"*Parbleu*! When people like you roll in gold and money!"

"To indirectly keep Vandel from taking your job, my father had the idea to return the strongbox and all it contained to him."

"I don't see how that might keep him from having the idea to retake my position."

"What? If you had those eight hundred thousand francs that, yesterday, not later, after your request that I presented to my father, were carried to Vandel's home Rue Barbette, would you care about remaining the head of the Secret Bureau?"

"I? Perhaps not. But Hulet's ego won't let him want anything less than being fully reinstated into the functions that he occupied in the past, with good fortune. He's a man who loves power for power's sake."

"Oh!" Matiphous said, "he has aged, and with the years, one acquires a taste for *farniente*."[176]

"That's all well and good, but after all the services that I have rendered your father, he should have been interested in a more direct way to help me, one more sympathetic to my posi-

---

[176] Doing nothing.

tion. You see how we live here, and my wife's fortune is very far from being able to afford us this luxury."

"Think about it, my dear fellow, and there is perhaps a way you can use the information that I gave you. As far as I'm concerned, I believe that we have done a great deal to bring the competition that is threatening you to a standstill."

'But if it isn't Vandel today, it will be someone else to-morrow. I'm not wanted anymore, and I don't hesitate to say so. The indiscretions of which I made myself guilty, to the benefit of the Marquis, weigh a great deal in the sum of all the irregularities with which I am accused."

"My father, on the contrary," Matiphous answered, "is totally convinced that nothing about him transpired out. He hasn't confided in anyone; on the other hand, he is also certain that you didn't gossip. So who, then, would have dared meddle in his affairs? You know by experience that he isn't a man to stand for that, and you know how he goes about dealing with people who could risk indiscretions toward him."

After that veiled threat, Matiphous broke off the interview in order to move to the piano near which Madame de Saint-Rambert was getting ready to sing. He was sure that, in speaking to Rempailleux about that eternally regretted strongbox, he had seeded the germ of an idea in his mind, in such well-prepared ground that it couldn't not produce fruits in the near future.

XVI. The Bibliophile

Hulet, it hasn't been forgotten, had a passion for books, and we once saw Lupiano use that passion to cause him one of the cruel bitterness of his life. Forced by an order of exile to leave France abruptly, he had sold, at the same time as his furniture, the greater part of his library. But included in that catalog were certain rare and precious articles which had been, for him, too great a heart-break to sell, not mentioning the fact that, to get rid of them in such a hurry, purely in terms of money, would have causes him to suffer an enormous loss. So

Hulet had then carefully packed them in a box and his book-binder had agreed to hold them, either until his return, or to have them sent to him where he would decide to settle permanently, supposing that his exile was indefinitely prolonged.

Upon his arrival in Paris, he opened in the hurry that can be imagined the box that he had left behind. Its contents were immediately reinstalled in a vast, new library hat Hulet, an ardent amateur of books, had hurried to acquire. It took a great deal of time before all the shelves could be filled. With a limited income, which the expenses of his voyages had made even less, it was only slowly that Hulet had been able to re-constitute his former rich library. However, his son-in-law, who was supposed to live with him, had wanted to remain in charge of all the household expenses, and his daughter, for whose dowry he had economized in the past, having made a magnificent marriage, without his having to spend a penny, he was still able to devote annually a rather hefty sum to satisfy his favorite taste. He had, therefore, been seen again at public auctions and in the bookstores. And right up to the moment when the revelations of the Marquis had come to bring trouble into his household, not a single day had passed without his having made some fortunate acquisition.

The day after Madame de Saint-Rambert's soirée, not-withstanding the worry that the revelation about his son-in-law still caused him, Hulet was busy arranging a rather large number of newly-bought volumes which were still awaiting classi-fication, when he was told that a person with a rather odd appearance was asking to see him in order to offer him what in the language of commerce, they call *a great bargain*.

Shown in shortly thereafter, that man, wearing a volumi-nous blond wig, *à la Titus,*[177] as it was then called, green

---

[177] In post-revolutionary France, during the Reign of Terror era, executioners cut the hair of those sentenced to death at the height of the neck to be sure that the guillotine did the job. Fashion, always capricious, was responsible for moving these haircuts to society: soon, lots of women in Paris at the time

glasses fitted with a *garde-vue* of green taffeta and a maroon suit buttoned so that nothing could be see of his linen, gave the appearance of an old scholar. Something, however, could contradict that diagnosis, in addition to the *in-quarto* volume that he held in his right hand, wrapped in an etui of silk, in his left arm, he was carrying a big sack of money.

"Oof!' exclaimed the unusual visitor, putting down his burden, "my left arm is all numb! Just think, Monsieur," he added, "I have just received rent payments from a shack that I own on the Rue Pastourelle. Impossible to persuade my porter, who acts in my name, to change them for me into bank notes. That good man still lives in the time of the Revolution, and bank notes for him are like *assignats*[178] And in this damned Marais, there's no means of finding a money-changer. So, it is an atrocious drudgery to collect money from that building."

"But," Hulet said, smiling, "it seems to me that you could take a carriage."

"Ah! Yes, let's talk about that. As a distracted man, what if it happened that I were in a hurry and left all my money in there to be stolen! The last time I took a cab, it cost me a thousand francs which I'm still trying to recover. You see, Monsieur, I need to feel a weight on my arm to remember that I'm carrying something. But let's deal with the subject of my visit—it's far more interesting than a bag of six-*livres* and a hundred-*sous* coins."

---

proceeded to adopt this look, leaving long hair in the front and cutting them very short at the height of the neck. For styling they used perfumed pomades to define their curls and locks and create a sophisticated tousled hair effect. The Classically influenced Titus was cropped short everywhere but at the front with curls combed forward onto the forehead to resemble the Roman Emperor Titus.

[178] i.e.: worthless. *Assignats* were paper money issued by the National Assembly in France from 1789 to 1796, during the Revolution, to address imminent bankruptcy.

"I understand you have come about a rare book that you desire to sell?"

"Desire is too strong a word," replied the newcomer." Say rather than I'm forced to sell, and I'll part with it only with great despair and sadness."

"But what forces you to take this path?"

"My eyes, Monsieur, are going. I recently had cataract surgery, but it was only partially successful; I can see where I am going, but it's now impossible for me to read. Because of that, my books have become a torture for me every instant. I am selling them, bartering them out. That's shameful to say, but that's how it is."

"Is your library very big?"

"No, about two thousand volumes, but all first-class.

"Shouldn't you consider a public auction? If you lavished on them the care that you took today, there would be a good chance that it might be more profitable."

"A public auction! So that my books could go I don't know where and to people I don't know? No, Monsieur, I'm like godmothers who don't give their cat to the first person who comes around without being sure that it will have a good home. If I didn't already know that you are one of the most eminent bibliophiles in Paris, believe me, my dear colleague, I wouldn't have come to you."

"Well, what is that book that you would like to sell to me?"

The old maniac carefully opened the box where his *inquarto* volume was enclosed, and, under Hulet's eyes, there appeared a magnificent volume bound in embossed red Moroccan leather.

"There, you see," he said, "is something you don't see every day."

Hulet opened the volume and read:

Opere
di Francisco PETRARCA
Cioë

Sonette et Triumphi;
Venetiis; Vindelinus de Spira
1470

"The Devil!" he exclaimed. "A Vindelinus da Spira[179] edition of Petrarch! That is a most rare article. Where did you procure that jewel?"

"Monsieur, in 1784, it sold for 1330 livres at the Duc de Valliere's sale. You can see his arms on it. Stolen, probably during the Terror from a magistrate whose library, after they had cut off his head, was confiscated by the State. It was sold to me by a street vendor. That man would have let me have it for 60 livres, but I didn't want it to be said that such a treasure had undergone such an ignoble depreciation, and paid for it the same figure than from the last catalog, and in cash, which at the time of the *assignats*, as we were then, almost doubled the cost of my acquisition. If you want it, I won't beat about the bush, 1500 livres is my first and last offer."

"But, Monsieur, don't you think that, in the somewhat suspicious provenance that you have pointed out to me, there may be some chance of trouble for the purchaser? The book, having once been confiscated by the State, the Royal Library, up to a certain point, might have some right to reclaim it."

"Oh! Yes, I know; you are a little like *Colas' cow*,[180] a former member of the National Convention, who finds that a

---

[179] The brothers Johann and Wendelin of Speyer (also known by their Italian names of Giovanni and Vindelino da Spira) were German printers in Venice from 1468 to 1477. Francesco Petrarca (1304-1374), a.k.a. Petrarch, was an Italian scholar and poet who was one of the earliest humanists. His rediscovery of Cicero's letters is often credited with initiating the 14th-century Renaissance.

[180] In 1605 in Chécy, a cow belonging to a man named Colas (or Nicolas) is supposed to have entered the temple of Bionne at the time of the preaching. Protestants would have killed it and eaten it. Since then they were nicknamed "eaters of Colas'

judgment of the Revolutionary Tribunal can still have the force of law today? Me, I respect all opinions; but I think that everything that was done at that time is now null and void. What's certain is that, for twenty-five years, I have had this volume in my library without ever being questioned about it."

"In fact," said Hulet, "in the case of moveable objects, the law states that possession is ownership. But from whom would I have the honor to buy it?"

"Monsieur, I will tell you my name, and I will even let you, for your greater security, come and pay me at my domicile, after you have had time to examine the volume. Will you, until then, check to see that there are no stains and no missing pages? Then, if its state of conservation is irreproachable, you can come and see me—or would you prefer for me to come back?"

"*Mon Dieu*, if you are good enough to leave the volume with me, I will examine it more at my leisure."

'Oh! Monsieur, I'm not distrustful. I now I'm leaving it in hands that know its true value. I don't have the least difficulty leaving it with you. Will you have had time to decide by tomorrow morning?"

"Yes, perfectly."

"Only, what I expect from you is discretion; that you will not say to anyone that I came to offer you that treasure. If we ended up not doing business together, if it became known that a connoisseur like you had turned me down, the book would be greatly depreciated."

"Believe me, Monsieur, I know my duty as a bibliophile."

"Well, until tomorrow then," said the unknown man, rising.

Before leaving, like a general who passes his troop in review, a magnifying glass in his hand, he glanced at the length

---

Cow," later shortened to just "Colas' Cow." In effect, Hulet is here being accused of being a Protestant or a Huguenot, being too preoccupied with morality.

of the bookshelves that filled the greatest part of the room where he had been received.

"Oh!" he said to Hulet, "you do have the most respectable collection, and from what I can see here, a great number of the book bindings of Thouvenin."[181]

A blind man's vanity! He pretended, upon a first and rapid inspection, to recognize the work of that famous bookbinder, when his glass could barely let him read the titles of the books. Otherwise, he would have given less summary attention to some of the rare copies passing under his eyes.

As he already was holding the door handle, Hulet said to him:

"You are forgetting your sack of money!"

"Ah!" said the bibliophile. "I'm incorrigible!"

The man took some steps to pick up his sack, then appeared to change his mind:

"But I still have several errands to run," he said. "This sack will only weigh me down. Could I ask you to keep it for me, with the book, until tomorrow?"

"Gladly," said the former member of the National Convention. "How much does it contain?"

"One thousand thirty-seven livres and thirteen *sous*. Or even better, perhaps you could change that sum into bank bills for me? Because a deposit between people who don't know each other is always risky—you don't know who lives and who dies."

"Oh, I much prefer that," answered Hulet. "I believe I am in a position to do you that little service."

And going to open the bottom panel of a bookcase, the upper part of which was fully shelved, he took from a wooden oak case a billfold where one could see that there were many more bills than the amount required. He counted out to the

---

[181] Joseph Thouvenin (1791-1834), one of the most prolific binders of his time. He was one of the three most important bookbinders of the 19th century and the Restoration in particular.

bibliophile the sum of a thousand francs, then gave the old distracted man two bills of five hundred francs.

"As for the change, you can put it in your pocket," he said. "That won't weigh you down too much."

"A thousand thanks," responded the good man. "I hope that you will have more than that to count out to me tomorrow. I warn you: I want to be paid in gold coins A Vindelinus da Spira is not paid in common silver, no, thank you."

"I have some gold, don't worry," responded Hulet, "but we will haggle about the price."

Thereupon, the two bibliophiles separated in a manner that made them believe that their business would be concluded the next day.

The next day, Hulet began to examine the precious volume, but in the middle of that pleasant occupation, which had kept him busy for several hours, he was interrupted by two letters addressed to him.

One bore the stamp of the Minister of the Interior and notified him that he would be expected in the office of the Minister that same afternoon. As he had not requested such an appointment, he guessed that it was probably to ask him for his decision with respect to to the overtures that had been made to him to become again the Head of the *Secret Bureau.* When he had been asked to consider that notion, in order to give himself time to think, he had used as a pretext the inconvenience that the marriage of his daughter was going to cause him, but apparently the Minister was now impatient and wanted a definitive yes or no from him.

The other letter had a stamp from Orléans, where his son, Victor, was waiting until his sister had been prepared for *her other happiness.* Included in it was another letter addressed to Helena. Following what had been agreed on, the interim husband was continuing playing his role, explaining his lengthy absence by some unexpected difficulties encountered in the affair which had forced him to go on that trip, that it was now necessary to finish well, since it had been started.

As for the letter ostensibly written for Hulet himself, it was unusual.

In fact, Victor Hulet had written, *I have not seen all that correspondence on which all the allegations of your officious Marquis are based. Now, you haven't kept me ignorant of the fact that that man has been your mortal enemy and that he had, at one time, begun to torture you with unbelievable refinements. Why that sudden change of feelings for you? Why did that warning arrive too late to prevent the marriage, but just at the moment after it was concluded? What if that correspondence was fabricated with infernal art, just to cause trouble in our family?*

With that person's immense fortune, and the unusual character he is said to have, with his patient coldness to prepare his vengeance, the supposition that I am making is not entirely impossible. It is, in fact, a great deal more likely than that delayed generosity of which he would suddenly be capable. However that may be, I want to verify this for myself. I plan to leave Orléans and arrive in Paris at about three a.m. No one in the house will know of my arrival. Wait for me at the door of the townhouse that opens on the Rue des Trois Pavillons, and let me in from that side.

When I have seen, with my own eyes, that the letters he brought to you are really from Mr. and Mrs. Bedloe, then it will be necessary to decide on a course of action, because the current situation is not tenable, and I see neither Helena nor I benefitting for any more temporizing. I am tired of staying here, and I don't know why, but my heart is telling me that we have been the plaything of a sick joke. For is it possible that, between the four persons involved in this mistake, the voice of blood was not heard by any one of us?

Besides, how is it possible that that strongbox, lost for six years, found itself in the hands of the Marquis at just this very point in time? Could he have been the one who stole it in the first place?

For another man, the eight hundred thousand francs that he brought with the return of the letters would give weight to one's generosity. But eight hundred thousand francs are nothing to the Marquis de Lupiano, when it is a matter of revenge. Besides, have you checked to see if the gold and the jewelry are not fake? etc., etc.

In four pages, of which we only give the substance here, Victor argued his point of view. And the result of his letter, was that the husband in him, that should have been killed with a word, was still very much alive, quibbling about his sacrifice instead of surrendering to it with grandeur and generosity.

The power of the false is such that it can create the illusion of the truth when it is presented and elaborated on with art. That argument made a certain impression on Hulet's mind. He had, for his own part, some arguments to add to those put forward by his son. He remembered the sudden manner in which the Marquis had ended their last interview, and the care that he had taken to have him leave by a hidden door. Not only, as Victor's letter had noted, had the Marquis not stated how the strongbox had come into his hands, but considering the whole matter closely, wasn't that death threat about the lock that the Marquis had warned him about, just one more elaborate trap of the kind that Lupiano's evil genius had shown itself so capable of in the past?

The Marquis had promised Hulet to give him the necessary instructions to neutralize the danger, but exactly two days had passed without his return at the Rue Barbette. He, however, had to return the manuscript he had been loaned, and that took only a few hours to read. Placed between suspicion and wicked interpretations, Hulet had, at least, one helpful inspiration; that was to go straight back to the puppet master whose influence grew from moment to moment in his imagination. A half-hour after receiving his son's letter, he had himself announced at Lupiano's townhouse.

As luck would have it, he was immediately relieved of one of the nightmares that he had made for himself. On entering the Marquis bedroom, he saw his leg extended on a stool and Lupiano in the hands of the Doctor, who was rubbing camphor on the foot that his client had sprained the night before.

"My dear neighbor," said Lupiano, "what the Doctor is doing explains why I didn't go to return your precious papers to you, and to instruct you against the danger pertaining to the lock of the strongbox that I pointed out to you. I am told that I will be able to go out again in a few days, but despite that, I was going to write to you."

"Then your accident wasn't serious?" Hulet asked.

"No," answered the Doctor. "Merely a pinched nerve. "The patient is doing better already."

"Doctor," said the Marquis, "would you have time to come back this evening?"

"Perfectly. I don't have any other serious patient, except for Madame de Camembert, and after having seen her at about six p.m., I'll come to spend the evening with you."

"So you think she is all right and the danger is past?"

"Yes. There are only some precautions to take, but those are significant. And, you know how stubborn she is! If she's not closely watched, she would soon do something imprudent."

"It really was pneumonia?"

"Yes! The worst kind, and without the strong treatment that I applied, she would have been lost!"

"Well, give her my regards, and also tell her that when she is able to have company, I will go and see her.

"Until this evening, then," the Doctor said on leaving.

The Doctor said goodbye to Hulet with that curiosity that one always displays toward for a man that one sees on a certain footing of friendship in a house where, an intimate there oneself, one encounters for the first time.

"To us, now," said the Marquis, when they were alone. "Where were we?"

"*Mon Dieu*! Still at the same point. I have not yet brought up the matter with my daughter. Another thing, here's what my putative son-in-law has just written to me…"

At the same time, he handed to Lupiano the letter he had received. After having read it, showing the least sign of trouble to the eyes of Hulet, who was watching him closely, he said:

"That is sad. There are not the words of a man who has accepted his part in the exchange to which he is condemned."

"We have to look at it from his point of view," Hulet replied. "He has not read the original letters, after all."

"That was a mistake that you made, not to take them with you and show them to him. When one is dealing with such a strange affair, you go forward with all your evidence in your hand."

"That is true, but I was in such haste to have him leave… And also, you told me that that strongbox was dangerous to open…"

"You should have taken the letters out and left the strongbox behind."

"But if, in the absence of tangible evidence, he had insisted that the writing was forged, what was I to answer to that?"

Lupiano looked at Hulet seriously and said:

"Wouldn't it also be somewhat your opinion that the letters might have been forged in order to support my claim?"

'I didn't say that, but I will admit, however, that in your conduct, so great and so generous, certain aspects of the matter still remain in shadows that I wouldn't be unhappy to see dispelled."

"Which aspects? Tell me."

"Two things struck me," Hulet replied. "First of all, the way in which, the other day, you made me leave your house so surreptitiously; and, then, you haven't told me how the strongbox came into your hands."

"Have you shown any desire to know that?"

"Not then, for I wasn't thinking about anything else at the time; but later, I wondered how you were so well informed, but it was already so late that there wasn't enough time for you to show me the secret of that lock that could bring death if it wasn't handled carefully."

"All right," said the Marquis, "I can see that your son's letter had an effect. You are still thinking about that box of insects that I sent you in 1809; *Timeo danaos et dona ferentes.*"[182]

"You have so many reasons to hate me!"

'Yes, Monsieur, and even greater ones than you know about. For instance, my son, who was returned to me, and to whom you owe the kindly feelings that have found their way into my heart—it wasn't enough for you to have wanted to make him perish at the moment of his birth, you also attempted to kill him a second time since then."

"Me, Monsieur?"

"And, if the other day, I had you leave so suddenly by a hidden door, that was because I didn't want you to find yourself face to face with a man who also has the right to hate you, but who hasn't pardoned you as I have."

"But, then, I would know your son?"

"Absolutely, and you made him a good part of that family curse of which that manuscript that you gave me to read, shows so well the progress and development. How will it all end? I don't dare foresee. Your son's letter frightens me, for I am beginning to see that, despite all my efforts, the race of the Pelopides, as you called us the other day, will still be the scene of great horrors."

"But, can't I know something more?"

"You know everything; I don't do things by halves, and there are enough horrifying secrets between us for me not to bargain with you about those that you still don't yet know. Have you known a man from Malta named Gregorio Matiphous?"

"Yes, a man that I had to punish."

---

[182] See Volume 1. Page 351; Latin for "Fear the Greeks, even if they are bearing gifts."

"That man, Monsieur, is my son, and by snatching out of the hands of Rempailleux that strongbox—an action for which you wanted him to pay with his life—he was able to give it to me, and I, in turn, to you, intact. Thanks to that theft, it was he who prevented the incest that was about to occur in your household, where, despite all this, someone else is still working to perpetrate it."

"Matiphous is your son!" exclaimed Hulet with stupefaction.

"What's so astonishing about that?" Lupiano replied. "Doesn't he spring from that same accursed blood from which we all spring?"

And then, the Marquis told in the greatest detail everything about Matiphous' behavior that could shed the most light on his past actions. He concluded with this:

"Our children, as you can you see, one by his inexorable hatred, the other by his foolish and criminal love in which he persists, put all the effects of our reconciliation in peril. It has to be ended, or that terrible secret, which you have for too long avoided sharing, will cause some deadly catastrophe. Bring your Victor to me tomorrow and I will convince him of the painful reality against which he can no longer rebel. As for Mademoiselle your daughter, her brother is right: time can do nothing to soften the bitterness of the revelation from which you are, in vain, trying to shield her. On the contrary, her strength is being sapped by the sadness of that separation that is being prolonged without her knowing why. Try to make her understand the truth through the services of her mother, her doctor, or her confessor, but do not make her wait any longer than tomorrow for her to know.

"As for your situation," Lupiano continued, "about which you consulted me the other day, my advice is for you to refuse those functions that you were offered."

"And what are your reasons?" the former member of the National Convention asked.

"That's because this inquisition of letters is in itself an odious and wicked business that has been the curse of our family. The way to turn away the wind of misfortune and death, which has never ceased to float over you and yours, is to avoid returning to its present source."

"That is perhaps true," said Hulet.

"If I were you," Lupiano continued, "I would break definitely with that awful past, that always tends to take you back and surround you. I would leave France. With the inheritance that your son has received, you now have large properties in America…"

"My daughter has been told that the climate there is not good for her."

"Well, then, come with me to India; I myself have large estates there, and I count on soon returning there."

"Your son hates me too much for us to ever think of living together in common harmony."

"My son still has a good heart," Lupiano responded. "Remember the day that he walked alone with you behind the casket of your son, Alexis. We all have too much to forget, but we can mutually recover from so much wickedness, since it wasn't the result of our own free will, but a latent and impulsive curse that compelled us to act as we did."

"Can we truly defeat that deadly curse?" asked Hulet.

"We must believe that," answered Lupiano, "since it has finally allowed us to meet and find out about it."

"May Heaven hear you!" said the former member of the National Convention. "What time may I come here tomorrow with my son?"

"At soon as it's daybreak," said the Marquis. "The day threatens to be rough. We can't begin it too soon."

He then returned the paternal manuscript to Hulet, excusing himself for not being able to accompany him in person to the door.

That afternoon, Hulet went to the Ministerial appointment which he had been given, and, following Lupiano's advice, he declined the offer of the functions that they wanted him to resume. Required to explain the cause of his refusal, he said that, since he had left the Secret Bureau, the whole organization had changed. The number of employees had been increased from twelve to twenty-two, which complicated the responsibility of the Director, and made it almost impossible to accomplish the narrow surveillance that it was his duty to exercise over his subordinates. He also complained that the positions in an organization where special ability and morality above all were necessary, had been given to men of tarnished reputation or old émigrés, who had used them only as sinecures or methods of intrigues, but in any case, with complete lack of care for any other duties. Finally, Hulet talked about the influence the Congregation,[184] a sinister power that was much in the news then, and which claimed to exercise some influence over the work which it was suggested that he should preside.

"Never," he continued, "could I be persuaded to have with the leaders of that association any direct relationship.

---

[183] An allusion to a study of the Scriptures, an inquiry into the doctrine of the duration of future punishment, particularly that of Hell's torment. See: Dr. Matthew Hornbery, Rector of Hanlake near Oxford, June 1773.

[184] Catholic organization founded on February 2, 1801, by the Jesuit priest Jean-Baptiste Bourdier-Delpuits (1734-1811), canon of Paris. It was made up of lay people and ecclesiastics, and played an important political and religious role in the defense of the Church, under the Directory, the First Empire and the Restoration, bringing together traditionalists and *ultras*. Criticized for its links with the Vatican, it was accused of spying, plotting, and was disbanded in 1809 by imperial decree, but it was restored in 1819.

Perhaps, without a doubt, the government could share with it some of the information that I would submit, but, as for my own participation in the matter, I could never lend my assistance to that narrow and squabbling inquisition, which is for the clerical party its principal method of action."

"But," answered the civil servant by whom Hulet was being interviewed, "it is exactly to remove the direction of that office from an intrigant who has become an agent for that party, that the Minister has thought of you. He knows your inflexible integrity, and by restoring your rights, in some fashion hereditary, in this function that, today, he is in sullied hands, he hopes to uproot that man, who still has his secret supporters. Perhaps only a meritorious candidate such as you have a chance to successfully close that breach."

"But as you can see," the former member of the National Convention replied, "it's not even a position that you are offering me; it's a competition against a miserable man against whom I am not even sure I have an advantage."

After a great number of words, turning in the same circle, since Hulet's resolution seemed unshakeable, the man interviewing him said:

"Be careful, however. The government can't see without displeasure a man who knows as many secrets as you do remain retired outside professional circles and beyond its power."

"Is it a question of sending me into exile again? I'm accustomed to it."

"No, but you are not unaware of the strict and threatening surveillance to which, in the past, the employees of the Bureau that ceased to work for it were subjected."

"Those times are past!" Hulet replied. "There is more gentleness in politics today: freedom of the press, the right to petition and make certain practices of an absolute government very difficult, if not to say impossible. What's more," he ended by saying, "it is improbable that I will long continue to reside on French soil, and that is one of the most decisive reasons I have for not accepting your offer."

"Then," the Minister's representative said, "you are going to condemn us to Saint-Rambert in perpetuity. You could
rid us of that man, and you will reproach yourself for not having done so."

"I don't think I have that much importance," Hulet said
modestly.

When he returned home, he spent a half-hour with his
wife and daughter without bringing himself to talk to them
about anything. Then, following a long-standing habit, at ten
o'clock, he said good night and went to his bedroom to go to
bed. But instead of going there immediately, he thought about
glancing again at the letters that, several hours later, would be
submitted to his son's examination. During his long career, he
had had many occasions to analyze handwriting, and could
promise himself that, if by some impossibility, the letters from
the Bedloes had been forged, as clever as that might be, they
would reveal certain details to him that would not escape his
experienced eye.

As a consequence of that decision, he went to pick up the
strongbox from the same bookcase from which, that morning,
he had taken out the bills that were exchanged against the old
bibliophile's sack of coins, and put it cautiously on his desk.
There, he began the process of verification that had just occurred to him. That examination only served to throw more
light on Lupiano's veracity. At first sight, the body of the writing appeared to the expert in handwriting that he was, remarkable by its openness and individuality. More subtle observations, bearing on the color of the ink and the paper, on the
formation of the characters and the down strokes, did not
change his first impressions. In addition, he concluded his
study by noting a point that summed up everything. The post-
marks on the stamps confirmed the places of origin and dates
in a way that was incompatible with the notion of forgery that,
in despair of any other argument, his son had favored.

In the middle of that work, during which a conviction
henceforth formed and took away all his concerns, Hulet felt
himself overcome by sleep, and he thought about going to bed.

For a long time, the direction of the *Secret Bureau* had accustomed him to long hours. He wasn't worried then about being awake for when his son would arrive. For more safety, he had an alarm clock that would be an infallible awakener. The room where he slept was also conveniently located so that he could, without making any noise, go and meet the traveler. Opening on the garden by a glass door, it was not directly accessible from any other room in the townhouse.

Before leaving his study, Hulet first had the idea of replacing the strongbox in the bookcase from which he had taken it, but feeling himself overcome by sleep, he was afraid that, by moving about that piece of furniture, made heavy by the gold and jewelry with which it was filled, he might do something clumsy. He decided then to leave it on his desk. The windows were protected by solid shutters. As for the door, he double-locked it and took the key with him.

That same night, a little before three o'clock, a rented carriage stopped almost at the corner of the streets of the Parc Royal and the Trois Pavillons. A man got out and immediately went down the second of these streets. He had just stopped in front of the outside door which, on that side gave access to the townhouse inhabited by the Hulets. But that man was not the son of the former member of the National Convention, because he had a key to the door, which he used to try to enter. He needed several attempts to make the lock open; however, it eventually ceded, and the door closed after him. He advanced cautiously, being careful to wipe out the trace of his footprints on the dirt, brushing them away with his handkerchief. He had, in addition, double-lined house shoes that allowed him to walk without making any noise.

A green lawn, surrounded by a walkway, occupying the greater part of the garden's surface, soon relieved him of the care of making the vestiges of his footprints disappear. Making his way across the lawn, he came to a place covered with dirt which extended across the façade of the townhouse, and he stopped to be sure that no window was showing any light.

Before going up several steps, the newcomer paid special attention not to leave any trace on the dirt he had just walked through and ran his hand several times under his shoes to rub off any gravel that could have made a sound under his feet. Next, he reached for the glass door that opened onto the room adjacent to Hulet's study. That study let in daylight, but did not open directly into the garden.

When it was a question of opening that second door, there was a problem. The key that had been used to lock it had been left inside the lock on the other side. Because of that, it was impossible for the nocturnal visitor to insert the one he had. However, with the help of a crook, he managed to bring the mechanics of the key exactly across from the opening of the lock. In that position, with the key he held in his hand, he pushed the other key out of the lock and made it fall inside the room where, thanks to a rug that he knew covered the floor, the sound of its fall was hardly perceptible. He could then enter, look for the key, put it back in its place, and use it to re-lock the door after him. The lock to Hulet's office offered no resistance. He was careful, as soon as he had entered, to lock it again with a double turn. After that, using a phosphorescent flint which he carried, he lit a small candle, called a *cave rat,* and got ready to examine the outlay of the place, that is to say, the bookcases, when, on his host's desk, he saw the strongbox that Hulet had left there.

Well! he thought to himself, approaching the object he coveted, *that good man wanted to spare me the trouble of ransacking his shelves; that's a delicate attention!*

Poor dear, he continued, *for a long time your beautiful eyes have made me die of love, or, if you prefer, how love from your beautiful eyes kill me.*

That man, as was obvious, showed that he knew his Molière, quoting from both *L'Avare* and *Le Bourgeois Gentilhomme.* [185] His eyes settling on the beloved strongbox,

---

[185] Two comedies by Molière: *The Miser* (1668) and *The Bourgeois Gentleman* (1670).

he began to inventory its contents. Next, he closed the lid, put the box under his arm and was on the point of leaving the room, when, with the bravado of a thief, he said to himself:

"Come to think of it, I shouldn't forget the Petrarch that I left him!"

He replaced his prey on the desk and rummaged around in the desk until he had put his hand on the Vindelinus da Spira which had allowed him to come and reconnoiter the surroundings, and at the same time, had allowed him to take an imprint of the locks and create a false key for them.

His moment of bravado over, the thief was going to definitely leave, and he already had his hand on the handle to one of the windows by which he intended to make his retreat, when he heard the sound of a rather inconvenient interruption. Indubitably, someone had moved about in the neighboring room. Shortly thereafter, a door opened and steps that someone was trying to muffle were heard in the garden. What could that bizarre incident mean? The thief couldn't believe that it was because of him. If his presence had been suspected, it was first of all toward the study that they would have come. Was it some amorous rendezvous of a servant? It had all the appearance of that, but there was no way to verify anything through the closed shutters unless he opened them, and the moment certainly seemed mediocrely opportune.

While our man, still listening with anxiety, deliberated as to what he should do next, there was more walking in the garden. Someone came into the house, and making their way toward the study. A great deal more belligerent than bibliophiles ordinarily are, the thief was resolved to do anything rather than give up his conquest of his golden fleece. He snuffed out his candle with his fingers wet with saliva, drew a dagger and was going to lie in wait behind the door, decided to strike at the inopportune person who was coming to disturb him.

Suddenly, he realized that, instead of one inopportune person, there were two of them, talking in a low voice, carrying a lamp that projected light under the door. Now, the game was not at all equal. It was a matter of committing a murder without almost any chance of succeeding, even if nothing worse happened.

He had to hide! A rapid glance around the room did not show him any hiding place. However, for Rempailleux—for our readers will undoubtedly have guessed the identity of the thief, and it is useless to remain mysterious any longer and hold back his name—there was still a way out of danger. That was the same method that we have seen him use fortunately and employ cleverly on the very day that began his relations with his adored strongbox. Although since that date, he had gained weight and become larger around the stomach, the instinct of self-preservation rejuvenated him. The former *Chauffeur* ran toward the fireplace, and, as that one was an older model, that is to say, huge and with a large opening, before the two trouble-makers had come into the study, he had managed to climb inside it and get himself installed there on two stones that he found under his feet, on his right and left. In that position that recalls that of the Colossus of Rhodes,[186] he could, without too much fatigue, wait to see what would happen. He had also taken care to situate himself at an elevation above the hearth that would allow him to be present, at least by means of his ears, during the scene that he was now curious to observe.

"Your calculations, my dear child," Hulet said, "as you're going to see, don't make much sense. All the letters bear the date of 1812 and 1813. How could you imagine that the Marquis de Lupiano could, at that time, have had enough foresight to set up a mine set off to explode today?"

"A letter is written," Victor responded, "on a little sheet of discolored paper, with whitish ink, and it's given the date of the year that's needed."

"But I'm not talking to you about the date on the inside; I'm talking to you about the date on the stamp put there by the post office."

"What if the stamp, too, was counterfeited?"

---

[186] One of the wonders of the ancient world, whose legs straddled the entrance to the port of Rhodes.

"Oh! This is becoming like a preposterous dream!"

"Why not? They say that man has audacity and depth!"

"All right, let's take a look," said Hulet, getting ready to take out the papers from the strongbox, the subject of the debate.

"Well, well..." he then said, "that's something unusual!"

"What's that, Monsieur?"

"I left the box open, but now it's locked."

"Then let's open it," said Victor.

"No, certainly not," the former member of the National Convention answered quickly. "It has a secret lock that is complicated by an explosive apparatus."

"A convenient way of stalling," said the young man in an ironic tone.

"What do you mean?" Hulet immediately replied. "That I myself locked this strongbox to avoid showing you the letters? That thought would be insulting if it was not totally unreasonable."

"What is certain is that the doors were closed; that everything here seems to be in order; and that no one has been in here, most of all not for the simple pleasure of closing a lid."

"I know that, on leaving my study," Hulet said, "I felt very sleepy. Perhaps I might have done it automatically? I really have no of memory of that."

"'There is no other kind of explanation possible," replied the young American. "But we have to find out the truth; I can't come here for nothing. I have the conviction that the secrets locked inside that box are essential for all of us to know, and in searching for a way of opening it, I'm sure we can find one."

"That would be a misfortune," said Hulet in a tone showing his firm resolution not to do anything foolish. "The Marquis," he continued, "who knows the secret of opening this box, and who is, besides, very willing to talk to you in order to dissipate all your doubts, told me yesterday that he would be available for us at whatever early hour we would wish. As soon as it is daylight, let's go and see him without anyone in the household having gotten wind of your presence,"

"But we could always try to open it now," insisted Victor.

"I repeat to you," Hulet answered, "that whoever tries, may well be killed. Since, in a few hours, your curiosity, rather vain, can be satisfied, it would be unreasonable to ignore the danger that has been pointed out to me."

"Very well, Monsieur, you are the master here," said the son-in-law in the tone of a man who resigns himself, but is not convinced.

"Now, if you will, let's take the strongbox into my bedroom, because, notwithstanding everything else, I still remain very intrigued at not having found it where I thought I had left it. Since there are still a few hours before we can go and see Monsieur de Lupiano, we can use them to get a little rest. You can share my bed, if you would like, or you can sleep in an armchair."

"All right," said Victor, "but I am still very sure that I could find the key to that mechanism."

Shortly afterward, Rempailleux saw the light disappear and heard the door to the study close. He then slid to the floor, disappointed, as is understandable, because that infernal strongbox always seemed to escape him, always fleeing before him. He didn't hide from himself, however, that this time it seemed final. A series of unusual circumstances had made it possible for him to first steal that treasure, gathered by the American whose suicide he had witnessed; but then he had lost it, and now, back after some long detours into the hands of its legitimate proprietor, it could be divided and shared in a way that would make it impossible for him to get it back. So it was now or never, during that very night, that had begun so well but had ended so badly, that it could be stolen.

Everything weighed and calculated, Rempailleux found that he had one last chance; that was to ascertain that the two dragons guarding the treasure had fallen asleep. But there were many difficulties with regard to entering an unfamiliar bedroom without waking its occupants! It was easy to imagine that, surprised in their bed, or at least with their eyes half-open, the two men could be easily strangled; but what sureness of hand would be necessary to attack them without their crying out, or engaging in one of those desperate fights that the instinct of self-preservation redoubles, and which in turn may rouse the whole household!

It would have been perfect if the shutters of Hulet's bedroom were closed, letting the light shine through. From the outside, the field of battle and the enemy could then be seen and evaluated. After about a half-hour of waiting, Rempailleux went up to see what opportunities there were for him. It took miracles of caution and cleverness to succeed in that reconnaissance without being betrayed by some sound. But it was in vain. The shutters were closed everywhere and not the least crack let a smidgen of light through. However, he heard not the slightest conversation, and that silence was a favorable circumstance that decided the robber to pursue his plan. There his problem became complicated, for he didn't know exactly where Hulet's bedroom was located. Some noise coming from inside it to help him would have been both a lucky strike as well as something to be feared, since it would have meant that the people that he had to catch asleep were, in fact still awake.

Orientating himself as best he could, Rempailleux crossed a dining-room, and listened at all the doors he passed without finding any indication. Then, at his last stop, he heard not only the sound of voices, but an animated conversation whose tone wasn't slow in becoming that of an argument. He applied his eye to the key-hole, and saw the bedroom, still lit, just in his field of vision. Hulet, like a man who had just left his bed in a hurry, wore no other clothing but his night shirt.

After a sudden movement that he made, widening his extended arms, a sudden explosion suddenly shook the house. Deciding to run the risk of the fight that he was prepared to have, sure of not being recognized under the layer of soot covering his face, in one turn of his hand, Rempailleux opened the door to the bedroom and rushed in desperation inside.

Thrown on the floor by the force of the explosion, a candle let him see the father and the son covered with blood and no longer giving any signs of life. Without a doubt, the son's imprudent and stubborn hand had taken advantage of Hulet's sleep to go over to the strongbox and try to open it. His efforts had awakened the unfortunate Hulet who had made a gesture of alarm to ward off the peril, but in vain.

What was strange was that, the evening before, after his interview with Lupiano, Hulet seemed to have had a presentiment of the impending catastrophe.

Going across that scene of carnage without stopping, holding his conquest, Rempailleux rushed out by way of the French window that he had the presence of mind to close after him. And before any of the inhabitants of the house were able to reach the place of the explosion, he also had time to lock the door of the garden behind him with a key.

The carriage that had brought him was waiting at the place where he had left it. He would have had some trouble explain his dark discoloration that his stay in the chimney where we saw him take refuge, had cast upon him, but before he had left, he had taken care to have his driver take a bottle of gin with him. So he found the man in a drunken sleep.

Rempailleux took the reins himself, and burning up the pavement, returned to the townhouse where he lived with his wife, Rue du Colisée. For the convenience of the nightly sorties required by his service in the *Secret Bureau,* he had the key of a door opening onto the commons, by which he could enter without being seen.

When he arrived in front of that secret exit, after having assured himself that that the driver still hadn't awakened, he got out of the carriage, gave the horse a strong lash of the whip, and, in that way, abandoned him to a frenetic ride that no human hand controlled any longer.

XVIII. The Ricochet

Lupiano first learned of the catastrophe when the Doctor came to dress his wounded foot. He didn't know any details at all. The Law was already at the Hulet townhouse, because some gendarmes, for lack of a Sergeant de Ville, a position which hadn't yet been created, were guarding all the entrances and exits.

Amidst the huge crowd of the curious that, for some days, continued to be stationed around the theater of the event, were recounted the most diverse explanations. According to some, the father and the son-in-law had fought a duel. The quarrel had been caused by the mad conduct of the son-in-law who had slept out the first night after his wedding. A misunderstanding would have been the cause of all the misfortune when, returning from a trip, the son-in-law, in order not to awaken anyone in the house, had come in through a door at the back; and his father-in-law, mistaken him for a burglar, had shot him, then killed himself with the same pistol, in despair, upon the realization of his mistake. A third version presented the father-in-law and the son-in-law as doing research on the philosopher's stone, and an explosion had occurred during a complicated chemical experiment, which had struck them both dead simultaneously.

Without being taken in by any of these ridiculous explanations, Lupiano understood immediately the fateful role that the strongbox had played, and as he was the one who had taken it to Hulet's household, he waited to see if some backlash wouldn't rebound on him. In fact, at about noon, a bailiff came to his townhouse, bringing an arrest warrant made out by the Investigating Magistrate. That was becoming serious; it was not as a witness. But as an accomplice to the explosion that he was being interrogated.

In another era, to gain time, he would have pleaded that his indisposition made it impossible for him to walk, but having solemnly sworn to himself to submit on every occasion to the law that, for such a long time, he had not recognized and defied, he saw there an opportunity to testify as to his respect for it. Having himself transported to his carriage, some moments later, he appeared before the Investigating Magistrate and the King's Prosecutor, who, since the morning, had been gathered clues from the Hulet townhouse.

After a long interrogation, the summons were converted into an arrest warrant, and, at about four o'clock, Lupiano was taken to the Conciergerie.[187]

Matiphous, who had not slept at Lupiano's townhouse, walked in just as his father was leaving, following the bailiff who had brought the summons. He immediately went to the Hulet townhouse on the Rue Barbette, but coming up against inflexible guards, he wasn't able to enter and remained in the street, mingling with the crowd of bystanders, until the great door of the courtyard opened, letting through the Marquis' carriage.

"They've arrested someone!" cried the crowd, getting in the way of the horses instead of letting them go through.

Matiphous wanted to jump to look through one of the windows of the carriage, but he couldn't get through the crowd. All he could see was the hat of the uniforms of two gendarmes who, seated at the front of the vehicle, were guarding the prisoner.

The kindness of a policeman having informed the perplexed Matiphous of the place of detention where his father was being taken, the man from Malta rushed to the Conciergerie, but it is useless to say that he wasn't even admitted past the first barrier. Roughly dismissed, he jumped into a carriage to go and see Lelouard, for whom he knew his father had particular esteem. On the way, he heard a newspaper hawker advertising *L'Etoile,* an evening pro-Government newspaper, which had rushed out a special edition in order to exploit the good fortune of the tragic and mysterious event

---

[187] Part of the Capetian dynasty's palace, which became a prison during the French Revolution. It now houses law courts and the Sainte-Chapelle.

which was exciting all of Paris. He bought a copy and read the following article:

Last night the inhabitants of the Rue Barbette, in the peaceful Marais neighborhood, were awakened toward 3 a.m. by a terrible explosion. After looking for some time for the source of the explosion, they found it in the townhouse of M. Vandel, a regicide and former member of the National Convention, recently recalled from exile by the inexhaustible clemency of His Majesty. Vander was found dead in his bedroom, with at his side, dead also, a young American, Victor Bedloe, who had just married his daughter.

What gives that event a mysterious character, is the manner, until now unknown, in which the victims were struck. From the debris, little pieces of glass and little square bits of lead with which the two bodies were riddled, it would seem that the explosive used was fulminate of mercury, a highly volatile substance, instead of the more common back powder. From that fact, one might be led to suppose the existence of a kind of Machine Infernale,[188] *but of it, there were no debris to be found.*

As soon as they reached the location, the investigators quickly searched to see if a robbery had been committed. Nothing showed any evidence of it. All the exterior doors everywhere were locked, and no valuables appeared to have been removed or taken from the bookcases where M. Vandel stored them. One circumstance, however, first drew the investigators' attention: a French Door, fitted with shutters, which, in the bedroom, the site of the explosion, opened onto the garden of the townhouse, should have been double-locked for the safety of the residents, but was simply shut. Furthermore, some foot-

---

[188] The expression *machine infernale* designates a single firearm built by Giuseppe Fieschi and the druggist Pépin in 1835 for an attack against King Louis-Philippe, but it also refers, thirty years prior, to another attack against Napoleon on the Rue Saint-Nicaise on 24 December 1800, nicknamed the "plot of the infernal machine."

prints found on the dirt in the garden below led to the suspi-
cion that the criminals had entered from that side. But after
having compared these with the victims' shoes, they found that
these matched exactly. Now, how did Mr. Bedloe, who, the
evening of his marriage, had left for Orléans, where he had
been retained, until yesterday, by an important affair, find
himself back in Paris without anyone in the house knowing of
his arrival? That is something, without a doubt, that will be
explained later.

While we are waiting for answers, we can reveal that the
notorious Marquis de Lupiano, a wealthy foreigner who has
been the subject of many conversations, has been arrested,
probably on very serious suspicions, and locked up at the
Conciergerie. The young Madame Bedloe, hardly recovered
from an illness that had seriously worried her family, has not
stopped having violent attacks of nerves, followed by fainting
spells, since the moment that she blundered into the horrible
spectacle that she was one of the first to discover Her family
fear for her life.

The journalist had naively concluded:

Some families are cruelly tried.

For Matiphous, as for his father, the instrument of death
was not in doubt, but without knowing everything, he knew
much more than the Marquis about the mysteries behind the
event. Obviously, Rempailleux had taken advantage of his
confidence and that must explain the disappearance of the
strongbox. As for his father's arrest, it could doubtless be attributed to Rempailleux's theft of that piece of misfortune in
Hulet's house. Matiphous reproached himself strongly for
having, against the paternal advice, persevered in his heinous
projects of vengeance against the former member of the Convention. Forced to hide his actions from him, Lupiano had
done what he had done in order to prevent the consummation
of the incestuous marriage—the product of a character of haste
and mystery that now had turned against him.

Matiphous' first inclination was to go put the law on the
trail of the thief, but Rempailleux might, after all, not be the

true guilty party; also, he benefitted from the protection of his functions and high patrons. Then, even supposing that he would called to account, he wouldn't neglect, in his defense, to bring down the man who had denounced him, who was far from irreproachable. Temporarily, then, Matiphous felt that he had no choice but to go and see the former *Chauffeur*. Perhaps his robbery having been successful, he would leave France and thus buttress the complain which could then be lodged against him without danger.

Everything considered, Rempailleux couldn't be blamed for the spilled blood. He had not, before stealing the strong-box, used it to strike and kill Hulet and his son, who had, without doubt succumbed due to the curse attached to their family. He was then not a murderer, but simply a thief, to whom Matiphous felt temporarily disposed to give the benefit of the doubt. However, in the new complications by which he saw himself everywhere surrounded, the man from Malta saw a cruel lesson: it was then that he understood how wise his father had been when he had preached clemency to him, say-ing:

"Don't get mixed up in any bad business now that a hap-pier direction has been given to your life."

On arriving at Lelouard's bank, where the arrest of the Marquis was already known, Matiphous found assembled: Montalvi, the Doctor, and most of the former *Red Brother-hood*, all men concerned by the news. A frightened note from Madame de Camembert, whose state of health kept her in bed, testified of the same solicitude and apprehensions. No one at the gathering knew about the connection between Lupiano and the Vandel family. They were discussing, therefore, in the dark. Some of them supposed that the Marquis had, on his own, for himself, undertaken some revenge where his usual manner of operation had been recognized. Others attributed the rigors of the law to the casual and cavalier manner in which he had received the police when they had come to ask him to give an account of the pretended poisoning of the stu-dent Maisonneuve. Others, finally, went even so far as to get it into their heads that, by whatever means, the present affair was related to the executions carried out by the Brotherhood, now dissolved. Had the police, interested in them for a long time, finally picked up their trail?"

Without adding anything further, Matiphous calmed a great deal of their terrors by affirming that, to the best of his knowledge, the relations between his father and the Vandels were positive, even friendly. They resolved, temporarily, to remain calm, waiting for the communication that, without a doubt, Lupiano would find the means to pass to his son or to someone among his friends. And they liked to persuade themselves that, the victim of some misunderstanding, he would soon be freed. That confidence, however, didn't prevent some members, on leaving the reunion, from secretly making plans to leave Paris within the briefest delay.

The next day, Matiphous renewed his efforts to get to the prisoner, but he was certain that he had been confined *incommunicado*, that is to say that any communications from him to the outside and vice-versa were strictly forbidden. Lelouard, to whom Matiphous had gone to report the futility of his actions, told him that anything was possible with money. And, in fact, two days later, an assistant to the Clerk of the Court, for the round sum of 25,000 francs, passed on to Lelouard, if not the content, but at least the substance, of all the interrogations which the Marquis had already undergone in front of the Investigating Magistrate.

We will reproduce here the text of that interrogation, condensing it as much as possible:

Asked if, the day of the marriage of Mademoiselle Vandel, during the wedding dinner, he had come to see the father of the bride, carrying even to the point of indiscretion his insistence to be received, Monsieur de Lupiano answered that he had gone on that day and at that hour to the home of Monsieur Vandel, and had asked for him to be told that he had things of the greatest importance to tell him.

Asked as to what were those things, Monsieur de Lupiano answered that a letter written by Monsieur Vandel's son-in-law the evening before his death, revealed a secret that, as far as he is concerned, because of the immense sadness of a family already too unhappy, he is repugnant to disclose.

The Investigating Magistrate having affirmed that no letter of that kind had been found at the scene, Monsieur de Lupiano responded that it had to be found and one should look for it in the papers left by Monsieur Vandel. He himself had seen it with his own eyes.

Asked if it was true, as affirmed by a servant with whom he would later be confronted, that, the day of his visit to Monsieur Vandel, he had given said Monsieur Vandel a strongbox, Monsieur de Lupiano answered that a confrontation wasn't necessary and that he would admit without difficulty that he had indeed given such a strongbox to Monsieur Vandel.

Asked as to what that strongbox contained, Monsieur de Lupiano responded that it contained about 800,000 francs in diverse forms in addition to valuable papers.

Asked as to why that strongbox was not found at the scene, Monsieur de Lupiano answered that he didn't know anything more than the police on that subject.

Asked if the aforementioned strongbox, as has been known to happen in the annals of locksmiths, had not been fitted with a security mechanism against thieves, Monsieur de Lupiano answered that, to his knowledge, it had indeed been fitted with such a device, and, as a consequence, he had given it to Monsieur Vandel already opened, and warned him not to close it until he had shown him the secret.

Asked as to why he had not shown him that secret at that time, Monsieur de Lupiano answered that the demonstration was long and difficult, and that there wasn't enough time then for Monsieur Vandel to be shown its operation.

To the observation of the Investigating Magistrate that the lack of time that he was mentioning was improbable, Monsieur de Lupiano responded that Monsieur Vandel had already been away from his guests a long time reading the papers in the strongbox, and that even before beginning that reading, his wife had come to remind him that he had been absent for some time from the wedding dinner.

Asked about the contents of these papers, Monsieur de Lupiano answered that those papers fully revealed the secret that was mentioned in Mr. Bedloe's letter, a letter that should be found in the dossier, and which the Investigating Magistrate promised to look for.

Asked where he had obtained that strongbox, Monsieur de Lupiano answered that he did not have to explain himself on that subject.

Asked if between Monsieur Vandel and himself there existed some motive for mutual enmity, Monsieur de Lupiano answered that, while they had been enemies in the past, Monsieur Vandel and he had reconciled, and he gave as proof of that fact the care that he had taken to return the aforementioned strongbox to Monsieur Vandel, containing an important sum of money and making him at the same time of a secret not less important.

To the observation that Monsieur Vandel and his son-in-law had paid with their lives their lack of knowledge about that secret, Monsieur de Lupiano answered that he much regretted that fact, but, first of all, the police had to prove that the strongbox had actually been the cause of death, and that in the absence of that strongbox, that proof would be difficult to establish; and subsidiarily, that he had done all that he could to warn Monsieur Vandel of the danger.

To the observation that, having appeared to warn him, he might in reality have relied on Monsieur Vandel's lack of caution, Monsieur de Lupiano answered that he had only to explain himself with regard to the facts presented in evidence, and not any suppositions or insinuations.

To the observation that, in making known the contents of the papers contained in the strongbox, the accused could successfully nullify the basis of the accusations against him, Monsieur de Lupiano replied that, although this might be true if said papers were in the hands of the law, but in their absence, revealing their contents was an act that he found repugnant, especially after having had the chance of seeing himself accused of lying; that the best thing for him was to wait; and that he would wait, etc., etc.

Lelouard couldn't understand some of the legal gobbledygook. As for Matiphous, he immediately noticed two things: one, the care that his father had taken to not compromise him in refusing to tell the manner in which the strongbox had come into his possession; two, the noble attitude of the accused, preferring to risk seeing his captivity prolonged rather than to cut it short by revealing, without it being absolutely necessary, the terrible secret that could prove deadly for the already unhappy Helena Vandel. But most of all, Matiphous was struck by the remark that, in the absence of the letters written by the Bedloes, Lupiano's defense remained difficult. Besides, even if, driven by the needs of his defense, he was to reveal their contents, the law could still maintain that these were purely made-up, and even that his story lacked plausibility.

At that point, the Bedloe correspondence must be in the hands of Rempailleux, and it was therefore most urgent to recover it. To a man who wanted money, they had almost no value. According to all appearances, it therefore shouldn't be too difficult to get them back from him. But in any case, a means to lead him to surrendering them should be found.

On leaving Lelouard, to whom he didn't think it useful to confide anything, Matiphous told his coachman to take him to the Rue du Colisée.

XIX. Rempailleux in Check

From the time Britannicus' presence in Paris had become known to him, Matiphous had formed the habit of always having loaded weapons in his carriage. On approaching Rempailleux' domicile, he thought that he was going to confront a dangerous person, with whom the negotiation that he was proposing to initiate could easily turn into a conflict. He then found it prudent to take two pocket pistols with him that he had at hand.

Provided with those defensive weapons, he presented himself to Saint-Rambert's concierge, asking if his master was at home. If he had been told that Monsieur de Saint-Rambert was on a trip, he would not have been surprised, since that was one of the chances that he had already accepted with respect to his unannounced visit. But not having smelled anything fishy on the horizon, Rempailleux hadn't found it useful to leave Paris. He was still at home, available, and therefore, a moment later, the man from Malta was shown into his study.

"My dear fellow," Matiphous said on entering, in order to give his actions a friendly turn, "it isn't exactly to see you that I've come. I owe a visit to Madame de Saint-Rambert, and in case I haven't chosen the hour to see her well, I began by asking to see you, so that it wouldn't appear too unseemly."

"What time is it?" said Rempailleux, looking at the clock. "And today is Monday... No, my wife is not at home; today is the day of the reunion of the charitable association of which she is the treasurer, and they usually meet at the home of the old Princess de G***. It's rather in the evening that you will have a chance to see her."

"Another time then," Matiphous said, "I will have more luck. Besides, right now, I don't seem lucky about anything. Have you heard what has happened since we last saw each other?"

"Don't talk to me about that!" said Rempailleux. "That's unbelievable. What does that arrest of the Marquis mean? There must be some mistake which will, without a doubt, be cleared up."

"Not at all. The affair is serious and is following its course. It's impossible right now to reach my father, who continues to be held in the strictest secrecy."

"But what are they accusing him of?"

"Of having taken that infernal strongbox to the Vandels."

"What strongbox?" Rempailleux responded, in a tone of the best acted ignorance.

"My God! *Our strongbox,* the one we talked about the other day at your reception."

"Oh! That!" said the former *Chauffeur*, with even more fake innocence. "So it would be the explosion of that fatal strongbox that...?"

Faced with the comedy being played out, which wasn't a good omen for the success for his negotiations, Matiphous became impatient. Interrupting his interlocutor in mid-sentence, he said to him straight out:

"You have without a doubt verified its contents?"

"What do you mean? The contents of what?"

"The strongbox you stole from the bodies of the Vandels. By my careless confiding to you, you knew that it had been taken to the Vandels, and you weren't a man to let someone else steal it."

"Oh! My dear fellow! Are you joking? If I had done that job, do you believe I would be here calmly chatting with you?"

"I did, in fact, have the notion that, now well-off with your loot, you would have skipped town, but you probably told yourself that I am the only one in the world who might suspect you, and counting on my discretion, you made the right calculation. My intention, I'm telling you this right off, is not to create any problems for you."

"Ah! Really!" said Rempailleux, laughing. "You haven't thought of making yourself the assistant to the King's Prosecutor? Well, you're a good fellow, and I should be deeply grateful for your clemency."

"Let's just talk about my silence. I repeat to you that you will have it, but on one condition, however."

"A condition! Please! I might have, for a moment only, appeared to join you in your foolish notion, but anymore insistence on your part, I warn you, would disoblige me. If then you don't have anything else to say to me, I would like to ask you to cut short our conversation."

"Do you really want me, when I leave here, to go straight to the Prosecutor you were talking about a minute ago? I'm telling you that you don't have a choice: either you render me a small service of no consequence to you, or you risk seeing your virtues, which are not too immaculate, put under the clairvoyant glance that I will provide to them.”

“But, my dear Monsieur, those virtues that are shining in you aren’t too brilliant either, and frankly I don’t see, for Your Excellency, any great interest in going to play the simpleton in the courts of Lady Justice.”

“I know what I’m exposing myself to. You will claim that I appropriated the inheritance of the American. My intention is to confess to that before you accuse me of it. But, in my case, I restored that inheritance, while you stole it a second time, in a pool of blood. You could very well find yourself in a heap of troubles because of my revelations.”

The resolute way in which Matiphous had laid out his plans, which were of rare simplicity, had without a doubt given his opponent something to think about, because, completely changing his attitude, he replied:

“That’s positively an *idée fixe* of yours, to keep me away from that damned Pandora’s box. But it is said that one shouldn’t argue with a madman, so tell me what service I may render you, because, in truth, it is your mental condition that I find interesting.”

“Beside the eight hundred thousand francs that I shall leave intact in your hands,” said the man from Malta, “you found some correspondence in the box. It could become useful in my father’s defense, while at the same time being of no interest to you. I have come to ask you to turn it over to me, so I can produce it in case the Marquis’ legal situation becomes worse.”

Seizing on the opportunity now given to him to renew his request for some kind of subsidy, Rempailleux replied:

“After all the devotion I showed your father, it wasn’t very nice of him to refuse to show me a sign of his gratitude!”

“Is that, in your turn, a condition that you put on your cooperation?”

“I can’t ask anything for those letters, since I don’t have them. But, even if I did, wouldn’t I have the right to say to the Marquis, ‘My dear fellow, it’s a matter of give and take.’”

"Yes—if the Marquis had anything to do with this negotiation, but he's not the one talking to you, I am; I who have
just *given* you a fortune, and who, in exchange, have come to
say to you, *take* some scraps of paper that, really, have no value except to me and give them back to me."

That distinction wasn't to the taste of Rempailleux, who
replied:

"I have told you just now that I was talking purely by
way of hypothesis. What you want from me, I don't have, so,
as they say in the Chamber, I now demand a closure, because
it's tiring to always go over the same subject."

"Listen to me," Matiphous said excitedly. "I'll get right
to the point. You are bold, but you are not brave. I saw you
tremble before death in London."

"That's charming," Rempailleux replied, "when it was a
question of hanging me behind closed doors!"

"Now it's not the King's Prosecutor that I'm threatening
you with," the man from Malta continued. "You still have
some good hopes of getting out of his clutches, and even looking at things in the worst way, what do you risk from him?
Jail? A jail from which you can escape."

"As you say, my dear fellow," Rempailleux replied insolently.

"But when dealing with me, just think about it, it's your
life that you're gambling with. As God is God, if you don't do
what I ask, in the middle of one of those glorious receptions
organized by Jack Ketch's daughter, I will slap the face of her
illustrious husband. We will see then, Monsieur Society Man,
if, without having to fight me, the scar that I will have let on
your cheek can be displayed in the salons!"

"My dear fellow," responded Rempailleux, whose vulnerable side had just been found, "you don't need to get it into
your head that your bullying airs have frightened me, but I see
that filial piety is a passion with you, and a passion that has
always seemed to me too respectable not to find a way into my
heart. Those letters that you want at any price, it's not absolutely impossible that I could procure them for you. But if the

Devil himself was here to ask me for them, I couldn't give them to him on the spot..."

"Why?"

"Because they aren't here."

"Where are they?"

"Somewhere. That should reassure you, and if you want to come back in a day or two..."

"Yes, to give you time to set up some trap for me."

"You would think that I was setting up one for you if I were to ask you to come with me right now to pick them up where they are."

"I suppose it's rather natural that you immediately felt the need to hide your loot. Where have you stashed it?"

"Outside of Paris, with a friend."

"How far from Paris?"

"Very near, only a few hundred steps from the barrier. "

"Let's go there. I have my carriage and some weapons with me."

Matiphous showed Rempailleux the pistols that he was carrying.

"Oh well!" the former *Chauffeur* said ironically. "You will be as well protected as if we were crossing the Bondy forest."[189]

"What direction are we going?"

"We'll go to the end of the Faubourg du Temple, then onto the outside boulevards, between the barriers of Belleville and La Chopinette."

"That's very easy to find," said Matiphous. "I actually have some business in Belleville, a visit that I have been guilty of putting off for too long."

"Ah, yes! To the family of Commandant Lefebvre, whom you knew in Madagascar"

"How do you know that?"

---

[189] The Forest of Bondy was a notorious lair of thieves and other dangerous brigands.

"From Britannicus. Being more caring than you were, he brought news of the Commandant to those poor people that you neglected. He's in good standing in that household, and I wonder how you will be received there, because he wasn't slow in telling them about your more than your casual conduct toward your *legitimate wife* that you have abandoned."

"I must beat that miserable man to death with a cudgel," Matiphous said angrily.

Seeing that Rempailleux had stood up to ring for a servant, Matiphous said:

"No, please, don't call anyone."

"Do you think by any chance that I have some squadron of guards here ready to tie you up?"

No, but even a man to whom one whispers something, or to whom one just makes a sign, can go up ahead, or follow our trail. You being a clever man are certainly not without having at hand men who would understand implicitly such orders!"

"I just wanted to tell my wife that she should go without me to meet an important personage with whom we have a meeting from three to four. Because you should know that, even despite Vandel's death, my position as head of the *Secret Bureau* is still compromised, and your father is truly cruel in not helping me out of this predicament."

"Bah!" said Matiphous, turning a deaf ear to the ways Rempailleux never ceased reminding him of this. "Women are much better than us at asking for favors, and Madame de Rambert, I am sure, will come back to you with excellent news on that account."

"At least, you will allow me to fetch my hat and gloves?"

"Here is a bijou of a bedroom ideally suited for a mistress," commented Matiphous who had followed Rempailleux into the next room.

"Yes," said the ex-*Chauffeur*. "I believe I would now have trouble returning to the lifestyle with which you threatened me earlier. All done!" he added energetically. "Let's go."

"The Belleville Barrier," said the man from Malta to the carriage driver, after his master had sat down in the two-seater that Rempailleux had entered first.

Conversation between the two travelers was only slightly animated; it's hard to talk in a carriage, deafened as one is by the noise of the wheels on the pavement, and then, each man had his own preoccupations to think about.

Matiphous didn't hide from himself that, although armed and seconded by two servants, he could still be led into a trap. For his part, Rempailleux, if he was meditating something, must have mulling bitterly over the kind of threats to which he had just been subjected. Nevertheless, during the climb of the Faubourg du Temple district, the horses returned to a steady pace and the conversation became livelier, especially when Matiphous had the thought of asking what had become of *Monsieur* Britannicus.

"Britannicus," Rempailleux calmly replied, "you'll see him in a moment."

"How's that?" asked the man from Malta, rather intrigued.

"It's to his place that we're going, providing he has not gone out."

"Monsieur de Saint-Rambert," Matiphous asked, "we're dealing honestly with each other, right?"

"I don't think anyone could have put his cards on the table more honestly than I. It was to Britannicus, who has a charming little hide-away, that I took my find. I am telling you my secret; what more do you want?"

"I find all that perfectly normal, but it was also by you that I was advised about the bad intentions of that man towards myself."

"Are you afraid? If so, let's turn around and go back."

"I am not afraid, but suspicion, as you know, is the mother of safety."

"You have weapons, two of your men are accompanying us, we are in open daylight, and we are going to one of the most populated places in the suburbs. Besides, Britannicus. as you have already experienced, isn't a very dangerous kind of assassin. If, all that considered, you still feel the need to be worried, that's because you are overly cautious."

"I'm not, but allow me to show my surprise that you had the idea to confide the secret of your, er, *find* to this peculiar fellow. After all, I am here to prove to you that he's a man whose loyalty is more than doubtful."

"You understand, my friend, that I don't usually share my business with the sainted Brothers of Saint Vincent-de-Paul. That Britannicus was one of my protégés in Rochefort.[190] He has a great deal of respect for me. I could then, without putting his discretion in doubt, take advantage the convenience of his lodgings to store something that I found inconvenient to keep at my house. After that, if you are too disagreeable to meet with that man, let me out here; I will go alone to his lair. During that time, you can pay your visit to Lefebvre's family, and the first one to return to the barrier will wait for the other one."

"No. While I've got you," Matiphous said good-naturedly, "I prefer not to let you go."

"Damn, my good fellow, you can see how accommodating I am. But there is one thing for which I can't answer: Britannicus may not be at home. Perhaps he is in Paris, where he goes almost every day. Your *legitimate wife* gives him almost as much money as he wants, and the fellow spends it as much to have a good time as to occupy himself with the terrible plots that he is said to be organizing, at great expense, against you. It's possible that he won't return until very late at night, and even, as it sometimes happens, he may not sleep at home."

"Let's go to his lodgings," said Matiphous, resolved to carry the adventure to its end.

---

[190] See Volume 3, Pages 183 seq.

On arriving at the barrier's toll booth,[191] the coachman stopped the horses and the footman went to the check to see if that was where one paid to cross.

"My dear fellow," Rempailleux then said to the man from Malta, "if I were as prone to injurious and malicious suspicions as you are, I might give you some advice."

"What would that be?" Matiphous asked.

"To leave your carriage here; we are going to enter a lower-class neighborhood, where carriages and lackeys in livery don't smell like perfume. The people of Belleville are on their own here, and don't like to see the superior classes come there showing off their luxury beside their rags"

"At the most, we will get some jibes," replied Matiphous, who couldn't keep from recognizing a basis of reality in Saint-Rambert's concerns.

"As you like," Rempailleux responded. "Then tell your coachman to take the boulevard to the left of the barrier and order him to go at a slow pace."

XX. The Camp de la Loupe

Sunday is the official day of rest. It is less rigorously observed by the worker than Monday, the day of feasting and liberty that the worker has himself decreed, and to which he finds a particular attraction, that of the forbidden fruit.

The slow pace advised by Rempailleux, which Matiphous ordered his coachman to follow, was, in every way, prudent, because it was on a Monday that their excursion took place on the outskirts of the La Courtille neighborhood.[192] Now, not only the side streets, but also the sidewalks of the

---

[191] The reader must remember that, at the time, entry into Paris proper was taxed.

[192] The neighborhood of La Courtille (today, near Ménilmontant) was, at the time, outside Paris limits and was a dangerous area frequented by criminals, drunkards, and, especially thieves.

exterior boulevard that the carriage was traveling, were encumbered with a compact mass of impatient pedestrians going toward outdoor restaurants and neighboring cabarets, who wouldn't have allowed the horses to go at a trot and disturb their long lines and their ownership of the street. Despite the discreet slow pace with which the carriage was moving, Matiphous, following what he had foreseen, received more than one curse, addressed as much to him as to his servants. Nevertheless, the carriage arrived without difficulty to a kind of garden, surrounded by a wall with a worm-eaten wooden gate that separated it from the street.

The only things missing from this enclosed garden were trees, flowers and a lawn; but the ground there appeared to have miraculously produced rows upon rows of tables and benches, to the point that there was hardly any space to walk between them. Sitting at these tables, a huge crowd of drinkers enjoyed some kind of purplish wine served in small jugs of glazed terracotta. To avoid the possible complications caused by patrons disappearing suddenly, the establishment asked for the drinks to be paid upon serving.

The name of the establishment was advertized on a large sign that bore above it the picture of a Flemish feast, and just below it, the clumsily drawn sign:

AU CAMP DE LA LOUPE
FEIGNANT, Wine-Merchant

Louper in the popular slang of the drinking establishment of the time, meant, to like to drink; a *loupeur* was a man who drank much and often; the *loupe* was the universal brotherhood of drunkards. The entire notion was thus summed up in one word, which might have found its origins in the popular word *loupe*, which meant an excess growth, and *louper* therefore become synonym with drinking excessively, because it is only in its excess than one can recognize a professional drunkard.

Thus the Camp de la Loupe was the permanent rendezvous of the *boit-sans-soif*, those who drank without being thirsty. And let's admire the name of the master of this place, that of the wine-merchant called: *Feignant*, a word meaning lazy, slothful, an open call to revolt against the notion of work, the enemy of the laborious classes. *Feignant* was the man who not only would not work, but was prepared to do anything to avoid working and, like the wealthy, escape the harsh necessity of having to earn one's daily bread.

Therefore we must rush to add that the clientele of the establishment was a faithful representation of the cold cynicism of its sign. One didn't find there hard-working laborers or diligent and honest women; what one saw was misery in rags, naked vice, and folks either on their way to or back from jail. Always turbulent and often the scene with bloody fights, this loathsome open-air *cabaret* was constantly under the surveillance of the police, which tolerated it because they found it useful to conduct regular searches and seizures, for the people who have business with the law also have the strange habit of congregating together in such places, thus making easier to be caught together at the same time.

"We've arrived," said Rempailleux when the coach stopped before the establishment we have just described.

"You called this a *charming little hide-away*?" said Matiphous, starting at the Bacchic pandemonium.

"His house is just at the end of that street," explained Rempailleux, pointing at a narrow passage between the *Feignant* establishment and another neighboring *guinguette*.[193]

"Will we stay here very long?" asked the man from Malta?

"A half-hour to three-quarters of an hour at the most," Rempailleux replied. "The thing is buried in the garden."

"You will wait for me here," Matiphous said to his servants, "and if I haven't returned in an hour, go to the barrier and ask for four men and a corporal to come to the house that is at the end of this passageway, because Monsieur and I will likely be prisoners there."

---

[193] Open-air café.

"The Devil!" said Rempailleux. "It's a pleasure to see your confidence."

"What does that matter to you, if you are straight as a die?"

"Ah!" said Rempailleux, "that's certainly all the same to me; but let's finish with this. Will you follow me?"

The little passage that Matiphous walked along, following the steps of his interlocutor, ended in a rather vast unoccupied space where big weeds and high nettles were an indication of little circulation. Beyond, there appeared a house of rather sad appearance. One story with an attic, it had three windows in the front, closed at the moment by green shutters. The door was reached by three crumbling steps, eaten away by moisture.

"This house," Matiphous remarked, "doesn't seem to be inhabited."

"I told you that it was possible that our man wouldn't be here to receive us," replied Rempailleux, pulling a doorbell formed of a rusty piece of wire from which a crowbar was hanging,

At the tingling of the bell, the door was soon opened by a young mulatress, in whom Matiphous recognized Britannicus' daughter, that he had brought to France with her father.[194] Born toward the end of 1808, in the chateau that Lord Stuart possessed on the Isle of Mainland, that child, very developed, as it happens to all those who inhabit tropical regions, was then reaching her twelfth year. Despite the African type that she had inherited from her father, in a number of other points, she resembled the blonde Kitty, whose terrible adventure at the Florence masked ball at the Pergola Theater hasn't been forgotten.[195]

"Well, Sadou," said Matiphous, who liked that young girl, "you're here, too?"

---

[194] See Volume 3, Page 186.
[195] See Volume 3, Pages 142 seq.

"Yes, good master," said the colored girl, "and very happy to see you again."

At the same time, she was about to take Matiphous' hand to carry it to her lips , but was roughly interrupted.

"Your father," asked Rempailleux, "is he at home?"

"He is here," responded the mulatress, throwing an angry look at the man who had just roughly interrupted her.

"Well! Tell him to come here; we need to talk to him."

At the same time, he opened the door of a room giving access to a corridor, leading to the rest of the house. Matiphous then found himself in a dining-room which looked out on a little garden made up of some thick clumps of lilacs and a long sandy alley. At the end of that alley, over the low walls, the fields could be seen, and further away the pleasant greenery of Pré-Saint-Gervais.

Britannicus wasn't long in appearing.

"Ah! Master has finally come!" he exclaimed on seeing Matiphous. "That's good; we're going to have a good laugh."

"Where did you bury the treasure I entrusted to you?" asked Saint-Rambert.

"Down there, just under the trees; it's enjoying the fresh air."

"Joker!" Rempailleux said. "Go get your tools." Then, speaking to Matiphous, "Will you follow me to the garden?" He added, "we're going to dig up the box."

"So you didn't even know where it was buried," said Matiphous, seeing Britannicus leave, "And you had to ask that fellow?"

"Well, I was very pressed for time and I left him the care of arranging all that."

"A strongbox that's enjoying the fresh air?" said Matiphous suspiciously.

"Why not, my dear fellow? That's a malgache joke. Were you afraid that he wanted to speak to you about your *legitimate wife*, who has come to chase you all the way to here?"

"That certainly seems like it," said the man from Malta, hearing a great deal of movement in the house.

"Well, why shouldn't she?" said Saint-Rambert. "She has rights, after all, that respectable woman, and she would be correct in pursuing them."

"Yes! But you, Monsieur, who have led me into this trap, believe that we still have some unfinished business left between the two of us."

Saying this, Matiphous cocked one of his pistols and made his way toward the door, but before he had time to reach it, it was opened from the outside, letting Britannicus enter, accompanied by three robust men from Madagascar, that were part of the personnel of the delegation dispatched by His Majesty the King of the Hovas. Those men, it goes without saying, had taken the part of the Ambassadress against her unfaithful spouse. In an instant, without having been able to use his weapons, Matiphous was thrown to the ground, tied up, and carried triumphantly to the feet of their mistress. Instead of finding herself weeping in Madagascar, Georgiana's rival had, it seemed, come to Paris to pursue her vengeance.

By marrying the first cousin of Queen Ranavalo, Matiphous had made a marriage of convenience, since in no country in the world, in Europe or in Madagascar, would Ravine-Vol (that was his wife's name) could have passed for a beauty. Born of a Hovas father and a Sakalave mother,[196] this Malgache Ariadne had inherited her looks primarily from the maternal side; that is to say that her complexion was chocolate-colored; she had high cheek bones; she had little, sparkling, intelligent eyes; her nose was somewhat flat; her lips were thick; her teeth protruded, but were remarkably white. As for her hair, that she wore with a great number of little tresses, rubbed with rice oil, it was black, curly, without being wooly. Ravine-Vol had, in addition, extremely delicate arms and legs. Her breasts were small, but, as if in compensation, at the bot-

---

[196] The Hovas and the Sakalaves are amongst the numerous peoples of Madagascar. (Author's Note)

tom of her back two large prominences would have allowed her without too many disadvantages to compete with the *Hottentot Venus*.[197]

In the shade of a group of trees, where she had gone to seek refuge from the heat of a June day, Matiphous' *Vadi-Bé* (legitimate wife) was seated on a *toutourane,* a rug of white cotton with blue fringes, made in the country of the Hovas. She was dressed with a *simbou,* a kind of silk toga with alternating stripes of brown, yellow and white, that in Madagascar was worn by both men and women, but that women draped coquettishly around their feet, their legs, their arms and their naked shoulders. These disappeared under an enormous quantity of silver chains, coral bracelets, and necklaces made from pieces of money pierced and strung, while, hanging from her ears, were two enormous golden rings. Without a doubt to show her unfaithful husband that she wasn't too desolated by his abandon, when he appeared in her august presence, she was having her women dance at the sound of a *bobre*, a national instrument that used a little piece of wood to put the metallic cord in vibration.

"So, it is you, traitor?" she said, putting her musical instrument in Sadou's hands. "As you can see, I did not return home, as you thought I might!"

"That wasn't an order that I gave you," replied Matiphous. "You are no longer my wife. I cannot command you to do anything."

"Ah! I am your wife no more? Me, a princess of royal blood! You think I can be repudiated like a *vadi-sindrangou* (a female slave). It's not going to happen! And first, you'll come back with me."

---

[197] Sarah Baartman (c.1790-1815) was the most well known of at least two South African Khoikhoi women who, due to their large buttocks, were exhibited as freak show attractions in 19th century Europe under the name *Hottentot Venus*—Hottentot was the then current name for the Khoi people (now considered an offensive term.

"I most certainly shall not," Matiphous replied. "I have a family here and my interests are in France. I will stay here."

"Then you did not do well to come here; because if you entered, you won't leave."

"That's rather improbable. I've taken some my measures. If in a half-hour, I'm not back, the guards from the barrier will come to my rescue. Ask that honest man who took care of bringing me here."

Thus called to testify, Saint-Rambert, who was delighted to be present at the interview of the two spouses, was content to answer with a comically respectful inclination of his head.

"So," continued Ravine-Vol, "you do not want to return to your marital duty?"

"I call on you again," Matiphous responded, "not to keep me here any longer. You are not in a country where you can exercise your own justice, and you could be sorry for any violence done to me."

"That's true," said Rempailleux, with a mocking tone. "Sequestration of a person; that's hard labor, as per Article 341 of the Penal Code."

Like most criminals, the former *Chauffeur* was very familiar with the criminal code.

"I don't care about your Penal Code," replied the woman from Madagascar. "Take that villain to the prison we made ready, until we leave."

Then, to show her spirit, she added:

"Sadou, give me my *bobre* so I can make my girls dance."

The place made ready to receive the prisoner was just the cellar of the house where, remembering the melodramas that he had seen played out, Britannicus had placed some straw for a bed, a jug of water and a morsel of bread.

Held tightly by strong ropes, and having heard a strong door close behind him, Matiphous would have been more worried if he had not counted on the coming intervention of his men. However, time passed and no one came to his aid. He then was becoming somewhat worried when the door of his cell opened and Rempailleux walked in. Britannicus, who accompanied him, carried a chair, which let it be supposed that the conversation would be of some duration.

The Negro left almost immediately. Rempailleux had some trouble finding a place on the uneven floor for the chair. Before sitting down, he went to the door that he carefully opened half-way, to be sure that there was no indiscreet listener. Britannicus was not hiding behind the door to overhear his words. He then returned to sit down and had with the prisoner the following conversation.

XXI. Blackmail

"You see, my dear fellow," said Rempailleux, "what ingratitude gets you! You father imprisoned on one side, and you here; that's what you've earned by rejecting my just demands."

"If you had been given a stipend," Matiphous answered, "you would, even so, still have stolen the strongbox, and it's because it wasn't found after the death of the Vandels that it was the cause of the Marquis' arrest."

"No, don't be difficult. If you had been just and accommodating with me, I probably wouldn't have begun taking risks again. But, in any case, I would have been in a hurry to give to the police the papers that you came to demand from me with threats. Let it be said in passing that you have not very nicely succeeded in that."

"So," said Matiphous, impatiently, "what are you getting at? Because you surely have a reason to be here, honoring me with your company."

"I wanted, my poor fellow, to make you see your position up close. You perhaps aren't exactly aware of it. So, you thought that you had done marvelously well in putting yourself under the protection of your men. But, I'm telling you that, a little at my instigation, they got into a quarrel with the interesting population of the *Camp de la Loupe*. Right now, your carriage is impounded, and far from being able to help

you, attacked and beaten by a mass of false testimonies for
having posed as agitators, your men have been taken to the
violon,[198] where they are waiting for you to come get them
out!

"I know," said the man from Malta, "that you are a clever manipulator of plots."

"Not at all! I am as naïve as a new-born child, and the
easiest man to deal with when you want to come to terms with
me. Your wife and Britannicus have been here for more than a
month, offering me fabulous sums if I would deliver you into
their hands. I've always put it off, thinking that the Marquis
would finally listen to reason. But this morning, you came to
my house playing the braggart. My word, to calm you a little, I
made use of the little intelligence that Heaven has given me.
However, we aren't Turks, and things can always be arranged."

"And on what basis does that arrangement seem to you
possible?"

"Well! The calculation is very simple. The Madagascar
woman has offered me fifty thousand *écus* if I would put you
at the mercy of her revenge. Offer me the same amount and I
will give you the preference. And if you even go to the round
sum of two hundred thousand francs, I will throw in that correspondence that's so important to you."

"I see. With the eight hundred thousand francs already in
the strongbox that would bring you up to exactly a million!"

"Well, yes, my dear fellow; if I have to admit it to you,
to bring my fortune right up to a million has always been the
dream of my life. It's only with that amount that one begins to
be distinguished from the masses. And when an opportunity to
crown me a millionaire presents itself, wouldn't I be stupid to
let it escape?"

"But, first of all, I don't have two hundred thousand
francs on me. To get them, it would be necessary for me to
leave. And still, even if you let me out of here free as a bird, I

---

[198] Slang for jail.

would be hard pressed to know where to get them. If my father were free, I don't say..."

"Bah! Don't you have an open account at the Lelouard bank, where the Marquis is a silent partner?"

"Yes, for a few hundred Louis—that much, I could get there, but two hundred thousand francs, that's something else!"

"You will explain the need for that advance by the necessity to get free of your shrewish wife, and the need to send her back to her country. It's not to the son of a Croesus like the Marquis that anyone will bargain about such a relatively modest sum, especially when it's a question of getting rid of such an obstacle in your his life. Besides, why don't we give it a try? You will write this note; I will give it to your footman, whom I will have released. How long will it take him? Two hours at the most to go and get back here. He will give you the money; you will count it out to me still warm, and you will be released immediately."

"And once I'm free, aren't you afraid that I will carry out my threats?"

"No, because you are an honest man, and there would have been a transaction between us. Besides, I have another defense against you. Right this evening, I intend to leave Paris with the Malgache delegation, God knows when I shall return!"

"What! After betraying my charming wife, you propose to leave with her?"

"Of course! It will be made clear that you were freed by an Act of God, completely independent of my own will. And since I am supposed to have compromised myself in the service of your other half, by making her horribly afraid of the consequences of our failed plot, I should be able to convince her to leave forthwith and shelter me under her wing!"

"You are truly a man full of resources," said Matiphous, with admiration.

"What do you expect, my dear fellow! When you have nothing under the sun, you have to know how to work hard at any little job."

Saying that, Rempailleux took a notebook out of his pocket. He tore out a page and said to Matiphous:

"All right! You're going to write that note. A message on a little piece of paper scribbled in pencil will look more compelling."

"But," the man from Malta said with amusement, "I'm not like the armless man that you see on the Pont-Neuf writing with his stomach."

"So, my good man, I'm going to untie your hands," responded Saint-Rambert, getting busy unknotting the ropes.

When Matiphous was able to write, he said:

"How am I going to phrase it?" he asked. "Lelouard is a tight and suspicious man."

"Well!" Rempailleux said, coming to bend over the prisoner, "nothing is simpler. Write: *My dear Monsieur Lelouard, It is necessary that, without any delay...*"

"On my word, no!" Matiphous suddenly said. "I will not write this note."

"What! You refuse?"

"Yes. With a man like you, there is no guarantee, even when carrying out the most serious plans agreed on. In addition, I don't like this kind of blackmail that you are using on me. And since my hands are now free, I prefer to use them to keep my promise to you."

And he applied a strong back-hand slap on Rempailleux's cheek, that was within his reach.

Rempailleux' first reaction to that slap was to throw himself on Matiphous, but showing admirable self-possession, he said:

"Monsieur le Comte, despite the information that I have been good enough to give you, you continue to believe that your deliverance is near, and it is certainly with that hope that you have perpetrated the audacity of your insolent brutality.

But be careful! Our plans are well made, and if you push me too far..."

Without answering, Matiphous was actively busy trying to remove the ropes that held his feet.

"Ah! No, no!" said Saint-Rambert. "I won't allow that."

At the same time he ran to the cellar door.

"Britannicus!" he shouted. "Come back here with all your fellows!"

The Negro not being slow to appear, followed by all his confederates, Rempailleux said to them:

"Come and see how badly you have tied up Monsieur le Comte!"

A desperate fight between the man from Malta and the Malgache delegation ensued, the outcome of which couldn't be in doubt. However, as it lasted for some time, the overexcitement of Matiphous gave him the strength of desperate resistance.

"Beat him a little, that fellow!" shouted Rempailleux, who was keeping himself out of the range of the blows being exchanged.

Britannicus and his men hadn't waited for his permission to deliver the most violent brutalities to the man who wouldn't submit. Soon unable to make any movement, Matiphous was replaced on his bed of straw.

"That's good, my children," said Rempailleux, dismissing his *gendarmerie*. "Leave us now, so that I can reason a little with that bad boy!"

When he found himself alone again with the prisoner, he said:

"We'll continue our conversation, my dear fellow, and I must repeat to you: if you believe in your impending deliverance, you are sorely deluded. Your servants, I am willing to admit, can't be held indefinitely, and as soon as they are free, they will take action to find out what happened to you. But by then, you will already be far away from here, on your way back to the kingdom of that excellent King of the Hovas, whose goodness you have so well repaid. Now, since that's what you want, you will be the one to leave, and I will stay, very decided, I warn you, to *care* for your honored father's affairs as they should be taken care of."

"Oh! That? I warn you," Matiphous said. "You should think twice before confronting him, and it will be too bad for you if you succeed in sending me back to Madagascar, because his vengeance will be terrible."

"What do you mean, *if I succeed*? But, my dear boy, it's already taken care of! You can consider that you are already there!"

"It will take a great deal of imagination to persuade me of that. I am not yet even in Bordeaux."

"Bordeaux!" exclaimed Rempailleux. "But that's not your departure port, Monsieur my sworn enemy! It would be too difficult to drag you that far. We have taken the time to make alternative arrangements, and it's from Le Havre that you will be departing. It's a great deal nearer Paris, and the boat that brought you here is, at this very moment, waiting for you."

"To Le Havre, then; but I'm not yet there."

"Agreed, but for that short journey, we have taken additional precautions. As soon as it's night, a carriage will transport you, gagged and solidly restrained, to a seldom frequented quay on the banks of the Seine where there will be a boat like the one we used in 1814, if you remember, on the Ostend Canal."

"And then?" Matiphous asked in contempt.

"There, once in the hold, you can rant and rave as much as you like, but with very little chance of being heard. Then you will very gently go down the Seine right to Le Havre, to be immediately carried aboard the *Franklin,* where you will have been preceded by your darling spouse and all her suite. Then, it's set sail for Madagascar! As for what awaits you there, that's beyond my ability to tell you, but I understand that they have various ways to cause people pain."

"Are you finished?" asked the man from Malta, whom the exposé of that plan had only very moderately affected.

"Yes," said Rempailleux, getting ready to leave. "I leave you with the regret that we weren't been able to come to an understanding. But it was written that we would never do business together. I'm going to tell Ravine-Vol, who charged me with negotiating the terms of your departure, that despite being preached at, beaten, and still stubbornly unchanged, you want to die unforgiven. It's your Papa who, on leaving his prison—if he leaves it—who will be somewhat astonished not to see his son anymore."

"He will leave it," said Matiphous, "and what he didn't do to you in the past in London, you can be sure that he will do this time."

"We'll see about that!" responded Rempailleux, leaving. "His goose is almost cooked, that good man, and I'll make sure the dish lasts even longer."

XXII. The Deliverance

The kidnapping project that Rempailleux had given himself the pleasure of recounting to Matiphous in its smallest details, was not, as it might be believed, an immediate product of his imagination. Actually, the plans that he had just laid out had been set up for a long time to satisfy the furious jealousy of the woman from Madagascar. At Bordeaux, when she had only suspected her husband's relationship with Georgiana, it hadn't taken much for her to want to use poison to cut short his infidelity. The rage of her African passion can then easily be imagined when she found out about Matiphous' disappearance with her rival.

She had immediately sent Britannicus to Paris where it was likely that the couple had taken refuge. A former acquaintance of Saint-Rambert, whose address he had known since 1814, the Negro first had the idea of seeing him to help him in his search; it would have been difficult for him to have chosen a better assistant.

Rempailleux, to whom Lupiano had indicated the rupture of their relationship and the suppression of his stipend, was naturally curious about what had caused that sudden determination. He therefore was not long in learning of the affiliation with Matiphous. As for the liaison of Matiphous with Georgiana, the man from Malta had surrounded it with such publicity that it was not a secret for anyone in Paris. Britannicus, in a few days, was completely informed, and he had immediately conveyed the result of his search to Ravine-Vol. In the meantime, the woman from Madagascar had received a letter from Matiphous in which, having sent her the money and the goods that he had brought with him to defray the expense of his diplomatic mission, her ex-husband had instructed her not to wait for him and to return alone to her country.

That definitive notice had transported the abandoned woman to her highest paroxysm of anger, and she had immediately resolved to get to Paris. Following the advice of Saint-Rambert, to whom very effective seductive offers of money had been made so that he would consent to be an intermediary in her revenge, the African woman had avoided the publicity with which her trip would normally have created. Just like the Osages Indians some years later,[199] she could have walked down the Rue de Rivoli to the Terrasse Hotel, and it is certain that, with her following, comprised of Britannicus and Sadou, three Hovas men and three Hovas women, she would have made on the Parisian idle on-lookers at least as much a sensation as these American Indians. Who knows but if, like them, presented at the Tuileries, she wouldn't have had the honor of being received by King Louis XVIII and by the Duchesse d'Angoulême et de Berri?

But such a great success at court would not have been long in coming to the ears of her unfaithful husband, and then he would have been put on the defensive. Unless she wanted to carry the news of her conjugal unhappiness to the foot of the throne or before the tribunals, the best thing for her was to

---

[199] This refers to a visit by a group of four Native American men and two women to France and their arrival in Paris on August 13, 1827.

retrench herself in the strictest incognito. It wasn't without some trouble that Saint-Rambert had managed to persuade her that, to have recourse to the King or to the Law, which had been her first thought, would have necessarily been fruitless. The cousin of Queen Ranavalo-Menjaka, Ramine-Vol believed that she had such a high place in society that her displeasure would be of interest to the Magistrates and the Crown, even though, in Madagascar, as Matiphous had explained to his father, marriage was an institution that was essentially temporary, of the type that we would call *mariage au treizième.*[200] Ramine-Vol couldn't accept that such a law, good, at the most, for the riffraff of her island, should be applicable to a princess of royal blood. In order to persuade her to take a less public form of her revenge, it had been necessary for Rempailleux to threaten her that, if she wouldn't follow his advice, he would take away his help and protection. Once it had been agreed that they would proceed quietly, when the date of the departure of the Madagascar woman for Paris had been decided, it had been necessary to find, for her and for her companions, a suitable dwelling where her arrival would not become an event. And it was then that the house where Matiphous let himself be drawn into had been chosen.

That property was owned by the Deputy Mayor of Belleville, a detail that will bring us back to the family of Commandant Lefebvre, because the reader will remember that they lived in that town, but now in conditions very different from those in which we have seen them in the past. Having become Madame Joseph, Amanda Lefebvre, with a thousand qualities of mother and spouse, had justified the rare devotion of which she had been herself the object. It would be in vain that a happier household could be found than that of the young foreman. The girl, once seduced and gone astray, had become the woman to whom Joseph could safely trust all the future of his life. Two children, the pride and the joy of their grand-mother, Madame Lefebvre, were not slow in crowning the happiness

---

[200] See Note 57.

of that union. And as if God had wanted to recompense him for his sacrifice, that, contrary to all the ideas of society, had provided him with inspiration and courage, everything had miraculously succeeded for him.

First of all, the owner of the factory where he worked had given him an interest in the business. Then, he had made him his partner; and, finally, with the payment of a life annuity, stipulated between them, he had sold him the factory. In that way, Joseph had become, in the common vernacular, a *major manufacturer*. The former worker had acquired in town such a considerable importance that, despite having scarcely reached the age of twenty-five, legally required to exercise municipal functions, he had been named Deputy Mayor. In 1819, at an Industrial Exposition, thanks to the superiority of his products, on the proposition of the Jury, the cross of the *Legion d'Honneur* had come to shine on his jacket.

Up until the time that the young industrialist had gone to take up lodgings in the buildings of the factory of which he had become the owner, with his wife and his mother-in-law, that he had wanted to have as a companion, he had lived in the house where we know Matiphous was being held prisoner. When Britannicus had arrived in Paris, even before having seen Saint-Rambert, he had hurried to go and visit the Lefebvres to give them news of the Commandant, something that the man from Malta, stunned by his new fortune, had neglected to do. That visit, one should note, wasn't purely disinterested on the part of Ravine-Vol's representative. While going to give the Lefebvres news of the Commandant, whom he had left in a good position in Madagascar, Britannicus had hoped that, having been preceded by Matiphous, he could obtain from them some information about the man he had been sent to find.

However that may be, and despite his rather bizarre behavior, his visit had been received with gratitude, and, naturally, when he had recounted the misfortunes of his mistress, he had created the strongest sympathy for that poor abandoned woman. After that, when it was a question of finding a lodging for her where she wouldn't be too much noticed, the Lefebvres had offered the house that they had ceased to occupy, thinking with good reason that, in Madagascar, Lefebvre would experience reciprocal goodwill since they were helping a relative of the King, in the service of whom the old soldier was now engaged.

The house was really a little too small to receive ten persons, but in Tananarive, capital of the country of the Hovas, civilization wasn't so very demanding that, to accommodate Madame the Ambassadress, the splendors of the Louvre were not necessary. It was then early Spring, and if her following weren't too comfortable, they could always find some place to camp out under the hospitable roof this made available to her. So, one evening, Ravine-Vol, with all her people had come to occupy the modest dwelling put at her disposal, and, except for Britannicus and Sadou, who, dressed in the European fashion, went out to buy supplies for the household, she and her people were condemned to absolute reclusion. No one in Belleville, suspected the existence of the new colony that had been settled there.

Only the Deputy Mayor, his wife and Mama Lefebvre had been permitted to pay court to the African aristocrat from time to time. And it must be said, once she had shown herself to them, they had understood better, and had looked on with more indulgence; the actions of her flighty spouse. Besides, visiting rather frequently the factory, where her gentleness and her beauty had gained her great success, the pretty Sadou spoke about Matiphous a great deal more favorably than Britannicus and his hateful employer. She was familiar with a thousand traits of his goodness; she recounted how he arranged for her education and, one day, when she had been threatened with being devoured by a crocodile, she escaped from that danger due to his courage. They had been set straight about Matiphous, and, as he had expressed the desire, the day he had fallen into Rempailleux's trap, if he had gone to see the family of his friend Commandant Lefebvre, according to all appearances, he would have been very nicely welcomed.

But he was going to make their acquaintance in another way, because, the evening of the same day, while the family of the manufacturer was finishing dinner, suddenly Sadou rushed into the dining-room where they were all gathered. She was out of breath, her clothes were rumpled, and everything about her indicated great emotion.

"Monsieur, Monsieur," she shouted, "come quickly. They want to kill him!"

"To kill whom, my little Sadou?" asked Amanda and her husband at the same time.

"Monsieur Matiphous! He's tied up in the cellar! They beat him; they're very bad men! And now, they want to take his life! "

"But who is it that wants to take his life?"

"His wicked wife and the men from Madagascar. My father the other man whom brought him said that it would be bad business, and it would be better to take him where he could be killed later, at their convenience, but Ravine-Vol and the men from Madagascar want to do it immediately. She said that she is mistress in her own house, and that she can do justice to a traitor in whatever way suits her.

"Oh! Oh! Like in *Christine à Fontainebleau!*"[201] said the Deputy Mayor, who had some knowledge of history. "We're going to take care of all that, my child. But you, my poor Sadou, when they know that you've come to warn is, they are going to mistreat you."

"I came out by way of the garden," the young girl answered, "and I can go back the same way, perhaps without anyone knowing that I went out."

---

[201] Drama in five acts in verse by Frédéric Soulié (1829) dealing with Queen Christina of Sweden who, while in Fontainebleau, and theoretically under French law, had one of her squires, Monaldeschi, killed on November 10, 1657.

"Then go back to the house quickly. Give me just enough time to put on a jacket and get my scarf and I will be right with you."

"You'll come quickly, won't you?" asked Sadou, reaching the door.

"Yes, yes, but leave now, and take care to see that no one sees you get back in."

The poor child left, running.

"To go alone among those savages who have a taste for blood," asked Madame Emile, "is that wise?"

"I don't know if it's wise," said the manufacturer," but it's my duty. Can I let a man be murdered two steps from me without interfering?"

"Go there, but with the gendarmes," said Madame Lefebvre.

"Not at all. I'm going to introduce myself as having been brought by chance to pay a visit to Ravine-Vol. I am going to settle the situation without a scandal and without the intervention of the law, because, after all, she believes that she is within her rights, that miserable woman, and I don't want to give her a jail cell in exchange for the hospitality that I have given her so far."

"Then, let me go with you," said Amanda, "that would seem more like a regular visit."

"That's true," said Madame Lefebvre, "I'm going with you as well."

"Not at all. That would be too many; but what you must do is tell the foreman and our servant to hold themselves ready. If in a good half-hour I haven't returned, you can send them to me as reinforcements."

I didn't take more than ten minutes for the Deputy Mayor to reach the door of the house. It was Sadou who opened the door when he rang.

"You've come in time," she told him, "and no one saw me re-enter."

"Can I see your mistress?" Monsieur Emile asked Britannicus, who had appeared almost immediately.

"My Mistress is not be seen," the Negro answered. "She has a very bad headache; she cannot see you, Monsieur."

"Ah! She has a migraine, like the ladies in Paris?"

"Yes, that right, a migraine—she must sleep."

"Well, then, my friend, so that my visit serves some purpose, you're going to take me to the cellars."

"To the cellars?" Britannicus asked, flabbergasted.

"Yes, just lately, the mason told me that he'd noticed a big crack in the foundation of your, er, *palace*. I want to go down to look at it."

"I don't have the key," answered the Negro.

"What do you mean, you don't have the key? Go look for it."

"I don't know where it is. We looked for it earlier, but couldn't find it. No find. Now I should go and work on dinner."

"Come now, that seems very suspicious. Are you by any chance hiding something in the cellar?" asked the Deputy Mayor.

"What, me, hide something?" Britannicus asked with a false laugh.

"I've been told, my friend, that, taking advantage of how close the barrier is, you bring contraband brandy into Paris every day. You understand that it wasn't for that use that I loaned you my house."

"No, no, I don't do contraband. They lied those who said that."

"Now, are you or are you not going to look for that key? Otherwise, I'm going to call the gendarmes whom I just saw a few yards away from here."

During that time, standing behind her father without being seen, Sadou, with her little hands, was making applauding gestures for the clever way Monsieur Emile, without compromising her, was preparing for the deliverance of the prisoner.

"I'll go again and see if can find that key," said Britannicus, going away rapidly.

"So, no one saw you come back in?" the manufacturer asked Sadou, who remained alone with him.

"No, they were all in a *kabar*.[202]. No one paid any attention to me."

"And who is that man that brought Monsieur Matiphous here?"

"I don't know him. He has never come here before."

Rempailleux himself was going to take charge of answering the curiosity of the manufacturer, because a moment later, he appeared, accompanied by Britannicus.

"Monsieur Deputy Mayor," he said, "my name is Comte de Saint-Rambert. Can I have a word with you in particular?"

"By all means, speak, Monsieur," said Emile, going into the dining-room, where, some hours earlier, Matiphous had been received.

"Monsieur," Rempailleux began, "I bless your appearance, because it gets me out of one of the greatest embarrassments that I have ever experienced in my life. In the interest of good manners and good harmony, that it is always sad to see disturbed between spouses, I persuaded Ravine-Vol's husband to have an interview with her and I accompanied him here in hopes of bringing about a reconciliation. But everything turned out badly, and following a very bitter discussion, not content with keeping Monsieur Matiphous prisoner, that band of enraged savages were talking about having him murdered. That's what's done, apparently, in princely manner in her country."

"Yes, but in a constitutional country like ours, we don't grant such privileges to Princess Spouses, and today, I would order the arrest even of Queen Christine of Sweden herself if she wished to apply her own brand of justice to her squire M. Monaldeschi.

"That is perfectly true, Monsieur, but I would dare ask your indulgence for a native who does not know the limitation

---

[202] Note from the Author: A council where business is discussed; a frequent usage in Madagascar.

of her rights. Even more so since, if I am not mistaken, your father-in-law is himself in the service of King Radama, and, as you know, that Ravine-Vol is a near relative of His Majesty.”

“I do not need any family considerations,” said the manufacturer, “to avoid a scandal. As you have said it very well, that woman doesn’t know what she is doing, and we have to be content with requiring that she set Monsieur Matiphous free.”

“Your presence, Monsieur Deputy Mayor, has done more than all my arguments for the past two hours. They are right now freeing your protégé, and I would even ask you, since we understand each other so well, for your permission to not wait for him. He must be very exasperated by some of the bad treatments he has received, and although, after all, he owes me his life, because without me you wouldn’t have had time to intervene, I would prefer not to see him at this moment.”

“Very well, Monsieur, I approve of your prudence.”

“What’s more, if by some chance you need my testimony, I will tell you again that I am the Comte de Saint-Rambert and that I live in Paris, Rue du Colisée.”

Rempailleux had no sooner made his exit, than Matiphous, freed, found himself face to face with the Deputy Mayor, who had gone to meet him.

“Monsieur,” said the manufacturer, “you are free; I am the Deputy Mayor of Belleville, and you have nothing more to fear. You are under the protection of the law.”

“Then, Monsieur,” said Matiphous, excitedly, “you would be willing to hear my complaint?”

“That’s my duty, but not here. Let’s first leave this cut-throat area. If I may, I would have the honor of receiving you in my home and offering you some refreshments, which you surely must need.”

XXIII. How One Becomes a Great Citizen

Various explanations ensued between Matiphous and Monsieur Emile, who, with grand airs, gave himself the noble role of liberator. Nevertheless, it was established that Rempailleux had slipped through his fingers, but since the manufacturer's intention had not been to give a judicial follow-up to the affair that he had just been settled so fortunately, that little deception mattered little to him. Then, thinking about the rather sad figure that he would make in case a lawsuit should come about, the man from Malta also came to the opinion that he should leave Saint-Rambert in possession of his impunity for the time being. Also, that lack of punishment was only temporary. He planned on, very soon, finding a way to repay the harsh and unmerited treatment that he had been subjected to. So it was not quits, but just a delay that his mortal enemy had gained.

At first greeted rather coldly by Amanda and Madame Lefebvre, when he was introduced to them by the manufacturer, Matiphous excused himself as well as he could for his negligence in not bringing them news of the Commandant immediately. He explained that, if he hadn't brought any letter to them, it was because when he had embarked for France, Lefebvre was absent from Tananarive. A revolt had broken out among one of the tributary populations of the King of the Hovas, and Commandant Lefebvre had been forced to leave suddenly on a mission to suppress it. Little by little, the reception of the mother and of the daughter became more cordial and Matiphous was consulted about the question of whether Madame Lefebvre should go and join her husband.

"If I decided to go back there," Matiphous answered, "I could take you with me, and I wouldn't hesitate to advise the trip to you, but it is not my opinion that you should go alone or in the company of Britannicus or Ravine-Vol."

"Also," said Madame Lefebvre, still possessed with her ideas of jealousy, "my husband must not lack women in that country of savages, and perhaps he wouldn't be very pleased to see me arrive."

"You are mistaken, Madame," said the man from Malta. "He positively charged me with bringing you back. But once he knows that I won't return, he will, less than ever, think of staying forever with King Radama. Therefore, it's better that you wait for him here."

"Besides," Amanda said to her mother, pointing to her children, "could you ever decide to leave these little angels?"

"No, grand'mama," the two children said at the same time, "we don't want you to go."

"Now, now, that's all right," said Madame Lefebvre, embracing them, tears in her eyes. "I won't leave, since these dear ones don't want me to, but, my son-in-law, you must get busy bringing my husband back."

"Whenever he likes it," responded the Deputy Mayor. "I have never stopped writing to him that, since my business has taken a turn for the better, he has a bed and a place at the table here."

"Yes, but Lefebvre is proud, and he fears being a burden."

"There are things to keep him busy here," responded Monsieur Emile, "but I can't make him Minister of War like the King of Hovas."

After having been present at that family scene, Matiphous, following some other conversation, asked the Deputy Mayor for his help in reclaiming his carriage and his men.

At eight o'clock in the evening, he returned to the Lamoignon townhouse. There was no news of his father, but a letter was waiting for him, almost from the time he had started out for the beautiful journey that he had just finished.

Once the letter opened, he read:

Mademoiselle Adelaide de la Salle, asks Monsieur le Comte de Lupiano to come to her house. She has things of the utmost importance to communicate to him.

She gave as her address Rue Barbette, at the townhouse occupied by the Vandel family. Matiphous didn't find the hour too late not to go where he had been invited, since the offer was of a nature to greatly intrigue him. So he immediately went to the address indicated.

While the servant to whom he had given his name went to get Mademoiselle de la Salle, the man from Malta, who was waiting in an antechamber, had a strange vision: a door opening to let in an ecclesiastic; in the room from which that man came out, he saw a catafalque surrounded by candles near which a priest was praying.

Five days had passed since the death of the two Vandels, and it was to be expected that, by then, they should have been buried. Was it then the unfortunate Helena, whose health, described in the article published in *L'Étoile*, had been presented as very fragile? Who had died? While still in doubt, Matiphous was told that Mademoiselle de la Salle was waiting for him. She received him in the study of the dead man, in which the reader has been several times introduced.

"Monsieur," said the old maid, "in the relationship that the Vandels and your father find themselves today, it will perhaps seem strange to you that I have asked you to come here."

"I believe, Mademoiselle," the man from Malta answered, "that a judicial error has given to our relationship a very different character than the one it should have had, and perhaps, today, better informed, the Vandel family..."

"The Vandel family," Mademoiselle de la Salle interrupted, "at this moment, Monsieur, is me: A mother dazed by sorrow, and a daughter who, from the moment she saw herself face to face with the cadaver of her husband and father, had a nervous crisis that the physicians call, I believe, catalepsy. Those are the people with whom you would have had to deal, if I, a very old friend of the poor widow, had not come to take over the management of the house here."

"Then," said Matiphous, "the funeral arrangements that I saw a moment ago, do not announce a new misfortune that befell this house, already so cruelly struck? The newspapers had written about Mrs. Bedloe's health as being seriously affected."

"No, Helena, thank God, is alive, and her present situation doesn't appear to threaten us with a deadly conclusion, but the sad spectacle that you saw is the result of a new complication that's come about in the fatal destiny of the unfortunate Vandels. For five days, the trouble that his burial has created for us has been infinite."

"How is that?" asked the man from Malta.

"You knew that, before his marriage, he had been in the holy orders?"

"Yes, I knew that, Mademoiselle."

"Since before his death, he hadn't reconciled with the Church, they felt that they should refuse him their prayers, and his widow was told not to send his corpse to his parish, where it would not be accepted."

"That's an odious act of fanaticism!" exclaimed Matiphous.

"For Victoire, an extremely pious woman, that's a misfortune worse than the death of the man she is mourning. Already, from the first communion of her daughter Helena, the irregular situation of her husband had been the cause of the refusal of the sacrament, a decision against which, fortunately, had been countermanded by a superior ecclesiastic authority. I have tried, me and all my friends, to similarly obtain the revocation of that cruel order, but the time of the burial was set, and before I could know the outcome of my efforts, the funeral services had come to take the corpse away. There then was a terrible scandal, a riot by the friends of the family, people coming to intervene to oppose the dead man's being taken directly to the cemetery. But on that day, the burial of Mr. Bedloe went ahead; since he was a protestant, there were no difficulties."

"But," the man from Malta said quickly, "Mr. Bedloe was a Catholic."

"What do you know about that?" Mademoiselle de la Salle asked, not less quickly. "Everything leads us to believe the contrary. His father and mother were both Protestants. His friends present at the ceremony said so."

"Yes, but unless he had abjured," Matiphous repeated, "I shall swear that he was born in the Catholic religion."

"Then, you know something of his past?"

"Yes, Mademoiselle, and it is possible that soon I will explain myself more thoroughly, but before I do that, please finish telling me what happened in the posthumous persecution directed against your unfortunate friend."

"Well, while our solicitation continued to the Archbishop, as the situation was becoming prolonged, we were compelled to have his mortal remains embalmed, which were then placed in a sort of chapel of rest, where all of Paris came to visit. Partisanship got hold of the affair; the status of our dear departed as a former member of the National Convention and regicide became a reason for the liberals to get involved. I told Victoire, but in vain, that all those political gestures were the surest way lose our support in our solicitation to the Archbishop, but her sadness found immense consolation in the type of homage rendered to her husband. Finally, the order came to allow him an ecclesiastical burial, but on the condition of immediately closing the doors of the townhouse, to put an end to the public displays of emotion which, due to the great number of visitors, were being propagated to the neighboring quarters. The burial will take place tomorrow morning and may Heaven grant us that it will not be disrupted by some disorder!"

"Was it for something related to those events that you wanted to see me?"

"No, Monsieur, what I wanted to tell you is that I have come to think that, by involving Monsieur your father in that sad affair, the police, influenced by information that was given to them here, might very well have made a serious mistake. A few explanations that I expect to receive from you, truthfully, will, I like to think, reaffirm my conviction on this subject."

"I am ready, Mademoiselle, to answer your questions."

"Monsieur your father, if I understand correctly, during his interrogations by the Investigating Magistrate, retrenched himself several times behind a letter allegedly written by Mr. Bedloe the evening of the event. It was understood that, the

letter coming from one of the victims, could provide explanations that he, himself, was reluctant to give. The Investigating
Magistrate has asked Victoire to look through her husband's
papers to see if she could find that letter, that was claimed to
be useful in finding out the truth, adding that, in respect for
Madame Vandel's mourning, he thought he should not come
himself to proceed legally for that search."

"I like to hear," Matiphous said, "that my father's sug-
gestion inspired the Investigating Magistrate with that discreet
reserve."

"As you will understand, it is I who was charged with
going through the inheritance papers and perform the required
search. As of yesterday, I have searched everywhere, and the
letter to which he alluded appears to be this one."

"Well, well, Mademoiselle!"

"But apart from the fact that it didn't seem very clear to
me, by checking it with another document that I also found, it
caused me unbelievable astonishment. So, while it spoke of a
mortal enmity that existed between Monsieur your father and
Monsieur Vandel, a will by the latter, written only a few days
before his death, stands as follows:

"*I give and bequeath to Monsieur the Marquis de
Lupiano, whom I know is curious about rare things, the manuscript placed under eight seals, alternately red and black, that
will be found in one of the bookcases of my study and that will
be given to him without the seals having been broken.*

"*In addition to the above, I also give and bequeath to
said Marquis de Lupiano my valuable collection of books, but
knowing that, for him, money means very little, I hereby authorize him to appraise the value of my library and to give the
price that he will have assigned to it, either to my wife, or if
not to her, to my daughter Helena, my only heir.*

"That will," said Mademoiselle de la Salle, finishing her
reading, "is as beautiful as that of Eudamidas of Corinth,[203]

------

[203] Eudamidas of Corinth had two friends, Charixenus, a
Sicyonian, and Aretheus, a Corinthian. When he came to die,

because it implies liberality by the Marquis. But, then, between the two men who acted that way toward each other, how could that hostility that Mr. Bedloe spoke about have existed?"

"It was only after having had much to hold against Monsieur Vandel, that my father rendered him the most outstanding service. Now, it was the generous act done by my father in that household which became the point of departure for the accusation for which he has had to answer today."

"Now I am beginning to see the light," said Mademoiselle de la Salle.

She then added, giving the letter of Victor Hulet to the man from Malta:

"Now, please read this and tell me if you understand something about what Mr. Bedloe wrote from Orléans."

"I understand everything," said Matiphous, giving back the letter, "and since you are an intimate friend of Madame Vandel, I think I shouldn't hide anything from you of the terrible secret to which that letter alludes. My father, right now, is trying to see that this terrible revelation, coming out in the middle of a judicial debate, doesn't add to the sorrows of Mademoiselle Helena and her mother; but my intention—you can somewhat understand that—is not to let the Marquis stay indefinitely accused of a capital crime So if he doesn't talk, it must be I who will speak, and speaking to you without reserve, I hope that you will find a way of bringing together his justification with the care and attention due to your unfortunate friend."

"You have, I believe, Monsieur, qualified as terrible," Mademoiselle de la Salle said with curiosity, "the secret that you are thinking of sharing with me?"

---

he being poor and his two friends rich, he made his will thus: "I leave this to Aretheus, to feed my mother and support her in her old age; this to Charixenus, to see my daughter married and give her the biggest dowry he can." The scene was depicted in a 1648 painting by Nicolas Poussin.

"Yes, Mademoiselle, and it is necessary to return to the darkest of antique fatalities to find the equivalent of the cruel revelation that I now have the duty to share with you."

Matiphous then told Mademoiselle de la Salle who Mr. Bedloe really was, and the way in which the Marquis and he had found out that information.

"Oh! *Mon Dieu!*" exclaimed Mademoiselle de la Salle, joining her hands in prayer. "What a terrible abyss your father kept those unfortunate people from falling into. They could truly be called an accursed family! Now, the unusual conduct of Monsieur Vandel the evening of the marriage is clear to me, and the letter of the so-called Mr. Bedloe is also clear to me. But that strongbox that contains the proof of the kidnapping that happened at Orgères, do you have any idea where it could be found?"

"I am working on that, Mademoiselle, and I am not without some hope of succeeding. However, the most absolute discretion is necessary for my actions. I can't very well make you the judge of the chances that I still have in order to bring about the result that I am looking for."

"Yes, I see," said Mademoiselle de la Salle. "That your father would have taken the strongbox from Monsieur Vandel's body doesn't make any sense. He obviously had no interest in doing that."

"I regret to see," said Matiphous, "that my frank explanations may not absolutely convinced you."

"Oh, not at all, Monsieur! I believe you, but in the middle of such shadows, who among us wouldn't be flinching? I speak all my doubts aloud and from this, you will see how little I believe them. And the proof that I consider you a friend of the Vandel family is that, shortly, you will receive a letter from them which, in inviting you to be present tomorrow at his funeral, will be the beginning of the justification of the Marquis, your father."

"I will fulfill that sad duty," Matiphous responded, "as in 1814, I fulfilled it for poor Alexis Vandel, another son that your friend lost at that time. But you, on your side, Mademoiselle, will you please be responsible for taking Victor Bedloe's letter to the Investigating Magistrate?"

"Let's talk about that," said Mademoiselle de la Salle. "Is that really the best way to proceed? That letter, once in the dossier, the terrible secret that it is so important to hide from Madame Vandel and, most of all, from Helena, would we still have control of it? Those *robins*,[204] when it's a matter of handling delicate situations, sometimes they have very heavy hands."

"On the other hand, however, if we don't inform the police, how could the appearance of guilt, because of which my father was arrested, be overcome?"

"First of all, by Monsieur Vandel's will, which clearly evidenced his good feelings towards the Marquis. Next, one could talk to the Magistrate, and if he is a person whom one could trust, we could speak to him as a man, and not as a magistrate, to whatever degree would seem appropriate."

"You are perhaps forgetting, Mademoiselle, that during that time, my father would still be in prison, incommunicado."

"No, I do not lose sight of that fact. But to proceed as I propose, isn't that to follow the path that the Marquis himself has laid out? If he had wanted to talk, he could have done so, but by his generous silence, he demonstrated that, above everything, he was preoccupied with not compromising the memory of an unfortunate man."

"In any case," said the man from Malta, "there is nothing to be done this evening. Tonight, we will think it over, and, if you will permit it, after the ceremony, I will have the honor to meet with you again to know the plan of action that you will have chosen."

"Until tomorrow, then," said Mademoiselle de la Salle.

It has to be agreed that, if Matiphous' day hadn't been pleasant, it had at least been amply filled. The next day, the man from Malta went to the funeral home, and he found gathered there, in the midst of an enormous crowd, scandal-

---

[204] Old slang for magistrate, derived from the robe they wear.

mongers from the liberal press. He couldn't keep from admiring the self-deception of some of the persons present. Without that refusal of a Christian burial, that had become, for some, a *cause célèbre* to demonstrate their hostility towards the government, nothing would have been gloomier, more obscure, and more forlorn than the funeral services of Hulet, to whom scarcely ten persons would have come to pay their last respects. And if the functions he had fulfilled during the greatest portion of his life had been known, instead of that passionate deployment of sympathy, what curses would have followed his casket!

As there were no relatives there, the ceremony was officially carried out by two American friends of the so-called Mr. Bedloe, who had been the witnesses at his marriage, and by Adolphe Levillain. Thinking that he should justify his presence, Matiphous went to greet Levillain in the drawing-room where the guests were being received. By the way in which the painter greeted him, he could be sure that Mademoiselle de la Salle had taken care, in advance, to explain his presence at the ceremony.

"It should be up to you, instead," the artist said to him, "to take charge of the honors, since Monsieur your father is the heir of the deceased."

Matiphous declined the role offered to him, and he went modestly to become part of the crowd, but he was happy to see that the diligence of Mademoiselle de la Salle had begun a reaction in the Hulet family against the accusation to which his father had to answer.

On leaving the church, someone tapped him on the shoulder, and, on turning around, he came face to face with a little old man, whose voluminous curly blonde wig, tie *à la* Talleyrand, a great number of rings and jewelry, in short, all the trappings of an *Incroyable*[205] from the time of the Direc-

---

[205] One of the nicknames given to the man-about-town of that earlier period whose dress carried contemporary fashion to an extreme.

torate, made him difficult to forget after having encountered him once. Matiphous immediately recognized in him one of his former colleagues from the *Secret Bureau,* with whom he had lived in the best of relations.

"Hello," the old employee said to him, holding out his hand. "You aren't like all these messieurs who have been hostile toward fulfilling their obligations toward the deceased. You practice the cult of remembrance, even though you didn't have many reasons to praise Monsieur Vandel."

"Well," said Matiphous, "before the tomb, all hatred must cease."

"Are you going to the cemetery?"

"Of course."

"We should try to catch up on things in a carriage, which won't be easy, because it seems to me that all of them are taken."

"That's not necessary," said Matiphous. "Mine is just a few steps from here."

"Good! That's marvelous! We can chat."

When he was installed in the two-seater, the older gentleman said:

"*Fichtre*! My dear fellow, you possess a most gentlemanly carriage! So you must have made quite a fortune in England where that excellent Monsieur Vandel was good enough to send you?"

"Yes, after a great number of crossings, I finally arrived at port."

"But a port, it seems to me, where you have been very pleasantly sheltered."

"But you, my dear fellow, are you still employed *over there?*"

"Yes, for my misfortune, my friend, because today, it's in the most frightful chaos."

"Monsieur Vandel, in fact, as I was told, wasn't very well replaced."

"That is to say, quite openly, that we have a former convict as our boss."

"How is that possible?" said Matiphous, pretending to be incredulous.

"I'm not speaking metaphorically," continued the old employee. "Our director is a man who has actually done hard labor."

"How could you allow them to force a person like that on you?"

"We tried to resign *en masse*, but the Minister us told that we should beware, because he would be appointed anyway, and they might take us to our word and let us go, so we had no choice but to submit. Against a man who has a pretty wife and who is supported by the party of priests, you can understand that this wasn't a battle we could win."

"In any event, even a bandit can be intelligent. How does that one manages the *Secret Bureau*?"

"He first began by creating ten additional positions; so instead of twelve employees, we now have twenty-two, and it's useless to tell you that all the newcomers are a collection of incapables of little value and intriguers who don't have the least scruple about meddling around with the secrets that pass through our hands. Then, this Monsieur named as his deputy a former regimental major, so that instead of one master, we now have two, and you should see how those grand dignitaries act toward their subordinates!"

"So, that kind of republican equality that was one of the good sides of the *Bureau*, and that Vandel managed to cultivate despite the superiority of his functions and of his title, has been abolished among you?"

"We have become so much a monarchy," the employee replied, "that Monsieur le Directeur has had a throne made for himself."

"What! A throne? Are you speaking figuratively this time?"

"No, my dear fellow, a throne, or if you prefer a pulpit. You remember the layout of the room: a big oblong table, at the high end of which Vandel sat with us?"

"Yes."

"Well!, Monsieur the ex-convict didn't think it was fitting to work side by side with his colleagues, so, at the back of the room, up against a wall, he had a kind of platform erected with several steps going up to it, where he now sits in a little enclosed space with a pulpit on it."

"I understand," said Matiphous. "Like a university professor."

"Precisely, and from there, Monsieur gives his orders and we make up the class. 'Monsieur this, you're not doing that well.' 'Monsieur that, you're not resealing that envelope carefully enough,' or 'your summary is too wordy,' or 'it is too short.' The supervision was going so well that, with all that wonderful surveillance, one of his recruits on resealing the envelope of a letter addressed to a Monsieur Chaudon, a merchant, carelessly put in another letter stamped from the post office and meant for a good old nun named Madame Sainte-Placide. [206]The merchant, who was not a great admirer of the government, realized the mistake and wrote to the *Courier Français* to reveal that fact to them, and with great strength of logic, they deduced the existence of the *Secret Bureau.* There followed questions in the Chamber of Deputies, much embarrassment from the Head of the Post Office, and finally the decision to remove the not-so-Honorable Monsieur de Saint-Rambert."

"So he is no longer your boss?"

"Not at all! The Congregation,[207] the business of which we've almost exclusively taken care of since he became director, got up in arms and claimed him as one of their most cherished creatures. His wife, a Catholic who had abjured Protestantism, began a campaign for their side and, after having been for an instant shaken, the miserable man is now more solidly installed and more insolent than ever."

---

[206] Notre from the Author: As reported in the newspapers of the time.
[207] See note 184.

"I have already heard that about that man," said Matiphous, "but what you don't know is that he has powerful enemies, who have decided to strike him at any time."

"Ah! Parbleu! If I knew them, I would gladly offer them my help."

"How many do you think are against him?"

"Just the other day, I was saying to one of my colleagues that we must not have had any courage to let ourselves be bossed around by such a shady character, and since that rascal wants to play the dictator, one fine morning, like Caesar, we should stab him in his curule chair."[208]

Matiphous couldn't keep from smiling at the idea of that Brutus in a wig.

"Laugh if you will," said the little old man, "but I would do it myself just as I told you, and it wouldn't be too difficult either to carry out. If everyone lent a hand, they wouldn't send the whole *Secret Bureau* to the Assizes for the murder of a disreputable character like Saint-Rambert. They know that we hold too many secrets. Besides, if this miserable man, as you say, has enemies, it could be expected that people from outside would help."

"That would be difficult," Matiphous objected. "That sanctuary can't be entered by just anybody, and that Monsieur, de Saint-Rambert who has modified everything, has doubtless thought to multiply the precautions to assure the secrecy of the office."

"Not at all! Nothing in that regard has been changed since you left, and a man who, like you, familiar with the people and the house could enter without any difficulty."

"Please believe me," said the man from Malta. "I have no desire to try that; I suffered too much in your lair to think of ever returning there."

The conversation ended there. They had arrived at the cemetery, where, over the tomb of the regicide, some passably anarchistic words were pronounced. In reprisal, the police,

---

[208] The ivory chair that some Roman Emperors sat in.

which, it is not necessary to say, had deployed a great number of men around the cortege, arrested some troublemakers who had shouted seditious cries.

As for his former colleague, Matiphous was careful to lose him in the middle of the crowd. He didn't intend to renew a relationship that placed him again in face of one of the most humiliating memories of his life.

XXIV. Rempailleux' House

A month had gone by since Lupiano's arrest, and the processing of his case had gone forward without freeing him. It must be believed, however, that Hulet's will and the letter of his son, Victor, had been communicated to the Investigating Magistrate, since, several times during the interrogations the accounts of which we have seen, those papers were mentioned. But, far from producing the effect that had been expected, from one day to the other, the Magistrate had shown himself more set against the accused. Without revealing the source from which he had gathered such information, he asserted that he knew many nebulous things about the Marquis' past, many shocking things, and he made him understand that, in addition to the crime of which he was accused, he was considering him a man to be watched and a dangerous adventurer.

Something more threatening was soon added to those bad portents. Lupiano was advised, based on the report of the Investigating Magistrate, the Chamber of the Council, having found his detention sufficiently justified, had issued an arrest warrant against him that was going to be submitted to the chamber of indictment of the Royal Court. In other words, his appearance before the Court of Assizes had already been decided.

At that time, there was no longer any reason to hold the accused incommunicado. Several days had already passed since he had ceased to be subjected to that strict regime. Matiphous not having appeared at the prison, Lupiano then began to sadly consider his son's lack of hurry to take advantage of the liberty that he now had to communicate with him, when, one morning, a guard mysteriously brought him a rather voluminous package of papers that bore his name. When the envelope was opened, Lupiano's surprise could easily be imagined. It was the correspondence between the two Bedloe spouses that was stored in the strongbox at the Hulet house the night of the death of the former member of the National Convention that had just been brought to him!

A thought naturally came to his mind, that his son, whose absence then could be explained, had taken care to re-cover the papers that he had now passed on to him. But why then had he not brought them himself, and why had he not accompanied them with a note? That was something unusual that would, without a doubt, have to be explained later. Per-haps such action had been made necessary by motives of cau-tion that were easy to imagine. Whatever the answer, Lupiano's innocence was now easier to prove, and if he had listened to his instincts, the upset that he would have brought into the case would have been attributed to those gestures of eccentricity with which, from times immemorial, he had stamped his life.

The role of a man unjustly accused, who, by a *coup de theatre*, dismisses all the charges amassed over his head, would have quickly drawn attention to himself, and he would have willingly let things run their course right up to his ap-pearance before a jury. There, with the publicity that the jour-nalists never missed giving to such a notorious trial, an ac-cused, no matter little he knew how to defend himself, would find himself placed on such a high pedestal that immense cu-riosity would be excited, and sometimes he might even enjoy displays of even warm sympathy.

But at the same time, by using that method, although he would have established his innocence in the most resplendent fashion, Lupiano knew very well that the frightful secret sus-pended over the lives of the Hulets would suddenly become known throughout all of Europe. Now, that was precisely what he didn't want to do. On the contrary, his desire and his thoughts were to put the least possible number of people into the confidence of that horrible misunderstanding, the effects of which he had neutralized, although at his risk and peril.

As a consequence, he asked to have a meeting with the Chief Prosecutor of the Royal Court, a man whom he had heard spoken of as a magistrate equally distinguished by character and intelligence. The correspondence that he showed him, accompanied with some necessary explanations, couldn't leave the slightest doubt in the mind of the Prosecutor. The next day the Prosecutor made his report to the Court and the magistrates who comprised it. Such was the authority of his word that, just by affirming on his word that the innocence of the accused was as clear as day, without having to produce the documents upon which his conviction was based, he obtained a verdict of *non-lieu*.[209] When he declared that the documents he had seen with his own eyes were not necessary to discover the truly guilty person, at the same time that they had just established Lupiano's innocence, adding that they contained evidence capable of destroying the honor of a family already too unfortunately stricken by an attack as profound as it was unmerited, the documents were then classified as secret.

Finally returned to freedom, the Marquis de Lupiano was unusually surprised when he learned that, two weeks prior, his son had gone out in the evening after midnight, on foot, and not reappeared at the townhouse. He reassured himself, however, with the thought that Matiphous had spent the night with Georgiana, but at the lodgings of the girl another surprise was waiting for him. On precisely the same evening that the man from Malta had left the Lamoignon townhouse, he had come to see his girl-friend and had had a argument with her. The subject of the argument was not known. Then, immediately after his departure, Georgiana, also after midnight, had left on foot without wanting anyone to accompany her, and since that moment, no one had seen her.

---

[209] No Bill; given when insufficient evidence has been presented to indict someone arrested for a crime.

At Lelouard's, where the Marquis went in haste, they hadn't the slightest news about the objects of his concern. The father's anxiety increased, and despite his little taste for the police, he was getting ready to call on them when a little illumination appeared in the middle of the shadows. As he was at his townhouse, considering whether he should go to the Prefect of Police, Monsieur Emile, the Deputy Mayor of Belleville, was announced.

As soon as he was in the presence of the Marquis, the manufacturer excused himself for his clumsiness in asking for Monsieur de Lupiano, without using his title. He should have said that he wanted to speak to Monsieur le *Comte* de Lupiano, not Monsieur le *Marquis*, for it was with him he had the honor to be acquainted with, and whom he meant to visit.

During the explanations that followed, the Deputy Mayor let it be known that he was the son-in-law of Commandant Lefebvre, and recounted the manner in which he had rescued Matiphous from the trap into which he had fallen. From that, the Marquis came to believe that it was, without a doubt, Rempailleux who was responsible for his son's disappearance. But a moment later, he had a doubt when the manufacturer added that, without the help of Monsieur le Comte de Saint-Rambert, Matiphous would have been murdered before he had had time to come to his aid.

In any case, it was clear that it was now a matter of going to Rempailleux for information, Immediately after the Deputy Mayor's departure, the Marquis de Lupiano was taken to Rue du Colisée. Getting to see the former *Chauffeur* was easy; but with that man whom he knew to be clever and wily, the Marquis thought he should use a great deal of caution, and, without stating the precise object of his visit, he told him he had come in search of information.

"Monsieur Marquis," said Rempailleux, "please allow me to congratulate myself on my good fortune, because it's not every day that even a man with a noble heart is able to answer with a good action the cruel and humiliating behavior from which he has suffered."

"What cruel and humiliating behavior?" the Marquis inquired.

"I'm talking about you cutting e off, without any warning, the annual payments that had been stipulated between us in exchange for information."

"It doesn't seem to me that it had been stipulated between us that I was agreeing to a payment in perpetuity. The services that you had agreed to render me were no longer needed, so very naturally their remuneration came to an end."

"Without a doubt, but you, Monsieur le Marquis, are so rich, and yet you didn't even consider a period of transition, or a one-time indemnity, for a poor man like myself!"

"A poor man! With a 25,000 francs salary and your wife's fortune?"

"*Mon Dieu*! Everything is relative, and you know that money doesn't stay in my hands."

"As a testimony to that, there were the ten thousand Spanish quadruples that I authorized you to go dig up in the Virgin Islands, and which, after a few years, you had completely squandered."

"That's true," said Rempailleux. "Your gifts to me date from long ago, and that's why I was astonished to see them so suddenly stop."

"Well, my dear fellow, if my gifts are so precious to you, you have a very simple way to be sure they will be great again. Give me news of my son who has disappeared for several weeks and about whom I am mortally worried."

"But, Monsieur le Marquis, you didn't entrust his protection to me!"

That sentence wasn't said with the insolence of a Cain,[210] who first used a similar argument. On the contrary, it was delivered with a smile and the air of a capable man who, well informed, wants only to be begged a little and even, perhaps,

---

[210] Cain who, when questioned by God about Abel, his brother, whom he has just murdered, replies: "Am I my brother's keeper?"

paid a little, before telling the inquiring party what he wants to know.

"Without a doubt," replied Lupiano, "I didn't entrust Gregorio's protection to you, but you do know that a woman from Madagascar and the Negro Britannicus were here crafting the most sinister plots against him."

"How would I have known that?"

"Because you yourself admitted it to my son when you charged him with presenting your request to me. Because, later, he was taken by you to a den of iniquity where, for a moment, his life was at stake."

"Monsieur le Marquis, I challenge the offensive insinuations contained in your words. If I put your son in contact with his estranged wife, who had come to Paris to look for him, it was only with a thought of reconciliation. He voluntarily accompanied me to see her, in his own carriage, with his own servants, and whoever informed you, should have also told you that I was so far from wishing him ill, that without my strong intervention, his life would have soon been terminated in a way that would make the search that you are now undertaking entirely useless."

"But a plan that didn't succeed at first may be tried again."

"I don't think that your son's disappearance can be attributed to the people whom you suspect. The same evening of the day when the attempted murder took place, the woman from Madagascar and Britannicus left Paris. I had made them so afraid of the officer of the law who had come to help me save the prisoner that they cleared out."

"Yet, apart from the intervention of those miserable creatures, how do you explain that, two weeks ago, Gregorio and the woman with whom he has an intimate and loving, relationship, each left, in their own direction, without leaving any trace behind them?"

"Are you saying that Mademoiselle Georgiana has also disappeared?"

"Yes, the same day, and almost at the same hour, as my son."

"Ah! Then, I see a light! Do you know that woman's handwriting?"

"No. I have never had an occasion to see it."

"Neither have I. That's annoying, because we could immediately have found out the truth. But I can still tell you an idea that just came to me. If that supposition turns out to have some truth in it, my inspiration will be doubly fortunate."

"What is that idea?" demanded Lupiano,

"Look at this, Marquis," said Rempailleux, going to take an envelope of large dimensions from a piece of furniture which seemed to hold its precious contents.

"Well?" asked Lupiano, after having glanced at the envelope which bore the inscription: *The Widow Vandel, Rue Barbette, Paris.*

"That address," Rempailleux replied, "is obviously in the handwriting of a woman; and what's more, notice the postmark on the stamp: *London, England.*"

"Do you mean to say that you think that the two fugitives have gone to England?"

"It certainly seems so, and you will perhaps be of my opinion when you know what that envelope contains."

"Then tell me, if you want me to know."

"It really is something," said Rempailleux, simpering, "that is shameful to say to people to their face. I rendered you a service; it would be better guessed."

"I will certainly not guess because I don't have the slightest idea of what you're saying; so say the thing straight out. My gratitude in bargaining with you won't depend on the amount of delicacy that you use to bring the truth to me."

"Very well, then! Let's go straight to the facts. You understand, Marquis, that since the beginning of your arrest, I must have received instructions to carefully survey all correspondence addressed either to you or to the Vandel family?"

"Of course. That's understood."

"Now, three days ago, the envelope that I have just shown you was unsealed by my own hands, and inside that folder, I found a stack of papers of which, at first, I understood absolutely nothing."

"But later," Lupiano asked, "you did understand?"

"Yes, because everything that I unseal, I have the habit of reading, and reading well. The result of that reading was that a certain act of kindness which I committed in the past, in the Chartres country, for a certain American named Bedloe, had turned out in the most regrettable fashion. I only intended to steal a child from the Vandels, and my conscience didn't at the time reproach me too much, since, in reality I had arranged for the poor little one a fate infinitely more brilliant than the one he would have had with his birth parents. And to sum it up, and the thing is horrible to say, in giving in to the Bedloes' desire, I sowed the roots of incest."

"The papers that revealed that tragic consequence of the kidnapping you carried out, weren't they the letters exchanged between the husband and the woman whose agent you were?"

"Precisely. But while going through them, I made another discovery. In the content of one of those epistles, which was the will of Mr. Bedloe, I recognized that they had been kept in a strongbox, whose possession, in the past, Monsieur, your son and I disputed, and that, finally, fell into the hands of my fortunate rival. So it became infinitely probably that he told you about the correspondence that I am now holding in my hands."

"And from all that, you conclude?"

"That you have been, Monsieur le Marquis, the victim of your good heart. Very much aware of all the details of the proceedings in which you were accused...."

"I see," said Lupiano, interrupting. "So you're the one who spoke to the Investigating Magistrate."

"What makes you suppose that?"

"The fact that he was given certain rather compromising details about me pertaining to my stay in England during the time we were there together, details that he would have had difficulty getting from anyone but you."

"On my word, my dear Marquis," Rempailleux exclaimed, "how can you have such suspicions about me, since I am the one to whom you owe your freedom today?"

"To you?" Lupiano asked with a rather marked tone of incredulity.

"But, of course, Monsieur, to me, who intercepted those letters addressed to Madame Vandel, placed them in another envelope, and hurried to get them to you by a safe way. Can you say that they were not useful to you in securing evidence of your innocence?"

"No, of course not; but I don't know that I owe that obligation to you."

"You do, Monsieur le Marquis. You have to make up your mind, and that envelope, that I've kept, won't let you have a doubt. Knowing that, in the absence of the strongbox, which you gave to Vandel the day of his daughter's marriage, you would have difficulty making the Law accept the respectful and devoted nature of the visit for which they were now asking you to account, I immediately felt that I had the sway to put an end to your trial, and I didn't hesitate to snatch it in order to get it into your hands."

"I thank you, and I will gift you a token of my gratitude. But to come back to my son, from the parcel you intercepted, how did you deduct the probability of his having gone to England?"

"You will certainly admit," said Rempailleux with insolence, "that the strongbox that disappeared from the Vandels must have been stolen?"

"That's my opinion," Lupiano replied.

"And after having made the haul, the thief wouldn't have wanted to remain in France, since the Law had already intervened in the affair. It would have been stupid to run such a great risk when he was already so well-off."

"That appears rather likely."

"From that, I merely supposed that your son would have gotten wind of the retreat where the thief had taken refuge, that he would have followed him beyond the Channel, and that

Mademoiselle Georgiana would have wanted to be part of this voyage."

"All these deductions hold together rather well."

"Now, who could have any interest in sending back those papers that had immediately brought about your release to France? Obviously, your son and only your son, because only he could have known the value of that correspondence. But when I see, moreover, that, accompanied by his mistress, he used a female's handwriting to write the address on the envelope, I said to myself: Those are people, obviously in contact with the thief, in negotiations or perhaps involved in a rather complicated chase, are proceeding with extreme caution and don't want to return to France before having seen the outcome of your case."

"But how do you explain the fact that my son addressed that parcel to Madame Vandel? To hide her family's misfortune, she could have very well suppressed those very compromising letters and left me in trouble?"

"That's exactly what I feared," Rempailleux answered, "and I even add that it would sadly have been very human to repay you in that way for your zeal. But notice that you were in solitary confinement, and therefore to send them directly to you would have been to throw them into the hands of the Law."

"Finally," asked the Marquis, "do you have have any other information, except these conjectures, that, I recognize, may have a certain degree of probability?"

"Marquis, you know the proverb about the most beautiful girl...[211] But I promise you to keep an eye on what preoccupies you. In my position, you discover a lot of things."

"Will you give me some ink and paper?" Lupiano asked.

Once those objects put at his disposition, the Marquis wrote, dictating to himself aloud:

---

[211] French proverb: The most beautiful girl in the world can give only what she has."

Monsieur Lelouard, will you please immediately pay, from the funds I have in your bank, the sum of fifty thousand francs to the order of Monsieur...

"Should I say Comte de Saint-Rambert, or just Saint-Rambert?" he added, turning toward Rempailleux.

"But, Monsieur le Marquis," Rempailleux replied, "that was a favor that I intended to do for you. I don't charge for my favors. When I do some actual work for you, that will be different."

"Don't act like a child," Lupiano replied. "Your trouble deserves payment."

"No, I assure you, you would absolutely offend me."

"Would you prefer that I have fifty thousand francs worth of diamonds sent to Madame de Saint-Rambert? I must acquit myself in some way."

"Well, then, please put Comte de Saint-Rambert," said Rempailleux, resigning himself.

The Marquis was careful to write across the check *good for,* and after having signed his name, he placed it in the hands of the most disinterested of informants. He then took his leave, after having again received the assurance that at the least sign of a discovery, he would be immediately told.

XXV. The Good Shepherd

The reader would be mistaken if he believed that Lupiano had accepted as anything but provisional the store of information that had been given to him by Rempailleux. His mind was too sharp not to see that there was something shady and complicated mingled in it. However, he was the first to have thought that his son could be somewhere occupied with gathering the means to prove his innocence. And he was too desirous to have guessed right not to have caressed with a certain complacency anything that supported that version. In summary, neither the complete frankness nor the duplicity of Rempailleux had been expressly proven to him, and, in doubt, the completely credulous attitude that he had shown to satisfy the avid appetites of that man could only be good for the future of their relationship. After all, what were to him the sum fifty-thousand francs? If the former *Chauffeur* had helped him with no ulterior motive, he considered that he owed him that recompense. If, on the contrary, the good help that he had rendered him masked some kind of dastardly plot, sooner or later, there would be an account to settle between them, and in that context, to assuage the caution of his adversary by the liberality he had shown him was a clever and well-thought-move.

Whatever the situation, Lupiano was not less worried about the fate of his son, and so he sent one of the former members of the *Red Brotherhood,* a very clever investigator, to London with the order to spare no expense in order to be able to gather some information.

Parallel to this, when going to thank the Prosecutor for the kind oversight that had led so rapidly to his release, the Marquis spoke to him about his paternal worry, and he obtained from him the promise of his using his important influence to discover the traces of the absent son. In the same visit, the Magistrate and he took up the question of what they should do take with respect to to Madame Vandel and her daughter. They were both of the opinion that to reveal the secret of that terrible marriage, followed by the death of the groom, would be gratuitous cruelty. Lupiano went so far as to express the wish to destroy the correspondence of the Bedloes. But the Prosecutor pointed out to him that the crime of which he had been accused, and whose author had not yet been found, might lead to other criminal charges, where the fact that the letters had been preserved might be useful. It then was agreed that they would be placed in the hands of the President of the Appeals Court, who would take charge of destroying them when it would be demonstrated that the public prosecution had ceased to be interested in their existence.

Those dispositions having rendered obsolete the former relationship between the Marquis and the Vandels, after all that had taken place between them, Lupiano would have had no desire to visit the townhouse on the Rue Barbette, if, a few days later, the Justice of the Peace of the neighborhood had not told him that a will, found in the domicile of the late Monsieur Vandel, named him as his heir. He was at the same time told that, the next day, following the requirements of the law, the will would be given to the President of the Local Court, a formality at which he had to be present.

That parcel, carefully sealed, that Lupiano was to inherit according to the the will, was brought to be identified. It was, as we might have guessed, the manuscript of the family genealogy that he was to inherit. Not wanting to destroy it, since it was the respected work of his father, Hulet, by the posthumous gift that he had made, had arranged that, in the event of his death, his wife and his daughter would not know the position that he had occupied at the head of the *Secret Bureau,* which had always remained a secret to them. The Marquis was therefore made the custodian of the precious documents. As for the deceased's library, the President of the Tribunal authorized him to take possession of it as soon as it was convenient. But Lupiano understood that, to be considerate of her, he had to ask Madame Hulet when he could go visit her, and he wrote to her about that subject.

Mademoiselle de la Salle, who continued, it appeared, to support her friend in everything, was charged with answering Lupiano's letter, and thus, she was the one he met. From her, he learned about the interview she had had with his son the evening of Hulet's burial. She had taken care to give the Investigating Magistrate the will of the former member of the National Convention as well as the letter written by young Mr. Bedloe from Orléans. Mademoiselle de la Salle recounted also that Matiphous had showed extreme irritation when he had learned that, even after she had accomplished her mission, the magistrate still passionately disposed to see as guilty any accused person, so that the two very conclusive pieces that she had brought to prove the innocence of the accused hadn't seemed to make any impression on him.

"Since he requires the other proofs I have told you about," Matiphous had then said to Mademoiselle de la Salle,

"I know where to get them, and I will procure them at any price."

Lupiano was happy to receive those words because they fit very well into his and Rempailleux' supposition. In announcing that he would get the correspondence of the Bedloes at any price, didn't Matiphous indicate that he knew who had the strongbox, and that he foresaw a long and difficult fight to recover it, which could explain his absence.

Thus reassured, Lupiano had more time to become preoccupied with the misfortunes of Madame and Mademoiselle Hulet, and asked about them with interest. He then learned that the sad Helena had also paid tribute to the evils that weighed on the name of Hulet. Since the fatal night when she had suddenly discovered the bodies of her father and her husband, she had undergone long periods of catalepsy, almost without pause, which had finished by coming close to insanity. There appeared to be little chance of a cure. In any case, the doctors had declared that the cure would be long and that, in her interest, the sick woman should have total isolation. Madame Hulet, then, who had nothing more to do in the world, had decided to re-enter a convent. In vain, to persuade her against such an idea, her friend Mademoiselle de la Salle had spoken to her of her son, whose return she had been left to hope for, or of her daughter, whom she must care for, at least until the time of a second, happier marriage, after she recovered her reason.

Attributing all the misfortunes of that family to her and Hulet's violation of their monastic vows, the poor woman persisted in her idea of retreat. But it wasn't to the Benedictine order, where she had formerly been a nun, and that, in 1814, had been re-established in the former buildings of the Temple by Mademoiselle de Condé, that she intended to complete her expiation. Out of humility, as if she had been a prostitute, she had asked to be received into the Good Shepherd convent of the Repentant Girls. It was there that she intended to finish her life. In the presence of that unshakeable resolution, Mademoiselle de la Salle, had a doubt, and she told that doubt to the Marquis.

"Should the terrible secret of the marriage of her daughter be revealed to Madame Vandel, or should she remain ignorant of it?"

Lupiano had already discussed that question with the Public Prosecutor, and, at first, it didn't seem to him that it could be handled in any other way than what they had done. However, when Mademoiselle de la Salle had objected to him that Madame Vandel, in believing it was her imperative duty to be reintegrated into the religious life, was still keeping through her children a tie to the world that could become an obstacle to the total quietude of her spirit, he became less convinced of the excellence of his solution.

"Very often," the old maid said to him, "in the middle of the solitude and of the saintly practices of the cloister, Victoire will experience a sharp pain of maternal feeling. She will think of her son, of whom you told her a trace had been found; of her daughter, that she will reproach herself for having abandoned; and her conscience will be overwhelmed. On the contrary, if we tell her everything, she will know that she should no longer wait for her son. In Helena's insanity, she will see a benefit rather than a punishment of Providence; she will accept that, by the loss of her reason, the unfortunate girl did not pay for the knowledge of that detestable union too dearly. At that point, seeking her consolation and refuge only in God, without sharing it, she will surrender herself to Him, and, at the cost of that final moral suffering, what we shall tell her will cause her to find if not happiness, but at least repose for the rest of her life."

"You are perhaps right," said Lupiano, struck by the justice of that insight.

And it remained agreed that, first prepared by Mademoiselle de la Salle, Madame Vandel would soon receive a visit from the Marquis. Under the pretext of lifting the suspicions of which he had been the object, he would tell the recluse the purpose for which he had come to the Hulets, the evening of their daughter's marriage, and, at the same time, he would take up with her the business of the library, which he said would be worth one hundred fifty thousand francs, although, reasonably, it could have been reasonably appraised at only a third of that price.

Several days afterwards, in the company of Mademoiselle de la Salle, the Marquis went Rue du Faubourg Saint-Jacques to the Good Shepherd convent, a sad building, the look and style of it seemed to be somewhere between cloister and prison. Received in a dark and humid parlor, he had an interview with the former Benedictine in which, using all the circumlocutions possible, he revealed the terrible secret to her. The unfortunate woman heard him without any outburst of sorrow. She was content to say:

"So God has willed to punish us… and I, who, for a moment, believed that we had been pardoned!"

Absorbed in the interior contemplation of her disaster, so frightfully complete and irreparable, she understood nothing of the generosity that Lupiano had shown in the settlement of the legacy that he declared he was willing to accept.

"Everything that you will do, Monsieur," she said to him, "will be well done. I would only ask you to be willing to let me keep the little prayer book that Monsieur Hulet had the habit of using."

Then she changed her mind.

"No," she added. "It would be better for you to keep that book; it would remind me of a past that should be forever banished from my memory."

At that, Mademoiselle de la Salle, wanting to create a diversion by telling her the excellent news that she had received, she said, about Helena, Madame Hulet answered:

"You are deceiving me. My daughter will not get well. She is the child of misfortune and of crime. In order for God to take pity on her, I must begun the expiation by which I must be pardoned for her birth."

These words disquieted Mademoiselle de la Salle. She thought that her unhappy friend was contemplating terrible austerities, and, after Madame Vandel had taken leave of them, the old maid asked Lupiano to let her speak to the Mother Superior of the convent, that was immediately summonsed. The Mother Superior was seriously indisposed and couldn't come to the parlor, and, in her place, she sent the Mistress of the Novices, a still young nun who had her complete confidence and whose appearance was as welcoming as her manners were distinguished. Mademoiselle de la Salle told her about her apprehensions and asked that the Mother Superior use her authority to repress the ardent zeal for mortification that she thought she had sensed in her friend.

"You can be reassured," the nun told her. "Mother Superior is absolutely opposed to any kind of body *maceration*.[212] I, myself, shortly after my entry into the convent, having a great many more faults than our dear sister, believed that it was my duty to subject myself to some practices of that kind. They were severely forbidden to me. Here, only actual faults are punished."

With that reassurance, as Mademoiselle de la Salle and Lupiano were about to leave, the Mistress of the Novices asked:

"Would I dare, since the opportunity presents itself, ask about a little question of common interest?"

Oh! Those nuns, thought the old maid, who wasn't a great admirer of the cloistral life, *they never forget the worldly matters!*

At the same time she answered:

"Speak, sister. What is it about?"

"Our new sister has a daughter, I believe?"

"Yes," Mademoiselle de la Salle answered, drily.

"Do you have any idea of the fortune that Monsieur Vandel left?"

"I couldn't say the exact amount. The estate hasn't yet been liquidated."

---

[212] The practice of asceticism to punish oneself for one's sins.

"Here is the purpose of my question. On entering here, our sister stated the desire to make a gift of eight thousand francs to the convent, more than double the dowry that we usually receive. If her situation of her fortune allows our new sister that liberality, and that it would not be an appreciable loss to her relative, we would willingly accept it, because the convent has a great number of expenses. But in case the generosity seems exorbitant to you, we would reduce it to the sum that is usually paid by the postulants. Mother Superior essentially seeks to not to want to have any difficulties with the family."

"Eight thousand francs," replied the old maid, who was not expecting such disinterest, "doesn't seem an exaggerated figure to me. Without counting what might be found in the inheritance, Monsieur de Lupiano, here, was shortly acknowledging himself her debtor, to a sum of one hundred fifty thousand francs."

"Monsieur de Lupiano!" exclaimed the nun. "Monsieur is the Marquis de Lupiano?"

"Yes, sister," said the Marquis. "Do I have the honor to be known to you?"

"Oh! Monsieur," continued the saintly girl, "how good God is to allow me to see you and to thank you. The future of two poor children assured, and I, myself, snatched from the cesspool where my life had been spent—all that, without a doubt, has left your memory?"

"Are you that young person to whom, about two years ago, Notre-Dame-de-Bon-Secours and the Priest of Saint-Leu took an interest in?"

"Yes, Monsieur, I am that unhappy girl of whom you had the profound delicacy to say, when you gave the most splendid alms, that you were the debtor. My young brother has very recently been accepted into the naval school. The other little one has been reared in a family where the most excellent woman is willing to serve as a mother; and I, myself, am so calm in this holy house, and, according to Mother Superior, so rehabilitated! That is what I owe you for your charity."

"So, you placed yourself here, and certain ideas of mysticism that bothered your protectors no longer have empire over your mind?"

"I am no longer anything but a humble servant of the Lord, and all the past is very far from me, except, however, my gratitude, that never, please believe me, Monsieur le Marquis, will be forgotten."

"Well!" said Lupiano. "I ask for your prayers. I am worried about the fate of someone who is dear to me. Obtain for me from God that my son will soon be returned to me."

"Oh! It isn't from the prayers of a sinful woman like me that you must expect very effective help, but I am going to tell Mother Superior that I have found my benefactor, and the whole community will unite with me."

"Thank you, sister, I am also happy to have seen you. We recommend Madame Vandel to you. She's a woman that Heaven has very much distressed."

"I have come from further away than she," said the nun. "Let us hope that God will also send her consolation, and since you are concerned about her, I will put all my zeal into making her life endurable in the asylum that she has chosen."

"Thank you once again," said Lupiano, giving his arm to Mademoiselle de la Salle.

"Marquis," the old maid said to him. "We have not known you very well!"

"Oh!" Lupiano responded, "to do good with money, the merit isn't very great; it requires neither virtue nor great warmth of heart; it requires only money."

That encounter, and the other reasons that the Marquis had thought that he had to reassure himself, suspended his apprehensions for several days. But when, after two weeks, the agent whom he had sent to London returned without any news, his most sinister thoughts returned and he visited the Prosecutor to find out if he had obtained some results from the investigations that he had promised he would launch.

Received politely, he nevertheless felt that he noticed some restraint in the magistrate.

"You should see Monsieur, the Prefect of Police," the Prosecutor said to him several times. "He is in a position to know a great number of things more than I do."

So Lupiano went to see the Prefect, who asked him for several days to gather information.

The next day, the Prefect sent the following note in an envelope, without even including a cover letter:

The twelfth of last June, a man from Malta, successively known in France, where he has resided several times, under the names of Gregorio Matiphous, Deschamps and Comte de Lupiano, took out a passport for London in that last name. He was accompanied by a woman whom he claimed was his wife, but was later found to be none other than the Demoiselle Georgiana, daughter of a complotter known as the Princess de Bevillacqua who, in 1814, was murdered in the woods of Vincennes woods. Said Demoiselle Georgiana resides in Paris as a Kept Woman.

Arrived in London, where he had the imprudence of going to inquire about an affair unknown to us, the man about whom Monsieur le Préfet seeks information, appears to have been identified by the English Police as a former convict, once condemned to deportation to the penitentiary colony of Botany Bay, from which he had escaped several years ago.

Following his arrest, the so-called Comte de Lupiano appealed to the French Ambassador, who wrote to the Minister of Foreign Affairs. That high official obtained information from the Bureau of the Prefecture of Police in the form of a written report dated of last June 25th, which is attached to the dossier of the above-named individual.

The information furnished by our services having been only negative, our Ambassador in England declared that he would no longer be concerned with this man's fate, and there is every reason to believe that he was again deported to Sydney, Australia, accompanied by the Demoiselle Georgiana, who had asked to follow him. That favor was easily granted, since there is a shortage of women in the colony.

It must be pointed out to Monsieur le Préfet that a man who calls himself the Marquis de Lupiano, and who claims to be the father of the personage in question, was recently compromised in the assassination of Monsieur Vandel and the American Mr. Bedloe. The Marquis was released for insufficient evidence, but everything leads us to consider him a dangerous adventurer. He certainly wouldn't risk appearing in England, where we believe he also has major accounts to settle with British justice.

When he received that note, Lupiano tried again to see the Prefect, to whom he wanted to explain himself. But the Prefect refused to see him, having him told that he had nothing to add to the information he had asked for and which had been furnished to him.

Three days later, following a long conference with Lelouard, who remained in charge of all his interests, the Marquis was in Southampton, where he embarked on a vessel ready to sail for Australia.

XXVI. Captain Nichols

Having set sail at the beginning of 1820, toward the end of that same year, after a crossing as fortunate as rapid, the ship on which Lupiano had taken passage came to dock at Port Jackson.

That was not the first voyage that the former corsair had made to Australia. Having spent a great part of his life in the most distant and the most adventurous wanderings, he had come to Sydney where he had recruited some of his most resolute subordinates for the *Red Brotherhood*. So, in that city, at the other end of the world, where he had disembarked without even a servant, he didn't find it any harder for him to find his way than he would have in London or Paris.

In order not to draw attention, he took accommodations in a furnished house of cheap appearance, and immediately started the quest for the one for the love of whom he had not hesitated to undertake a voyage of 3,000 leagues.

In case Matiphous really had been returned to the penitentiary colony, it wouldn't have been very clever to ask information about the subject from the authorities. But, from Mistress Aston, his former acquaintance, whom he had every reason to believe was in Australia, the Marquis hoped to procure the necessary information. In 1814, as Matiphous had told him, that woman had been condemned to ten years of deportation. She hadn't then finished her term of exile, unless death had shortened her exile, which was hardly likely, considering the robust health she had always enjoyed, so she could be expected to be installed somewhere in that country,

Lupiano wasn't long in encountering in the streets an old convict dressed in the yellow cassock that identified the most incorrigible kind of condemned man, most of all when in big, readable letters on various parts of his clothing there was printed the gracious epithet, *Thief*. He thought, with good reason, that this emeritus criminal would be able to give him news of a woman who, among the corporation of London thieves, had gained such great popularity.

"Jack Ketch's sister-in-law," said the old convict when he was interrogated on the subject of the former Providence of Newgate. "Certainly, yes, I know her, and if Your Lordship wants, I can take you to the superb establishment that Mistress Sedley founded two steps from the big hospital."

A gold piece put in the hand of the obliging *cicerone*[213] confirmed that his services had been accepted, and shortly afterward, Lupiano's eyes were struck by the glorious sign of *The Bottle and the Magpie*. In Sidney, as in London, Mistress Sedley had placed on that ensign, which she had raised very high, the picture of a bar with rum and other incendiary liquors.

"Mistress Sedley," said the convict, opening the door to a vast tavern where it was not yet the hour when many drinkers came together and giving the mistress of the place the name of

---

[213] A tourist guide, in reference to Marcus Tullius Cicero, Roman statesman noted for his erudition.

her last husband. "Here is a gentleman who wants to speak to you."

"Ah! Monsieur le Marquis," exclaimed the tavern owner, who immediately recognized Lupiano, on whom, thanks to his premature aging, the passage of the years had left almost no mar. "You have been good enough to remember me."

"But, of course," replied the former Marquis de Samaniego. "And I am charmed that you have transported here the respectable establishment that you directed with so much success in London."

"Do you know about my misfortune?" asked Mistress Sedley. "And how that monster, Gregorio Matiphous, took revenge for the trick that you helped me play on him with respect to the loves of my charming niece?"

"Yes, I know all that," replied the Marquis, "and it's precisely about him that I came to talk to you. I've been told that I would find him in Sydney."

"That's to say that he was here, and it would have been better for him if he had stayed, accepting the offer of my hand, that I had the kindness to make to him to compensate him for his unpleasantness with my pretty Kitty."

"Then he's no longer here?"

"Neither here, nor anywhere else, the poor boy!"

"How's that, neither here nor anywhere else? What do you mean by that?"

"Well! That he has gone to the other world, to join that good Broughton, whose death he caused by his gossip soon to be seven years ago,."

"You are saying that Matiphous is no longer alive?" Lupiano asked in an altered voice.

"Yes, Monsieur le Marquis, and if you have another trick that you intend to play on him to get revenge, it's too late, my good man. Our Good Lord was more in a hurry than you were and he called him back to Him."

"But where did he die, and when?" asked the Marquis in a tone that showed anger and a veiled threat.

"Ah! You don't have to get angry," said the tavern-keeper. "If you don't believe me, over there is Captain Nichols, who's playing *piquet*.[214] You can find out from him."

Lupiano quickly approached a table where a big and heavy-set man with a sun-tanned face, wearing little gold anchors in his ear lobes, was deeply absorbed in a game of cards with a colonizer.

"Captain," said the Marquis, "I'm told that you might have some news about one Gregorio Matiphous?"

"*Quatorze* of Queens," said the Captain to his opponent, without seeming to have heard.

"Monsieur," repeated the Marquis, touching him on the arm, "Mistress Sedley has just told me that you knew Monsieur Matiphous. I would like to ask you what you know of him. I am his father and, because of this relationship, I hope you will pardon my interruption."

"His father!" replied the sailor, continuing to shuffle his cards, while he glanced at Lupiano disdainfully. "It's his mother that you should have said."

That insolent allusion to his effeminate exterior made the Marquis lose control of himself.

"Monsieur," he said, "when I ask a polite question, I intend to be answered in the same fashion."

And with a violent movement, he scattered the cards that the sailor held in his hands.

Captain Nichols, tall and with the build of Hercules, remained for a moment stupefied by the insult that had just been made to him by a man who looked as if a slap on the face would be enough to render him unconscious. After he had recovered from his surprise, but before he had time to deliver some brutality, the tavern-keeper intervened.

"Captain," she said to him, "you were wrong. No one talks like that to the Marquis de Samaniego."

"Monsieur," asked the sailor, instinctively taking off his hat, "is the Marquis de Samaniego?"

---

[214] A card game.

"Yes, that famous corsair that you regretted so much not to have known, and whom no one, I warn you, shall insult in my house without punishment."

"But, little lady, when it comes to insults, it seems to me that I'm the one who should complain."

"No, Monsieur," replied Lupiano. "You answered with a gross joke a question that I asked you from the bottom of my heart. Gregorio Matiphous, I repeat to you, is my son, and when I asked you what you might know about him, you didn't even deign to pretend to have heard me."

"Matiphous, your son!" exclaimed the tavern-owner. "Is that possible!"

"Yes, my good Mistress Sedley, and it's to learn what happened to him that I undertook the journey from Paris to Sydney."

"Well, if I didn't answer you," said the sailor, taking advantage of the retreat which had been opened to him, "that's because I didn't have anything good to tell you."

"Everything," responded Lupiano, "would be less cruel to me than the uncertainty in which I have lived for almost six months."

"What do you want to know? Whether Monsieur your son is living or dead? I can't tell you that I saw him die, but I would be lying if I told you that I believe he is still alive."

"Then," said Lupiano, clinging to the dubious form of that reply, "you are not certain?"

"Certain, no, but a Frenchman, who is completely trustworthy, General Lefebvre, whom I met a short while ago in Madagascar, told me that, in the land of His Majesty, the King of the Hovas, something bad had happened to the one you are interested in."

"Then, he was kidnapped in France and taken to Madagascar?"

"Yes, by his legitimate wife whom he had abandoned for another woman, and, on my word, that African wanted to get revenge."

"But in a civilized country, one does not transport an unwilling man, or, it would have to be with the guiltiest connivance on the part of the captain of that ship."

"If I may, Monsieur le Marquis, when a sovereign signs a contract with the captain of a ship to take his ambassador to France and return the same ambassador to him; when that ambassador conducts himself badly in the country to which he has been sent, when he deserts his wife and the members of the embassy, and when it even happens that he becomes guilty of murder..."

"Guilty of murder! Matiphous! That's impossible!" Lupiano said, interrupting.

"Nevertheless, it had to be something like that for the French police to have intervened, and for it to have taken charge of conducting Monsieur Matiphous to Le Havre and that it consented to deliver to me, the Captain, in writing, a permit to transport said prisoner back to Madagascar, a permit upon which the accusation of murder was very clearly stated."

"So, Monsieur, it was you who were responsible for dragging my unfortunate son to his death?"

"That is to say that I was the one charged with taking him back to Madagascar, as was stipulated in a document in good form, which I was given by a representative of the French government. What's more, after we had left harbor, I demanded that he be given the best treatment and I didn't allow him to be put down in shackles in the hold, as was the idea of his amiable spouse."

"That permit from the French police, would you be able to show it to me?"

"Yes, Monsieur le Marquis; although I didn't request a copy, they gave me one and I kept it."

"And what happened after the arrival of the prisoner Madagascar; were you informed?"

"I was told about it roughly by General Lefebvre, who, some days later, came with a young lady and asked me to take him back to Europe. I told him I couldn't do so, since I was expecting important business in the vicinity of Cape Town; the same day, he took passage on another ship."

"A woman, in fact, was supposed to be with my son when he was kidnapped. Was she with Lefebvre when he came to you?"

"No. According to what the General told me, she was found to be to the taste of King Radama. He would have kept her amongst his concubines; and, on my word, I would have done the same, because she was a beauty of the first order."

"But, what about my son? What would they have done with him by the time Lefebvre came to find you?"

"I repeat, I couldn't tell you exactly, but it seems he was treated rather roughly, since it was because of that treatment, which he had in vain opposed, that Lefebvre left the service of the King of the Hovas. After that, Monsieur le Marquis, I must tell you something rather consoling. No one knows what happens in the Palace in Tananarive. Radama is a very secretive man. Your son, they say, had once been his favorite. It is therefore not entirely impossible that he had the news of his death spread about, which could very well be untrue."

"Captain," Lupiano then asked, "what sum would you ask to make your ship available to me?"

"Five hundred thousand francs, but that might perhaps seem a little expensive to you," responded the Captain, smiling.

"Five hundred thousand francs; it is agreed," said Lupiano. "Prepare everything. This evening we are going to set sail for Madagascar."

"That's a generous payment," said the sailor, "but I can't answer you on the spot. The business I mentioned to General Lefebvre is still hanging. I must first consult with some people with whom I came here to discuss something. Give me your address and tomorrow I will have the honor to see you, and at the same time, I can bring you the paper that the French police gave me."

Lupiano told him the hotel where he was lodged, and he retired less desolated than might be imagined. He had seen a small ray of hope.

The next day, instead of the visit from the Captain, he received a letter:

Monsieur le Marquis,

I pride myself on being a gentleman, and I don't want to steal your money. The voyage you are thinking of taking to Madagascar would, unfortunately, lead to nothing. Yesterday, I wanted to handle your feelings carefully and lead you gently to understand the state of things. There is no more hope, and you will not find your son alive. In addition, it isn't with a ship like mine that you could intimidate the King of the Hovas. You wouldn't go thirty yards beyond the harbor than you would be stopped short. If you want a distraction to your sorrow, I flatter myself that I have something grand to propose to you, and which will make you much talked about. I will come to chat with you about that this evening and I ask you until then to accept my respectful compliments.

Captain Nichols

Humanity wasn't the only thing that explained why the author of that letter had taken much care and consideration to surround the news of the death of the Marquis' son. Knowing from Mistress Aston what a terrible man the Marquis de Samaniego was, his facts and actions still resounding in England as a legend, he had feared the first explosion of his sorrow and tried to reveal his misfortune slowly as the antiquarians unrolled the *papyri* at Herculaneum.[215]

---

[215] Herculaneum was the site of a library that contained more than 1800 *papyri* found in a villa in the 18th century that had survived the eruption of Mount Vesuvius. Extreme care had to be taken to avoid destroying the *papyri* that had survived carbonization.

The precaution had been both wise and successful. Conducted by stages to understand the immense loss he had suffered, the Marquis, when Captain Nichols arrived at his boarding house, received him without being carried away by despair. Only from the short and threatening tone with which he demanded the paper that had been promised did he show that the bearer had done well to bring it; otherwise a severe reckoning would have been demanded of him.

After having read the document, the Marquis focused on the signature: *Isidore Graillet, agent,*

"Captain," said Lupiano, "you acted with great carelessness: *Agent* is not the title of any officially recognized French authority."

"But, Monsieur le Marquis, uniformed gendarmes were under that man's command."

"All right," said the Marquis impatiently, "let's finish with all your care and concern, and without reticence, tell me now how the murder of my son was committed."

"I can assure you that I have no details on that subject. General Lefebvre, if you return to France, could explain to you..."

"Yes, I will certainly return there. Are your preparations complete?"

"Your question, Monsieur le Marquis, leads me to inform you of the truly grandiose enterprise that places an obstacle to our setting sail for Europe together at once. You are a man of honor, and one can be candid with you without danger. With your immense fortune, and the prodigious things you have accomplished, you could, if you would become part of this enterprise, make our two names immortal."

"What is your project?" asked Lupiano, whose curiosity couldn't keep from being aroused. "What's it all about?"

"And even," the Captain continued, "if I may hazard a look into the future; who knows if, in some time, a fleet couldn't be put at your disposition to go and chastise that bastard King of the Hovas."

"Explain yourself," said Lupiano. "I don't like sentences which sound like they come from a sales prospectus."

"Sentences from a prospectus!" the seaman repeated. "Do you think that if Napoleon was restored to his throne by you, he wouldn't be capable of putting at your disposal four or five frigates in order to go and conquer a country like Madagascar on which France has always had designs?"

"To go rescue the Emperor from Saint-Helena," Lupiano quickly asked. "Is that what you are thinking about?"

"You've said it, Monsieur le Marquis," replied the Captain, lowering his voice. "And the enterprise is less difficult than you think."

Captured by the grandeur of the idea, Lupiano let himself be distracted from his sorrow for a moment and asked Captain Nichols how far his project had already advanced.

The seaman then explained, and history is there to confirm it, that the thought of rescuing the Emperor occupied the imaginations of all the captains of the Merchant Marine carrying the British flag who were allowed to put in at Saint-Helena.

Some of them, wrote the author of *The History of the Two Restorations,*[216] *warm-hearted chevaliers, gave way to their admiration for the captive and the pity that his misfortune inspired in them. Most of them got no further than the cost of the service, fixed invariably at a million, payable when the Emperor would have had reached the United States.*"[217]

Captain Nichols belonged to that second class of liberators, more in love with the money than the glory, but his plan,

---

[216] *Histoire des deux restaurations jusqu'à l'avènement de Louis Philippe (de janvier 1813, a octobre 1830)* by Achille de Vaulabelle, Paris, Perrotin, 1857.

[217] Of the numerous plots to rescue Napoleon from Saint-Helena, two bear some resemblance to the plot Rabou details here: the first was headed by Tom Johnson, a notorious British criminal; the other by Nicholas Girod, friend of pirates and criminals and former Mayor of New Orleans.

when he had developed it for him, seemed to Lupiano to be surrounded with enough chances of success that he asked him the reason that had prevented him, up until then, from putting it into action.

"The Emperor won't agree to it," answered the Englishman. "He has no confidence in it, but if a man like you were involved, and if Napoleon could be told the surprising things that you have done…"

"The Emperor knows me," replied Lupiano, becoming animated. "He knows that I was once a corsair under the tricolored flag and that, in the seas of India, I delivered terrible blows to the British Navy. Besides, more than one time I have put in at Saint-Helena, and I was capable, after having avoided the surveillance of warships, of finding a place to reach the island with a canoe."

"Well, then," said Captain Nicholas, "what's keeping you from putting yourself at the head of those ready for action? Knowing that you are so rich, the Emperor wouldn't fear that you were motivated by money."

"What holds me back," replied Lupiano, "is that I have now in Europe a project that comes before all others. Besides, only in Europe can I put together ten men entirely devoted to me in the way that is necessary for your enterprise."

"But that project that you say you have in Europe, shall it occupy you for a long time?"

"Eight days at the most, so here's what I propose to you: we will, while returning to France, dock at Saint-Helena. I will try to see Napoleon and come to an agreement with him. If he refuses, well, with the help of the devils incarnate that I will have hired to reinforce you group, whether he resists or consents will become irrelevant; we will kidnap him. In any case, the million that I have promised you will be yours. It will be paid to you the day of our departure from Le Havre."

"That suits me," said Captain Nichols. "When do we leave?

"Tomorrow, in the afternoon, if that's possible."

"Very well. I will leave you now to prepare everything," said the Captain, on taking leave.

Yes, thought Lupiano, when he was alone. *If the man whom I suspect is truly guilty, after my revenge is taken, there won't be anything worth doing in my life other than the great scheme that has just been proposed to me.*

XXVII. Longwood

The morning of the next day, Lupiano paid a visit to the tavern-keeper.

"My dear Mistress Sedley," he said to her, "yesterday, in my sad preoccupations, I forgot to give you news about Kitty, your charming niece."

"You have seen her, Monsieur le Marquis? And what has become of that charming child?"

"You knew that she had lost Lord Stuart, her first husband?"

"No, I didn't know that. So, like me, she is now a widow."

"Not quite. She has remarried, to a man who exercises some important administrative functions and with whom she lives in a splendid townhouse in Paris where she gives concerts and hosts the most elegant society."

"Ah! The poor dear!" exclaimed the tavern-keeper. "She always had such a lovely voice!"

"But there's something even better. In the midst of all her luxury and fortune, she hasn't forgotten her relatives: *My poor Aunt Aston,* she said to me some time before my departure, *how happy I would be to see her again and to offer her a suite in my townhouse.*"

"Is that true, Monsieur le Marquis? She told you that?"

"Indeed she did, my dear Mistress Sedley, and with tears in her eyes. So, finding you again here, all alone, an idea has come to me. Are you free to leave Sydney?"

"Oh! Totally! My impeccable conduct and the importance of my business have given me a sterling reputation among the authorities of the colony. Besides, it's widely known that I was falsely condemned. Also, it's been more than two years that my *emancipation* has been authorized."

"Well then, what prevents you from returning with me to France to see your niece? I'm sure that seeing you again would make her very happy."

"That's true," said Mistress Sedley, who had turned purple at the thought of all that good fortune. "But," she added, on thinking about it, "there's my devil of establishment."

"Well, sell it, then."

"When are you leaving, Monsieur le Marquis?"

"We're setting sail this evening at six o'clock. I've chartered the brig the *Franklin* from Captain Nichols. I'm offering you free passage on it. It will be t just as if you were at home."

"Well, it's not that between now and this evening, I can't find a buyer, even though the time is short. I've had many offers before, but I have one of my nephews here, one of the sons of Jack Ketch."

"Why is he in the colonies?"

"He's not here as a convict. Quite the contrary! He has the same job as his father in London."

"How is it that your Jack Ketch hasn't found a way to exercise his business in Europe?"

"That's exactly what he says, the poor boy, and he is so unhappy in this country; so much so that if he no longer had me at his side to encourage him to be patient, he would have given way to despair."

"Well, bring him along. There's room for one more on the ship. And your sister will be delighted to see him, too. She told me, I don't know on how many occasions, that after you, her brothers were whom she loved the most in the world."

"And you don't think that, because of his functions...?

"His functions? He doesn't wear them written on his face, does he? Didn't Papa Ketch come to see his daughter a year ago? She welcomed him with open arms, showed him off everywhere. With his serious face and his white hair, everyone mistook him for a member of the House of Lords."

"That's very good, but I still must think of one thing: he has no personal income, my dear nephew, and after he quits his job here...."

"I have the means to employ him," Lupiano answered. "Another idea has just come to me. And until he has found someone to marry, I will take care of him."

"Goodness! If you are arranging things so well, I'm going to have one of my prospective buyers come at once!"

"Do that. And at six o'clock sharp, be on board with your nephew. I warn you, I won't wait."

The voyage right to Saint-Helena offered nothing remarkable. Still feeling a somber sadness, but nevertheless full of goodwill for everyone surrounding him, after a few days, Lupiano was adored by the whole crew, to whom he distributed excellent rum daily. As for Mistress Sedley, she admired the particular kindness that the Marquis showed her nephew, an insignificant boy with carrot-red hair, for whom he seemed to have taken a particular liking. Often, for entire hours, he talked with him about the details of his strange profession.

Toward mid-February 1821, the *Franklin* dropped anchor in the natural harbor of Jamestown, the only side of the island that allowed access to Longwood. Captain Nichols, who, during two previous ports of call, had gotten friendly with the governor, Sir Hudson Lowe, by pretending to feel an entirely British hatred for his famous prisoner, hastened to go and pay a visit to that jailor, who has since become immortal. He let him know that he had on board a victim of the Imperial tyranny, imprisoned at Vincennes by the orders of Napoleon himself. That man, the crafty Captain told Lowe, had promised himself the great joy of mocking his former persecutor in his abasement, betting that the ex-Emperor wouldn't probably be very pleased by the visit of his former victim. That was enough to convince Sir Hudson to immediately deliver a permit to disembark to the Marquis de Lupiano, and a pass to climb up to Longwood.[218]

To Bertrand,[219] the general with whom he had twice conferred about the project of evasion, Captain Nichols' discourse was very different. He presented the Marquis as a former corsair who had once had the honor of approaching Napoleon. What's more, he knew the island and thought he was able to choose a spot where an escape would present the greatest possibilities of success. Consequently, the Marquis asked to be seen by the Emperor, which was, in addition, the only price he put on the success of the undertaking, of which he intended, before and afterward, to assume all the costs.

Bertrand hurried to do everything possible to see that the two visitors were received, but he didn't hide from them that their wish had very little chance of being satisfied. The Emperor was very ill and less than ever disposed to consider thoughts of escape. Taken to the gardens of Longwood, the Captain and Lupiano were left there while Bertrand went to receive orders from the glorious captive. Shortly afterward, he returned to tell them that the Emperor was too ill to see them, suggesting that instead, they deal with him and with

---

[218] Longwood House, originally a farm belonging to the East India Company, converted for holding Napoleon and those accompanying him.

[219] Henri Gratien, Comte Bertrand (1773-1844), French genera who accompanied Napoleon to Saint-Helena. Condemned to death in 1816, he did not return to France until after Napoleon's death, and then Louis XVIII granted him amnesty allowing him to retain his rank. Bertrand was elected deputy in 1830 but defeated in 1834. In 1840, he was chosen to accompany the Prince of Joinville to Saint-Helena to retrieve and bring Napoleon's remains to France, in what became known as the *retour des cendres* [return of the ashes].

Montholon,[220] about the project that they had intended to submit.

"But could he at least be seen?" asked Lupiano.

"That's difficult," he was told.

However, Bertrand told the guests to follow him and he led them within reach of the Emperor's habitation, maneuvering in such a way that they could see him, if he showed himself, without themselves being seen. They stayed there for some time vainly hiding, when, coming to them in a hurry, Saint-Denis,[221] one of the valets, said to Lupiano:

"The Emperor wants to talk to Monsieur."

"Me?" asked the Marquis.

"Yes," answered the valet. "Alone."

"The Emperor," Bertrand said to Captain Nichols, "must have recognized him when looking out the corner of a curtain, as he often does when he refuses to see people. His memory of faces is prodigious. It is enough for him just to see a man one time..."

---

[220] Charles Tristan, Marquis de de Montholon (1783-1853), French General who chose to go into exile on Saint-Helena with Napoleon. Despite the departure of his wife, Montholon stayed on at Longwood to the end of the Emperor's life (May 1821). He then spent several years in Belgium, and in 1840 acted as chief of staff to Louis Napoleon's attempted coup. He was condemned to imprisonment at Ham, but was released in 1847. He then retired in England and published *Récits de la captivité de Napoleon à Ste Hélène*. In 1849, he became one of the deputies for the Legislative Assembly under the Second French Republic.

[221] Louis-Étienne Saint-Denis (1788-1856), a.k.a. Mamluk Ali, faithful servant of Napoleon whom he followed to Saint-Helena. After his return to France in 1821, he managed a fairground carousel. In 1826, he published his memoirs and in 1840 joined the expedition organized for the return of the ashes. In 1854, Napoleon III made him knight of the *Legion d'Honneur*.

"Well," said the Captain a little enviously, "the Marquis' face is different enough to be recalled."

Lupiano was taken by the valet into a rather poorly furnished entry room, the walls of which had been painted a pale blue, where a dozen chairs, a table, a large sideboard, a dessert table, and a deep maroon rug, comprised all the furniture.

"Whom shall I announce?" asked Saint-Denis.

"The Marquis de Lupiano."

"Monsieur le Marquis de Lupiano!" announced the valet in a loud voice, opening the door to the drawing-room.

Accustomed to not being astonished at anything, the Marquis would have been mildly moved if he had found the same man who, in all his glory, had confronted him in 1810. But on seeing the Emperor as an ordinary middle-class man, fallen into a terrible state of thinness, showing on his pale face his long and profound suffering, he felt tears come to his eyes. The only thing he wanted to do was to keep, within the limits of the most respectful reserve, the expression of the sad astonishment and the immense pity that had filled him at the sight of that grand ruin.

"Monsieur," the Emperor said to him after making a motion telling him to sit down, "I have seen you somewhere before; but my memory finds some disaccord between the name I've just been given and your face."

"Sire," the Marquis answered, "I had the honor to be taken one evening to the Tuileries, into the office of Your Majesty. I was then called the Marquis de Saint-Faust."

"Ah! I remember it very well! The suicide man! Well, Monsieur, it seems to me that you are behind with your religion."

"The Emperor," Lupiano replied, "having overturned the temple and dispersed the Levites, the Grand Priest, temporarily, decided to live, and, for some time now, he would have liked to thank your Majesty with sincere gratitude for the violence done to him."

"So, consolation has finally visited you?"

"Yes, Sire, I've had my own return from Elba, and at the moment I least expected it, a son, lost to me for forty years, completely reconciled me with existence."

"You see!" said the Emperor.

"But, since then, he has been taken from me by a terrible blow of fate."

"Look at me, Monsieur. Hasn't my son also been taken from me, alive, and my wife, and so many very regrettable others? Haven't I lost them all without ever having recourse to your dreadful solution?"

"Nevertheless, Sire, some say that in 1814..."

"That's true. The bad days that you had foreseen had arrived. The fall was so rapid and so heavy that, for a moment, I became confused. Since the disastrous campaign against the Russians, in order not to fall alive into the hands of the Cossacks, I always carried around my neck a small sachet of poison that Yvan, my primary surgeon,[222] had prepared for me. One night, at Fontainebleau, in a veritable excess of mental alienation, I wanted to use it. But the poison was stale. It made me terribly sick without killing me. Saint-Helena was my destiny."

"Sire, Saint-Helena is still only a step for the Emperor. It's necessary to leave, and if Your Majesty will trust me..."

"To go where? To America, fifteen thousand leagues from Europe? I wouldn't be there six months before someone would assassinate me. On Elba already, there had been a plan to kill me, and if the head of the gendarmerie had not alerted Drouet, that project would have succeeded.[223] One must al-

---

[222] Alexandre-Urbain Yvan (1765-1839), French surgeon who entered the personal service of Napoleon in 1800. He became Chief surgeon of Invalides in 1811 (a place he held until 1832) and inspector general of the health service. His role in the suicide attempt committed by the Emperor on the night of 12 to 13 April 1814 remains unclear.

[223] Jean-Baptiste Drouet, Comte d'Erlon (1765-1844), Marshal in Napoleon's Army. There is no mention of a plot to kill Na-

ways obey one's lucky star; everything is written on high. Only my martyrdom can give the crown of France to my son and to my dynasty. In America, I can only see assassination or oblivion in my future. It is better to stay with my companions in exile on this rock, where the eyes and the pity of the world come to look for me. Jesus Christ would not have been God without his crown of thorns!"

"Sire, at fifty-years-old, the destiny of Your Majesty can't be finished!"

"Haven't you been struck by my state of decay? The climate, my prison, and that terrible governor, are killing me. I am at the end of my life; I feel it. My strength, my faculties are abandoning me; I am collapsing under the burden; I no longer live, I vegetate."

"Supposing that the physical strength of Your Majesty has weakened, your genius is still intact. The Emperor will perhaps make less war, that maybe he loved too much. He will have more time to give to the problems of government. He will doubtless find the way to reconcile the strength of power with liberty."

"Liberty!" responded the Emperor, becoming animated. "Who would dare say that I have constantly been its enemy? When you leave here with Montholon, go read the constitution that I dictated to him several months ago, with the reign of my son in mind. You will see if I haggled with the people of France over liberty."[224]

---

poleon in Elba. In fact, after Napoleon abdicated in 1814, Drouet did not join him in exile and transferred his allegiance to the Bourbons. He was given command of the 16th military division, but was soon arrested for conspiring with the d'Orléans party, to which he was secretly devoted. He escaped and during the Hundred Days, rejoined Napoleon, who by then had returned from exile.

[224] Note from the Author: see Montholon's *Récits de la captivité...* (q.v.) Vol. 2, p. 386.

"It is not your son, Sire, it's Your Majesty that must put his work in practice, and I repeat, if you will have a little confidence in me..."

"To put myself in the hands of a man of your energy and of your intelligence," responded the Emperor, "certainly, that is very seductive, but I have made my decision. I must die here, or France must come to get me."

"Sire," replied Lupiano, "Your Majesty in the past condemned me to life in prison in the dungeons of Vincennes. Well, I condemn you to reign again. Since the Emperor doesn't want to help me, my means today are insufficient. But in a few months I shall return, and unless I perish in that enterprise, I warn you, willingly or by force, I will take Your Majesty away."

"In several months, you will no longer find me. The sickness that has been unleashed makes progress every day. But it doesn't matter. I am still grateful to you for the warm devotion you have expressed."

Speaking thus, the Emperor had risen. He opened a box of necessary items, and took out a decoration of the *Legion d'Honneur*, adding:

"Marquis, you have fought valiantly under the tricolored flag. Take this ribbon from my hand. This is today no longer a decoration; but it will be at least a souvenir."

"Sire," responded Lupiano, "if it is not permitted for me to wear it in my boutonniere, please believe that I will wear it on my heart."

The Emperor made a sign of goodbye to him with his hand.

"Sire, not goodbye," said Lupiano, "but in a few months, your deliverance or my death!"

XXVI. Big Effects and Small Causes

Om April 11, 1821, Lupiano was back in Paris, and in one of the apartments of his townhouse, he had settled his young friend, the Sydney hangman, and Kitty Ketch's aunt,

Mistress Sedley, the tavern-keeper and former owner of *The Bottle and Magpie.*

Upon his arrival, his Hindu servant gave him a voluminous letter bearing the postmark of the Cape de Good Hope, written by Gregorio Matiphous. That letter was as follows:

Tananarive, Madagascar Island,
27 November 1820,
My noble and venerated father,

As you often told me, "When you are in port, don't do any bad business." And at the same time, you were preaching clemency and the forgiveness of past offences. You showed great wisdom in all this, and I wish I had listened to you!

Today is a grand kabar; *that is the name given here to an assembly of notables who decide affairs of great importance. I was found guilty vis-à-vis King Radama for having left his service without obtaining his prior agreement, and also guilty of adultery vis-à-vis my* vadi-be, *Ravine-Vol. As a consequence, I was condemned to the* Trial of the Caimans.

Here's that that trial consists of:

The Ipioka, a large river that flows through the area of Tananarive, is infested with crocodiles. Tomorrow, at dawn, I will be taken with great pomp to that river facing an islet covered with weeds which these odious reptiles use as a nesting place. After having taken off my clothes, an Ombiache, *a kind of seer or priest, will lead me, holding me by the hand, right to the edge of the water, where I must, three times, dive and swim the distance which separates the islet from the banks. If I am fortunate enough not to be attacked by any of the voracious reptiles to which I am thus given as prey, I shall be freed and able to return to France and again see those whom I love. If, on the contrary, which is more likely, I succumb to the beasts—then, it is adieu! My noble and revered father, I will have died thinking of you.*

You will see that it is for not having followed your advice that I find myself today so near my end. When I learned of your generous action toward Hulet, I was, at first, indignant that you had hidden from me what you had done. And in order that this man, whose side, it seemed to me, you were taking against that of your own son, would not reap all the benefit of your actions, I had the unfortunate idea of letting Saint-Rambert know into whose hands the strongbox, so long disputed between us, had passed. I was not mistaken in thinking that he would try to steal it, and, without a doubt, he was near completing his theft the night of the explosion in which Hulet and his son perished.

My first punishment was to see you accused of that misfortune, and to know that the letters that I helped disappear had now become necessary to prove your innocence. I went to Saint-Rambert again to ask him to return them to me. He began by denying that they were in his possession. Then, finally, pushed to the end, under the pretext that they were hidden in an isolated house in Belleville, he brought me to that house where, for several weeks, Britannicus and my so-called wife had been hiding, waiting for the result of the bargain made with that wicked man to hand me over to them.

There, I was subjected to despicable treatments. Not willing to withdraw the sum of two hundred thousand francs to the benefit of the author of that trap, I saw myself tied up and beaten like a slave. That day, without the assistance of the Deputy Mayor of Belleville, who came to my aid, I would have been murdered.

Having escaped from that peril, I no longer thought of anything but revenge. If Saint-Rambert had been a man to use the sword, I would have challenged him to a duel, and I would, in fair play, have taken his life, or he would have taken mine. But I knew that he didn't duel, and I was even more eager to get rid of him, since he had made your case worse. I calculated that, after his death, a police search, made inevitable by the functions he filled at the Secret Bureau, *would recover that correspondence that had caused that unjust accusation lodged against you.*

I knew that, since I had left the Secret Bureau, *nothing in the arrangement of the place had changed, nor had the pre-*

cautions taken to prevent an intrusion by someone uninvited. I could then go in, observe everything and set up my plan as a result.

As I have already mentioned, I noticed that, in the room where the unsealing of the letters was done, Monsieur de Saint-Rambert, in order to be better set himself apart as Director from his colleagues, had arranged a special place for himself, entirely separate. It was a kind of throne with a writing desk locked with a key, where, evidently, he kept the objects he used. He would have to open the desk each time he came to preside over the work of the Secret Bureau. *I began by making an imprint of the lock in order to have a duplicate key made. Next, with the knowledge of chemistry that medical studies have given me, it was not difficult for me to prepare a strong dose of fulminate of mercury, a very explosive substance which will detonate with enormous power at the slightest shock.*

After having put that mixture into a steel strongbox, I connected it to one of those firecrackers that schoolboys play with, and which explode when suddenly pulled. This percussion cap was itself attached to a string that passed through the keyhole of the desk lock. In that way, when Saint-Rambert would come to open his desk, he would set off a formidable explosion.

Once my preparations had been completed, the evening preceding the execution of my homicidal project, I went to see Georgiana. Because of the worry that your arrest had caused me, and because of all the other cares that preoccupied me, I had neglected her for several days. When I appeared at her lodgings, I had to go through a jealous scene, and when I stubbornly refused to stay with her until the next morning, as soon as I had left her, she followed me. She was so persuaded that I was going to another lover's rendezvous that, after seeing me return to my house, where I was going to pick up my makeshift bomb, and make some final arrangements, she was still not reassured.

By an unusual stroke of fate, persuaded that I would come out later, she had the patience to wait for me. Toward four o'clock in the morning, she saw me walking in the direction of the Hôtel des Postes. More passionate than ever in her surveillance, she followed my trail. Thanks to my natural preoccupation at the time, I didn't notice that I was being followed until the moment when, about to enter the secret entrance to the Bureau, *I discovered the unhappy girl beside me, asking me where I was going at such an hour, and what I was doing there.*

I only had a rigorously calculated time in order to accomplish my evil work and leave the Bureau *before the time when an old man, working there from time immemorial, would come to light the lamps. I couldn't leave in the street that poor girl who had come to give me such positive, although so untimely, proof of her furious attachment.*

"Come with me," I told her, taking her by the arm. And totally astonished, she accompanied me into a place where, before her, no woman, for certain, had ever had access. One my bomb had been set up, I hurried to leave, but God, who without a doubt, didn't approve of my plan, willed that, at the exit, the spring by which the door automatically closes, functioned with more difficulty than when I had entered. Finding resistance, I got excited. I tried to force it. In short, the door refused to open and there we were, prisoners.

The situation was becoming serious, but all was not lost, however. The table on which letters were unsealed was of vast dimensions and covered with a green cloth falling to the floor. Not having any other place, we could temporarily hide under there. Being careful to stay in the middle of the space covered under the table, there was no chance that the employees' feet could touch us. After having given the explanations necessary to my poor companion, and having made her understand that, at the least noise coming from us, it might mean our life, hearing the steps of the old watchman resounding in the corridors, I pulled Georgiana into our sad refuge.

While that man, singing, made his rounds, I wondered if I shouldn't show myself, force him to open the door and thus leave that dangerous place. But he knew my face, and later, after the bomb had gone off, through him, it would become known that I was the author of that disaster. I could still renounce the enterprise, and in retrospect, that would have been better. Unfortunately, I held to my vengeance. Besides, it would have been necessary, in the presence of that witness, to remove the bomb from where I had placed it. But I suppose that that old man wouldn't have guessed what it was. Still, because he was very religiously devoted to the interests of the Secret Bureau, *where he's worked for years, he would have told Saint-Rambert that I had entered the sanctuary, bringing someone there with me. Just that revelation would have threatened me with serious consequences. I then really had only one choice: have that man open the door for me, and then, to make sure of his silence, stab him. Nothing was easier for me; I was dealing with an adversary who was a weak old man, but I couldn't make myself decide on that cruelty. I had held back from the idea of making the entire ignoble office explode in an act of mass destruction, and I had only resolved to take Rempailleux' life because I could strike him alone. I therefore let the poor devil leave, never suspecting the danger that he had escaped, and we waited.*

Soon, having arrived at their post, the employees started their work. Assisted by a sub-director whom he had appointed, Rempailleux only came in much later and didn't immediately take his place at his desk. He walked a long time around the table, making several observations to those under his orders. My heart was beating because, despite that delay, each moment drew us closer to the catastrophe. My plan was then, after the force of the explosion would have extinguished all the lamps, when the terrified employees would have dashed in disorder toward the door, to take advantage of the obscurity and the confusion to leave with them.

But how things in this world turn out! Until that point, Georgiana had conducted herself very heroically. One of her hands in mine, she had been waiting patiently and coura- geously for the end of the strange position in which we were placed, when suddenly, everything was compromised by the most ridiculous unexpected event. In that underground room, three-quarters of the time uninhabited, the wood-panels with which the walls were covered served as a refuge for numerous nests of mice. Just with the envelopes thrown about, when the unsealing had been botched up, they had found ample materi- al to nibble on. One of them, when running across the floor, had gone under Georgiana's skirts. The surprise, the disgust, mingled with terror that contact with these animals cause, made her cry out. There was immediate commotion among the employees.

"There's a woman here!" some of them exclaimed.

"Look under the table,!" Rempailleux said. "That's where the voice came from."

At that moment, we were discovered, and, before I could stand up, ten assailants surrounded me so that all resistance was impossible.

Taken with Georgiana into a solidly closed room situat- ed under the post office building, I thought, my most noble and venerated father, of your prison in Malta, and not knowing exactly what treatment was in store for us, I wondered if, sus- pended for some time, the curse of the "Bloodied Girl" had not finally resurfaced again.

We saw no one during the whole day, not even to bring us food. Had they reserved torture by hunger for us?

A little before night fall, Rempailleux appeared.

"Dear Monsieur," he said, "it seems you have absolute- ly wanted to prove that your legitimate wife, who continues to wait for you at Le Havre, was correct. You will be taken there along with Mademoiselle. This time, your transfer doesn't offer any major complications. I had only to see the Prefect of Police, who will have you escorted there. What the Devil of an idea you had, knowing how strict our rules are, to want to satisfy your mistress' curiosity, that she no doubt expressed,

by showing her our "holy sanctum." No one is more cocky than you!"

"Monsieur," I then said to Rempailleux, taking him to one side, "I ask nothing for myself. I admit that I am as vain as you say; therefore, I must pay for my lack of caution. But it would be an abominable cruelty to link my fate to that of a woman, I swear to you, who doesn't even know the real nature of the place where you've found us; and to support what I say, I submit the stupid jealousy of Georgiana which led her to accompany me there."

Seeing that I wasn't making a great impression on the man I was talking to, I added:

"Do you want to bargain? Grant me Georgiana's freedom and I will give you life, because I swear to you, if you refuse, tomorrow you will be a dead man. You understand very well that, by risking to come to this place where you have found me, I did not come without a purpose, and that couldn't be merely to satisfy a woman's curiosity. Tomorrow, once again, if you do not come to terms with me now, you will have ceased to live tomorrow. You know what the Marquis is capable of. He directs everything from the depth of his prison."

Rempailleux was very upset by my revelations, to which I had put a singular tone of truth.

"But if the Marquis is involved," he said to me, "he wouldn't care for the freedom of your mistress; it's only yours that would bring about his intervention."

"No," I replied, "guarantee me Georgiana's freedom and I shall give you important information that will put you out of danger."

"I can't decide alone," Rempailleux finally said to me. "The Prefect of Police has been called. I'm going to consult with him."

An hour later, he returned and said to me with good will:

"The Prefect gave me carte blanche. *But do we always have to think of killing each other? What sense does that make? All right! Come with me, both of you. You must be dying of hunger; you've been forgotten all day. Let's go together*

to a nearby bistro and seal a reconciliation which, I hope, will be frank and durable. After having eaten bread and salt together, even among savages, it is said, you can no longer hold a grudge.

Saying that, Rempailleux took us to Very, a restaurant where we enjoyed an exceptional dinner, and he had the good taste to not speak of the revelation that I had promised him. It was I who, the moment we got up from the table, had the honesty to say to him:

"In the Bureau, don't open your desk with the key. Lift the cover from the back side and tell the worker not to use a hammer. That could set off an explosion."

"Fichtre!" exclaimed Rempailleux. "I had a narrow escape!"

Then we left by a backdoor of the restaurant. We hadn't taken four steps in the little street which that entry leads to, when we were surrounded by two gendarmes and the police. They forced us into a rented carriage that had been waiting there. A policeman and two gendarmes sat beside us. Just at the moment the carriage started off:

"Enjoy Madagascar!" said the infamous Rempailleux, showing his hideous face at one of the carriage windows.

Traveling with extreme speed, the next day we were at Le Havre, and aboard the Franklin.

The Captain, who hadn't taken us on board without taking the precaution of having received written orders from the Police, didn't let us be maltreated by Ravine-Vol, but he put me under arrest in my cabin and separated me from Georgiana, to whom, I since then found out, he paid assiduous court during the entire time of the crossing. I like to believe that it was in vain.

When we arrived in Madagascar, if I had had to deal only with King Radama, I believe I could have made him see reason. Lefebvre defended me with all his strength. His credit since my departure had become very great. But Queen Ranavalo detested the foreigners. My vadi-bé *was her relative, and you know how all women support each other. She plotted*

*so well with all the local chiefs that Radama had his hand
forced. My fate was no longer in doubt.*

*The daughter of Kitty Ketch and Britannicus, a charming
child who, in Belleville, went in peril of her life to fetch the
Deputy Mayor and thus saved my life, found a way to reach
me, despite the strict seclusion in which I had been kept since
my condemnation. I knew through her that Lefebvre continued
to petition, with all possible zeal, Radama, and that he even
threatened to leave his service. But I hoped nothing from that
side. To escape from the crocodiles, I had to have confidence
only in myself. Brought up in Malta, among fishermen, I swim
like a fish. If those villainous beasts didn't follow too close
after me, I could, perhaps, cheat them of their dinner.*

*From all the details that I give you, father, you can judge
whether I envision my fate with equanimity. I have received
great consolation from the presence of a Lazarite Missionary,
who turned out to be Monsieur de Limeuil. You will recall that
I brought up his wife on the Bell Rock Lighthouse. His words
were full of kindness, and he put my soul in a state ready to
appear before God without fear.*

*I have done many bad things in my life, but basically I
was never bad toward anyone who wasn't already so with me,
and still, I often pardoned them. I will do the same with
Rempailleux. I do not want you to take revenge on him. Sooner
or later, things will turn out bad for him without your putting
a hand on him. I haven't spoken to you of Georgiana; I think
that she will stay here. Radama, who is passionate about
women, will put her among his concubines. So, she will end up
in a harem, just as she began. Now, good-bye one more time,
my noble and venerable father, or, if God wills it, see you
soon.*

To Matiphous's long letter, there was a note added by
Monsieur de Limeuil, who had written:

*I have the sad duty to inform you that on the morning of
November 28, Monsieur your son was put to the barbarous*

trial reserved for him. For a moment, we all thought that he might be saved from the danger. He had successfully crossed the river twice, but on the third attempt, he disappeared from sight.

I had not left him for an instant from the time he had been sentenced, and I can tell you that he died as a good Christian, feeling the most respectful and tender affections toward you. Someone who had experienced the great generosity of his heart had strongly recommended him to me on his death bed. Having been thrown outside his path, I didn't have the opportunity to render him any of the good offices that I would have liked. Heaven willed that, having become an evangelical worker in Africa, at last I found myself there to support him in his last passage. A brother, Monsieur le Marquis, wouldn't have been for me the object of a more affectionate and devoted zeal.

Please accept, etc.,

Anatole de Limeuil
Lazarite Priest.

When Lupiano finished reading those two letters, a visit from Lelouard was announced. At his arrival, Lupiano had asked him to come. The two friends embraced each other silently. Then, as Lelouard knew from Lefebvre, who had been back in France for more than a month, all the details of the kidnapping and death of Gregorio Matiphous, he began a series of condolences.

"It's not a question of moaning about the one we have lost," the Marquis quickly interrupted, "but of avenging him. Our former associates, what has become of them?"

"Hernandez and the Armenian," Lelouard answered, "got frightened after your arrest. They left Paris and I haven't seen them since. As for the others, they come very promptly to cash their monthly subsidy. But I strongly doubt that you can count on the help of Montalvi and that of the Marquise."

"What makes you think that?"

"About four months ago, Madame de Camembert became the Princess of Bevillacqua."

"Ah! Ah!" said Lupiano, "you see that I was right in not sending them together to Bordeaux. But just because you get married, is that any reason to break off former relations?"

"They haven't exactly broken with the Doctor and with me, but they do turn a cold shoulder to us and keep us at a distance. Montalvi required the dissolution of our commercial enterprise. Bringing as dowry to the Marquise his title of Prince, he probably thought that such a high aristocratic title should no longer be attached to a banking house. So we liquated the company, and he walked away with a million we'd made while handling the capital that you entrusted to us."

"I'm very comfortable with that," said the Marquis. "So I am now even with him. Then, in your opinion, with the fifty thousand livres of income that Montalvi set up for himself, and the sixty thousand that his wife brought him, he might be too rich to want to run adventures with us?"

"On the contrary, his wife and he intend, as in the past, to undertake something on their own."

"Have they contacted our stipend holders?"

"Yes. They have presented some kind of plan to some of them. And there's an even more conclusive indication. The new Madame de Bevillacqua has restarted in her role as a fortune teller or seer. She knows better than ever the vulnerable sides of people's private lives. From that, I conclude that Saint-Rambert is again furnishing her with some information."

"Why does she waste her time," Lupiano said quickly, "getting tied up with that miserable wretch. However, Montalvi wouldn't allow her to pay him in the same coin that she once gave Lefebvre. And he charges a big price for his indiscretions, that Monsieur Rempailleux. He cost me more than three thousand louis."

"I suppose that Madame de Bevillacqua pays him in social favors. Rempailleux's wife has a salon where she has never been able to attract the feminine portion of the noble *Faubourg*. Since she's back in fashion more than ever, our former friend has lifted that interdiction. She has been seen at the concerts of Madame the Directress of the *Secret Bureau,* whom, for her part, she has deigned to entertain. The other day, when I was visiting with her at the Bevillacqua town-house, the Princess strongly insisted that Saint-Rambert should not miss showing up at the ball that she is giving the day after tomorrow to celebrate a great Royalist anniversary, that of the return of the Comte d'Artois to Paris."[225]

"But, for me," exclaimed the Marquis, "that liaison is something monstrous. Does she, that woman without a heart, ignore the account that Rempailleux will have to settle with me?"

"I like to believe it," responded Lelouard. "What's more, Saint-Rambert doesn't show himself there. They say he even has the good taste and the discretion to seldom appear at his wife's receptions."

"It doesn't matter," said Lupiano. "In everything that concerned my son, Madame de Bevillacqua has always had unfriendly or unfortunate initiatives. She had better be careful! She may pay dearly for the attitude she has taken. So we won't count on her, or Monsieur her husband. As for the rest of our men, can you get them together this evening?"

"Absolutely," Lelouard answered.

"Well, this evening, let them all come to the Doctor's place. Not here, because that would be advertizing my return before I have had an opportunity to talk to them. More than ever, after the information that you have just given me, I need to surround myself with mystery. Please convey my instructions to the Doctor."

"But why couldn't the reunion be held here at my place?"

"Because I intend to keep you out of the danger that I'm going to throw myself into again. You're our banker, my dear friend, and since, for what I have to do, I foresee that I shall

---

[225] The future king Charles X.

need a considerable amount of money, you shouldn't be mixed up in my more risky enterprises."

"I don't like that role. I like to share my friends' danger."

"This isn't just in your interest," answered the Marquis. "It's in all of us. That's why I'm giving you an exceptional role. When you know everything, you will agree with me."

Lupiano's first concern, after Lelouard had left him, was to have himself taken, in a rented carriage to the Rue Jean-Jacques-Rousseau (formerly Rue Platrière) to that house with the impoverished appearance which, in the past, had served as the entrance to *Secret Bureau.* It will be recalled that, at one time, the shop of a liquor salesman communicated by an underground passage with the room where the unsealing of the letters occurred. It offered employees an entry as secure as it was convenient. Later, that subterranean passage had been abandoned. Montalvi, in order install there the political society of the *Grand Firmament,* had purchased the house to which it was attached, and, in place of the liquor shop, had opened the famous Lottery Bureau.

Under the Empire, after Montalvi's arrest and the dispersion of the secret society of which he had been the head, the suspicious house had remained closed for some time. Then, the State, which had confiscated it, had rented it to a man from the Auvergne who, for many years, had a business there as a boilermaker. Since then, his business that had gone through several highs and lows. The Marquis knew its history from Montalvi. And it was the Auvergnat, its current renter, that Lupiano had come with some solemnity to see, asking him for a moment's interview. The reader will later learn the object of that interview, but what can be stated now was that, the next day, the boilermaker's shop did not open at the usual time. That unusual situation was explained by a polite note attached to one of the shutters, on which passers-by could read the following information, written in bad Auvergnat spelling: *Clozed for Repers.*

After leaving the Auvergnat, the Marquis had himself driven to Belleville, where he found the now *General*

Lefebvre living in his son-in-law's household. Lefebvre recounted to him how, indignant at the treatment that Matiphous had received, he had told Radama that he was resigning from his service, and how the King of the Hovas had been delighted to let him go, considering the disquieting influence that his military knowledge had eventually had on the Madagascar army.

Lefebvre then introduced the pretty Sadou to the Marquis. After having saved the life of Matiphous in France, the poor child hadn't wanted to stay in Madagascar, where she had seen the man who, at another time, had saved her from a similar death thrown to the crocodiles. Cleverly taken by Lefebvre, who had helped her with what she wanted, she had returned to Europe to find her mother, whom Britannicus had always refused to introduce to her, even though he never stopped talking about her.

"I will take you there myself, my child," the Marquis told her, "and if she doesn't receive you in a proper fashion, don't worry, you will have a dowry with which Lefebvre and Monsieur the Deputy Mayor will have no trouble finding a good husband for you."

Then, taking Lefebvre to one side, the Marquis confided to him the secret of the enterprise that he was contemplating to help the prisoner of Saint-Helena, and asked him if it was convenient for him to associate himself with that gigantic operation. Lefebvre accepted enthusiastically.

"Well!" Lupiano then said, "the day after tomorrow, come to me in the evening with Sadou. I will have taken care to send her a ball gown. All three of us will go and visit your former lover, Madame de Camembert, now married to the Prince de Bevillacqua. I'm sure she will be very happy to see you again."

"That remains to be seen," responded Lefebvre, recalling the reception given to Lelouard, who had come on his behalf.

"I'm telling you," replied the Marquis, "that she will receive you with the greatest pleasure. Besides, it's absolutely necessary to make an appearance at that gathering that is tied to the grand scheme I have just told you about. After you have shown yourself there for a moment, you will take Sadou back to Belleville. You will then travel to Le Havre, where you will go immediately on board the *Franklin* that is scheduled to take us back to Saint-Helena. If I don't make it, just in case, I will give you a letter for the Captain. But you do realize the extent of the difficulties and the dangers that we will be running?"

"It still won't be more perilous than the great retreat from Moscow," Lefebvre answered.

"Then it's agreed. I am counting on you. The day after tomorrow, come and get me, around nine o'clock, Rue Pavée, in the Marais, at the Lamoignon townhouse."

Back home, Lupiano filled Mistress Sedley with joy when he told her that, two days from then, in the evening, he would take her to see her adored niece, Madame la Comtesse de Saint-Rambert. As for John Ketch, he almost fell over backward when the Marquis, sending him in gold the sum of twenty five thousand francs, told him that, for a simple service, he would be ready to send him triple that sum that he had already received.

That evening, as Lelouard had promised him, all the former *Red Brothers,* minus Montalvi and the two deserters, were gathered at the Doctor's place. After having told them that he was putting himself again at their head, never again to be separated from them, Lupiano asked them if, when he had finished the business he had come to carry out in Paris, they were willing to become part of a distant enterprise that would resound around the entire world.

"You must be told the truth," he continued. "We will have to surmount great dangers, but at the end, if we succeed, you will gain a large, honored, happy existence, and, thrown into the bargain, glory, for those which that fleeting thing can attract."

After an acclamation of agreement, the Marquis continued:

"Be ready then, in forty-eight hours to embark at Le Havre, where a brig is waiting for you. Once at sea, the goal of our journey will be revealed to you."

As for the more immediate work that had to be finished in Paris, it was well within the framework of the former operations of the *Brotherhood*. Lupiano immediately distributed all the roles and set up all the necessary arrangements. It is not necessary to give any explanations to the reader yet. He will soon see the effect of the dispositions taken. To let him know the details now would be to commit what might be called a tautology in narration.

XXIX. The Expiation

On the day of the masked ball given by Madame la Princesse de Bevillacqua, the servants of Madame de Saint-Rambert, who had orders to come pick her up there at three o'clock in the morning, were somewhat surprised to see her come back a long time before midnight, in a rented carriage, and as her maid said when commenting on the incident with the concierge of the townhouse, *with a completely upset face.*

When she was barely in her apartment, she had her husband's valet called.

"Saint-Jean," she said to him, "you know where to find my husband. Go and tell him to come speak to me without wasting a minute."

"But, Madame, I don't know where Monsieur spent the evening."

"You are lying! You must have carried letters twenty times to the house where I know he goes every evening."

"I don't understand what Madame means."

"It's not a matter now of being unduly discreet, and you will be the cause, I'm warning you, of the greatest misfortune, if your master is not here in half an hour. With a fast carriage, it doesn't take forty minutes, going and coming, to pass by Rue de Bourgogne to the house of Mademoiselle Hortense Boulard, a renter."

When, despite the frightening precision of that information, Saint-Jean still seemed to hesitate, Madame de Saint-Rambert exclaimed:

"Go on, you miserable man, it's your master's life that is at stake!"

"If Madame believes," said the valet who had been convinced by her argument, "that Monsieur *may be* at the Rue de Bourgogne, I will try to go there and find him."

And he left, enormously intrigued.

Madame de Saint de Rambert spent the time of her feverish wait changing into a night peignoir from the dazzling ball gown in which, two hours earlier, she had left to go to the Bevillacqua townhouse. And while she took off her finery, so great was her preoccupation that, instead of putting a magnificent diamond necklace that she had just taken off from around her neck, back in her jewel box, she threw it carelessly on a love couch.

Saint-Rambert entered his wife's bedroom a half-hour later, agitated.

"Madame," he said, "I don't interfere with your pleasures. The Duke comes here whenever he pleases to council you on the ways of salvation. It seems to me just that I should be allowed to enjoy the same liberty, and that I shouldn't be tracked into the houses where it might be pleasant for me to spend the evening."

"You are absurd, Monsieur, if you suppose that I have jealous notions. Yesterday, in fact, an anonymous letter made me aware of your kindness toward a Demoiselle Boulard. Did I look upset to you about that? But it's really about something else that I must speak to you: Lupiano is back in Paris! Now, do you believe that this news was worth the trouble of disturbing you?"

"Where did you learn about his return?"

"From him, Monsieur, who, a while ago at the Princess' ball, played the the damnedest trick on me. I don't know how that miserable man has been able to assemble that terrible assemblage. All at the same time, he introduced to me my daughter, from Britannicus, my aunt Aston and my brother John Ketch."

"That man is the Devil!" shouted Saint-Rambert.

"The Princess also played an equal part in that infernal cortege which he brought, having them announced in a burlesque fashion as *Monsieur le Marquis de Lupiano and his company*."

"Who else did he bring to the Princess'?"

"That boorish soldier that you once had under you as an employee, and to whom that poor Madame de Camembert seems to have granted some of her favors in order for her to obtain information."

"Ah! Then this, too, was set up against us," Rempailleux remarked. "By placing the Princess in the presence of her former lover, that diabolical Marquis obviously wished to punish her for the relationship that now ties her to us. But Monsieur de Bevillacqua must have taken the joke badly?"

"Monsieur de Bevillacqua was tied up in a card game so much that he, at first, didn't know anything about what was happening. Besides, except for the dress of Mistress Aston, that this monster had amused himself by having her look like *La Tante Aurore*,[226] the presence of the people that he had

---

[226] Ma Tante Aurore is a playful comic opera with a subtle net of literary illusions by French composer François-Adrien Boieldieu (1775-1834) and librettist Charles de Longchamps(1768-1832). It premiered at the Opéra-Comique of Paris on January 13, 1803. The controlling aunt after whom the work was named is a colorful old woman who has been spurned in love and become addicted to the Gothic romance. She refuses to marry off her niece until the latter has demonstrated that she, too, can live in a world of literary illusion and romantic fantasy. The playful libretto contains a myriad of references to contemporary literature, including Fielding's *Amelia*, the story of Blanche de Castille, *Clarissa, or The History of a Lady* and *Pamela, or Virtue Rewarded*, both by Sam-

brought with him didn't at first make any sensation. It was only the Princess and I who understood the wickedness of what was happening. We greeted them with coldness by putting the best face possible on those detestable characters that that traitor had just dragged out of the past and placed in our path. My aunt and the mulatto girl even came to sit beside me. My neighbors, hearing their parentage being discussed, quickly left."

"I understand," Rempailleux said ironically. "That must have been in order not to stand in the way of your family reunion."

"I had just exchanged with my aunt some nice words, telling her that the place was badly chosen for getting together, but that the next day, I would take great pleasure in receiving her at my townhouse, when the Duke came to me in a very emotional state. Taking me to one side, he said to me:

" 'The strangest gossip is circulating in the ballroom. Is it possible that those two women seated by you, one is your aunt, a former deportee to Botany Bay; and the other, a daughter that you had with a Negro servant? Could it also be believed that the tall gentleman with red hair, who doesn't leave the Marquis any more than his shadow, is your brother, the Sydney executioner?'"

"Ah!' said Rempailleux, "we have here on our hands a deadly foe."

"I didn't need to hear the Duke's words," continued Madame de Saint-Rambert, "to perceive that something was happening. The whispering, the wicked glances, the void that was, little by little, made around me, had warned me of the impending explosion of a great scandal.

" 'Monsieur le Duc," I said to my illustrious friend, "please give me your arm to leave. That would be the best response to these infamous calumnies that, tomorrow, at my townhouse, I will explain to you."

---

uel Richardson, *Orlando Furioso,* and several popular Gothic romances.

"Good answer!" said Saint-Rambert, approvingly. "But during all that time, where was Bevillacqua? Was he dead?"

"As I crossed the last drawing-room, holding the arm of the Duke..."

"Ah!" Rempailleux interrupted. "He accompanied you? There, Madame, you have a true friend."

"...The noise of a lively argument," Madame de Saint-Rambert continued, "struck our ears. The Duke stopped, and, wanting to hear and see, he approached a group where Monsieur de Bevillacqua, enraged, was saying to Lupiano:

" 'All right! Our former friendship explains why you have come here without being invited, but since when, I ask you, is my house a country fair that, with your eternal need for eccentricity, you use to exhibit your personal menagerie?'"

"Very well put," Rempailleux remarked.

"Yes, but the Marquis' response was terrible:

" 'Since you have received here the wife of the Director of the *Secret Bureau*, a former criminal.'"

"If he said that, that insolent man," Saint-Rambert shouted, "his goose is cooked!"

"On hearing that," Madame de Saint Rambert continued, "Bevillacqua lunged to get at him, but he was held back by the banker Lelouard, Lupiano's doctor, and also by Lefebvre, who came between them, saying that the Marquis was a man who would give him satisfaction. Moving then to Lefebvre, Bevillacqua said:

" 'And who, Monsieur, are you to come into my house where you haven't been invited?'

" 'A former friend of Madame,' responded the boor, 'brought here by Monsieur le Marquis de Lupiano. My name is General Lefebvre.'

" 'Oh, yes, a general made in Africa!'

" 'Or, if you prefer, Commandant Lefebvre, made in France, Legionnaire by the Emperor's own hand. If you would like to know more about me, I live in Belleville, at the home of my son-in-law, the Deputy Mayor.'

" 'Come away, Lefebvre,' Lupiano then said. 'Let's take the ladies away, because I see that we are decidedly unwelcome here.'

"At the same time, he offered his arm to my aunt Aston, and, shortly afterwards, while he packed my friendly relatives in a splendid *landau*[227] that had come forward to the bottom of the steps, seeing us pass by, the Duke and I, he affected to give us the most respectful greeting."

"That doesn't matter," said Rempailleux, "by speaking publicly about the *Secret Bureau,* he has put himself in a very bad position. From a private quarrel, he has made it a matter of state. It's only a question of putting the police on his trail."

"And that's what you should do," said Jack Ketch's daughter. "That's why I took it upon myself to disturb you in your nightly routine,"

"I'll do it right away," responded Saint-Rambert, getting up from the love couch where he had been sitting.

But as he left it, he felt something under his hand. Recognizing his wife's diamond necklace, without her noticing anything, he slid it subtly into his pocket. In that single act, he had the revelation of a plan of action.

Rempailleux had for a long time wondered what he would do in case Lupiano reappeared. Until then, he had played it rather well, but he knew that, on his return, the Marquis would know everything, that he had had Matiphous kidnapped, while the Marquis, transformed into a reverse Telemachus,[228] had made a voyage of ten thousand leagues in search of his son. That was more than was enough to create a very unpleasant adversary.

---

[227] An evolution of the ordinary carriage both in practical use and in elegance. It had four wheels, seats for four with two pull-down seats and could be hitched to two or four horses.
[228] The son of Odysseus and Penelope who goes searching for his father who has not yet returned from the Trojan War. Here, it is the father who is searching for his son.

The former *Chauffeur*'s instinct had been not to wait for a man whose revenges were known to be terrible, and to go abroad incognito. If, despite that wise intention, he had been caught, surprised, still in Paris, it was because his prudence had finally slumbered in his passion for that Demoiselle Hortense, about whom his wife had shown herself so well informed. He had fallen stupidly in love with that girl, without reason and reservation, something more frequent perhaps in the last stages of maturity than in the ardent passion of youth. But with the blow struck by Lupiano, he had just awakened.

My skin before everything, he said to himself, and in his terror, instead of wasting his time to call the police, his real intention, upon leaving Madame de Saint-Rambert, was to take to his heels, after having equipped himself with the six or seven thousand francs in bank bills that he always kept at the ready, in case he should have to make a quick departure. That's why he had the inspiration to add the theft of his wife's diamond necklace to his money for the journey, and why, in parting, he had made his farewell in that way.

Rempailleux' consternation can easily be imagined when, a moment later, after opening his strongbox, he found that a billfold, which two hours earlier he had checked with his own hands, had now disappeared! An expert in that matter, he carefully examined the piece of furniture where he had kept it. There was not the single trace of a breaking and entering-it was a theft, to use his expression, *as neatly carried out as possible!*

Naturally, Rempailleux immediately suspected Lupiano, who had first struck him through his wife, and had now come to strike through his fortune, waiting to strike his life. With what he knew of the terrible ways in which the Marquis operated, nothing was more logical for him than that sinister progression. His fright was at its greatest when Saint-Jean came to tell him that an old woman was asking to see him immediately. Since it was close to midnight, the hour was at least odd. He immediately smelled some new plot from his dangerous adversary. But despite it all, he ordered that this unexpected visitor be allowed to enter. To protect oneself from an attack, it is better to see it coming first.

"Who are you?" asked Rempailleux, when he saw a woman with an honest appearance, but rather poorly dressed, enter.

"I am the sister-in-law of the concierge of Mademoiselle Hortense Boulard Monsieur. My brother-in-law and my sister couldn't come here because the police are at their house."

"What are the police doing there?"

"It's for a murder that has just been committed."

"A murder! Who has been murdered?"

"It costs me a lot to tell you, Monsieur, but, still, you have to be told."

"Yes, yes, who has been murdered?" Rempailleux asked emotionally.

"Murdered isn't quite the right word; the victim is only wounded, but the doctor says that she won't live through the night."

"Killed or wounded, who is the victim?"

"Mademoiselle Hortense Boulard."

"Come now!" said Rempailleux, shrugging. "It hasn't been an hour since I left her."

"It's exactly that. The murderer was waiting in the street for Monsieur to leave, and then he immediately went up."

"What fairy tale are you telling me, my good woman. As if Hortense would receive a visitor at such an hour!"

"Unfortunately, it's not the first time, Monsieur, and the poor girl has now paid dearly for that. But what do you expect; she's young; she doesn't know how to hold onto a respectable man. It even seems that the more these emptied-headed girls are showered with good things, the more they are in a rage to cheat."

"But supposing that all that is true," Rempailleux said with distrust, "what did the murderer look like?"

"Not more than twenty-five years-old, Monsieur; a dark, handsome man, but that's not important, because when the police commissioner searched him..."

"Ah! So he has been arrested?"

"Yes, Monsieur, by my brother-in-law, who, having heard the girl cry out, had the forethought to pull the emergency cord, so that the murderer was caught as if in a mousetrap."

"And then, they told to to come and tell me?"

"Yes, my brother-in-law and my sister aren't enough to guard the door, seeing that there is a crowd in front of the house; the whole neighborhood is in confusion."

"Well, what can I do about that?" asked Rempailleux, who still didn't believe a word of that story. "Mademoiselle Hortense has a doctor with her; I'm not one."

"Ah! Monsieur, you couldn't have the hardness of heart to refuse to let her embrace you on her death bed. You are the only one she asked to see."

"Leave me alone. Hortense, I am sure, is as healthy as you and I. I know very well who sent you."

"Well, Monsieur, I didn't expect such cruelty. To pretend not to believe me just so as not to be disturbed. The murderer, is not much of a man, but since he struck the blow—likely motivated by jealousy—he wants to kill himself and shows such emotion that the police have put him in handcuffs. Still, that thief has a better heart than you, a man from the high society!"

"You said, he is a thief? Did he rob her before striking her?"

"No, Monsieur, but when the commissioner searched him, he found on him some false keys and a billfold containing more than a *myon* [229] in bills."

"That billfold," Rempailleux quickly asked, "did you see it?"

"Yes, very well. It was a red billfold with a small steel lock, but without a key, so that, on opening it, the bills that it was stuffed with fell to the ground. I, who am talking to you, helped pick them up. There was also a lock of hair wrapped in fine paper with two dried flowers."

---

[229] Million.

At that information, Saint-Rambert recognized the bill-fold that had been stolen from him, and at that point, his thoughts took a completely different turn. Now, it was not only through his wife, through his purse, but also in the dearest of his affections that Lupiano's implacable vengeance was following him. He did not doubt that, at his instigation, Hortense had been murdered by the same man who had robbed him, and if he would not find his mistress alive, he had at least every hope of recovering his billfold. He then decided to rush to the Rue de Bourgogne, promising himself that he wouldn't approach the house except with the necessary caution.

"All right, my good woman, I'm going to get dressed and follow you."

"Then, Monsieur doesn't want to take advantage of the carriage that I have down below?"

"Ah! You came in a carriage?"

"Damn, with my old legs, would I have been able to come any other way?"

Rempailleux thought a moment. If someone wanted to draw him out of his house, would he be safer in his carriage than in the one he would get into with that woman? On the other hand, to go on foot, would the danger be less? Nevertheless, he had to go out, because, if everything he had been told was true, his billfold would be returned into his hands, not counting the fact that, if Hortense was dying, some suspicions about her faithfulness had been aroused, had reached his heart, and he sought to learn more.

In the middle of those uncertainties, unexpected help seemed to have been sent to him by his lucky star. Laverenette, that former army major whom he had, at first, made his right arm, and then the sub-director of the *Secret Bureau*, had added to his functions as an opener of letters, that of an agent of the secret police. A report had been made to the Prefect of Police about the strange scene that had taken place at Madame de Bevillacqua's ball, and about the imprudent words spoken by Lupiano regarding the existence and the direction of the *Secret Bureau*. Immediately called to the Prefecture, Laverenette had read that report, and, with another agent, had been charged with going immediately to Saint-Rambert's house to verify its truthfulness. It was usual for the Prefect, before taking any action, when it was a serious matter, to proceed with that precaution, nothing being so common as the exaggeration, the inaccuracies, and sometimes even the complete lack of truth, contained in the report submitted to his administration

When Rempailleux felt himself backed by two men from the police, he felt that he was invulnerable and disdainfully sent away the old woman. After having made Laverenette and his colleague believe that he needed to go to the Rue de Bourgogne to get more information about the affair that he had just been told about, he gave them weapons and ordered them to accompany him, not hiding from them that he wasn't without a certain apprehension of encountering some kind of ambush on his way.

After some objections that didn't show their courage under any good light, the two policemen got into Saint-Rambert's carriage with him. Although the shortest route from the Rue du Colisée to the Rue de Bourgogne was to go by way of the Champs-Elysées, since that direction, at the time when our story takes place, didn't offer the security that it does today, the coachman was ordered to go down the Faubourg Saint-Honoré as far as the Place Louis XV, that he then had to cross in order to reach the bridge of the same name.

After both bridge and square had been crossed, Saint-Rambert felt himself out of danger. At the Bourbon Palace, located at the entry to the Rue de Bourgogne, there was a station of army veterans; two steps further, Rue Saint-Dominique, near the Ministry and the townhouse of the Minister of War, there were two more stations. Just let someone try something against him in a neighborhood so well guarded!

He continued on his way with no other concern than that of knowing what was waiting for him at Mademoiselle Hortense's house. Suddenly, almost at the turning of the quay, past the first houses on the Rue de Bourgogne, his carriage stopped. Putting his head immediately out the window, Rempailleux saw the door to a big townhouse open. Almost at the same moment, a man came out of nowhere and grabbed the reins of the horses of his carriage. The carriage was then quickly pulled forward into a badly lit courtyard. Darkness and fear made the objects there appear larger. The courtyard, the doors of which had been immediately closed, appeared to be full of armed men pointing the barrel of their pistols at the carriage. Rempailleux lacked the courage to use his weapons, as did his acolytes. It was with a sense of submission full of terror that he followed the injunction to get out of his carriage. Then, in the man who opened the carriage window and lowered the dashboard, he recognized the Marquis de Lupiano!

As each of the prisoners stepped to the ground, he was searched, relieved of his weapons, and a slip-knot, the kind used by the *Thugs,* the notorious Stranglers of India, was slipped around his neck.

In their stupor, the prisoners let themselves be led without saying a word into a huge room with blue and gold paneling, but in which they noticed only a few chairs and a wooden desk with implements necessary for writing,

"Messieurs," Lupiano said to them, "you will forgive me for receiving you in this way in an apartment without furniture. I have only been in possession of this house since this morning. I only rented it as a place to put Monsieur de Saint-Rambert, since he couldn't be made easily to go where his heart and his money called him. I thought it was useless to furnish the place, since I will probably never occupy it, although I had to pay a deposit for a three, six, or nine years' lease."

By then, Saint-Rambert had recovered some of his composure.

"What does all this violence mean, Monsieur?" he said to Lupiano. "Take care; the police are on your trail. The two gentlemen with me have the honor to belong to them. From one moment to the next, they will discover the place where, after having robbed me, you are now holding me prisoner."

"Ah!" Lupiano exclaimed. "These gentlemen are from the police? I am truly delighted. Their presence will give what is being prepared an official character. First of all, Monsieur le Directeur, I must reassure you. Your billfold is in the hands of Mademoiselle Hortense Boulard, who is in marvelous health, and couldn't be more appreciative of the gift you sent her. As for the men accompanying you, they can rest easy; no danger shall threaten them. I'm keeping them here only as witnesses."

"Monsieur le Marquis," said Laverenette, "we accept with pleasure your assurances of proper treatment, but if you intend to proceed with some rigor against Monsieur de Saint-Rambert, he was right when he told you that you would be taking a big risk. The authorities are alerted and what it has gotten it into their head to discover won't stay long hidden."

"So, Messieurs," Lupiano replied, "that's why I don't intend to retain you for very long.:

At the same time, talking to one of the men who had just entered, he asked:

"Is everything ready?"

"Yes, Monsieur le Marquis. The coachman is in a cellar where there is no way for him to be heard. The unhitched horses have been replaced by yours in the stable and the carriage is waiting for you."

"Messieurs," said Lupiano to the prisoners, "will you please follow me?"

"But where are you taking us?" demanded Rempailleux.

"Don't worry," replied the Marquis, "you're not being taken to the Plain of Grenelle to be shot. But since the trip is going to be of some duration, and you might have some vague desire to disturb it with some *inconvenient* demonstrations, you won't find it unusual that I employ with you the same procedure used on such occasions."

That said, despite his resistance, Rempailleux was tied up and gagged, so as not to be able to say a word, and carried into a large berline with six seats. Seated alongside him were the Marquis and three of his assistants. Another man acted as the coachman, and two as the outside valets. As for Laverenette and his companion, after having been advised to be silent and not to budge, on pain of feeling the slip knot still tied around their neck tightened, they occupied the two remaining seats in the berline.

After a journey of about twenty minutes, midnight having rang out from the Post Office clock, the berline stopped on the Rue Jean-Jacques Rousseau in front of the shop of the Auvergnat, whom Lupiano had met the previous evening. While the carriage disembarked its contents, with an excess of caution, despite the fact that the street, at that hour, was almost deserted, two carts filled with vegetables, looking as if they were going to the market of Les Halles, arranged themselves in order to form around the boilermaker's shop a blockade that made any approach almost impossible. The door soon closed, and the prisoners, preceded by Lupiano, went into a back shop where a man with red hair was asleep in an old armchair, in the company of a bowl of punch.

"John," Lupiano said to him, shaking him by the arm, "wake up, my friend! It's time."

After John had risen from his armchair, stretching his arms, the Marquis forced Rempailleux to sit in it. He made Laverenette and his colleague also take seats, while, to their great surprise, the armed men, numbering six, who had aided Lupiano in the trip from the Rue Bourgogne, walked to the other end of the room and disappeared successively through an obscure breach in the wall, slowly, by degrees, descending a staircase that must have been there.

"Monsieur le Directeur of the *Secret Bureau,*" said Lupiano to Saint-Rambert, "you do not know, I'm sure, all the territories in your empire. I found an entry into your *holy sanctum,* as you once called it to my son, which is probably unknown. In promising to that honest man from Auvergne, whose guests we are at this moment, that, while he went back to his *country* for a while, I would uncover and share half with him a treasure hidden in the cellars of his house. I received *carte blanche* for the search that I had in mind. In a moment, I will take you to be enthroned in the sanctuary for the violation of which you make the curious and the indiscreet pay so dearly."

Prevented from talking by the gag that was held in his mouth, Rempailleux struggled in the armchair where he was seated.

"Monsieur le Marquis," said Laverenette, "what you're going to do is serious. The police already know that you are more informed than is proper vis-à-vis the existence of the *Secret Bureau.* Take care that you don't find yourself face to face with them."

"Do you really think so?" responded the Marquis. "No, I think that we will be finished here before they have time to suspect anything. See, someone is coming to inform us...."

At that moment, the dark opening through which Lupiano's janissaries[230] had disappeared was lit up with a reddish light, and, in the back shop, six phantom-like figures, each carrying a torch in his hand, came to stand in a line. With their long red robes with their hoods pulled down over their faces, with two holes pierced at the level of the eyes, they could have been mistaken for red penitents, if that color was in usage.

"Let's go, Messieurs," said Lupiano, speaking to the two police agents. "You are going to be enlightened."

Two of the men dressed in red went ahead. Laverenette and his colleague followed, not without notable emotion. When it was Rempailleux's turn, he fought with as much resistance as the ropes with which he was bound would allow. Since he refused to walk, two of the Penitents had to carry him. The two others followed gravely. After them, the man with the red hair, whom Lupiano had called John, went into the subterranean passage that our readers will no doubt recognize as the one through which, during the Empire, Matiphous

---

[230] Members of an elite infantry unit, household troops and body guards, in the Ottoman Empire.

had escaped the vengeance of the *Grand Firmament.* The Marquis walked last.

With his prodigious energy and powerful genius for evil, of which he had given so many proofs, spurred by the loss of his son and an immense need for vengeance, with all the instincts of his wicked past, the Marquis de Lupiano, in two days, had conceived and put into action all the details of the dark drama whose denouement was now approaching. Notably, since the last meeting of the *Secret Bureau* had taken place, he had been able to enter, through the passage that, at this moment, we are seeing him follow, the place where the unsealers of letters worked. He had taken advantage of their absence, which always lasted twenty-four hours, to make preparations for the most terrible of expiations.

When they reached the cellars where the letters were unsealed, the six red phantoms, in order to light the scene, attached the torches they carried to the racks fitted to the walls that normally held the hats of the employees. Lupiano then ordered that Rempailleux be divested of all that hindered him. Speaking to the two witnesses that chance had arranged to be present for his revenge, he said:

"Messieurs, in 1799, the man that you see here was condemned to be hanged. His lucky star snatched him from that destiny, which, at that time, he had well deserved. Since then, I had the kindness to return him to grace..."

"Your son made an attempt on my life!" shouted Rempailleux. "Laverenette! You know very well about the bomb that would have blown up all of us!"

"Ah! I see that Monsieur," said Lupiano, "belongs to your honorable company. Well, then he is going to find out where the path he is presently following may lead him some day. As I was saying," he continued, "that man, who had once experienced my clemency, sent my son to a terrible death..."

"I delivered him to his legitimate wife, whom he had abandoned," Rempailleux interrupted, "that all."

"And the crocodiles of Madagascar shared the shreds of his flesh. And as for me, you miserable man, it seemed to please you to send me to Botany Bay, some five thousand leagues from here, to look for my son, whom you knew had been condemned to the most deplorable end. My voyage, however, was not useless. I brought back from Sydney an executioner, to be the one to effect my revenge. John Ketch, the moment has come to do your duty."

"That's impossible!" Rempailleux shouted. "Him! My own brother-in-law—hang me? John Ketch, think about it! I am the husband of your sister!"

With the most marvelous English composure, John Ketch had gone toward a rope hanging from a pulley attached to the vaulted arch which stood rather high above the floor.

"Coward!" the condemned man shouted.

Then, addressing Laverenette:

"And you! You calmly let your friend be slaughtered!"

And he struggled in the hands of six red phantoms, who dragged him under the pulley. Laverenette was in no condition to answer, because he had partially lost the use of his senses. Almost inanimate, he was in the hands of his colleague, who, by the attention he was giving him, was only too happy to divert his attention from the horrible spectacle.

Because of their relationship, John Ketch, who was a man distinguished in his art, had decided that he wouldn't let the victim linger. He had arranged the noose in a manner so as to cause asphyxiation in the briefest time possible.

A minute had scarcely passed that, having consigned his villainous soul to God, Rempailleux, like the pendulum of a clock, oscillated, suspended six feet above the ground.

"Messieurs," Lupiano then said to the two witnesses of the execution, "I regret to leave you in a not very pleasant company, but if I gave you back your liberty immediately, you would feel bound by your conscience to go and report what has just happened under your eyes. And you can understand that I shall need to have several hours before me in order to avoid any further discussions with the administration of which you are a part."

While he was giving that explanation, the rope joined to
the pulley had brought the hanged man down within reach of
the *Red Brothers,* who placed on his forehead a stamp of the
same color, it will be recalled, with which they usually indicated the number in the order of their vengeance—in this case,
the number 5. Then, around the neck of the tortured man, was
placed a small chain of bronzed steel, at the end of which was
a sign made of ebony wood on which were inscribed, also in
red ink, the motives for the condemnations carried out by the
Red Brotherhood. Written on this one were the words: **Every
Crime.** After that funeral orison, Rempailleux shortly thereafter began again to swing in space.

Having left through the subterranean passage, the *Red
Brothers*, by means of two strong oak planks that they carefully and solidly fixed to the wall, firmly shut the means of
communication between the letter-opening cellar and the shop
of the Auvergnat.

Once alone, Laverenette and his colleague counted on
escaping through the usual exit, but Lupiano had been careful
to block all the exits leading to the Rue de Verdelet. When,
some hours later, the employees of the *Secret Bureau* came at
the usual hour, they discovered that entrance, as well as exit,
had become impossible. Before communication could be re-
established, some work was necessary that would require great
discretion. Given the hour, and the choice of workers employed there, Lupiano consequently knew that he had a good
thirty hours head start. The authorities were not in a position
to act against him. From the *Franklin,* he was in a position to
defy all the Prosecutors and Judges of the world, as well as all
their arrest warrants.

XXX. Too Late!

Embarking with his people a little before mid-April, the
Marquis de Lupiano should have been able to reach Saint-
Helena by mid-June, but his crossing was horribly impeded by
bad weather, followed by hopeless calms. A wind storm that

the *Franklin* experienced when in sight of the Canary Islands forced her to put into Santa Cruz de Tenerife for repairs. All plans for the journey had been so thrown into disarray that, in the second week of June, the expedition had not yet passed the Cape Verde Islands.

There was nothing to reproach Captain Nichols, however. He was a solid and strong navigator. Besides, to tell the truth, the control of the ship did as well in the hands of the Marquis as in his. Before they came on board, Lupiano had counted out to him the million they had agreed on. The Englishman had shown himself filled with the most respectful deference, and Lupiano had been consulted in every difficulty encountered.

Lupiano explained to himself the delays that desolated him by a rather bizarre superstition. For him the number *thirteen* had something mysterious about it, and he attributed some kind of good luck to it, entirely the opposite of the bad superstition that is usually associated with it. His *Sleepers' Club,* his *Brothers of Death,* each had had thirteen members. On reading the Hulet family manuscript, he had noticed that the *Apostles of Nuremberg,* and after that, the *Secret Bureau,* founded under Louis XIV, were established with the same number. Now, when he had thought of immortalizing his *Red Brotherhood* by rescuing the prisoner of Saint-Helena, that number had sadly been reduced to nine. For one thing, the Brazilian Hernandez and the Armenian had deserted. For another thing, he had not been willing to invite Montalvi on board. And Lelouard, by his order, had been told to stay in Paris, in charge of the Society's account.

"We won't succeed," he said one day to the Doctor, who had volunteered to be part of the voyage. "I should have filled our ranks to return to our former number before embarking. Here, where the entire group would be hard pressed to be sufficient, I am operating with only a fraction of it."

Another reason for him to be more seriously worried was the attitude of said *fraction.*

Once out to sea, Lupiano had revealed to the *Red Broth-ers* the goal that he was proposing, but that information had not provoked any enthusiasm among them. They had apparently thought that he would be leading them toward the conquest of some golden fleece.

"To free the Emperor!" said that sad gathering of sordid materialists. "After that, we'll only get a pension and a room at the Invalides![231] No, thank you!"

A great attack to sack one of the villages in South America which were said to be gorged with gold, or to intercept some galleons, would have been more to their taste.

That bad morale was even more inflamed when Captain Nichols, following the bonus that he had just received, felt obligated to distribute some hundred francs among the men of his crew. The question of receiving a similar treatment was then roughly proposed by the *Brothers* to Lupiano. It was known that he was generous. But that display of greed raised his emotions and he took it as a matter of ego to not answer it.

Boredom, that all sailors feel when crossings are prolonged, intensified that situation, and it wouldn't have taken very much for the Marquis to find himself in the position of Christopher Columbus, hardly able to prevent a revolt among the adventurers that he was leading to discover the New World.

At the Doctor's insistence, Lupiano finally relaxed his position not to submit to any demand, and after they had passed the Canary Islands, he quieted all the bad moods and seditious dispositions by signing over to each of his seven rogues[232] a gift of one hundred thousand francs to be redeemed by Lelouard, his banker. The promise of strong devotion had

---

[231] A complex of buildings located in the 7th arrondissement of Paris, France, containing museums and monuments, all relating to the military history of France, as well as a hospital and a retirement home for war veterans, the buildings original purpose, initiated by Louis XIV in 1670.

[232] Nine minus Lupiano and the Doctor, obviously.

followed that liberality, greeted with shouts of *Long Live the Emperor!,* and after that, everything went better. But the Marquis nevertheless kept a bitter memory of the kind of violence with which he had been threatened, and as Lefebvre, who had embarked with them at Le Havre, was complimenting him on that liberal concession, he said:

"Certainly the Emperor comes before my ego, but these cutthroats, these miserable wretches, will pay me back, for that insult."

Contrary to Lefebvre's opinion, another incident wasn't long in demonstrating how wrong the Marquis had been when he had departed from his inflexible habits. On the morning of the day that they expected to reach the Cape Verde Islands, Captain Nichols took him aside and told him with embarrassment that his crew was upset; that having found out about Lupiano's magnificent liberality to the men following him, they had given way to a feeling of envy. In short, the conclusion was that, to satisfy the morale and the good will of the English sailors, a new blood-letting of the *inexhaustible* Marquis' purse was deemed necessary.

"I believe," Lupiano responded, "that I have done things properly. With the sum I paid you, you have, it seems to me, enough to satisfy your men and even keep a fortune for yourself."

"Without a doubt, Monsieur le Marquis, but I already gave them a part of the million that I got from you. I can't distribute another hundred thousand francs to each of them, as you have done to your group."

"These sordid money details, compared to the great project that should occupy us, are shameful. I cannot distribute the sums I took with me when we embarked, because they shall be necessary when our mission is executed. Thirty thousand francs to be shared between your money-famished crew, is all that I can let be extorted for."

"Ah! Monsieur le Marquis, that's a harsh word."

"Your request isn't any less so, and you shouldn't pretend otherwise. Did we, or did we not, agree on a million?

Then our agreement should be carried out religiously, just as the one which you made with the King of the Hovas."

"I see very well," the Captain then said, "that you haven't forgiven me for having taken your son back to Madagascar."

"No, Captain! Neither you, nor your crew! You, all of you, were the instruments of horror. We have come together for a purpose; that's understood. But afterward, we shall no longer be partners. So, do you accept the thirty thousand francs I have offered you?"

"Gladly. My men will be very content with that."

"Very well. Take them, but don't get anyone go ashore at Porto Praya. You know sailors: as soon as they'll have their money, they won't come back on board. We would lose even more time. The Doctor and General Lefebvre will go ashore to buy any supplies that might be necessary."

"That's understood, Monsieur le Marquis. Before night we will be within sight of Santiago. I will drop anchor at some reasonable distance from Porto Praya. Besides, that's a shanty town that anyone could perfectly well do without seeing."

An hour before sunset, land was sighted. Having recognized the island of Santiago, the Captain dropped anchor, and shortly thereafter, a skiff started toward Porto Praya, having aboard Lefebvre and the Doctor.

There was a splendid sunset. As it disappeared from the horizon, huge clouds accumulated in its space, filling the sky with butterfly colors of purple, rose, violet and emerald green. When the sun's flaming disk was just about to be extinguished, the firmament seemed to have been hung with crimson, and then a band of gold continued to illuminate the western coast until the last shadow had disappeared.

"Beautiful opera decoration!" said the Captain. "But even so, it's bringing some wind."

At that moment, the sailor on watch duty announced a sail. They soon recognized a ship under the English flag. It was moving rapidly with wind behind it. Soon, holding a spyglass, the Captain could read the name. That wasn't a fortunate sign for she was the *Acheron*.[233]

"Hallo! The Ship!" Captain Nichols shouted when the whip was alongside the *Franklin.* "What's the news?"

"*The Emperor is Dead,*" the crew answered with one voice.

It seemed that each sailor wanted to have the honor of that immense news. And, with no more details, the ship sailed by.

"Well, there we are!" said the Captain, addressing Lupiano, that the news had prostrated. "And on top of the bad weather that's coming in tonight. We were wrong to send someone to land. It will be the devil to stay in place. In what direction now are we now going to sail? And where do we have to take you, Monsieur le Marquis?"

"Nowhere," answered Lupiano, with a stifled voice.

"Nowhere is not a place," retorted the Captain. "Yes, as a matter of fact, he was a great man, but the world doesn't stop because he has died."

Seeing that the Marquis didn't answer him, he left to organize his crew for the bad weather coming.

In his moral being, Lupiano had just felt like a man who is suddenly lacking air to breathe. Now unable to deliver the Emperor from Saint-Helena, he no longer saw any other purpose for his existence, and knew of no other reason to live. The last thing that had connected him to the material things of the Earth had just been broken.

After walking about for some time on the bridge, roughly sending away his men who had tried to come to confer with him about the news that had modified all their existence, the Marquis retired to his cabin.

For more than two hours, while the ship was violently shaken by the storm, which raised and caused the anchor to move about, he seemed not to know what was happening.

---

[233] In Greek mythology a river that flows through Hades which the dead must cross to enter the place of rest.

At about nine o'clock, the storm calmed, but the sea was still too choppy for the boat sent ashore to rejoin the ship. While waiting, Captain Nichols drank a glass of grog with his second mate. Then, having taken a look around at everything, he went to bed.

He had been asleep for about a half-hour when he was awakened by the officer in charge of the wheelhouse who said in great excitement:

"Captain, come quickly! It's all over for us! Your damned Marquis has been possessed by the Devil. You know that he normally doesn't smoke, and yet he's just got into his head to light a pipe and go down with it into the powder room."

"Then we've got to stop that fool!" exclaimed the Captain, getting up quickly.

"It's not possible! He's locked himself in. We've been talking to him for ten minutes, without success."

"F*** [234].acquaintance I made there!" exclaimed the Captain, rushing out of his bedroom. "I'm going to see if I can talk and reas…"

He couldn't finish the word. A horrible explosion shook the vessel and terrified the Doctor and Lefebvre, who, with the men in the skiff, were watching from Porto Praya, waiting for the moment when the sea would let them come back on board.

The next day, at daybreak, they could no longer have the slightest doubt about the extent of the disaster. Every minute the waves brought some debris from the ship. Several bodies were identified, among which that of Captain Nichols, but Lupiano's was not found among their numbers. [235]

---

[234] Rabou leaves the word incomplete here. He probably means to use the word "*foutre*," a vulgar interjection expressing excitement or dismay.

[235] Rabou is being coy here. Who, then, is the mysterious narrator who, in 1833, as told in the *Avant-Propos* of Volume 1, narrates the entire story of the Hulets and the *Secret Bureau*?

Two days having passed, and the sea not having brought anything else to shore, his two companions despaired of being able to render him the last rites. At that point a frigate coming back from Cape Town arrived. It had put in at Saint-Helena and was spreading the *news* around the island. The Doctor, who knew the Marquis very well, explained the fate of the *Franklin* and, with Lefebvre, took passage on the ship that offered to them to return them to Europe.

The Doctor disembarked at Southampton. He didn't find it prudent to return to France before learning what had happened after the execution of Saint-Rambert. But in fact, nothing at all had happened. On finding their Director hanging from the ceiling of the letters unsealing room, the employees had been more horrified than saddened by what they saw. The little old man that Matiphous had encountered at Hulet's funeral, had stated very bluntly that *it was a job well done.*

Not having caught Lupiano and the *Red Brotherhood,* whose secret had finally been revealed to them, the police took the greatest care to stifle the entire affair. Rempailleux was said to have hanged himself and was buried quickly and quietly.

Mademoiselle Hortense Boulard genuinely believed that she owned the billfold that Lupiano had had carried to her. But Laverenette intervened and forced her to cough it up for the benefit of the inconsolable widow. However, when, following the judicial search of Saint-Rambert's house, after his death, as Matiphous had foreseen, the Law discovered the correspondence of the Bedloe couple, that he had kept, so that, in one way or another, he could profit by it, Rempailleux was found to be the thief of the strongbox and the sums it contained.

Was it the Marquis himself, who somehow managed to cheat death? Or was it Gregorio Matiphous (ditto)? As indicated in our epilog, we personally subscribe to the latter hypothesis But somehow, one of the two must have survived. (*Note from the Publisher.*)

Mademoiselle de la Salle, informed of that fact by the Prosecutor, had Adolphe Levillain appointed the guardian of Helena Hulet. With his assistance, an arrest-seizure was carried out against Madame de Saint-Rambert. Having simply accepted that the community of property established between her and her husband by their marriage was sufficient, she was then obliged to return the sum of eight hundred thousand francs, that is to say a hundred thousand francs more than what Mademoiselle Hortense had already returned to her.

Her explanations that, after Madame de Bevillacqua's ball, she gave to the Duke, her zealous *converter,* not having appeared satisfactory to the latter, a break-up followed, and, without having shown the least interest in seeing her daughter again, Madame Rempailleux went to bury the stains of her very eventful life in the depth of the Orkneys, where she still had some property inherited from Lord Stuart, her first husband.

John Ketch, his task completed, and with a hundred thousand francs in his pocket, went immediately to find his aunt, to whom he recounted the drama and the role he had played in it. The only thing Mistress Sedley said was this:

"That damned trickster of a Marquis, he's always the same! As for Kitty, it serves her right, because she tried to act like a Princess with us."

The same night, with her nephew, she found it prudent to go to Calais and, from there, back to England.

Upon his return to Paris, Lefebvre, whose dispute with Montalvi will be recalled, wrote to him in order to make himself available for a duel, but Lelouard kept the affair from going forward. Informed of all the bloody griefs that Lupiano had against Rempailleux, Montalvi finally understood the crime of *lèse-amitié*[236] that he had committed. The scene that Lupiano had made at Madame de Bevillacqua's ball was

---

[236] A play on words: *lèse-majesté* is the crime that consists in insulting or attacking the King; the word "Majesty" being here replaced with that of "friendship."

therefore found sufficiently justified, and, in any case, Lefebvre had only been an instrument in Lupiano's hands. So peace was made between the two adversaries that Lelouard wanted to keep from dueling each other, when he asked them to lay down all their feelings of hatred for each other on the tomb of the one they had both loved.

After the disaster of the *Franklin* and the death of all those aboard had been legally verified, Lelouard produced a will that Lupiano had left with him the day of his departure, having finished writing it while he was waiting for Rempailleux in the house on the Rue de Bourgogne, rented specially to set up an ambush.

Since that will serves very usefully to settle with our readers all the details that remain in this story, the essential elements of it are reproduced below:

Today, on 14 April, 1821, in Paris

This is my last will and testament.

About to take part in an enterprise in which I have decided to succeed, or to lay down my life, I intend that the sums belonging to me, which today should amount to forty million francs, kept in French and American banks (as detailed in the attached statement), should be distributed in that various ways that follow.

1. I hereby give and bequeath to the hospitals in the Kingdom of Hanover, where the Kormer family, now extinct, originated, the sum of eight millions.

2. Ditto with the hospitals of Paris, for the sum of five millions.

3. Ditto with the hospitals of the City of London, for the sum of five millions.

4. I hereby give and bequeath to François-Etienne Lelouard, banker in Paris, whom I also charge with being the executor of my will, the sum of five millions, not including the other sums that I may have invested in the banking house that he directs with as much intelligence as honesty. I hereby give him receipt for these sums.

5. I hereby give and bequeath to Jean-Hyacinthe Lefebvre, retired Battalion Leader, member of the Légion d'Honneur, charged with being my second executor, the sum of a million.

6. Ditto with Monsieur Emile, manufacturer of chemical products, Deputy Mayor of Belleville, and member of the Légion d'Honneur, for the sum of five hundred thousand francs.

7. Ditto with the poor of the above-mentioned commune of Belleville, for the sum of five hundred thousand francs.

8. Ditto with the Demoiselle Sadou, recently returned from Madagascar, now a guest of Madame Emile, wife of the Monsieur the Deputy Mayor of Belleville, for the sum of two millions.

9. Ditto with Madame Emile and Madame Lefebvre, respectively wives of Monsieur Emile and Commandant Lefebvre, each for the sum of two hundred fifty thousand francs, in payment for the care that they will continue to give Demoiselle Sadou until the day of her marriage.

10. I hereby give and bequeath to my servants the sum of a million, to be shared as found just by the executor of my will.

11. Ditto with my Hindu servant, Raganot, for himself alone, the sum of five hundred thousand francs.

12. Ditto with the Religious Community of the Repentant Daughters, in the person of Sister Herminie Daliron, whose religious name I do not know, for the sum of a million.

13. Ditto with young Monsieur Daliron, the brother of the aforementioned Sister, student at the Naval School, for the sum of five hundred thousand francs

14. Ditto with another child, whose name I do not know, but whom Sister Daliron will be charged with designating to the executors of my will, who will believe her affirmation, the sum of five hundred thousand francs.

15. Ditto with John Ketch, former executioner of the city of Sydney (Australia), the sum of five hundred thousand francs.

16. Ditto with Mistress Sedley, aunt of the aforementioned John Ketch, for the sum of five hundred thousand francs.

17. Ditto with Jean Valsivière, coppersmith and boilermaker, to whom I promised to help find a treasure, for the sum of five hundred thousand francs.

18. Ditto with Monsieur Maisonneuve, law student, for the good grace he showed during the 1820 Carnival by participating in a bad joke, for the sum of five hundred thousand francs.

19. Ditto with Mademoiselle Adelaïde de la Salle, for the sum of five hundred thousand francs.

20. Ditto with Madame Lacombe, laundress, former concierge at the Cour de France, *for the sum of fifty thousand francs.*

21. Ditto with the blind man who plays the clarinet at the foot of the third tree on the Avenue de Marigny, for the sum of fifty thousand francs.

22. Ditto with the Demoiselle Georgiana, nicknamed the "Bloodied Girl," for the sum of fourteen million francs. Said sum shall be invested in State Bonds, until the time the legatee comes forward. In case said fourteen million francs have not been claimed after eighty years have passed, it will be remitted the Office of Charity in the neighborhood where the Lamoignon townhouse, my last residence, was located.

23. I hereby give and bequeath all my books and manuscripts to the Royal Library located on the Rue de Richelieu.

24. I hereby give and bequeath to the widow Camembert, Princesse de Bevillacqua, all the furnishings of the Lamoignon townhouse that she was not pleased to accept at another time.

25. I hereby give and bequeath to my "excellent" friend, the Prince de Bevillacqua, a lottery ticket that I charge my executors to buy from the Lottery of Bordeaux for the drawing that follows the day of the opening of my will. Said ticket must be for the sum of 25 francs and must be placed on the odds of winning four numbers in a row.

26. I hereby give and bequeath to Doctor Adalbert, in gratitude for the good care I have received from him in health and in sickness, the sum of two millions.

27. I hereby give and bequeath the remaining three million, after all of the above stated dispositions have been fulfilled, to Signore Zambalo, a fisherman on the island of Gozzo, near Malta, or to the children born of his marriage, if he has passed. In the event that neither the fisherman Zambalo, nor any of his children have survived, the sums bequeathed to them shall be divided among the twelve Offices of Charity of the city of Paris.

The present will, written entirely by my hand, is signed and sealed with my stamp.

Maximilien de Kormer
Marquis de Lupiano

It is useless to specify here what commentaries that last will of the Marquis provoked. The wealth that he left, the great plan he had conceived, and the mystery that surrounded his death, continued the popularity with which his name had always been connected, as did certain *bizarreries* in his last dispositions.

All the legacies were accepted, except for those made to Monsieur and Madame de Bevillacqua. Without acknowledging the Prince's refusal, the executors of the will bought, in his name, a lottery ticket, and the bizarre nature of fate made four numbers come out in a row. The odds were put at seventy-five thousand to one. A *quaterne* bet paying seventy-five thousand times the amount of the bet, that was ore million eight hundred seventy-five thousand francs that were offered to Montalvi, who refused them.

That bit of haughtiness brought him bad luck. Badly managed, his fortune and that of his wife soon dissipated. Two years later, they filed for separation and ended up ruined. Monsieur de Bevillacqua then threw himself into political conspiracies and perished miserably. The small discoloration of the skin that Lelouard had once warned Madame de

Bevillacqua about, reappeared later on her face, and despite all the care of the Doctor, who had returned to practice in Paris, the discoloration became cancerous. After a long sickness and the most painful operations, the beautiful Marquise de Cam-embert remained horribly disfigured and she went to bury her remorse and disfigurement in a far-off province.

The relationship that the liquidation of the will and the succession of Lupiano brought about between the executors and the various heirs drew Lefebvre's attention to the student Maisonneuve. He found that young man would be a perfectly good match for Mademoiselle Sadou. As soon as the former habitué of the *Chaumière*[237] finished his law studies, everything was arranged. He was soon appointed to the position of Auditing Judge because, despite a great fortune, young people must have something to do.

Lefebvre's idea was successful, meaning that, despite its claims for being unusual, the present novel, like many others ends foolishly with a marriage.

---

[237] Fashionable restaurant where Maisonneuve wasted his time as a law student in Paris.

Two Letters: An Epilogue of sorts
By Jean-Marc Lofficier

To His Excellency the Director of the Congregatio Missionis
of the Lazarite Order,
The Vatican, Rome
Your Excellency,

Acting on your instructions, I save facilitated the successful rescue of Gregorio Matiphous and his female companion, Georgiana.

It was clear that Matiphous was not supposed to survive the barbaric trial of the crocodiles; and had he, by a miracle of the Lord, survived it, there was no doubt that his spurned native wife would have soon arranged for him to be assassinated.

I therefore instructed Matiphous to submerge beneath the waters during his third attempt at crossing the river, and swim downstream towards a small bend hidden from view where two of my acolytes stood ready to save him. The same acolytes had previously deposited in the river, upstream of the reptile-infested islet, an oxen carcass that drew the crocodiles away from their intended victim.

In the meantime, a small pouch containing a few fine diamonds, taken from our secret cache in Cape Town, convinced the King of the Hovas to release the girl Georgiana.

Both dressed in robes of our order, Matiphous and Georgiana were then taken to Cape Town, where they embarked on a steamer departing for New York.

As instructed, I have kept the entire operation shrouded in the greatest secrecy, and impressed upon the two survivors that they should appear to remain dead to the eyes of the world.

Anatole de Limeuil
Order of the Lazarite

Tom Brown,
New York
        (...)
The strange character of the so-called Marquis de Lupiano had already come to my attention, and our brother the Marquis de Rio Santo had already appraised me of his probably doomed scheme to rescue the ex-Emperor. Knowing that the mercurial Marquis obeyed no will but his own, I did not consider him for a position on our Council, until an unexpected opportunity arose to save the life of his son, an equally resourceful but perhaps more malleable individual.

Our contacts in the Vatican were more than happy to oblige in executing this small favor for us, and just today, I heard that our future associates are en route *to New York, even as I write this. There has never been any doubt in my mind that the future of our brotherhood lies with America, which will dominate the next century. It is, therefore, important to secure talented and loyal individuals to help us build our empire there. Under their new identities, this Gregorio Matiphous and his woman, will no doubt prove invaluable in that task.*

Follow the instructions attached to this letter and I predict that there will be light tomorrow!

Michele Bozzo-Corona
Rue Thérèse, Paris.

Sherlock Holmes, Fantômas, Lupin, Raffles and More: The Spanish Plays (stage plays)

Jean Petithuguenin. *The Adventures of Ethel King, The Female Nick Carter*

P.-A. Ponson du Terrail. *The Immortal Woman; The Vampire and the Devil's Son; The Police Agent*

Georges Price. *The Missing Men of the* Sirius

Charles Rabou: *The Secret Bureau: The Secret Bureau: The Brothers of Death*

Antonin Reschal. *The Adventures of Miss Boston, The First Female Detective*

Henri de Saint-Georges. *The Green Eyes*

Norbert Sevestre. *Sâr Dubnotal: Jack the Ripper; The Astral Trail*

Eugène Thébault. *Radio-Terror*

P. de Wattyne & Y. Walter. *Sherlock Holmes vs. Fantômas* (stage play)

David White. *Fantômas in America*

Pierre Yrondy. *The Adventures of Thérèse Arnaud of the French Secret Service; The Adventures of Marius Pégomas, Marseille Detective*

www.ingramcontent.com/pod-product-compliance
Lightning Source LLC
Chambersburg PA
CBHW031926110726
47902CB00001B/50